THE FORGOTTEN

THE
FORGOTTEN

by

R. L. King

MAGESPACE PRESS
San Jose, California

To Dan, who understands me

Contents

Prologue

In the darkness, her eyes flew open.

Disoriented, she lay still for a moment, holding her breath. Around her there was no sound. The room was quiet and dark, the curtains still against the closed window, the soft glow of her alarm-clock face illuminating a few inches of her battered nightstand.

3:27 a.m.

She waited for several seconds, reaching out with all her senses. Something had awakened her. She didn't just wake up for no reason in the middle of the night. Was it the sound of one of the staff walking past the door? The closing door of one of the residents returning to his or her room after a trip to the bathroom? The blare of a too-loud radio or television in the far-off common room downstairs? She didn't think it was any of those. They were all normal sounds around here, part of the fabric of her existence. There was no reason why any of them would start affecting her differently now.

So what was it, then? A bad dream? God knew she had enough of those, but it still didn't seem right. Those kinds of dreams tended to jolt her awake in a cold sweat, the vestiges of whatever horror had sought to disturb her calm still alarmingly fresh in her mind.

She took a deep breath, rolling over and pulling the covers up so she could snuggle under them, cocoon-like. When she was a little girl back before things had all gone to hell, she used to think that nothing could hurt her as long as she was bundled up in her safe warm bed, the covers wrapped around her as tight as mummy wrappings. A lot had changed since those days, but the feeling still brought her comfort. Okay, she told herself. Just go back to sleep. It'll be morning soon and you'll forget all about this. *To quiet her mind, she began to play an old game* her brother had taught her many years ago – think of a category, then pick a random letter of the alphabet and try to think of something that fit the category. She usually fell back asleep before she hit ten letters.

Okay, *she thought again*. Wild animals, and P. Possum. Q. Ugh, I hate Q. Oh, wait—quail! Moving on to R—how about raccoon? S, then —

Scream.

She gasped, jerking fully awake. No mistake that time – she had *heard it. It wasn't close, but it was there. The desperate, inarticulate scream of someone in terrible pain, or fear, or both. Somewhere inside the house. Downstairs, maybe?*

For a moment she just lay there, trying to quiet her breathing, listening to see if the scream was repeated. It wasn't. She'd heard plenty of screams during her time here – everybody had. Kids were always coming down off something, having nightmares, detoxing. Hell, she'd produced a few of those screams herself, on some of her bad nights. That had been awhile, though, thank goodness. Most of the residents here had been here for awhile, and most of them had worked through most of their demons to the point where nights were usually pretty quiet. The worst she'd heard in the last month had been an argument between Ryan and Charles after Ryan had decided to blow off some assigned chores.

She took a deep breath. The easiest thing to do would be to just roll over, pull the covers over her head, and go back to sleep. Now that she knew what had awakened her, she could easily rationalize it as somebody having a bad night. It wasn't her concern. You learned early not to get too involved around here. Just focus on your own thing, and leave the rest of it to the staff. That's why they were here. Getting involved could get you in trouble, or worse. You just pretended you didn't see things, and pretty soon they went away. If you were lucky, anyway.

But yet something about that scream – it had sounded very young. Too young to be here. She knew everybody in this place, and the youngest resident was fourteen, three years younger than she was. That scream had not come from a fourteen-year-old. She would have bet a lot of money on that, if she had any. What a child was doing here, she had no idea.

Still trying to stay as silent as possible, she swung her legs free of the covers and sat on the edge of the bed. The wooden floor was cold on her bare feet – it would be winter soon and the air was full of a constant low-grade chill. They couldn't afford to run the heater all the time so they did what they could.

She didn't need to turn on a light – she knew every inch of this place like it was the home where she'd grown up. Quietly she padded across the room, pushed open her door – no locks here – and stepped out into the hallway. On either side of her were a row of closed doors; to her left a stairway led down to the kitchen, rec room, and other common areas. The hallway was deserted.

Still moving slowly and silently she crept toward the stairs, then stopped to listen. Nothing. The house was as still as she'd have expected it to be at nearly 3:30 in the morning.

It's not too late, she told herself. You can just turn around and go back to bed. Nobody's seen you. You won't be in trouble.

But the child – such pain for one so young. And the scream – why hadn't everyone heard it? Why weren't all the doors being flung open, people running out to see what was going on? She couldn't have been the only one who heard it.

They told her that she heard things – saw things – sometimes things that nobody else could hear or see. They tried to tell her that they weren't there, but she knew better. They were there, all right. They were everywhere, all around. She even suspected that they were here, but she couldn't be sure. They hid their traces well. She had found evidence, almost like a leftover trail of body odor or perfume that remained in a room long after the person had left, but nothing definitive.

Nobody believed her, of course. She learned that a long time ago, and stopped saying anything about it. She'd been in places like this long enough to know how they worked. You kept your head down and your mouth shut, you did what you were told, and you tried to find ways to get by without attracting attention. She'd gotten good at that.

And now, if she kept up her current course, she could end up losing all the credit she'd built with the staff, all the trust she'd earned. It would be so easy to just turn around and go back to her room.

She thought of her brother then. She'd been close to him years ago, when she was a little girl and he was a teenager. She'd idolized him, loving the way he'd take on neighborhood bullies or barking dogs to protect her. He protected everybody. That was just the way he was. And she wanted to be just like him – a protector of the weak, not a coward who'd slink back to her safe warm bed at the slightest sign of danger. She'd never be able to live with herself if that child was injured.

She was at the bottom of the stairs before she realized that she'd been moving. Again she stopped, again she listened.

More silence. Had she just been hearing things? Had it just been the tail end of a particularly vivid dream, perhaps brought on by the cry of a bird outside her window? That was –

Wait.

What was that?

She froze, standing just inside the open entranceway that led to the kitchen and the dining room.

Had that been a whimper? The sound of someone desperately trying not to cry?

There it was again! It went on for a couple of seconds, then cut off abruptly as if purposely muffled. Then she heard the low rumble of a male voice.

It was coming from somewhere in the direction of the kitchen. Of that much, she was certain. She was also certain that there was no way she could give up now. She had to know who this mysterious child was, and what this man was doing to him. The male voice hadn't been loud or distinct enough for her to recognize it, if she'd ever even heard it before.

Practically tiptoeing now, knowing that if she made even the smallest of sounds she'd be discovered, she moved across the kitchen like a ghost in flannel skully pajamas. There wasn't much past this point: just the pantry closet and the door to the basement, which was always locked. She'd never been down there – when she'd asked, she was told they kept things like yard care items, cleaning chemicals, and other supplies there, and it was off limits to residents. She hadn't much cared; she had a normal amount of curiosity but wasn't in a big hurry to poke around a smelly, spidery basement.

Now, though, she noticed to her surprise that the basement door was open, just a bit. The tiniest crack of light poked out into the kitchen, softly illuminating a few of the blue and white floor tiles. And as she stopped near it to listen, she heard the whimper again.

It was definitely coming from down there.

She stopped, her breath coming a little faster. What was a distressed child doing in the basement with the weed whackers and the toilet cleaner? And what was a man doing down there with her? She couldn't think of any possible way that this could come out sounding good.

What to do, though? Should she call someone? Somewhere around the house at least one of the staff should be doing rounds soon; she could find them and bring them here. But what if they didn't believe her?

Or worse – what if they were somehow connected with whatever was going on?

She closed her eyes for a few seconds, willing her brain to calm down and let her think. Call the police? They'd never get here in time. Even that time when Johnny had ODed on some bad stuff he'd somehow gotten hold of and freaked out in the dining room, the cops had taken nearly twenty minutes to arrive. By that time Johnny had injured two residents and a staff member. So no, cops were out of the question.

Did she dare check it out on her own? Maybe if she sneaked down there –

Looking around the darkened kitchen she tried to find a weapon. The only light came from the tiny shaft from the basement door, the scant moonlight coming in from the window, and a small Mickey Mouse night-light plugged in near the toaster, but it was enough to show her that no weapons were forthcoming. Naturally they kept all the knives and other dangerous implements locked up. Even things like rolling pins were locked away out of reach.

She could sneak back to her bedroom and look for something there, or —

The child screamed again, loud and piercing. This time the scream started out with words: "Nooo! Please...don't — "

That was it. Tossing all caution away, she flung the door open and pounded down the wooden stairway, looking wildly around for the source of the scream —

— and stopped dead.

There were no yard-care implements here. No chemicals. No spiders.

There was only a featureless gray room with padded walls and a hard, concrete floor, illuminated by a bank of harsh fluorescent lights overhead.

In the middle of the room stood a man, his back to the stairway, holding on to a young boy perhaps nine years old. The man didn't appear to have noticed her, the sound of her descent having been muffled by the child's screams. As she watched, momentarily shocked into immobility, the man laughed and touched the boy's forehead.

He screamed even louder this time, a sound of such transcendent agony that rose to a shrieking crescendo and then abruptly stopped. For the space of barely a second the boy's eyes met hers — pleading with her to do something, anything — and then —

— he was gone.

Just like that, the space where he had stood was empty. There was nothing left but a faint smell of ozone in the air, a heap of disarrayed clothing, and a tiny charred pile of what looked like ashes at the man's feet.

"NOOOOOOO!" Her own scream, of defiance and shock and disbelief at what she'd just seen, was almost as loud as the boy's. She rushed forward, having no idea what she intended to do but not caring. She had to do something.

The man wheeled around, and she nearly stopped in her tracks again. His face was wild, almost inhuman in its ferocity. His eyes blazed with some weird inner light, and his mouth was stretched wide in a grin straight from the pits of Hell. He reached out toward her, his fingers seeking her.

"Get – OUT!" she yelled. It was as if something alien had taken over her mind – she felt like whatever was happening, she was just along for the ride now. Instead of shrinking back from the madman lunging toward her, she held her ground. Clasping her hands together and pointing them at his head as if she were shooting an invisible pistol, she forced out with her mind. She felt something, some kind of power, emanate from her fingers and contact the man. For a moment a nimbus of strange foggy light formed around him. He screamed, clutching his head and dropping to his knees.

She did step back now, staring dumbly at him as he writhed there, obviously engaged in some massive interior struggle. Then all the life went out of him and he dropped bonelessly to the floor. As she continued to watch, some sort of nebulous pur-plish...thing...wafted up out of his body and hovered momentarily in the air above him. It seemed to orient itself briefly, then shot toward her.

"NO!" she yelled again, and forced out with her mind as she had done before. She had no idea how she was doing this – it was instinctive, like breathing or crying. But it had its effect – the floating thing changed direction, darting around the room for several seconds and then heading straight up through the ceiling.

She didn't move for nearly a full minute. She stood there, rooted to the spot, her numb gaze taking in the room, the pile of *ashes and clothes, the unconscious (dead?) man. The weird insane expression had left him; he looked now like nothing more than a nondescript middle-aged man in a suit.*

When the compulsion to remain standing in one place left her, she did the only logical thing she could think of: she ran. Pelting up the stairs, her only thought was to get away from the man, to find someone on the staff, to bring them down here and show them the man and explain to them about the ashes and the boy and —

— She flung herself out the door into the kitchen. She didn't see the shadowy figure standing there until she collided with it.

1.

There are good ways to be awakened. These include things like your favorite song on your clock-radio, the soft caress of a lover, or maybe the cheerful trilling of birds outside your sunlit window.

Jason Thayer was pretty sure that they did not include things like the sound of a nightstick clanging off the bars of your cell.

Struggling blearily to wakefulness under a thin blanket, Jason realized simultaneously that every bone in his body hurt, and that somebody was yelling something at him. "What...?" he mumbled.

"Get up, lazy!" came the voice. Male. Harsh and gritty like somebody who'd smoked way too many cigarettes in his life, but also amused. "You don't think the good people of this fine city are going to put your useless carcass up forever, do you?"

Jason sat up, running a hand through his hair. "Yeah, yeah," he grumbled. He felt like he'd been run over by a truck, and his mouth tasted like he'd been chowing down on the choicest of aged roadkill. And whiskey. Never a good combination. "By the way, Stan, just so you're aware: the maid service sucks around here, and the room service guy brought me the wrong thing again. You should look into that. I pay your salary, you know."

Stan chuckled, opening the unlocked cell door. "You know, kid, you're gettin' a little old for this. Every time I toss you in here you look a little worse in the morning. Maybe you should stop pissin' off gorillas at bars, eh?"

"Where's the fun in that?" Jason muttered, hauling himself to his feet and crossing to the door. "Did I win, at least? I can't remember."

"Nah, but the girl's friends showed up and got her out of there after the guy took you apart. So I guess you could say you distracted him. With your face," he added after a moment, examining Jason's puffy left eye.

Jason grinned, probing at a tooth with his tongue and determining that it wasn't sufficiently loosened to worry about. "Hey, that's a win by me, then."

Stan sighed and slammed the cell door shut, eliciting a grumpy, "Hey, can't a guy fuckin' *sleep* around here?" from one of the two occupants of the drunk-tank two cells down. "You know," the cop said, shepherding Jason along the bare hallway to the front desk where he handed him his leather jacket, an envelope containing his wallet, belt, keys, and watch, and a clipboard with a sheet of paper attached, "I was kidding back there, kinda. But you really do need to lay off this stuff, kid. It ain't always gonna work this way. Either somebody's gonna pull out a gun and blow you away, or the good citizens of San Buena-ventura are gonna get tired of this shit and the brass are gonna tell me to knock it off. Which might end up with you doin' real time instead of sleepin' off bar fights in my spare cell."

"Yeah, I know that." Jason scrawled his signature at the bottom of the sheet of paper, tossed the clipboard on the desk, and began stuffing his belt through the loops on his faded jeans. "But what was I gonna do, Stan? I don't like assholes who mess with people who can't fight back."

"That's why bars have bouncers," Stan pointed out.

"Yeah. I know that too. I've been one, remember?"

Stan rolled his eyes. "Yeah, I remember. And that worked out so well." He clapped Jason on the back. "Go home, kid. Clean yourself up, take a shower, and go to sleep for awhile. Then find yourself something to do that doesn't involve beating anybody up."

Jason caught the bus home. He wasn't sure exactly where his motorcycle was; he supposed he'd need to find out pretty soon. Maybe Stan knew, but he didn't think this would be the best time to ask him about it. The shower idea sounded really good right now — standing under hot water for about an hour would be just the thing to cheer up his bruised body and make him feel marginally human again.

The first thing he noticed when he opened the door to his apartment and tossed his keys on the cluttered coffee table was that the message light on his answering machine was flashing. He took a deep breath. Couldn't today just leave him alone for a little while? In his experience, flashing lights on his machine never meant good things. It was never "Congratulations! You won the lottery!" or "Hey, buddy, I'm out with this really hot chick and she's got a hot sister who's dying to meet you." No, not for him. It was usually more like "Where's the rent?" or "I'm gonna fuck you up when I find you, asshole!" or "I never want to see you again!" So it was with understandable reluctance that he slumped down on the couch and poked the flashing red button, then picked up a motorcycle magazine and idly started to page through it. Maybe he'd be lucky and it would just be a bill collector. He was getting good at ignoring those.

"Jason?"

The single word jolted him like an electric current. He tossed the magazine aside and stared at the machine's tiny speaker.

"Jason? Are you there? If you are, please pick up. It's me." There was a several-second pause, then the voice continued, faster and more frightened. "Jason? Oh, God, you're not home. Or maybe you're just not answering. But — oh, Jason, I need help. There's something going on at this place and it's wrong and I'm scared. I have to get out." Her breathing quickened again as another pause stretched out. "I can't talk long — I'm not supposed to be using the phone and I don't know how long it'll be before they find me. Charles says I have to go. It's not safe here anymore." Another pause, then: "Somebody's coming. I have to go now. Oh, God, please, Jason—help me! You're the only one I can trust!"

There was kind of a scuffling sound, the sort you might hear when somebody is fumbling around with the phone receiver, and then a soft click and the line went dead. Then the little red light went out, and another one appeared next to "No new messages."

"Oh, shit..."

That, or some variation of it, was his usual response to hearing that particular voice. He felt bad about it, but it was true. That voice had not brought him anything but trouble for years, and it was looking like this was no exception. Restlessly he got back up. "I gotta think," he muttered aloud. Shower forgotten, he went to the tiny kitchen, started to reach for a beer, changed his mind and grabbed a soda, and threw himself down in the single chair of his kitchen table, shoving drifts of old bills and outdated magazines and folded newspaper sections out of the way.

He really wished he didn't feel this way. A long time ago, back when he was a kid and his dad was alive and the world hadn't yet gone to shit, he and Verity had gotten along great. He was too old to hang around with her much—the 7-year difference in their ages made that pretty much impossible, especially since she was a girl. But as much as they could be as the kids of one of the local cops, they were both wild and daring and got into all kinds of society-approved kid hijinks. She'd been more gothy, dressing in all black and writing terrible poems about death and vampires, while he'd been the classic gearhead, always strewing the garage with machines and vehicles in various stages of disassembly. She'd hang around, watching him with her big dark eyes as he worked, occasionally asking a question that they both knew she didn't give a damn about the answer—she just enjoyed hanging out with him.

All that changed five years ago. He had no idea what had caused it, though it did coincide with the time when things really started to go downhill for the world in general so he supposed it was sort of going around. Around about that time, only a few months before Dad was killed and a few more before Jason had gotten himself kicked out of the Academy, she'd gone...funny. Dad thought it might have something to do with puberty, and the doctors he took her to agreed, but nobody could figure out how to fix it. They'd searched her room looking for hidden stashes of drugs or booze, and found neither. And it wasn't like that anyway—Jason, who'd had plenty of experiences with alcohol by that point and had enough friends who experimented with various drugs that he recognized the classic stoner look—could have told them that. Sometimes she'd be fine for a few days, but she'd always go back to staring off into the far distance, rocking back and forth, and going on about seeing monsters.

Jason knew he didn't want to do it, but Dad had really had no other choice—as a single parent (Mom had died years earlier of some sort of female-type cancer that Jason hadn't delved into the details about too deeply) he had to work to support the family, and the insurance wouldn't cover full time home care. So that meant the only option was to put Verity into some sort of program. Dad found several, checked them out and seemed satisfied with one, but Jason still remembered Verity's shrieks and screams the day she'd gone away. It was like she'd come up out of her little world long enough to figure out that they were rejecting her.

The first facility had been only about twenty miles from home. They'd gone to visit her when they could. Jason hated the place—it made him feel weird, and he couldn't help wondering (but at least having the good grace to be ashamed about it) whether whatever V had was hereditary, or contagious. He didn't go often because by that point he was busy with the Academy, but whenever he did, she didn't seem to recognize him. She just stared at him in mute accusation.

And then Dad was killed. Just like that—one failed drug stakeout and Jason was fatherless, and suddenly responsible for Verity's care decisions. Dad had left enough insurance money for awhile but Jason, who by this point was no longer at the Academy, didn't feel anywhere near mature enough to handle all of this. He attended the funeral in a daze and afterward he just threw himself into the various odd jobs he was doing now and tried not to think about his problems.

And then she ran away.

That phone call had come on a Tuesday afternoon, and caught him still in bed after an all-night marathon poker game with some of his buddies. She'd disappeared, they told him. Had he seen her? Heard from her? No, he'd said, all the while his brain spinning out of control. What the hell was he going to do? How was he going to find her? She was barely fifteen.

Turned out he needn't have worried. She showed up on his doorstep later that evening, dressed in jeans and a dark shapeless hoodie that made her look like a small and very lost young boy. Begging for him to take her in. Telling him she was cured and that they were horrible to her at "that place." Pleading with him not to send her back there.

He'd tried it for awhile, and for a few days it worked. He'd called back the facility and told them that she was there and that they were going to give it a try, since she did seem better and more lucid. They'd advised against it and told him to call them back if, as they suspected, it didn't work out. Verity assured him that she'd be good and everything would be okay.

The first inkling he got that all wasn't well was the next night. He'd awakened after hearing odd noises in the front room, and when he got up to investigate he found her sitting in the middle of the floor, staring at something he couldn't see. When he'd tapped her on the shoulder to see whether she was sleepwalking, she'd turned her head, looked right into his eyes, and said conversationally, "They're all over the place, you know. You might even know one of them. You might even *be* one of them." Then she got up and walked out of the room. She remembered nothing about any of this the next day.

This had freaked him right the hell out, but he'd tried to hold it together and do the right thing by his sister because he knew that's what their dad would have wanted. But then he caught her breaking into his liquor stash. When confronted, she said simply, "It helps me make them go away." When he asked her who "they" were, she couldn't tell him.

The final straw, though, had been when she'd attacked the mailman. The whole thing sounded pretty absurd when Jason looked back at it—like she was some kind of rabid dog that couldn't be trusted in polite company. But facts were facts—she'd dived out from behind some dumpsters one day and tried her best to slam the guy face-first into the concrete, yelling something that was mostly incoherent but sounded like, "You're not gonna get me!" Luckily she didn't seem to be allowing for the fact that he was twice her size, so even crazy strength couldn't do the job. He hadn't pressed charges, on the condition that Jason's dangerous and unpredictable little sister be sent back to a place where they could look after her.

He didn't really have a choice after that. She screamed and ranted and threatened to run away again, and he had to take her seriously. After all, she'd already done it once. He consulted with her old doctor (boy, *that* felt weird: Dad was the one who did things like that, not him) and even talked to Dad's old friend Stan (the same Stan who would later serve as doorman for Jason's occasional overnight stays in Chez Pokey). In the end, he decided to go with a facility up in the Bay Area that claimed good results in dealing with cases like hers, and provided a level of security that would prevent another case of wanderlust. It had taken most of the rest of the money Dad had left to set her up there, but money wasn't important to Jason. He told himself it was because he wanted Verity to have the best care, but there was also another element he was less willing to cop to: she spooked him more than he wanted to admit, and having her locked up several hundred miles away meant that the odds were good she wouldn't show up on his doorstep again.

He'd gotten regular progress reports from the place over the next couple of years: she was definitely improving. Whatever treatment program they had her on was helping her, and the frequency of strange or violent incidents had dropped down to a couple of times a year. The doctors had reported that she'd had a couple of run-ins where she'd been caught with marijuana (the place was high-security but it wasn't a prison—visitors could and did smuggle in contraband fairly frequently) but aside from that she'd been pretty much a model patient. Earlier this year they had recommended that she, having just turned seventeen, be moved to a sort of "halfway house" facility in Mountain View, where she would have more freedom and would start learning the skills she'd need if

R. L. KING

she was going to live on her own. That had been six months ago, and after he agreed to the move he had only gotten one other progress report: she was doing well, fitting in, and seemed to be a good candidate for transition to outside living once she turned eighteen.

She hadn't called or contacted him once in all that time. And he felt pretty guilty to admit that he hadn't contacted her either, except to send her rather uninspired Christmas and birthday presents, sometimes late. Oh, he'd thought about calling a few times: he'd picked up the phone, or got out some paper to write her a letter, but something always stopped him. He just kept telling himself that they were taking good care of her, that he'd see her when she was out—maybe he'd even ask her to come back down here and stay with him till she got back on her feet. He didn't need to get involved—in fact, he rationalized, doing so might set her off again, and that would be bad for her recovery. *Yeah, right.*

"You're the only one I can trust," she'd pleaded on the phone. But was he? He stared down at the litter of papers on the kitchen table ("Midland National Bank fails," read one headline. "Unemployment at 12% nationally," said another) and sighed. *Why does she think she can trust me when all I've done is shove her out of my life because she wasn't convenient?*

On the small table next to the couch, the phone sat silently. Even the little red "no new messages" light had gone out now. *It's all you, buddy,* it seemed to say. *Whatcha gonna do?*

He had to hunt around for an embarrassingly long time before he located the number of the halfway house—he finally found it on a torn-off piece of paper buried under a stack of bike-parts catalogs and skin mags on his nightstand. Before he could change his mind, he perched on the edge of the couch and dialed the number.

It was a long time before anyone answered. Then, "Hello?" The voice sounded young.

"Uh, yeah, hi. Is this—" he consulted his slip of paper for the name "—New Horizons?"

"Yeah."

This wasn't going to be easy, he could see. "Can I, uh, talk to somebody in charge?"

"In charge? Oh. Uh, yeah. Just a sec." There was the sound of the phone being tossed down on a table, then the far-off call of "Dr. Delancie, some guy wants to talk to you!"

Another long pause—Jason was beginning to think the kid had wandered off and forgotten about him—and then somebody picked up the phone. "Good afternoon. Who is this, please?" This time the voice was male and sounded older.

"Who's *this?*" Jason responded. "I need to talk to somebody in charge there."

"That would be me," the man said smoothly. "Dr. Edward Delancie. And you are?"

"I'm looking for my sister. She's a resident there. She called me last night—left a message on my machine. Sounded like she might be in trouble."

Pause. "Who is your sister?"

"Verity Thayer. She's seventeen."

"Ah, yes, Miss Thayer. Lovely girl. What did you say your name was again?"

"Jason."

"Well, Jason," Edward Delancie said, "I'm sure if you're familiar with your sister's case, you're aware that she suffers from certain...delusions."

For a moment he wasn't sure how to reply. "Yeah, I know that," he finally said. "I thought she was doing a lot better, though."

"Oh, she is, she is," Delancie assured him. "She's making wonderful progress. But sometimes she has — moments of backsliding. I hope you understand. They're coming with less and less frequency as time goes on, but they still happen. And I regret to say that last night was one of them."

Jason took a slow deep breath. "So — you're telling me that whatever she said last night, she was making it up? That she's not in any trouble?"

"Well...technically she *is* in a spot of trouble, since we have strict rules here about unauthorized use of the telephone. She's currently in what we call 'time out.' "

"What the hell does that mean?" Jason demanded. He was growing more and more convinced that he didn't like this guy, but he wasn't sure why.

Delancie didn't miss a beat. "It means, Jason, that she's had certain privileges suspended for two days. No telephone, no television, and no visitors. You understand, I hope, that our treatment methods are carefully designed, and unfettered contact with, shall we say, 'the outside world' can cause severe setbacks."

Jason glared at the phone. "So you're saying she's in some kind of — what — solitary confinement?"

Delancie laughed. "No, no, no! Of course not! She still has access to our library, and she's able to move around the facility just as she always was. She's simply not allowed television privileges nor any contact with anyone outside until Friday."

"So I can't talk to her?"

"You're welcome to give her a call on Friday, or to write her a letter. But until then, I'm afraid that won't be possible."

Again, Jason took a deep breath. It was all he could do not to growl at this oily son of a bitch. "So how do I know she's even still there? She said something about needing to get out—about how it wasn't safe there anymore. She could be dead for all you're telling me!" His voice rose a bit at the end, and he could feel his temper rising along with it.

"Jason, please." Delancie still sounded utterly unruffled. "I understand that you're upset, but there's really nothing I can do. Rules are rules, and they're put in place for the benefit of the residents." He was silent for a moment, then added, "I'm sure you know this, as you signed the papers to have your sister come to live with us here at New Horizons. Or perhaps you've forgotten over time, since I don't show any record of your ever having visited your sister here."

You smarmy fucking bastard. "Listen up, *Ed.* Maybe I haven't visited before, but I'm coming up there now. And if you know what's good for you, you'd better let me see my sister. You got that? Have her ready to go, 'cause I'm taking her out of that place. I don't really think a pretentious ass like you is the kind of guy I want looking out for her." His mouth was running away with his good judgment again, but for once he just let his brain go along for the ride.

"You do what you think you must, Jason." Apparently this Delancie character was incapable of being pissed off, which pissed Jason off even more. "You are, of course, responsible for making these sorts of decisions for your sister until she reaches the age of eighteen. But may I submit that, since I have been overseeing her care for the past several months, that perhaps I might have a better idea of what's required to, as you say, 'look out for her' than you do. Let's make an appointment and we can chat, then you can make an informed decision. Is that acceptable?"

Jason gritted his teeth and forced himself not to start yelling into the phone. Smarmy or not, the part of his mind that actually made rational decisions had to admit that the guy made sense. Verity *could* be a handful sometimes—he knew that from firsthand experience. And she had certainly been known to overreact to things that didn't even exist. "Okay," he grumbled. "We'll talk. But I want to see her when I get there. That's not negotiable. I want to make sure she's okay."

"Fair enough," Delancie agreed cheerfully. "When shall I expect you?"

"When I get there," Jason told him. And he hung up, which was strangely satisfying.

Two hours later he was on the road. It would have been sooner, but he figured he really should be kind enough to his battered body (and anybody who might be near him) to at least take a short shower, and then he had to go back down to the station and figure out from Stan what had become of his bike. As it turned out, they'd picked it up from the parking lot at the bar and had it in the impound lot. "You leavin' town?" Stan asked, eyeing Jason's duffle bag.

"Yeah, for a while. Change of scenery might do me good." And then, because the cop was looking at him like he didn't believe a word of it, added, "Going up to the Bay Area to check on V."

Stan's expression softened. "She doing okay?"

Jason shrugged. "Who knows? That's what I'm headed up there to find out."

"Take care, kid. And take care of her. Lemme know if there's anything I can do, okay?"

"Might take you up on that."

Jason Thayer had loved everything about motorcycles since the time he'd been a small boy playing with toy versions. He loved reading about them, looking at them, fixing them — but mostly he loved riding them. The sensation of being out on the open road, the wind whipping through his hair, made him feel the closest he would probably ever get to flying. Plenty of people had asked him why he didn't have a car, but he'd always just shrugged. It's not that he couldn't have had one if he'd wanted one; with his mechanical talent and knowledge of all the area junkyards, he could have bought some trashed junker and had it purring like a kitten in a couple of months. If he needed a car for something (like one of his infrequent dates), he just borrowed one from a friend and paid them back by doing their wrench monkey work for them.

"The roads aren't safe," some people told him. "Life's not safe," he'd usually respond. Sure, they were right — he knew he took his life in his hands every time he went out, especially these days with so many bums and lowlifes hanging out on the roads, but he couldn't explain it to anybody who didn't understand. He felt like if he let them keep him off his bike, then they won. And he was just stubborn enough that he couldn't let them do that.

He was heading up 101, making good time. This particular bike, his current baby, was a 10-year-old Harley Super Glide. It ran well and looked like crap, which suited him just fine — for one thing, he was much more concerned with mechanicals than aesthetics, and for another, it made it a much less attractive target for thieves. They were everywhere nowadays. Even in relatively tranquil Ventura area he had to be careful where he parked it. But down there he mostly just rode it around town, doing whatever odd jobs or errands he lined up. It had been a long time since he'd just gotten out on the road and opened her up. He knew he was going to have to stop soon, though—even though the bike ran well it was still a Harley, and Harleys shook. It was part of their charm. After last night he would have traded a lot of charm for a nice mellow touring bike, but he had what he had, and that meant more frequent stops.

The rest stop wasn't the kind of place he'd normally choose to pull off, but he was getting hungry and aside from its effect on his bruised body, the rumble of the bike's engine was also making him realize he needed to find somewhere to have a piss pronto or things were going to get ugly. It was already starting to get dark; at least the place still had lights—a lot of them didn't nowadays. He pulled in, parked the bike next to a picnic table, and headed off toward the bushes. There was a bathroom but he didn't trust it: unlike the parking area, it didn't have any lights. The illumination from the overheads revealed graffiti sprayed on its walls—the usual ganger scrawls along with some odd symbols that Jason didn't recognize. Just not worth taking the chance.

When he got back, intending to just toss down a couple of energy bars and a bottle of water from his pack, he froze. Two dark shapes stood near the picnic table, between him and the bike. One was large, shapeless and imposing looking, while the other was smaller and oddly twisted. Jason slipped his hand into his pocket for his knife, wishing now that he'd brought his pistol. He wasn't technically supposed to have it anymore, but if it saved his life he'd have been happy to worry about the legal details later.

The two shadowy figures didn't move as he slowly approached them, keeping the picnic table between them. "Can I help you guys with something?"

"Yeah," said the big one. His voice was low, doleful, almost apologetic. He stepped forward, and the light revealed a large Hispanic-looking guy in a ski cap and a shabby overcoat that was, amazingly, too big for him. "You got anything to eat? We're real hungry."

"Real hungry," echoed a quavery voice. The smaller figure moved up next to his friend: he was an old man, hunched and skinny, with bright manic blue eyes that shone dazzlingly out of his wrinkled apple-doll face.

"Uh..." Jason paused, looking them up and down, gauging his ability to get to his bike before they could catch him. The old guy he could take easily, unless he had a gun hidden somewhere. The big guy he wasn't so sure about. They both looked a little—not quite right, but not necessarily threatening. He glanced around for a vehicle, wondering how they'd gotten here in the first place, and saw none. Finally he decided to play along. "That's all you want? Something to eat? You're not gonna hassle me?"

"Naw, man," said the big one in his ponderous tones. "We just hungry, y'know?"

Jason had thrown several of the granola energy bars in his duffel bag so he could make quick stops instead of having to waste time and money stopping at fast food places. Keeping a close eye on the two strangers to make sure they didn't come any closer, he dug two bars out and tossed them on the table. "There. Now you gonna let me get on my way?"

The old guy darted forward and snatched up the bars before Jason could change his mind, flipping one to the big guy and immediately ripping the wrapper off his own and wolfing the bar down like he hadn't eaten in weeks. The big guy looked at Jason. "Thanks, man."

Jason nodded. He watched the old man finish his bar and nibble at the inside of the wrapper for crumbs, while the big one carefully unwrapped his and took slow, purposeful bites. After a moment, Jason opened the duffel again and put two more bars on the table. "Looks like you guys could use them more than me. How'd you get here, anyway?"

This time, the big guy picked them up and pocketed them with another nod of thanks. The old one looked hungrily at his friend's pocket but seemed to under-stand—save them for later. "Travelin', travelin'," the big guy said noncommittally. He looked Jason in the eyes, though his wandered a bit. "Listen, you're a good dude, so I'm gonna tell you something."

Jason cocked his head, keeping his hand on his knife inside his pocket. In these times, too much trust could get you killed even if things looked like they were mostly okay. "Oh yeah? And what's that?"

"You don't wanna hang out here," the big guy said, gesturing around. "This ain't a good place."

"And how do you know that?"

The old guy pointed toward the bathroom as if the ac-tion was self-evident, then shuffled back behind the big guy.

"You see that, there on the side of the crapper?" The big guy waved in the same direction his friend had.

"What? The tags? This ganger turf?"

The big guy shrugged. "Don't know nothin' about that. Don't care. But you see that circle thing with the X through it and the squiggly line?"

Jason shot a quick glance in that direction without tak-ing his eyes off the two bums for longer than a couple of seconds. Sure enough, one of the odd symbols he'd no-ticed before looked just as the big guy had described it:

"Yeah," he said. "What's it mean?"

"Means this ain't a good place. Means you don't wanna camp here."

"You know that from just that symbol? Who put it there?"

"I dunno." The big guy seemed to be losing interest, his attention wandering. "Hey, man, you got anything to drink? Beer, maybe? Little whiskey?"

"Or maybe a smoke?" the old guy asked hopefully, poking his wizened face out from behind the big guy's sleeve.

Jason sighed. "Sorry. Hey, listen, I gotta go. Thanks for the tip, and you guys take care, okay?" He began moving slowly in the direction of his bike, ready to leap to instant action if they tried anything. He hoped they wouldn't—he still hurt quite a bit from last night.

They didn't. They just stood aside and watched him as he fired up the bike, strapped his duffel to the back, and threw a leg over the seat. He was about to put it in gear when the big guy yelled over the rumble: "Hey, man!"

"What?" Jason sighed a little to himself—he wished these two weird bums would just let him get away from here. He wasn't allowing his stress and readiness to ramp down as long as they were still near him, and it was starting to make him feel lousy.

The big guy took a couple of steps closer, holding his hands up placatingly. "No hassle, dude, no hassle. I just wanted to tell you—my name's Manuel. This here's Edgar. You run into any trouble up north, maybe you mention our names, yeah?"

Jason didn't completely succeed in keeping his incredulity off his face. Two random bums at a rest stop were suggesting he invoke their names if he got into trouble someplace they didn't even know where he was going? Yeah, right. That was gonna happen. "Uh...sure. I'll do that. Thanks." *Don't antagonize the headcases...*

He was a mile out of the rest stop before he realized that he hadn't had anything to eat or drink himself.

2.

He rode straight through the rest of the way with only one stop for gas and a quick meal eaten in the parking lot of the station. He took the first exit labeled "Mountain View" and pulled off into the parking lot of a grocery store to consult his map. He hadn't been up here since he was a kid and had no idea where he was going—he knew the whole area was one big urban sprawl, with one town running into the next one with barely a border. Wasn't looking much better than Ventura, either, he noted, spotting things like the overflowing dumpster that he could smell from here and one of the grocery store's windows covered with plywood and tattered fading flyers for local concerts. "Things are tough all over, I guess," he muttered to himself.

Much as he would have liked to show up at New Horizon's doorstep right now and maybe wipe what was undoubtedly a pasty smile off Ed Pretentious Delancie's face, he decided for once in his life that he'd use a little discretion and make his appearance first thing in the morning. He doubted that being sweaty and covered with dead bugs would make any kind of positive impression. Intimidating, maybe—but he knew that he didn't have the only say about whether he could pull V out of that place. He'd at least make an attempt to placate ol' Ed. If that didn't work, punching him in the nose was definitely not off the table.

He fired up the bike again and cruised down El Camino Real, the main drag that tied most of these indistinguishable towns together. There weren't that many cars on the road, fewer motorcycles, and quite a number of people huddling in small groups in shop entranceways. Jason took a deep breath and let it out slowly. It was worse up here than it was back home, by a long shot. He knew this area used to be fairly prosperous — a lot of the new high technology companies had been based around here, luring people in search of good jobs. But all that had gone sour, like everything else, five years back. Things were a lot different now. His eyes darted back and forth, taking in the billboards ("DRINK BUZZ!" proclaimed a barely-dressed chick, wide paper strips of her skin peeling necrotically away from the faded neon background) and haphazardly-placed posters ("The End is Near!" one screamed in thick black letters, while the electric grin of some TV philanthropist shone out of another).

There were a lot of motels along El Camino, ranging from high-class chains that he knew he couldn't afford to ramshackle establishments that looked like they'd been around for fifty years and might have changed the sheets on the beds a couple of times during that period. He had enough money to last him for a little while if he was frugal, but...yeah. Even he had standards.

The glow of a neon sign off to his left caught his attention. "MOTEL - CHEAP ROOMS," it read in a font that had gone out of style when his dad had been a kid. "What the hell," he muttered, and flipped a turn into the driveway.

The parking lot was full; he had to leave the bike down at the end of the row from the office and trudge back. Ignoring the scrutiny of a couple of leather-jacket-clad teenagers who were lounging near the ice machine, he continued on his way. He'd almost reached the office when a small white symbol chalked on the curb near the office door caught his eye. At first his gaze just slid over it as part of the background scenery, but then something clicked in his mind and he stared at it wide-eyed.

It was the same symbol he'd seen back at the rest stop — the one the two bums had told him meant "a bad place."

No, that's crazy. It's got to be a coincidence. I'm just tired. I'm seeing things that don't mean anything. But all the same, it spooked him a little. It was definitely the same symbol, a symbol he'd never seen in his life before today, and had now seen twice in the last several hours.

Back when Jason was a kid, his dad had once told him, "Jase, don't let anybody ever tell you not to listen to your gut. Sometimes it's all you got, and it might save your life someday. Brains are great—you should never disengage your brain. But your gut's gonna be what saves you." Right now, looking at that innocuous little symbol chalked there on the curb, he understood what Dad had met. He felt a little stupid doing it, but he took one last glance at the office door, then turned around and headed back for the bike.

The two teenagers who'd been next to the ice machine weren't there anymore. Instead, they were standing near the Harley, silently inspecting it. Jason got a glimpse of some kind of red and black logo on the back of one of the jackets. "What do you two want?" he demanded.

They looked startled to see him back so soon, but shrugged. "Just lookin'," said the older one, turning to face Jason. His head was shaved and covered with colorful tattoos that extended down to his forehead. "Ain't illegal, is it?"

"Okay, you had your look. Now clear out."

Shrugging again, the two of them sloped off back toward the ice machine without another word. Jason watched them go, glanced around to make sure they didn't have any friends lurking in the shadows, then rumbled off again still pondering the weird symbol.

First thing the next morning he was on the road again. He'd found a symbol-free motel a couple miles up El Camino and settled in; a shower, a quick meal from the fast-food place next door and a good night's sleep had done wonders for his outlook, and by the next day as he spread his map out over the room's tiny table and memorized the route to New Horizons, he'd pretty much forgotten about things like creepy bums and strange graffiti. All he was thinking about now, as he carefully watched for street signs, was Verity.

New Horizons, when he finally found it, was a two-story gray Victorian style home in a marginal residential neighborhood. All around him, Jason could see signs that the people who lived here weren't doing all that well: peeling paint, roofs missing shingles, broken-down swingsets, junker cars that looked like they barely ran. New Horizons itself was in decent repair but had the threadbare look of a place that was being kept up haphazardly as the money became available. There was no sign or placard announcing its name, only the house number. Almost without thinking about it, Jason glanced around looking for chalked symbols, then felt embarrassed about it. Still, he was heartened by the fact that he didn't see any.

Next to the large double front doors was a button with an intercom speaker. He stabbed the button. "Hello?"

The seconds stretched out in silence. Jason waited nearly a minute, then knocked insistently on the door before hitting the button again. "Anybody in there?"

Again several seconds passed, and then a female voice crackled out of the speaker: "Yes, may I help you?"

"Yeah. I'm Jason Thayer. I'm here to see my sister. Verity."

Pause. Jason was beginning to wonder if anybody in this place ever did anything quickly. "Verity's not here," the voice said at last.

Jason froze. "What the hell do you mean, she's not here?"

"She's not here," the voice repeated. "She left a couple of days ago."

Jason took a long, slow deep breath in lieu of kicking down the door. "Okay," he said slowly, measuring every word. "I don't know who the hell you are, but I want to see my sister, and I want some straight answers. Get Delancie out here. And open this damn door."

"Hold on a minute." The speaker went silent again.

Jason waited. A minute passed. Two. Three. He looked down at his watch: he would give them two more minutes and then he was going to beat his way in. He had mad visions of them spiriting Verity out through the back door while he waited like a sucker on the front porch, but he knew if he gave in to those, he'd be moving into territory it was hard to get back out of. So he waited, following the second hand on his watch as it swept its way toward his deadline.

With fifteen seconds to spare, something rattled on the other side of the door, and then it swung open. Jason jerked himself back to attention.

"Mr. Thayer? I'm Edward Delancie. It's good to meet you." The man inside extended his hand. He looked almost exactly like Jason had expected him to: middle aged, white, brown hair just beginning to go gray, wire-rimmed glasses, caring-professional sweater. His eyes crinkled with kindness, but his perfect white teeth reminded Jason more of a used car salesman. He stepped forward, and only then did Jason notice that he was flanked by two other men, identically dressed in jeans and New Horizons-logo light blue button-down shirts. One was bald, black, and overweight; the other was short, white, and muscular. They both looked like they could handle themselves quite well in a fight.

"You need your thugs with you to talk to me?" Jason demanded, cocking his head toward the two.

Delancie smiled, shrugged. "You sounded pretty belligerent, Mr. Thayer. You scared poor Melissa when she answered the intercom. These aren't thugs; they're members of my staff. But all the same, if you give me your word that you won't do anything violent, I'll be happy for us to have our chat just you and me."

"I want to know where my sister is," Jason said stubbornly. "When we talked yesterday you said she was in some kind of time-out, but the chick on the intercom said she was gone. Which is it? I want to see her now, and then we can talk."

"Erm." For a moment, Delancie looked uncomfortable. "Mr. Thayer, come with me. Let's talk in my office. Charles, Tony, I don't think you'll need to stick around. I'm sure we can discuss this like civilized folks."

For a second something in Jason's brain pinged — something he thought he should remember — but then it was lost in the anger again. "Is she here, or isn't she?"

"Well...no." Delancie raised his hands in a gesture of surrender as if he expected Jason to hit him. "Come with me, Mr. Thayer, and I'll explain everything. There's been a terrible oversight, and I take full responsibility." He indicated for Jason to follow him. Charles and Tony looked uncertain about whether they should come along as well. Delancie waved them off.

It was all Jason could do not to start busting heads, but he knew that wouldn't get him anywhere — at least not until he had all the information. He sighed and stalked off behind Delancie toward a door at the end of the hallway.

"You see, Mr. Thayer," Delancie said as he settled himself behind a cluttered desk in an office that was surprisingly small and unimpressive for somebody as obviously full of himself as he was, "I was given incorrect information, and I passed that information on to you without checking on it. By the time I'd discovered my error, I tried to reach you but you had already left."

"What the hell are you talking about?" Jason demanded, planting his hands wide on the edge of the desk and leaning over it to tower over the seated Delancie.

"Please, Mr. Thayer, sit down." Delancie's expression of calm concern didn't change. "I'll explain everything."

Jason, giving up for the moment, threw himself into one of the high-backed wooden chairs in front of the desk. "Okay. This better be good. And it better be fast, because if Verity's not here, I need to get out there and find her."

"I assure you, we're already looking. We've alerted the authorities and we feel it's only a matter of time before we locate her. But let me tell you what happened. As it turns out, I was given a report that said that Miss Thayer was in time-out, written by one of our part-time staff who fills in when I must be away. I didn't check the report. Since in the past when given time-out, Miss Thayer tends to remove herself to her room and stop interacting with the other residents, I assumed that she was doing the same this time. It wasn't until this morning that I discovered that she had left the facility."

"So you don't—I don't know—*check* to make sure your people are here every day? Don't you have some kind of roll call? Don't they have to go to school or something?"

Delancie sighed. "Mr. Thayer, we do what we can. We don't have a lot of money here, and our staff is somewhat—shall we say—a skeleton crew lately. Because Miss Thayer is one of our older residents, and because she has been improving so dramatically over the past few months, we generally don't keep as close a watch on her as we do some of the other younger or more—er—emotionally fragile residents. As I mentioned, Miss Thayer still has occasional episodes, but it's been quite some time since she's had one."

R. L. KING

"So you think she might have had one and it caused her to take off?"

"It's quite possible. She did make an unauthorized phone call, as you know, which tells me that she might well have suffered a setback. Some of her particular delusions involve paranoia — the belief that certain people mean her harm."

"Certain people? Who?" Jason leaned forward. "Have people around here been mistreating her? Bullying her?"

Delancie shook his head. "No, no. In fact, the few times I've seen her under this impression, the focus is invariably upon different people each time. Sometimes it's random people who walk by. Sometimes it's a staff member, or a resident. Once it was me. It's not an uncommon problem, and she's not the only one who suffers from it."

Jason sighed. "Well, whatever's going on, I need to find her. And when I do, I'm taking her home with me, back to Ventura. This place obviously isn't working for her." He glared at Delancie. "I want the number of the local police department, and I want to talk to her friends here."

"I'll be happy to provide you with all the information I've given the police about the case, and put you in touch with the detective who's responsible for it. But I'm afraid I can't let you talk to any of the residents here." Delancie looked genuinely rueful. "I doubt they would know anything anyway, but regulations prevent it. I can't allow you to compromise their treatment programs by interrogating them."

Jason almost growled. "But you're okay with compromising V's treatment program by not keeping a close enough eye on her that she can't bolt without anybody seeing a damn thing, right?"

"Mr. Thayer —"

"No, no, never mind," he said, shaking his head violently and standing. "Forget it. I can see I'm not gonna get anywhere with you. Give me the police info and I'll get out of your hair. Next time you talk to me, it'll be with my lawyer. If you can't run this place well enough to keep track of a seventeen-year-old girl with mental problems, maybe there needs to be somebody who can." Jason was bluffing, but he hoped Delancie didn't know that. He didn't even *know* any lawyers. Maybe Stan did. But in any case, he couldn't afford one.

"Again, Mr. Thayer, you'll have to do what you must," Delancie said, rising also. "Let me get that information for you. And if there's anything else I can do to help you that doesn't require compromising confidential information —"

Jason was about to grunt out a negative when he realized there *was* something. *Let's see how much Mr. Sharing-and-Caring really* does *want to help.* "Yeah. There is, actually. Do the kids here have their own rooms?"

"Some of them do, yes."

"Did Verity?"

"Yes, she did."

"Okay, then. I want to see it. If she doesn't have a roommate then that shouldn't compromise anybody's confidential information, right? I'm my sister's legal guardian, so I should have access to her stuff, right?"

Delancie didn't answer for a moment, appearing to be mulling over Jason's request and searching it for ulterior motives. Finally he nodded. "All right, Mr. Thayer. I'll take you there. But I must insist that I remain in the room with you while you look."

"Yeah, whatever. Let's go."

They were heading out the door when a young girl around fourteen came barreling down the hall. "Dr. Delancie," she called, skidding to a stop. "Davey Chen is having an attack. Martha said I should come get you."

Delancie looked ruefully at Jason. "I'm sorry, Mr. Thayer, but I do need to attend to this. I hate to ask you to wait, but I can't let you go to Verity's room alone."

Jason was about to protest when another voice sounded from behind him. "I'll take him up there, Doc." He turned to see one of the two guys who'd come to the door with Delancie—the bald black man. "You go deal with Davey. It'll be okay."

Delancie obviously didn't like this idea, but he got one look at Jason's expression and sighed. "All right. Thank you, Charles. Just make sure that he just goes to Miss Thayer's room, that he doesn't take anything with him when he leaves, and that you both come back here when he's done. I'll be up when I can." With another sigh, he quickly headed off to follow the girl.

"Let's go," Jason told Charles. "I gotta get out there and start looking for her, so time's wasting."

Charles nodded, leading him back down the hall to the common area, then up a flight of stairs. "This way." Jason noticed a kid about fifteen sitting at the top of the stairs, his arms wrapped around his knees, rocking gently back and forth. The kid didn't even appear to notice him and Charles as they passed.

Verity's room was second from the end of the hall. Charles pushed the door open—"We don't let the residents have locks here," he said in answer to Jason's questioning look—and motioned him in. "Like the doc said, you can look around but I can't let you take anything with you."

Jason got started right away. First he stood in the middle of the room and just looked around. There wasn't much to look at. The room was quite small, barely large enough to hold the twin bed, dresser, nightstand, minuscule desk, and chair. A tiny window on the far wall was covered with institutional white curtains, and the opposite wall had another narrow door that Jason assumed led to a closet. A small shelf over the nightstand contained a few paperback books, with some gaps in between. There weren't many decorations, either: a shaggy purple rug next to the bed, an alarm clock with a blue glowing face and a small teddy bear on the nightstand, a couple of album covers on the wall featuring gothy bands with attractive but scary-looking female singers, but that was it.

He started with the desk, which had only one drawer. No help there — nothing but empty notebooks, pencils, a couple of candy bars ("She's not supposed to have those," Charles said, but he didn't seem too disturbed by it and he didn't confiscate them).

In the dresser's two drawers he found some underwear, three folded sweaters, a few books that looked like textbooks, a couple of hats, ticket stubs from long-ago movies she must have seen. "She didn't have much stuff, did she?" he asked Charles. "Do you know what she took with her?"

"She had a bag — I think she took some clothes, a few books, her portable CD player and some discs...I don't see this ratty old stuffed tiger she had, so she must have taken that too. She didn't have a lot of stuff. She wouldn't have had a lot of time to pack, either — the staff do rounds once every hour and they'd have caught her for sure if she didn't get out fast."

Jason nodded, feeling more and more stressed. There were no clues here. He found no notes hidden in the underwear drawer, nothing stuck between the pages of the textbooks. "You guys already went through here, I assume, yeah?"

"Yeah, after we discovered her missing. Sometimes they leave notes. Didn't find anything, though."

Jason sighed, lifting up the mattress and glancing underneath. Nothing. Ditto the pillow. The last place to look was the closet, and he wasn't holding out much hope. This turned out to be justified—nothing there but jeans, T-shirts, one dress that looked like it had never been worn, and two pairs of shoes lined up next to each other on the floor. "Well, this was a bust," he said at last, after going through the pockets of the jeans and finding nothing.

"Coulda told you that," Charles said. "But it makes sense you'd want to look for yourself."

Jason glanced up. Charles was scribbling in a small notebook he must have taken out of his pocket. "What are you writing there?"

"This? Oh, nothing to do with Verity. I keep notes about stuff I need to do so I don't forget." He motioned toward the door. "Hey, listen, if you're all done here we'd better go. I gotta get back to work, unless you want to see anything else—?"

Again, Jason sighed. "Nah, that's okay. I guess my next stop is the police station." He looked at Charles. "You knew V, right?"

"Yeah, I've worked here for awhile. You get to know the residents."

"Did she seem upset about anything? Was anybody hassling her? Do you have any idea why she might have wanted to leave here so quickly?"

Charles thought about that for several seconds, then shook his head slowly. "Not that I know of. She was always kind of a quiet kid—listened more than she talked, and seemed sad a lot. But nothing different than usual lately." He paused. "This is a good place, Mr. Thayer. They take good care of the kids here. And she was on track to get out on her own soon, too. It didn't make any sense for her to take off." He offered Jason his hand. "You take care, Mr. Thayer. I hope you find your sister. I'm sure

Doc Delancie's doing the best he can to track her down, but havin' family involved can move things along, you know?"

Jason took the offered hand and shook it. He almost jerked, startled, when he felt the small piece of paper touch his palm, but managed to suppress the reaction. He shot a questioning look at Charles's dark eyes, but the man merely made the most imperceptible of head-shakes and smiled. "You ready to go back down now?"

"Uh...yeah. I'm ready." Jason pocketed the little piece of paper and followed Charles back down the hall and down to the common room.

Delancie was just coming out another doorway, looking a little frazzled. Jason was strangely satisfied to see that the man was *capable* of being frazzled—it made him somehow more human. "Did you find anything, Mr. Thayer?"

Jason shook his head. "Nope. I guess my next stop is the police. You got that contact info?"

Delancie nodded. He pulled out a notebook similar to the one Charles had, quickly copied the information from a business card onto it, and handed it to Jason. "Lt. Arrelli is handling the case. Talk to him, and he should be able to tell you more than I'm allowed to. Good luck, Mr. Thayer. I assure you, this kind of thing happens occasionally, and we've always had the runaway back here within a few days, safe and sound. I'm confident the same will be true for your sister."

"Yeah..." Jason grumbled. "I hope you're right."

He waited until he was back at his motel room before he looked at the paper Charles had slipped him. Carefully unfolding it and spreading it out on the table, he stared at the hastily-scrawled words:

Kona Club, 8 p.m.

Quickly he scrambled to the nightstand, yanked out the local phone book in the drawer, and riffled through the business section. There it was: Kona Club, on Monterey Road in San Jose. He found a pen and wrote down the address below the penciled note, then pulled out his map. That was a few miles south of here. Sounded like some kind of bar. *What the hell — ?*

Why would this guy want him to go there? Did he know something about V? Or was he part of whatever was going on, and wanted to get him on his own turf? Who was this Charles guy anyway, and why did he —

The thought that popped suddenly into his head almost made him cringe in embarrassment. All at once he could hear Verity's voice on his machine, clear as if he was playing the recording again: "*Charles says I have to go...*"

He could have kicked himself. He had somebody who was connected to V, who might even know what the hell was going on, right there alone in a room with him and he'd spent his time pawing through her underwear drawer and looking for clues in her textbooks! "Idiot!" he said aloud to the empty room.

Okay, then, of course he was going to have to go. But eight o'clock was a long time away, and he still had the cops to talk to. Maybe they'd already found her.

He didn't really believe that, and thus wasn't surprised when he went to the precinct station and got the story from Lt. Arrelli. He had to wait awhile, but eventually a short balding guy with a moustache and an outfit that practically screamed "harried overworked civil servant" showed up and asked him what he was doing there.

Jason explained things to him, and he nodded. "Yeah, I know. She's definitely on our radar, and we've got word out to the beat cops keep an eye out for her. But I gotta tell you, Mr. Thayer, with all the violent crime going on around here these days it's not a high priority. Girl almost eighteen who runs away of her own free will—I know you don't want to hear this, but when I got gangers killing each other every day, guys dismembered in alleyways, women getting gang-raped, bums and hoboes everywhere...one girl who's eighteen in a month who took off on her own—" he shrugged. "We'll do what we can, that's all I can promise you."

Jason sighed. He couldn't even dredge up his usual anger at the man. He'd been a cop's kid—he knew all about how some crimes got investigated more than others. Police departments were almost always strapped for funds, and they had to make the hard choices every day. Especially these days, with the government in bad shape and so many people unemployed and not paying taxes. "Did you talk to her friends, at least?"

Arrelli consulted his notes. "Yeah, I sent a guy out there to do some interviews, but nothing definitive. They said she'd seemed fine, nothing out of the ordinary. She hadn't said anything about wanting to leave, or thinking about doing anything drastic. In fact, according to one girl they were going to try to catch a flick with the staff the day she took off." He shrugged again. "It happens, Mr. Thayer. According to what I've got here, your sister had some emotional issues, but nothing that meant she couldn't live a normal life at this point. They said she was due to leave the halfway house when she turned eighteen, and that she had a good shot at making it on her own. Maybe she just decided to leave a little early and start a new life somewhere else. I see that all the time. Things are just fucked up all over these days—everybody thinks they can find something better somewhere else."

"Yeah..." Jason sighed. "But you *are* looking for her, right? You haven't just written her off because you think she's fine?"

"We're looking for her, Mr. Thayer. I just wanted to be straight with you."

Jason nodded. "Fair enough. And I'm gonna be straight with you—I'm gonna be out there lookin' for her too. Because I don't believe she's fine. And if you'd heard the message she left on my machine, you wouldn't either."

"I can't stop you from doing that," Arrelli said. "Just don't get in the way of my investigation, and don't do anything illegal. I know you're worried about your sister, but don't become my problem. You got that?"

"Yeah, I got it."

"Oh, and Thayer?"

"Yeah?"

"Be careful. I know you're not from around here. I don't know what things are like down where you come from, but this area—it's more fucked up than the garden variety burbs. There's a lot of dangerous characters out there on the streets, and we ain't got the manpower to keep 'em all under wraps. So take care of yourself, especially at night. I s'pose it won't do me a damn bit of good to tell you to just go home and leave this thing to the professionals, will it?"

"Not a damn bit," Jason agreed. "But thanks for the advice. I'm pretty good at lookin' out for myself."

"That's what they all say," the cop muttered.

3.

The day passed with agonizing slowness. Jason had quite a few hours to kill, so he used them doing research: studying his map of the area (he liked to be familiar with the streets in case he had to get out of a bad situation in a hurry) and then heading over to the nearest library to take a look at the last few weeks of local newspapers. He doubted it would do any good, but he figured he'd see if there were any other suspicious looking missing persons stories or anything else that might catch his eye. It was another thing he'd learned from his dad and Stan — sometimes it was the thing that seemed totally unrelated that ended up breaking the case. He asked the librarian for the previous two months' worth of papers, then took the stack off to an empty table in a back corner and spread out the most recent one.

Two hours later he had gotten through them all. He just stared at the neat stack he'd finished with for a long time: Arrelli had been right. This place was seriously screwed up for an area that was supposed to be mostly bedroom communities and computer companies. Practically every paper he'd opened had had a story about at least one missing child, escalating gang activity (the predominant gangs around here seemed to be branches of something called Dead Men Walking and something called the Blood Warlocks, who were locked in a bitter turf war, but other smaller gangs were getting in on the fringe action as well), rapes, murders, violent armed robberies — sure, this was a large area and large areas had crime, but this was crazy.

Even that wasn't the strangest of it, though. Jason doubted he'd have noticed it if he hadn't been looking through the papers sequentially, but two other types of stories caught his eye as well. They were less frequent, maybe once or twice a week at most, but they seemed so odd that by the time he got through the first month he started looking for them specifically.

One had to do with a significant uptick in the number of transients who'd showed up in the area and seemed to be settling in, with more turning up every week. Jason was no stranger to these—they had them back where he came from too. The rotten economy over the past few years as businesses failed and the government couldn't stop squabbling among itself long enough to come up with a plan to help out meant that more and more people were unemployed, and many of those, especially the ones who didn't have safety nets or family ties, were taking to the roads in search of something better elsewhere. They'd even revived the old hobo trick of riding the rails to get around. Jason didn't have anything against most of the ones in Ventura—he'd even gotten to know a couple of them who hung out Downtown and been fascinated by the stories they'd told him in exchange for a fast-food meal or a bottle of cheap booze. But he knew, too, that they weren't all just unemployed people looking for work. A significant number of them—higher than you might expect, Jason realized now—weren't right in the head. It had gone from the old days with the occasional bag lady walking down the street talking to her shopping cart to whole camps of them who had somehow found each other and huddled together for mutual protection. Jason tended to avoid this type when he encountered them—he felt a little ashamed about it, since none of them had ever approached him in a threatening manner—but he just didn't want to get involved. He had enough of that to deal with with Verity. His mind flitted briefly back to the two bums he'd met at the rest stop.

The other type of story that caught his eye—it was hard to miss—was the accounts of horribly violent crimes.

These were less frequent than the transient stories by far, but much more shocking. Jason remembered something Lt. Arrelli had tossed off in his list of things the department had to deal with: "guys dismembered in alleyways"—he'd thought at the time that the cop was exaggerating for effect. But no, there it was, right there on page 3 of the paper from three weeks ago next to a cheery ad featuring a grinning used-car salesman: "Gruesome murder claims man near Sunnyvale bar." This was a respectable local paper so they didn't go into the gory details, but it was clear enough: the man, who had been a regular at one of the nearby bars, had indeed been dismembered, his limbs spread out over a one-block area, his intestines ripped out and wrapped around his neck. Jason stared at the words, eyes wide. That wasn't the kind of thing you saw every day. That was fucking Jack the Ripper territory. You'd have to be pretty damn pissed at a guy—or a class A psychopath—to do something like that to him. The police, said the article, had no leads but advised members of the public to be careful and to avoid going out alone at night. *No shit, Sherlock*, Jason thought wryly.

He found two similar stories five and six weeks back: the first was a businessman who had suddenly and inexplicably tossed a fifty-year-old female stranger in front of a commuter train, and the second was a small camp of transients who'd all been slain around their campfire, their throats cut and their bodies laid out in a wheel-spoke pattern with their feet facing the fire. The businessman was in custody and as of the article's publication date was on suicide watch—he claimed he had no idea why he'd done it and had immediately collapsed, distraught, as the train had crushed the screaming woman's body. No suspects were in custody for the hobo camp murders. Cynically, Jason wondered how high a priority that would be, given the nature of the victims.

He sighed, tossing the last paper on the pile. Of course, all of this had nothing to do with Verity — except that it made it even more imperative that if she was out there, he'd have to find her fast. Sure, she'd been a resourceful kid when they were growing up, but she'd spent the last five years living mostly outside normal society. The thought of her out on the street with gangers and dismembering murderers and mentally unhinged bums made his blood run cold. Why was he sitting here reading newspapers when he should be out there looking for her?

Gathering up the stack, he headed back toward the front desk to drop them off with the librarian. As he walked, he looked around. Before he'd been so focused on his task that he'd barely noticed his surroundings, but now he saw that the place was mostly empty except for a couple of high school kids doing homework at one table, a bespectacled old man sitting in a chair by the fireplace reading a book, and an odd-looking group huddled around a table at the end of the fiction section. Jason stopped for a moment to look at them through a gap at the top of one of the shelves. There were five of them — three men and two women. All of them wore shabby clothes and had various bags on the floor next to their chairs. Two of the men and one of the women seemed to be having a hushed and urgent conversation, while the other woman, barely into her twenties, stared dreamily out the window and the other man scribbled something on a piece of paper with such force that he broke his pencil and had to dig in his grimy coat for another one. Even from where he was standing, Jason could smell the funk of unwashed bodies. He glanced over at the librarian, who was watching the group with distaste. She caught

Jason looking at her, shrugged, and returned to stamping books.

Jason moved to her desk and dropped the stack of papers on it. "Thanks," he said.

"You're quite welcome," she told him. "I hope you found what you were looking for."

"Not really, but thanks anyway." He cocked his head toward the table with the shabby group. "They come in here a lot?"

Her nose wrinkled. "Almost every day. I don't think they have anywhere else to go."

"They bother anybody?" He was thinking of the news stories about the growing groups of transients.

The librarian shook her head. "No, they're always quiet and keep to themselves. I just wish they'd bathe occasionally."

Jason nodded sympathetically. "Eh, probably just in here tryin' to stay warm." He waved farewell to her and was halfway to the door when something occurred to him—one of those sudden intuitive insights that his dad used to refer to as "cop flashes." He stopped and turned back, heading over to the transients' table.

The three having the conversation looked up as he approached. One was a leathery middle-aged man whose bearing suggested ex-military and whose florid cheeks suggested current alcoholic; one was an older woman with wispy gray hair and watery blue eyes, and the third was a bookish-looking young dark-skinned man in his mid twenties with a scraggly beard. It was the middle-aged man who spoke, his voice authoritative and a little challenging: "Somethin' we can do for you?" The other two looked fearful and seemed to be doing their best to melt into the scenery. Meanwhile, the young girl and the scribbling man continued with what they were doing, ignoring Jason completely.

"Maybe you can," Jason said. He moved to the edge of the table and hunkered down—he knew from experience that when you were trying to get something out of somebody, towering menacingly over them wasn't the best approach. "I'm looking for somebody, and I thought maybe you guys might have seen her around."

"We ain't seen nobody," said the younger man, but he didn't look at Jason.

"It's okay, Benny," the middle-aged man said, his tone surprisingly gentle. His squinty gaze settled back on Jason. "What makes you think we might have seen anybody?"

Jason shrugged. "She disappeared around here. Figured if you guys know the streets you might have spotted her. I'm not from this area." He forced himself to keep his expression neutral—up close, this bunch positively reeked with the mingling odor of unwashed clothes and bodies, heavy cheap perfume, and the whiff of alcohol. He was surprised there wasn't a little green stench cloud hovering over the table.

The old lady giggled. "Not from around here? Never would have guessed."

"Well," the middle-aged man said at last, "I doubt we seen anybody. We keep to ourselves." Benny nodded, still not meeting Jason's eyes. The young girl was still looking out the window, and now she'd started humming to herself. The scribbling man forked a furtive glance at Jason, then returned with a vengeance to his project, breaking another pencil with a loud *snap*. He looked frantic for a moment until the old lady reached down, rummaged in her large flowered tote bag, and produced another pencil. He snatched it up and resumed his scribbling.

Jason watched him without seeing him, seriously beginning to think he'd made a mistake coming over here. He glanced at the clock on the wall: 5:45. He'd planned to grab some dinner and then head over early to the Kona Club so he could get the lay of the land before the meet. He'd have to leave soon if he was going to do that. "Uh...that's okay," he said, rising and turning to go. "Sorry to bother you."

"What's she look like?" Benny asked suddenly.

Jason turned back, startled. "Huh?"

"Your sister. What's she look like?" Now the young man was looking at Jason. His eyes were eerily steady, dark and unreadable.

"I—uh—didn't say anything about her being my sister." Suddenly Jason was on his guard, the little hairs on the back of his neck standing up as a chill ran through him. "How'd you know that?" he demanded.

Benny shrugged. "What's she look like?" he asked again.

"Benny knows things, sometimes," the old lady said apologetically. "He don't mean no harm."

Jason took a deep breath, and realized to his shame that he couldn't give a very good answer to the question. It had been three years since he'd seen Verity. "She's...uh...seventeen. Dark hair, big dark eyes...probably dressed in black. Kinda gothy-looking, you know? She was always into that."

Benny digested that information. "Lotsa girls like that on the streets," he said at last.

"Girls not safe on the streets," the middle-aged guy said, sounding almost indignant. "Somebody snatch her, or she run away?"

"Ran away," Jason told him. "She was—staying at a halfway house." He felt like he was losing control of the conversation, and didn't want to give too much away to a group of strangers who might well be dangerous or un-predictable. "Listen, if you happen to see anybody who looks like her, ask her if her name's V, okay? That's what she goes by. Tell her that her brother's looking for her. Put the word out. Librarian says you guys come here a lot— I'll check in. You find her for me, I'll make it worth your while, okay?"

For several seconds all three of them looked at him. Then the young girl who'd been looking out the window turned to face him too. "He's good," she said dreamily. "He's a good one..." Then she turned back to the window again and said no more.

Oddly that seemed to solidify a decision for the middle-aged man. "We see her, we'll tell her," he said. "Not likely we will. If she's got any sense she'll stay away from strangers. If she hasn't got any..." he shrugged. "What'd you say your name was?"

"Jason. Just tell her Jason wants to talk to her. Tell her she doesn't have to go back." He looked at the clock again. "I gotta go. But I'm serious—I'll be back. And—thanks."

It wasn't until he'd pulled out of the parking lot and was halfway down the street that he realized what he'd noticed only subliminally when he was inside: the man scribbling with the pencil had been drawing, over and over, a series of symbols that looked very similar to the ones he'd seen at the rest stop and the motel.

4.

Heading back to the motel room to change clothes after grabbing a quick dinner, Jason couldn't help feeling more than a little freaked out by the strange group at the library. The way that guy Benny looked at him — it was like he could see into his brain. *That's crazy*, he told himself angrily. He's *probably crazy. The whole lot of them probably are. I bet they're having a good laugh about the whole thing right about now.* And the symbols the guy had been scrawling — was he just seeing things that didn't exist, and making connections that weren't there? Or was there some correlation between the people at the library and the two bums at the rest stop?

He didn't have time to worry about it, though — he had to pick his way through traffic because there was an accident on his way back to the motel (he shuddered as he passed it — a small white-sheeted form laid out in the middle of the street next to the mangled remains of a bicycle) and by the time he got there it was already almost seven. He'd have to hurry if he wanted to get his early start. He was glad now that he'd taken the time to study the map so he had an alternate route to avoid the accident. He just wished again that he'd brought his pistol along too.

Monterey Road was a long drag, full of seedy businesses, nightclubs, trailer parks, and abandoned buildings. Definitely not the nicer end of town, but that didn't surprise Jason too much. Obviously Charles wanted to meet up with him someplace they wouldn't be likely to be seen, which made Jason wonder just what kind of information he was going to be divulging. His nerves were jangling, his brain spinning out all sorts of possibilities of what might have happened to Verity when he finally spotted the Kona Club.

At least it was there and still open. He'd sort of wondered about that, actually. The lights were even on, including a couple of flickering sodium-vapor floodlamps casting weird illumination over the parking lot. A big neon sign in green and yellow near the door announced the club's name along with a jaunty palm tree whose fronds spread out over the letters. Below the sign, another smaller one in red proclaimed "Cocktails - Live Music." The whole place looked like it stepped bodily out of some sort of time warp from about thirty years ago.

The lot was about half full, mostly with older cars and a few bikes. Jason debated whether to park somewhere conspicuous or somewhere hidden, and decided that he'd take the chance on someone seeing him here in order to be sure his bike was still around when he came out. He parked near the door, then slipped a ten-spot to the gorilla checking IDs inside the door. "Keep an eye on it for me, will ya?" he asked, hooking a thumb back in the Harley's direction. "I'd appreciate it, man." He couldn't really afford it, but it was a lot cheaper than having to get a new bike. The guy merely nodded, pocketed the bill, and waved Jason in. It was 7:45.

Inside, the Kona Club was pretty much like every other dive bar Jason had ever visited (and he'd visited quite a few): smoke-filled main room, vague battling stenches of beer, cheap perfume, piss, and BO, shabby mismatched tables and chairs. Same neon beer ads on the walls, same boozy low-life patrons, same tiny stage near the back where a three-piece band was in the process of setting up their instruments. The only thing that made this place a little unique was the Polynesian theme—a dusty stuffed parrot in an oversized faded lei perched on top of the ancient TV above the bar, some nonfunctional tiki torches had been deployed in various corners, and a sign near the cash register flanked by two fake coconuts with colorful umbrellas stuck into them exhorted customers to "Try Our Special - You'll Never Get 'Lei'd' This Cheap Again!!"

Jason moved through, thankful that he looked intimidating enough that nobody would casually try to hassle him. He wondered if Charles was here yet, or if he'd even be here. Maybe he was sending somebody else. Maybe he wasn't coming at all. All Jason could do now was wait and see. He ordered a beer and took it to a table as far back as he could go and still be reasonably sure he'd be able to hear conversation over the band when they fired up. Settling himself in a chair against the wall where he could keep an eye on both the front and the back entrances, he waited.

He didn't have to wait long. Only a few minutes after eight, someone slipped through the crowd and dropped down into the chair across from him. "Wasn't sure you'd come," the newcomer said. He looked a little out of breath, and more than a little nervous.

Jason hardly recognized Charles. Instead of the neat button-down New Horizons shirt and dark blue jeans, he now wore an oversized Oakland Raiders jersey under a leather jacket, a do-rag covered his bald head, and he held a pair of dark sunglasses which he tossed onto the table. He looked more like one of the gangers that Jason had seen on the street than a respected staffer at a halfway house for kids with issues. Instantly he was on his guard. "What's—going on?" he asked, making sure to continue checking out the ways in and out in case there were any unexpected surprises in store.

"I wanted to talk to you," Charles said, leaning forward and speaking under his breath. He needn't have bothered—the band had just started to play, and Jason practically had to read lips to understand him over the din. "It's about Verity."

R. L. KING

"I figured that." Jason took a swig of his beer and tried to look nonchalant—just a couple of buddies having drinks after work. "But why slip me a note? Why not just tell me when I was there?"

"Look," Charles told him, glancing around. "I don't want to stay here long, so just listen, okay?"

"Do you know where Verity is?"

"Yeah, I'm pretty sure I do. But listen to me." He leaned in closer. "That place—New Horizons—there's something going on there. Something bad. I think Verity saw something she shouldn't have, and it scared her."

Jason stared at him. "Something bad? Bad like how?"

"I dunno, man. I'm not sure I want to know. But every once in awhile we get kids in there—they show up for a day or so, then they disappear. We got our long term residents, like your sister—they're usually okay. But the new ones—orphans, mostly. They come in, and then they're gone."

"Where do they go?"

"I don't know. Delancie says they get handed off to the proper authorities—like they've done something wrong. Maybe they have, I don't know. But it's happened too many times. Always with kids under 13. We haven't had a new resident in a couple of years, 'cause we're full up. But yet these kids still show up. And the weird thing is, they usually show up secretly. Like, nobody sees 'em come in."

"But you do?"

"I watch, man. After the first time, I just kinda keep my eyes open. I don't say anything—you get the impression real quick around there that if you want to keep your job, you just do what you're told and don't make waves." Again, Charles looked over his shoulder as if he expected somebody to be sneaking up on him. "But they always come in at night, or in the early morning, when the residents are still in their rooms."

"So what's this got to do with V? You think she saw one of these kids show up? You think she saw what happened to 'em?"

"I just know she was scared to death that night. When I saw her I was making rounds—she was on her way back to her room, and she was white as a ghost. Eyes were like half her face. She talks to me sometimes—it's like I can get through to her best, 'cause I listen, and I'm not big on judgment unless it's something that might be dangerous. Anyway, she wouldn't tell me what she saw, but whatever it was, it scared the hell out of her. She told me she had to get out before they caught her."

"Before *who* caught her?" Jason demanded.

Charles shook his head. "I don't *know*, man, and that's the truth. Might be Delancie...might be Tony...might even be the director of the place. He ain't around there that often, but he shows up occasionally. All I know is that I believed her."

"You said—Delancie said too—that she gets delusions sometimes. Hell, I know she does. I've seen 'em myself. So how do you know this isn't one of those, and you didn't just help a mentally unstable girl run away to who the hell knows what?" A little anger was creeping into Jason's voice now.

"Listen, Mr. Thayer—" Charles said, his dark eyes boring into Jason's.

"Jason."

"Jason. I've been around. I've had this job for three years now, and before that I was into some bad shit. Gangs, drugs, booze—I've seen a lot of people during some pretty bad times in their lives. And I've seen Verity when she was having her episodes. I'd bet my job that she wasn't makin' this up, or seein' things that weren't there. She saw something, and I believed her."

"So you helped her get out?"

Charles nodded. "Yeah, when she couldn't get hold of you, I knew she had to go somewhere. I couldn't go with her—it would have looked too suspicious. But I gave her the name of a friend of mine who could put her up for a few days, and a little money to call a cab. There's a pay phone down at the end of the block. Told her to go to my friend's place and I'd check up on her when things died down."

Jason's eyes narrowed in suspicion. "Why would you do all this for her? You two weren't—you didn't have something going, did you? 'Cause you're, what, in your mid 20s, and that would be—"

Charles smiled, raising his hands to ward off Jason's words. "Nah, man, it wasn't anything like that. She was just a friend—we just liked to talk when we had a chance. Besides, I'm not her type."

Jason raised an eyebrow. "She's not into—what? Older guys? Black guys?"

This time, Charles almost chuckled. "She's not into guys at all."

For a moment Jason could only stare at him. "Wait. She's—?"

"You didn't know? Yeah, I guess maybe you wouldn't, since you haven't seen her in a long time." His brow furrowed and his expression suddenly grew hard, almost like he was the protective big brother and Jason was the interloper. "That a problem?"

"What?" Jason was startled by the question. "Why would it be? It just surprised me. She never told me, is all."

Charles nodded. "Anyway, that's the story. I think it'd be better if you found your sister and got her the hell out of here. Take her back to where you come from. Like I said, I don't know for sure if there's really anything going on at New Horizons, but I'd bet a lot of money there is, and I'd hate to see her back there. I'm gettin' out myself as soon as I get paid at the end of the month. I've finally saved up enough so I can make a move."

"If you think something's up there, why don't you call the cops?"

For a long time Charles just looked at Jason as if he were trying to decide if he really *was* that naive. "Come on, man. Be serious. For one thing, I can't prove a damn thing. For another, they don't even bother with stuff like this around here anymore. And most important—I'm not exactly the law's favorite guy, you know? Like I said, I used to run with a gang, and I still deal a little weed on the side for extra money. I ain't in any hurry to get myself locked up, not with the stories I've heard about what it's like inside these days."

"Fair enough." Jason sighed and finished his beer in one long pull. "Okay, so let's go find V. You got a car? She around here?"

"I'll take you to her, but we're gonna have to use your wheels. I got here on the bus. She's back up north, in East Palo Alto. That's where my friend lives."

"Why meet here, then?" Jason demanded. "You knew you were gonna tell me where she was—why not pick someplace a little closer?"

Charles shrugged. "Wasn't taking chances. Didn't want anyplace anywhere near New Horizons."

"You really *are* spooked, aren't you?" Jason could see the fear in the other man's eyes. Whatever he was saying, he believed it.

"Listen, man." Charles stood up and leaned in across the table. "This place has been getting worse for years. There's somethin'...*bad* about this whole area. I've lived around here all my life, and it was never this bad when I was a kid. Sure, there were gangs and crime and drugs and all the shit that you get in the big city. But the last few years..." He shuddered. "I know this is gonna sound crazy, but it's almost like folks around here just got *meaner*."

Jason got up too, digesting that as he shrugged into his leather jacket. "Well, crazy or not, I want outta here. I want to find V and get her back home. So let's get on the road. The faster I find her, the faster I can make that happen."

Fortunately the ten he'd slipped the door guy must have worked: the Harley was right there where he'd left it, and soon they were headed north back up 101. "You ever get back in touch with V?" Jason yelled over the sound of the wind.

"Not yet," Charles yelled back. For all his tough appearance, he didn't seem to be enjoying the motorcycle ride very much, his hands clenched in death-grips on the grab rail behind the seat. "Like I said, I was gonna contact her when the heat died down. I didn't want to lead the cops straight to her."

Jason nodded and turned his attention back to the freeway. By his reckoning they'd be on it for about twenty minutes if the traffic cooperated. It was surprisingly sparse—he guessed that whatever passed for rush hour around here was over. He forced himself to keep his mind on the road and not think about his upcoming reunion with Verity and what he was going to say to her. Even so, he was so focused on what was up ahead that he almost missed the headlights bearing down on them fast. He moved over to the right lane to let the car pass.

It moved over too, and the lights got bigger. It wasn't slowing down. "Shit," he growled.

"What?" Charles was so busy holding on for dear life that he wasn't paying much attention to surroundings. That, and he'd put his dark sunglasses back on which meant he probably wasn't seeing much anyway.

"Hang on tight!" Jason gave him a couple of seconds to firm up his grip, then dropped the bike down a gear and opened the throttle. He didn't like pushing the Harley this far—Hogs in general were built more for cruising than racing and he knew a couple of his jury-rigs would-n't survive sustained high speeds, but he didn't really have a choice. His eyes scanned the road ahead for an exit, but he didn't see one coming up.

"What the hell are you doing?" Charles screamed in his ear. "Tryin' to get us killed?" But at that point the fast-approaching car reached them and whipped over a lane, accelerating to pull up even with them. "Holy shit!"

Jason hunched down low over the bars and risked a quick glance to the side. Two figures hung out of the pas-senger-side windows of a battered old sedan, laughing and shrieking. One of them flung something at the bike, but fortunately his aim was bad and he missed. The car veered alarmingly toward Jason's lane.

"You better hang on!" Jason yelled. "This might get ug-ly fast!" Uttering a quick prayer to whatever gods looked after insane motorcyclists, he jerked the bars to the side, barely avoiding the sedan as it straddled the lane marker, half in Jason's lane and half in its own.

"Faster!" Charles cried.

"This is as fast as we got!" Jason protested. He was al-most on the shoulder now, but one quick look at all the debris there told him he didn't want to stay there long. The last thing he needed now was to blow a tire—if that happened at this speed they'd be picking pieces of him and Charles up off the freeway in a baggie.

The guy in the back seat of the sedan shrieked again, a high keening war-whoop, and chucked something else at the Harley. This time it connected—an empty beer bottle smacked into Charles' upper arm. For a moment his grip faltered but he quickly clamped down and leaned into

Jason's back. "Those guys are DMW!" he yelled. "Bad news!"

"Ya *think?*" Jason screamed back. He edged the bike back over into the lane, then risked another burst of speed to pull ahead of the sedan. If there wasn't an exit soon, they were —

It had almost flashed by before he saw it: an open roadway to the right. The exit sign, normally reflective, had been spray-painted over so he didn't see it in time, but that didn't matter. He was going on sheer instinct now. He flung the bike to the right at the last possible moment, missing the guardrail by mere inches and sending a plume of dirt and sand flying up behind them. The car, unable to react as fast, flashed on by. Jason could hear them screaming obscenities as they disappeared up the road.

He wanted to stop right there on the exit, but he didn't. Instead, he forced himself to keep going, hung a right onto the first available road and then down about another mile before he finally slowed and let the bike roll to a stop. He switched off the headlight but kept the bike running, just in case. He could feel Charles' labored breathing behind him. "You okay?" he asked over his shoulder.

"Y-yeah." Charles forced out between breaths. "Holy shit. Just—holy shit."

"What the hell *was* that?" Jason demanded. "You guys always get crazy people tryin' to run you off the road up here?"

Charles allowed himself a few more breaths before answering, pulling off his shades and trying to get his heart rate down to something approximating normal. "None of the roads are safe anymore," he said. "Especially at night. They don't usually hit the freeways, but it happens. The DMW — Dead Men Walking. They fuck with people 'cause they can — the cops are scared of 'em. They do what they can but—" he spread his arms in a gesture of futility. "Fact of life, man."

"So you don't think they were after us, then? Specifically?" Jason twisted in the saddle so he could meet Charles's eyes.

"I doubt it. They're equal opportunity assholes. They hassle anybody they think they can get away with."

Oddly, that reassured Jason a bit. At least it didn't look like the car was going to take the next exit and loop around to try to find them. "So we just got lucky, is what you're sayin'."

Charles took a deep breath. "You don't have a car, do you? Somethin' with four wheels?"

Jason's answering smile was a little manic. "Sorry, man, what you see is what you get."

"I was afraid of that." He let the breath out slowly. "I don't mind admittin' I came close to needing a change of shorts there for a minute."

"You and me both." Jason looked around, trying to find a street sign. This area was outside what he'd memorized on his maps. "Do you know where we are?"

"Yeah. We're actually not too far now. I can get us there from here."

"But not on the freeway."

Charles shook his head vehemently. "Man, you suggest getting back on that freeway and I'm walkin' home. It's safer."

5.

East Palo Alto, it turned out, had about as much in common with its more posh sister city as Jason did with the Queen of England. His gaze was constantly moving as he and Charles rumbled down side streets, taking in the rows of shabby houses, drifts of trash in the gutters, abnormally large number of abandoned cars parked haphazardly at the curbs, and small knots of loiterers on streetcorners. "Nice place," he muttered.

"This place hasn't ever been fancy," Charles told him, "but it's really gone downhill the past few years. Used to be a lot of working-class people—it was all they could afford. But then the gangs moved in, and the lowlifes, and the place went to hell like everywhere else."

"And your friend lives here?"

"She hasn't got a job—at least not a legal one. Her place isn't the greatest, but the neighborhood's decent by EPA standards. She does all right."

Jason wasn't convinced. More determined than ever to get his sister out of here before something happened to her, he returned his attention to driving. "Turn here," Charles told him, pointing to a street off to their left. "Then take the next right at the stop sign."

They both saw the flashing lights up ahead long before they reached the house. Jason stiffened, but Charles muttered in his ear, "Be cool, man. I'm sure it's fine. Cops come around here all the time. Just be easy and don't do anything suspicious."

Easier said than done, but Jason did as instructed. As they rounded the last street, though, his worst fears were realized: three police cars with their red lights flashing, along with an ambulance, were blocking the street. "Is that the house?" he hissed. "Your friend's?"

For a long time Charles didn't answer. Then, finally: "Yeah."

"Shit!"

Jason started to speed forward, but Charles grabbed his arm. "Listen to me," he ordered. "I don't know what cops are like where you come from, but around here they're bad news. At least most of 'em are. I want to help Verity but I ain't going to get hauled in tryin' to do it. Just be cool. Don't give 'em any excuse to hassle you. Got it?"

Every nerve in Jason's body was screaming defiance; he wanted to rush forward, knock down anybody in his way, and find Verity. But even as he slowed the bike down he realized Charles was right. He wouldn't be helping her by flying off the handle. He had to see what was going on first. Pulling off at the curb two houses down, he approached the scene on foot. Charles hung back, remaining near the bike.

Almost immediately, one of the cops moved toward him. "Nothing to see here, kid," he snapped. "Keep on moving."

Jason could already see a crowd that had gathered loosely around the outer fringes of the scene: mostly women huddled with kids in small knots, a few teenagers. His quick glance around didn't spot anybody who looked like Verity among the groups. "I think my sister's here," he told the cop. "I think she's stayin' here at this house. What's going on? What happened?" As he watched, behind the cop a couple of EMTs came out of the house pushing a figure on a gurney. They quickly headed in the direction of the ambulance.

Jason tried to do an end run around the cop, intending to get a look at the gurney's occupant. "Is that her? V?"

The cop grabbed his arm and shoved him back. "I said stay back," he barked. "This is a crime scene." He examined Jason for a moment, then said, "You know the people who live here? What's your name?"

Jason turned to say something to Charles, but the man had melted into the shadows and was nowhere to be seen. Turning back to the cop, he said, "No, I don't know them. I was told my sister might be staying here, and I'm tryin' to find her. She's seventeen. Dark hair, dark eyes. Damn it, tell me if that's her in that ambulance so I can go with her to the hospital if it is!" His voice rose in anger, but he didn't care. This cop was wasting his time — if that was Verity, he didn't give a damn about the rest of what was happening here.

The cop keyed the mic clipped to the shoulder of his uniform jacket, muttering something into it. He listened for a reply, then told Jason, "No dark-haired girl around here. Don't ask me for details — I can't give 'em to you. But I can tell you the victims are both older women, one black, one white. No teenagers."

"Can you tell me what happened?" He stared at the house as if trying to see through its walls. There was yellow crime scene tape stretched across the doorway, and cops and other personnel moved in and out like busy insects intent on their jobs. "Are they dead?"

"Looks like a home invasion robbery gone wrong," the cop said. He glared. "And I'm not telling you anything about their condition. It's none of your business. Now listen, kid — move along. I can't stand here yakking with you all night."

"Yeah, yeah. Thanks. But keep an eye out for her, okay?" He was feeling the bright edges of panic starting to claw at his brain now. If she wasn't here, where was she? Did they catch the invaders? If they'd gotten away, had they taken her with them?

He drifted away from the cop, doing his best to look nonchalant until the man moved back over to his patrol car and started to write something on a clipboard. Then he moved toward the crowd. Maybe if they lived somewhere near here they might know what was up. Where the hell was Charles, anyway?

He chose a couple of male teenagers standing next to each other near the fringe of the crowd, not wanting to spook the mothers with kids. He sidled up next to them, hands casually in his pockets like any other gawking onlooker. "Hey."

They looked at him suspiciously, but nodded.

"You know what happened here?"

"Somebody got killed," the younger of the two said. He was only thirteen or so and looked worried, though he was trying hard not to show it.

The older one, who looked like his brother, nodded. "Yeah. Somebody musta broke in, and—" he made a slashing motion across his throat.

"They cut her throat?" Jason asked, surprised. That was a little extreme even for a botched robbery.

The older boy nodded. "Yeah. I looked in the window before the cops showed up. Jimmy dared me to do it. She was layin' on the floor in the bedroom, all splayed out. Looked like blood everywhere."

Jason paused to digest that. "What about the other one?" he asked, pointing at the ambulance, which was pulling away from the curb with its lights flashing.

"Dunno. She didn't live there. I think she was a friend of Miz Barnes."

"That's the lady who got killed?"

"Yeah. I recanized her." Like his younger brother, the boy was looking a lot more spooked by the proceedings than he was trying to let on, but still relishing the opportunity to tell such an interesting story.

"But you didn't hear anything? You didn't see anybody else around here? Like maybe a teenage white girl?"

They shook their heads. "Nope. Miz Barnes, she had a lot of visitors. Usually at night. Sometimes she told fortunes, too, in the daytime. But no teenage girls. Mostly men at night, and middle-aged ladies in the daytime."

Hmm. So now he knew what Charles's friend's "not so legal" occupation was, at least. "You know when this all started? When the cops got here? Did you call them when you saw Miz Barnes dead?"

The boy looked at him like he was crazy. "Call the cops? Me? No, man. I just heard somebody scream—maybe an hour or so ago. I waited a few minutes, then went to check it out. That's when I saw her. I didn't stay too long—you don't want to get caught anywhere near something like this, trust me."

Jason nodded. "Okay. Thanks, guys. Listen—if you happen to see a teenage girl around here that you don't recognize—" he reached in his pocket, pulled out a stub of a pencil and a scrap of paper, and scrawled down the phone number and room number for his motel "—call me there, okay? I'll make it worth your while if you help me find her."

The older boy looked at the paper, then pocketed it. "Okay," he said.

"Oh—one other question. You said you heard the scream, then waited awhile before you came over. Did you see anybody leaving? Running away?"

The boy shook his head. "No. They musta gone out the back. We didn't see nothin'."

"Okay, thanks." Jason sighed, heading back toward the bike. Every time it seemed like he had a lead on Verity's whereabouts, something happened to snatch her away from him again. If he'd been a more paranoid type, he'd have to start thinking that somebody was doing this on purpose. As it was, he needed to figure out what to do next. Was she out on the street somewhere? Had she fled the scene when the intruders had busted in? Had they busted in at all, or were they "clients" of Miz Barnes's and something had gone wrong? The questions were definitely beginning to outnumber the answers.

As he approached the Harley, Charles detached himself from some shadows and nodded to him. "You find out anything?"

"Where have you *been?*" Jason demanded. "You kinda left me hangin' out to dry there."

"Sorry. I told you before—I can't afford to get mixed up in this and lose my job. Cops see somebody who looks like me around a crime scene and things start to get ugly."

Jason nodded. He didn't like it, but he didn't doubt it was true.

"What'd you find out? I take it Verity's not there? If that was her in the ambulance you'd be followin' it, not standin' here talkin' to me."

"Yeah, she's not there. You know somebody named 'Miz Barnes'?"

Charles's eyes widened. "Yeah. Melody Barnes. That's my friend, the one who took V in. Why? What happened? Is that her in the ambulance?"

Jason took a deep breath. He'd never been good at breaking news gently. "She—uh...I'm sorry, Charles. She's dead."

"What?" Charles gripped his arm hard. "What do you mean, she's dead? Dead people don't get taken away in ambulances!"

"That wasn't her in there. It was some other woman who was visiting her. Your friend—they said she was murdered. I'm sorry," he said again, and he genuinely was. Caught up as he was in the search for his sister, he had no reason yet to believe that she wasn't alive. This woman, whoever she was, wasn't so lucky. This was bad stuff.

Charles stared at him for a moment, then dropped his gaze. "Aw, man..." he muttered.

"You two weren't—?"

"No. We had a thing awhile back but it didn't work out. She was older than me, and we never quite agreed on her...uh...business. But she was good people. And you can bet those cops aren't gonna spend much time tryin' to figure out who did it. Just another black hooker dead—what the fuck do they care?"

Jason didn't know what to say, so he covered it by mounting the bike and firing it up. "I want to cruise around the area a little. I don't expect we'll find V, but I gotta at least try. I'm out of options, otherwise. After that I'll drop you off at your place. Where do you live?"

"Home? I don't want to go home. I want to go to the hospital. I want to see this friend. Maybe she can tell me what happened to Mel."

Jason nearly slapped himself. Of course! There was still somebody who'd been involved with this who was still alive, and he'd completely forgotten about them. "Yeah, okay, let's do that. Hop on. Maybe she can tell us something about V, too."

6.

Cruising the neighborhood and the couple of miles surrounding it for the next half hour or so yielded nothing except some suspicious stares from locals and a close call when a police car started to follow them but then veered off in another direction at a high rate of speed shortly thereafter. "You know where this hospital is?" he called back to Charles. "Aren't there quite a few around this area?"

"Well, they ain't takin' her to Stanford Med," Charles said bitterly. "Best bet is EPA General. It's close, and they take people who don't have insurance."

With Charles yelling directions over Jason's shoulder, they soon arrived at East Palo Alto General Hospital. It had definitely seen better days, that was obvious even this time of night. The found the front entrance and hurried inside.

The waiting room was packed with people of all types: parents hovering over sniffly kids, a group of teenagers with a friend who had a bloody bandage wrapped around his arm, a couple of small knots of bums keeping to themselves in the corners, and hospital personnel bustling in and out constantly. There were no available chairs in the waiting room. Charles cocked his head toward the desk. "You ask," he told Jason. "They aren't gonna take me seriously dressed like this."

Jason nodded, hurrying over. Three nurses were seated behind large admitting desk, two of them intent on making notes on clipboards. The third looked up. "Yes, may I help you?" Her expression clearly said, *you don't look like you're dying. Go sit down and wait.*

"Uh...we're here to see somebody who I think just got brought in. Maybe in the last half hour or so?"

"Name?"

Uh oh. "Uh...I don't know her name. She's a friend of a friend. There was some kind of robbery at her friend's house and she got hurt. We want to see how she's doing."

The nurse was looking suspicious now. "Sir, I'm sorry. As you can see, we're very busy here. I can't spend the time to try to track down somebody if you don't even know her name. If you want to wait, things tend to slow down after three a.m. or so. I might be able to help you then."

Jason sighed, glancing down at his watch. It was only a little after midnight. "Yeah, thanks," he said, hurrying back to Charles. "No dice," he told him. "You don't know this friend's name, do you?"

Charles shook his head.

Jason watched more people moving in and out of the waiting room, and a thought struck him. "Hey, if there are this many people here, I doubt they'd bring her into the main waiting room. She'd go straight to emergency, right? Maybe she'll still be there!" Without waiting for an answer, he ran out the way they'd come in, scanning the signs out front. He spotted one labeled "EMERGENCY" with an arrow pointing off to the right, and took off. He could hear Charles pounding along behind him, already out of breath.

Nobody bothered them when they busted through the double swinging doors and hurried down the hall, dodging gurneys both empty and occupied. If possible, this place was even more chaotic than the front desk area. At the end of the hall was a large open area filled with more people on gurneys, people sitting around moaning in pain along with worried-looking friends or family, and even more scurrying hospital personnel. It smelled like the faint scents of blood and vomit overlaid with a heavy sharp tang of antiseptic. As he and Charles stood there trying to figure out where to start, a loud voice called "To your left!" They leapt out of the way as a gurney bearing a blood-soaked male figure hurtled by, propelled by two ambulance attendants and a nurse.

"Busy place," Jason muttered.

"Yeah. Sad thing is, some of these people are probably gonna die waiting to get seen." Again Charles couldn't keep the bitterness out of his voice.

Jason didn't have time to worry about the socioeconomic implications of inner-city emergency care right now. His eyes darted around trying to spot any women on gurneys, but so far all of the patients were men or teenagers. Then he noticed an area off to their left that had been blocked off by movable dividers. "Let's try over there," he said, and hurried off.

He pushed aside one of the dividers just far enough for him and Charles to get through, and found himself in a wide open area that had been compartmentalized into a series of semi-private cubicles with more dividers. Each of the sections contained a hospital bed, and from what he could see, most of them were occupied by patients. There were aisleways between them, with doctors, nurses, EMTs, and the occasional civilian hurrying busily back and forth. Nobody seemed to be paying any attention to Jason and Charles as long as they stayed out of the way. "Come on," he muttered. "If we hurry we might be able to find her before they chuck us out. Should we split up?"

Charles seemed reluctant to do that, and Jason didn't press the point. He picked a direction and hurried down the aisle, glancing left and right quickly at each occupant and then moving on. Several bloody teenagers, an old lady with an oxygen mask, a little girl with a bandage wrapped around her head — she had to be here somewhere! They had to catch a break at some point during this whole mess.

R. L. KING

The area was like a maze of misery, filled with moans and beeps and the occasional scream of pain. Every once in awhile an opening would present itself to veer off left or right, and once the whole thing opened out into a central area with a large desk and a lot of medical equipment. Jason realized that the makeshift "rooms" were arrayed in a square pattern around the central monitoring area, giving the hospital people the quickest access to all four sides. He ducked back down the hallway, not wanting to be seen by anyone wondering why he and Charles looked like they had no idea where they were going.

"Hey, I think I might have found her!" came Charles's low voice over the moaning and beeping. Jason rushed back toward his voice, peering into openings, and found him standing next to a bed two cubicles down.

Jason stared down at its occupant. It was a woman in her mid-thirties, chubby and pale, with wildly curly dyed-blonde hair and garish, almost theatrical-looking makeup. Her eyes were closed and there was an IV line snaking from her left arm up to a bag of clear liquid on a stand. On the other side of the bed a monitor beeped steadily. The bedcovers were pulled down a bit to reveal a blue hospital gown and a bulky bandage that appeared to be wrapped around her right shoulder and the upper part of her chest. "You think this is her?" he whispered.

"Yeah," Charles said, looking down at her too. "She looks like the type Mel would hang around with. Hurry up, though—if it's not her we have to keep looking."

Jason's reluctance to try to wake the woman was overcome by his compulsion to find Verity. Gently, he reached out and shook her uninjured shoulder. "Uh...you awake?"

"Willow," Charles said suddenly.

"Huh?"

"That's her name. Says here on the chart. Willow Meadows." Charles was down at the foot of the bed, peering at a metal clipboard hanging there.

Jason let his breath out and nodded. "Willow?" he asked, a little louder, with frequent glances toward the opening of the cubicle. "Willow, can you hear me?"

The woman moaned a little and shifted position. That might have been a bad idea, as she grimaced in pain. Her eyes opened. They were green and bloodshot. "Mmm?"

"Willow, can you hear me?" Jason asked a little louder. "Are you a friend of Melody Barnes?"

That seemed to solidify her gaze a bit. "Mel?" she mumbled. "Is Mel okay? Is she — ?"

"I'm really sorry, Willow," Jason said patiently, "but we need to ask you some questions. It's really important. Can you help us out?"

"Mel? She's — she's dead." Tears formed in the corners of Willow's eyes. "Dead...they...they killed her."

Jason nodded. "Yeah..." he said, forcing himself to keep his voice gentle. "I'm sorry, she is. I'm really sorry. But we need your help, Willow. I need to know if there was another person at the house. A teenage girl."

Willow nodded, looking pained and weary.

"She was there?" Jason glanced at Charles, then back. "She was at the house with you?"

"Girl...V...Vivian...? Violet?"

"Verity?"

Again, Willow nodded. "Yeah...that's it...Pretty name. Odd...but pretty. Girl was...odd too. She was there...and Su...Susanna..."

"Susanna? Who's that?" Jason looked at Charles again, but the other man shrugged and shook his head.

"Friend...We...went to visit...Mel. Then...they came. Susanna...sensed it. Sensed...them coming. Mel...didn't believe her..."

Jason was barely breathing now, leaning in close to catch her every word. "So...what happened? Did Susanna leave?"

Willow nodded. Her already pale face was growing even paler under her makeup, and her breathing was getting more labored. Next to her, the steady beep of the monitor became a little more erratic. "Susanna...said we had to go. She...she grabbed the girl...and they tried to get Mel to go too. She...wouldn't. Then they were there..." Tears flowed freely now. "Poor Mel..."

Jason nodded. "Please, Willow. Do you know where they might have gone? Verity's my sister, and I'm really worried about her. She's not used to being on the streets. I'm afraid somebody's gonna hurt her if I don't find her. Do you know where Susanna lives?"

Amazingly, Willow chuckled at that. "Susanna...don't live anywhere. But...I think her group...might be hanging out at an...abandoned...fruit packing plant over on Broadway St. in Redwood City these days. You...know it?"

Jason looked at Charles, raising a questioning eyebrow. "That whole area's industrial," the other man said, surprised. "Most of it's abandoned now. Warehouses and manufacturing, I think."

"That's where she'd be?" Jason asked Willow. "That's where she'd take my sister?"

Willow shrugged, then her face screwed up with pain and the beeps became even more erratic. "Most...likely...unless they got her." She reached out and gripped Jason's arm; her grip had nearly no strength. "Listen...watch out for DMW. They're...bad news."

Jason's eyes widened. "That's who did this to you? DMW?"

Willow didn't answer. "Bad...news," she repeated. "Worse...than you know." For several moments she closed her eyes, and Jason thought she might have passed out. Then she opened them again. "Give me...pencil...paper..."

For a moment Jason didn't process what she'd said. Then he scrambled to pull the pencil stub out of his pocket and darted his gaze around looking for another scrap of paper—he'd given his last one to the kids at the house. Charles pressed his little notebook into Jason's hand. He quickly turned to an empty page and handed it to Willow. "What do you want to write?" he asked. "You can tell me, and I can—"

Willow shook her head, taking the pencil and notebook. Laboriously she wrote something on it, then let it and the pencil drop on to the bedcovers. Jason picked it up and stared at it. There were no words, just a single symbol:

"What is this?" he asked her.

"Look...for that," she said. "And...if you see Susanna...or anybody...show that paper to 'em."

"I don't get it," Jason said. "Show them this paper? Why?" He ripped the page out of the notebook, put it in his pocket, and handed the notebook back to Charles.

He didn't get an answer, though. Suddenly Willow looked stricken, her body jerking once and then settling back on the bed. The slightly erratic beeping grew even more erratic, and her breathing quickened and became labored. Jason stared, wide-eyed for a few seconds, then yelled, "Help! Somebody get over here!"

A few seconds later a nurse clad in green scrubs hurried in, followed by an orderly. "What are you doing here?" the nurse demanded, moving quickly to Willow's side and beginning to check her out.

"We're—we're friends of hers," Jason said quickly. "We heard she was here, and—"

"Get out," the nurse ordered. "Both of you, now!" She wasn't even looking at them, instead focused completely on Willow. She barked an order at the orderly who hurried off. "Move!" she said to Jason and Charles, and then, a little more kindly, "Go back to the waiting room. We'll let you know when we know anything."

They took that opportunity to get out before anybody else showed up and punched holes in their flimsy cover story. Nobody bothered them or even appeared to notice them at all as they hurried back out through the waiting room to the parking lot. Jason was breathing hard, keyed up and a little overwhelmed with everything that had happened in the last hour. For a few seconds he and Charles just stood by the bike and caught their breath. "You don't know this Susanna person, right?" Jason asked Charles at last.

Charles shook his head. "No, man. This is getting way out of my league now."

Jason pondered. "Listen—like you said, this isn't really your problem anymore. I'm really sorry about your friend. I don't know what else to say. But you got no dog in this fight anymore. I know you gotta get back to work tomorrow, and it's already late. Let me take you back to your place and then I'll head over and look for V at this building she mentioned." He wasn't really in a hurry to part company with Charles, but he had to reluctantly admit that there was really no reason for him to still be involved.

"No." Charles shook his head. "I'll see this through with you, at least for tonight. Like I said—I like V. She's a good kid, and I'd hate to see her get caught up in bad shit. I'm on call tomorrow so I can't help then, but I got a couple more hours before I gotta get some sleep. And I know the area a lot better than you do. Let's go. Maybe she'll be there and we can just get her back and call it a night."

After a moment, Jason nodded. "Okay, then. Let's get going." He paused a moment and pulled the paper Willow had given him from his pocket. He smoothed it out and showed it to Charles. "You ever seen anything like this?"

Charles stared at it for several seconds, then shook his head. "I don't think so. There's weird graffiti all over the place anymore, but most of it's gang tags. That doesn't look like a gang tag."

Jason decided against telling Charles about the weird symbol he'd seen at the rest stop and at the motel he'd almost stayed at. He was convinced that those and the one he held now were related somehow, but he had no idea how. He'd hoped to be able to ask Willow, but at this point he didn't think that was going to be possible. Instead, he swung a leg over the Harley and started it up. "Tell me where we're going," he told Charles. "Is it far?"

"Not too far. Few miles."

Jason nodded and pulled out of the parking lot. After a quick stop to gas up they were on the road again, keeping to city streets. "Did you hear what she said?" he called back over his shoulder. "About this Dead Men Walking gang being worse than we knew? Wonder what she meant by that."

"No idea. I know they're bad news. When I used to run with the South Bay Boyz, DMW were small potatoes — even smaller than we were. Used to be called the Zombies. They've been growing fast, though, over the past few years. That's hard to do. Usually smaller gangs that step out of line get knocked down fast."

"What do you think happened with these guys, then?"

"Nobody knows. Rumor is they got themselves a new leader and he was able to pull things together. A lot of people got killed back then. It was a bloodbath for awhile."

"And it isn't now?" Jason yelled without turning his head.

"That's when it started, is all I'm sayin'. Before that, the gangs mostly just fought among themselves over turf and biz. DMW just likes causin' trouble, and like I said, the cops are scared of 'em."

Jason just nodded, returning his attention to steering. They'd moved out of residential territory now and were entering an area that looked more like what Willow had described: light industrial and warehouses. There weren't many streetlights: most of the ones that weren't broken were out, and the few functional ones flickered crazily as if they might just give up at any moment. It didn't help that they were yellow and made the whole area look even more menacing than it already did. "Should be around here somewhere," Charles told him. "Broadway is some-where around here, but I'm not sure exactly where. Drive around and I'll watch signs."

Jason did as instructed. This whole situation was weirding him out and raising all kinds of red flags in the back of his mind. They hadn't gone that far from the hospital, but he was finding it hard to believe that two weaponless women could have made it this far on foot this quickly without being attacked by some street predator. From the look of things buses didn't come anywhere near this area, at least not at night, and he doubted that they had the cash necessary to convince even the bravest cab driver to venture over here. *Maybe they had a car,* he reminded himself. *Nobody ever said they didn't.*

"There's the street," Charles called, poking him in the shoulder and pointing. "Hang a left here."

Broadway Street was long, seemingly deserted except for a few derelict cars, and had even fewer working lights than the main drag had. The buildings were large and obviously long abandoned, set back from the street and towering up on either side of them like some kind of malevolent urban canyon. Jason kept checking his mirrors, unable to shake the feeling that somebody was watching their every move. In front of them, the beam from the Harley's headlight picked out drifts of trash blowing lazily across the broken asphalt.

"I don't like this, man," Charles said nervously.

"I don't either. Keep your eyes open—let's find this place. I feel like a sitting duck out here in the road." He was trying really hard not to think about snipers. Not that snipers were anything he'd ever encountered before except in books, but if there were any around this would be the ideal place for them. It would be nearly impossible to see a figure perched on one of these high roofs.

They cruised the entire street, and by the time they reached the tee intersection at the end of it, they hadn't seen anything resembling a fruit-packing plant. "You sure we got the right street?" Charles asked.

"You heard her too. Broadway." He pointed at the sign, which hung at a crazy angle on its pole. "That's where we are."

"Maybe we went the wrong way. Turn around and let's look again."

Jason executed a big lazy U turn and rumbled back down toward where they'd come from, his eyes constantly swiveling left and right. They'd gotten about halfway back to the intersection when he spotted it: a large building with corrugated metal sides, set far back from the street. One of the flickering streetlights happened to be nearby, allowing him to pick out the faded words "Del Valle Packing Co." on the large sign near its front entrance. "How the *hell* did we miss that?" he asked nobody in particular.

"Hey, look." Charles poked him in the shoulder again and pointed. Jason had to squint a little to see it, but over the riot of colorful gang graffiti that covered most of the surface, he made out the triangle-and-rays symbol that Willow had drawn on the paper in his pocket. It was spray-painted in white over top of the gang tags and looked relatively fresh. "She said look for that. This must be the place."

Jason nodded, already turning off the road and in to the plant's large parking area. The Harley bounced and juddered over bits of torn-up concrete and patches of bare dirt with small scrubby plants poking out of them. Behind him he could feel Charles' tenseness like it was a tangible thing. "See anything moving?"

"Nothin'."

"Well, they wouldn't be out here. They're probably holed up inside somewhere. Damn, I wish I had a flashlight. You don't, do you?"

"Sorry, man. Fresh out."

Jason parked the bike in the shadows near the front of the building. "Wait a sec, I might have something." He'd forgotten about a small tool bag he kept strapped to the back of the seat. Digging in it, he emerged with a flare. "Not a great solution and it won't last long, but better than dark. Let's save it till we need it, though—still need to find a way in."

The front doors were locked tight and chained up with a heavy padlock. Motioning for Charles to follow him, Jason moved along the front of the building to the left edge, then started off toward the rear keeping close to the wall. It was very dark here but he didn't want to use the flare until they were inside. He stumbled along, occasionally tripping over chunks of loose concrete but managing to maintain his balance. Charles was slower, huffing along behind him.

After several minutes they reached the rear of the building. They still hadn't found any way in — there were windows but they were too high up to climb to and none of them appeared broken or open, and a single smaller door, which was locked as tightly as the front door had been. The whole place had the deserted air of a building that had not seen any human contact for a long time. "You didn't pick locks in your days as a ganger, right?" he whispered to Charles.

Charles chuckled despite his nervousness. "I was more the 'stand around and look intimidating' type."

"Okay. Let's keep going."

The back part of the building definitely held more possibilities. The pavement sloped down and ended at a concrete loading dock with steps leading upward from ground level on the side nearest where they were. They could barely make out two large rollup doors, both of which were closed, and a stack of rickety pallets and broken wooden boxes piled haphazardly on the dock next to the corrugated metal wall. "Let's try this," Jason whispered. He headed up the steps to the dock, careful not to trip over the boxes and pallets. They were all over the place, all broken, but the biggest concentration seemed to be next to the wall. There was very little light back here, just the small amount that filtered over from the two barely functional streetlights on the road bordering the back part of the plant.

Charles moved over and tried to push one of the roll doors upright, but it too was locked down tight. Jason discovered that the other one was too, as was the smaller door to the left of them.

"Well, damn." Jason was beginning to get quite frustrated now. Either Willow had lied to them, they were at the wrong place, or whatever way you got into this place was hidden so well a team of bloodhounds couldn't find it. He even glanced upward to see if there were any broken windows back here, thinking he could pile pallets and make a suicidal attempt at climbing them, but he realized that there was no way Verity and Willow's friend would have been able to do that even if there had been windows. There weren't any.

"What do we do?" he hissed. He wanted to hit something, punch a hole through this wall and get *in* there.

Charles didn't answer; he was examining the small door but didn't appear to be getting anywhere. "Want to try the other side?" he asked at last.

"Yeah, in a sec." Jason moved back to the stack of pallets and boxes. It was fairly tall—almost as tall as he was. Seemed weird that they were stacked like that, not neatly but kind of just tossed there. None of them appeared to be intact, either. He leaned in a little closer and that was when he saw it. There were no gang tags back here, just a lot of dirt and grime. Carefully sprayed onto one of the larger sections of broken boxes was the triangle symbol. "Here," he called. "Help me move these, willya?"

Together, he and Charles shoved aside the debris piled near where the sign was. "Aha!" Jason whispered in triumph. "There it is!" He pointed at a section of the corrugated metal that appeared to have been cut away from the side of the building, then carefully reattached with the seams lined up. It would be hard to spot for anyone who wasn't looking for it, especially with all the junk in the way. "Keep a lookout, okay?" he requested, and squatted down to examine it more closely.

In only a few seconds he'd figured out how it worked: it was attached on one corner and spun on that point. So all he had to do was shove it aside and slip through the resulting opening, which was about three feet square. "You can come on in now," he called, scrambling further in to make room.

Charles, wider than Jason, had a little more trouble getting through, but soon the two of them were standing inside on the dusty concrete floor in what felt like an enormous empty space. Even though it was pitch dark in here, the area just *felt* enormous. "Light up the flare," Charles's voice came nervously from beside Jason.

"In a sec." Jason took a deep breath. "Verity?" he called "You in here? It's me, Jason." His voice echoed insanely around the metal interior of the cavernous space.

"Don't *do* that!" Charles hissed, fumbling around and gripping his arm tight. "We don't know *what* the hell is in here!"

"Shh!" Jason shook himself free of Charles's grip and strained his ears to listen for any sounds as the echoes of their voices died. All he could hear were the beating wings of some small flying creatures hurtling fearfully around up in the rafters, no doubt startled by the voices.

"Light the *flare,* dammit," Charles ordered.

This time Jason complied. He pulled off the top and struck it; instantly the immediate area around them was bathed in eerie red light and their eyes were dazzled by the sudden illumination. The light didn't extend out very far, but they could see that they were indeed standing in a large empty space. Looking at the floor, Jason could see the large bolts sticking up which undoubtedly had held down heavy machinery at one point, but that was all gone now. "Let's take a look around."

"They're not answering—maybe they're not here."

"Or maybe they *can't* answer. Maybe they're hurt." Jason held the flare out in front of him and began making his careful way across the floor, mindful of the many bolts and bits of debris strewn around. There was dust everywhere, but there were also footprints in it—*somebody* had been here recently. From the look of things, many somebodies. He checked his pocket for his knife and wished once again that he'd brought his gun. *If we don't find her tonight, tomorrow I'm finding a way to get another one,* he told himself. He pointed out the footprints. "Somebody's been in here," he said.

Charles nodded but didn't answer. He was staying close to Jason, not wanting to get too far from the single light source.

Jason continued to pick his way forward, frustrated that he couldn't see more than a few feet ahead of him. He vowed to throw a flashlight and some spare batteries in his tool bag tomorrow, and had to smile a little wryly at all these promises he was making to himself.

"Is that a door?" Charles's whisper broke the silence and startled Jason.

"Where?"

Charles pointed. Sure enough, at the far corner of the room, which they'd almost reached, appeared to be a small pod of a room attached to the wall. It had a door with a tiny window set into it, and a larger window that looked out over the plant floor. This larger window was broken, the glass spread out all over the floor in front of it. "Let's take a look," Jason whispered.

Together they moved over, and Jason shined the flare into the little room through the broken window.

It had clearly been an office at some point. A broken desk and a file cabinet without any drawers had been pushed back to the far wall to maximize the amount of available space. A closer look revealed why: spread out around the floor in the middle of the room were shabby blankets, one patched sleeping bag, a couple of tote bags, a number of empty grocery-store bags, food wrappers, and the remains of what looked like a hastily abandoned meal. The smell in the room was not just the musty disused odor of the rest of the area, but also included more than a whiff of unwashed clothes, and a smaller hint of something else—ketchup, maybe? Definitely some sort of food. "There was somebody here, and not long ago," Jason told Charles, pointing.

Charles nodded. "If there were homeless folks here, they wouldn't leave their stuff unless they had to get out in a hurry. Lot of folks, that's all they've got in the world."

Jason tried the door: it was open. He moved into the room, not sure what he was looking for but thinking he might know it if he saw it. "Why would they leave? Do you think somebody broke in here?"

"Hard to say. No easy way to tell if there's blood—not in that red light. But it doesn't look like there was a struggle..."

Jason shined the flare around trying to spot anything that looked like it might be blood, but didn't see anything. It was like whoever had been here had simply gotten up and deserted their meal in mid-course. "I don't think there's anybody in here anymore," he said, unable to keep the tone of defeat from his voice. "Damn it, where *is* she?"

He was about to take a frustrated punch at the drawerless file cabinet when he heard something. He put up his finger and glanced warningly at Charles.

"What—?"

"Shh!" he hissed.

This time they both heard it: a loud rumbling sound, coming from outside—from the front of the building if Jason's ears were accurate. "Shit!" he snapped.

"That's bikes," Charles said, suddenly more nervous. "Oh, man—Willow said to watch out for DMW. If that's them—"

"If that's them, we're fucked. And we're sitting ducks in here. Come on — we need to get out before they come around the back. *Shit!*" This time he *did* slam his fist into the file cabinet. "My bike's out there!"

Charles was already leaving, but he couldn't go any faster than the light source. "Come on, man. We gotta go."

They hurried across the floor as fast as they dared, still having to dodge bolts and debris. When they reached the hidden hole they paused, listening. The rumbling seemed farther away — either the newcomers had left or more likely they couldn't be heard this far back. "Let me go first," Jason said. "If they're already in the back we're gonna be vulnerable when we're coming out."

Charles had no objection to that plan, so Jason quietly swung the corrugated panel aside and slipped out behind the pile of broken pallets, trying his best to be as silent as possible. He stopped again to listen and heard nothing close, though the rumbling was more audible now that he was outside. Whoever was out there, they were still here. "Come on," he hissed back at Charles. Moving out of the way, he crouched down behind another pile of debris and kept watch on the nearest corner of the building. Reluctantly he doused the flare by putting the cap back on it. It would make it harder to see, but would also make *them* harder to see.

Charles emerged from the hole with much grunting and muttered swearing, but he too got out safely and joined Jason behind the pile. "What now? If they're up there we can't go back to get your bike."

"Lemme think." He took a deep breath, his brain spinning out one crazy idea after the other. He didn't want to leave the Harley up there, but a bike — any bike — wasn't worth getting themselves killed over. If he could get it back, though, they'd have a better chance of escaping than if they tried to do it on foot. At last he said, "Stay here. "I'll go back and scout around — see if I can figure out where they are."

"Like hell," Charles protested. "No way I'm stayin' back here. Let's just make a run for it. Sorry, man, but I ain't dyin' for your bike."

Jason was just about to reluctantly agree that was the best course of action when the rumbling started getting louder. More distinct now, it didn't sound like the low throaty rumble of a Harley, but the higher-pitched, more manic sounds of sportbikes. Multiple, from the sound of it. They were coming closer, straight up the same alley Jason and Charles had taken a short time before.

Jason grabbed Charles's jacket sleeve. "Come on," he whispered. "We'll have to risk going the other way. If they come back here maybe we can circle around and grab the bike before they come back."

Charles looked dubious but now that the intruders were coming, even making a run for it no longer seemed smart. Unfolding himself painfully from his crouch, he hurried after Jason.

It didn't sound like they'd left a moment too soon. The sportbikes once again got louder just as Jason and Charles disappeared around the opposite corner, then quieted a bit. Had they stopped? Were they investigating the back part of the building, looking for anybody hiding there? Jason didn't know and he didn't care. With Charles once again puffing behind him, he hurried down the opposite alleyway toward the front of the building.

There were some boxes and debris piled up along here too, and as they reached the front edge, Jason pointed at them. "Hide here for a minute. I'm gonna look around and see if they're gone. If they only left one I should be able to take him if I get the drop on him. You come lumbering along behind me like a freight train, that ain't gonna happen."

Charles glared at him with some indignation, but he was still breathing hard and couldn't exactly deny the charges. "Hurry up, man," he exhorted. "They come this way, I'm runnin', freight train or no."

"Deal," Jason muttered. He moved forward and peered around the edge of the building. He couldn't see anything—no lights or signs of movement—nor could he hear anything but the far-off rumble of the bikes in the back. He couldn't be sure, but it looked like his bike was still where he'd parked it. Keeping close to the wall he sidled along the front of the building toward it, eyes constantly in motion searching for potential threats.

It was still there. He took a few seconds to give it a quick visual inspection—it didn't look like anyone had touched it. The tires were still pumped up and as far as he could tell it was still in the same place he'd parked it. He turned back toward the corner he'd come from and motioned Charles to join him. With any luck they could just hop on the bike and get the hell out of here before the guys in the back even knew they were gone.

Charles crossed the distance in next to no time—the guy might be chubby, but he could move when he had to. "Shh," Jason whispered. "Let's—"

Lights suddenly appeared around the other side of the building, momentarily dazzling them, pinning them to the wall like two insects in a killing box. "Got 'em!" yelled a triumphant, strangely manic voice. "Get up here! We got 'em!" Almost immediately the other motorcycle sounds began to get louder.

Jason swore. He had a decision to make now, and he knew whatever he picked would likely mean the difference between whether they lived or died—if they even had a chance to live through this at all. He could dive for the bike, try to get it started and get them out of here, or he and Charles could make a run for it and try to lose themselves in the night. The bike itself didn't even matter anymore. It was worthless next to their lives.

As it happened, the guy on the bike made the choice for him. With a high-pitched, insane laugh, he reached into his jacket and pulled out something, which he chucked in the direction of the Harley. "Down!" Charles yelled, grabbing Jason's jacket and yanking him backward.

The object flew unerringly at the Harley, coming to rest almost directly in front of it and exploding. The sound ripped through the quiet night as flames erupted around the bike. The kid on the sportbike was laughing the whole time, as was his friend on the bike next to him. "Next one's for you, shitheads!" he yelled.

Jason could see light patterns approaching now — the other bikers were close. "Come on!" he yelled to Charles. "We gotta get outta here *now!*"

Charles wasn't arguing. He and Jason both took off back toward the corner they'd come from. It was only when they reached it that they saw more lights approaching from that side. Damn — boxed in! The only direction they had to run now was straight out through the front parking lot, and that would be a killing field if the bikers had guns.

The other bikes were emerging from either side of the building now: two on each side, making six in total. Two of them had passengers, including one who looked smaller than the others. Jason took all this in in the space of a few seconds. So far he couldn't see any guns, but he was sure they were hidden somewhere in the gangers' jackets. Lacking anything else to do, Jason pulled his knife from his pocket and flicked it open. If he was going down, at least he was going down fighting. Next to him, out of the corner of his eye, he could see Charles doing the same thing. "They DMW?" he muttered sideways.

Charles nodded. "Yeah." He sounded resolute and scared, like he was preparing to die.

"If we run they'll shoot us, won't they?"

Charles's answer surprised him: "Nah. DMW don't use guns. They like to get up close and personal. And they like to blow shit up," he added unnecessarily, cocking his head back toward the burning Harley.

The bikes were coming closer now, moving slowly, rumbling into a semicircle in front of them. "They don't use guns? You serious?"

"They're known for it. It's kind of their signature."

Jason drew in air through gritted teeth as one of the bikers in the middle of the semicircle reached inside his jacket. "I'm gonna do something crazy, then. Be ready, okay?"

"What the — ?"

But Jason didn't wait for him to ask questions. Instead, he spread his arms, yelled something unintelligible at the top of his lungs, and immediately turned to his left and sprinted toward the nearest bike, which happened to be the one with the rider and the smaller pillion.

Sometimes God or the universe or whatever runs things out there favors the idiots, and for one of the few times in Jason's life he got the benefit of that favor. The biker was so startled by this utterly inexplicable action that he hadn't even moved when Jason hurtled into him, grabbing him and tossing him off the bike. He scrambled to his feet quickly, but Jason had already tossed off his passenger as well (*a kid? Seriously? Nah, I must be wrong*) and leaped onto the sportbike.

The other bikers weren't as easily startled, though. The guy who'd reached into his jacket yanked out another of the small grenadelike objects and flung it in Jason's direction. He gunned the engine and shot forward, coming to a quick stop next to Charles, barely avoiding the explosion where the bike had been. "Get on!" he screamed. This whole plan was predicated on keeping his level of panic and adrenaline high enough that he didn't stop to think about how completely insane his actions were.

Charles hurried to comply, but he was a big man and there wasn't as much room on the back of the sportbike as there had been on the Harley. He stumbled and fell against the bike, his weight upsetting Jason's balance so he had to put his foot quickly down to avoid toppling over. "Fuck!" Charles yelled, scrambling to get his feet under him again.

The other bikers were getting closer. Jason knew he couldn't hesitate. "Take this, assholes!" he yelled, gunning the bike again and stuffing it through the open space between the two bikes in front of him. One held his ground, but the other peeled off to the side. Jason spun the bike around (these things handled a hell of a lot better than the Harley) and zipped back toward Charles.

Only Charles wasn't there anymore. He'd taken advantage of the gangers' momentarily lack of attention and made a run for it, back toward the corner of the building. "Get him!" yelled one of the gangers, turning his bike to get some light on the fleeing figure. Charles was only feet away from making it around the corner of the building. If he could do that, then maybe they might have a chance. If he—

And then the middle ganger leapt off his bike and did a very odd thing, all in the space of a few seconds. Jason got a look at his face as he went by—his eyes were cold and dead-looking, gleaming with some sort of malevolent fire. He didn't quite look human. Crouching down, he jerked up the figure of the smaller passenger from where he'd fallen. Then, with one hand on the boy and one hand pointing authoritatively at Charles's retreating form, he yelled...*something*. Something loud and so completely foreign that Jason couldn't even start to make it out.

Several things happened nearly simultaneously at that point:

The ganger's hand seemed to glow. A crackling nimbus that Jason wasn't even sure he'd seen properly appeared around it, and then arced out toward Charles.

Under his other hand, the boy's body began to shake as the nimbus surrounded it as well.

Some sort of glowing force jumped from the ganger's hand to Charles's head.

Charles screamed, clutching his head in agony. As Jason stared, his eyes so wide he had completely forgotten to blink, blood began to erupt from every hole in Charles's head. His eyes, his nose, his mouth and his ears began to spew blood so forcefully that it splattered the near wall of the building he was next to. All of this was surreally illuminated in the headlights of the other bikers' rides. Abruptly Charles's screams ceased. He dropped to the ground in a crumpled heap and didn't move. For a second or two afterward, another scream—higher pitched this time—echoed Charles's, and then that too was stilled.

Eyes still bulging with panic, Jason took a quick glance sideways at the guy who'd apparently caused all of this. He was standing there, a look of triumphant glee on his face. Jason realized with horror that he looked like a man experiencing an orgasm. All around him the other bikers had similar expressions. For a moment, Jason forgot to move too. He stared at the lead biker and noticed that the boy was gone as well. All that was apparently left of him was a heap of clothes and pile of what looked like ashes on the ground.

Suddenly, something slammed into him from behind and he was thrown sideways off the bike. He crashed to the ground, landing painfully on his right arm. One of the laughing gangers had recovered his senses enough to run his bike into Jason's, and was now towering over him, gunning his engine. "You like that?" he called. "You like that? You wanna see some more? We got lots of tricks!"

Jason struggled to scramble to his feet. His mind was still spinning, his heart pounding so hard he could feel it moving his ribcage. The bikers were surrounding him now. He turned in place, still holding the knife but so confused he wasn't even sure he'd know what to do with it. The lights were dazzling him. What the hell had just happened? What had that guy done to Charles? What—

Suddenly in the periphery of his awareness he heard the sound of screeching tires, and another set of lights appeared, approaching fast. More bikers? Oh, shit, not more—

A bright light, brighter than the bikes' headlights, erupted around two of the gangers and they dropped like someone had cut their strings, their bikes clattering down next to them. The other bikers spun around. A large black car had rolled up and screeched to a stop parallel to the scene. A shadowy figure leaned out the window. "Get in, you fool!" the figure yelled. "Hurry up!"

7.

Jason, still running completely on instinct, didn't hesitate. He vaulted over the car's hood and dived in through the open passenger door. He had no idea who his savior was, but he didn't care. Even if it was yet another enemy, at least he'd have another chance to get himself out, and he'd be more likely to do that against one than against six. "Go! Go!"

The bikers had recovered quickly, and four of them were now circling the car as the other two hustled their bikes back upright. One of them reached into his jacket. "Look out!" Jason yelled. "Go! He's got a—"

The shadowy stranger ignored him. Instead he stuck his arm out the window, directing his palm toward two of the gangers. Jason stared, wondering if he was finally succumbing to whatever hereditary madness had gotten hold of Verity, as a bright glowing shield appeared in front of the gangers. Too late to stop his throw the lead one tossed his firebomb, which impacted the shield, bounced off, and exploded right at his and his friend's feet. They flew off their bikes and hit the ground, bloody, aflame, and screaming, then lay still. For a couple of seconds Jason saw—or thought he saw (he couldn't be sure of much of anything at this point)—a shimmering effect blur the air above their bodies, then rise up and dissipate into the night.

"That's done," the stranger said grimly. "Now let's get the hell out of here." Jason only had time to notice two things—he had a British accent, and he sounded exhausted—before he gunned the engine and the car rocketed out of the parking lot. The remaining gangers, amazingly to Jason, didn't follow.

"Wait—Charles—" Jason protested. "We can't—" He couldn't get the image of blood erupting out of Charles's eyes out of his mind.

"He's already dead," the stranger said without stopping. "Nothing we can do about that now." The car careened down the street, fishtailing back and forth like it was being piloted by a drunk. Jason decided not to say anything about that. He glanced over at the stranger—he looked maybe mid-thirties, dark hair, dressed in a dark overcoat. The slump of his shoulders and the way he held his head told Jason that there was definitely something not right with him.

As if to punctuate this, the stranger jerked the car to the side of the road, hit the brakes, and threw it into park. "Drive," he ordered, already getting out. He swayed on his feet, leaning on the hood. "Can't—"

"You want me to—?" This guy he'd never met before wanted him to take the wheel? Things were getting weirder and weirder.

"You can drive, can't you?" the stranger snapped, impatient.

"Yeah, but—"

"Do it, then." He was already working his way unsteadily around the front of the car, and when Jason got out, he dropped into the passenger seat and appeared to momentarily pass out, his head lolling against the window. His face was pale and Jason could see tiny drops of sweat standing out on his forehead.

He looked back down the road in the direction they'd just come from, halfway expecting the DMW kill squad to be approaching with friends. Nothing there, but that could change any second and he knew it. He jumped into the driver's seat. "Where we going?" he demanded, hoping the stranger was conscious enough to reply.

"Drive to Palo Alto," he said without opening his eyes. "I'll be all right in bit. Stay off the freeways, and tell me when you get there."

Jason nodded. His heart rate was starting to return to normal now, as was his breathing. This beginning of a physical recovery brought with it the crashing down on his brain of everything that had just happened in the last few minutes. "What the—" he started. "How did—" He couldn't seem to get out a coherent thought. The enormity of events was threatening to overwhelm him. "You— they—"

"Hush now," the stranger murmured. "Just drive. Let me rest for a bit. I'll try to explain when we get where we're going."

That was hard for Jason to do, with about a hundred questions whirling around in his mind trying to force their way out. But he kept quiet, figuring he owed the stranger that much for saving his life. He drove, concentrating on watching both in front of them and behind and hoping that nobody bothered them. The car, which the logo on the steering wheel revealed to be a Jaguar of some sort, purred along obediently; he could feel the power under its hood ready and waiting if he needed to gun it, but he hoped desperately that he wouldn't have to. His nerves were about as frazzled as it was possible for them to be right now—any more shocks and he was afraid he might just spontaneously combust or something.

Like that kid. That guy touched him and he—

No, don't think about it. Just drive. Don't think at all. It's safer that way.

The stranger neither moved nor spoke for the next several minutes. Jason got the car back to El Camino—he didn't know the area well enough to navigate all the way to Palo Alto on back streets. As soon as the territory started to look familiar, he ventured, "Uh—are you there?"

The stranger nodded, pulling himself to a more up-right seated position. "I'm here. Going to have a frightful headache for awhile, but that's an occupational hazard." He looked around, getting his bearings. "Ah, good, you made it. We'll be there in no time now."

"We'll be — where?"

Instead of answering, the man merely gave him more directions. A right turn and then another half-mile or so of wending their way down narrow, tree-lined streets, and the stranger reached across to trigger a garage-door open-er under the sun visor on Jason's side. "Here we are. Just pull in here."

Jason did as he was told. The driveway sloped downward into a single-car garage under what looked like a venerable old two-story house. He stopped the car and handed the keys to the stranger, afraid to say any-thing because once he did, he knew he wouldn't be able to stop.

"Come on," the man said. He was sounding much more aware now, though still tired. "I'm sure you've had quite a night of it, and I could do with a cup of tea — or p'raps something a bit stronger — myself." Without wait-ing for an answer, he unlocked a door at the front end of the garage.

Jason followed him quickly up a short flight of stairs. The stranger removed his overcoat and tossed it over a hall-tree near the top, then led Jason into a kitchen that looked like it didn't see much use. "Have a seat," he said, motioning toward a small breakfast bar littered with books and old newspapers. "I'll have this tea on in no time and then we can chat."

Jason sat, taking a perch on one of the stools. He put his head in his hands and shoved his hair back, feeling very much like his brain was trying to either shut down or fly into pieces. To distract himself, he watched the stranger as he worked. He'd gotten the age right—somewhere between mid thirties and early forties. He was tall and thin, dressed in jeans and an old oversized black fisherman's sweater over a white T-shirt. Jason couldn't see his face at the moment, but his hair was dark brown, untidy, and slightly longer than the current fashion for a guy his age.

In a few minutes the tea kettle the man had put on was whistling merrily; he pulled out a couple of cups from a cabinet, puttered with them briefly, and set one in front of Jason. "Liquor cabinet's in the other room," he said. "Let's go out there and sit down, and I'll see about satisfying your curiosity before your head explodes. Amusing as that might be to watch, it would make a dreadful mess and Mrs. Olivera would flay me alive for ruining the carpet."

Jason chose not to answer this, wondering if he'd cast his lot in with yet *another* insane person. He did seem to attract them. Instead, he picked up the steaming cup and followed the man down another hall into a large room. "Sit anywhere you like," the stranger said, dropping down into an ancient leather armchair near one of the room's softly glowing lamps. "The good stuff's in the cabinet over there by the fireplace."

Jason just stared for a moment. He'd never seen a room anything like this, at least not outside of TV shows about people in England or somewhere in the old-money East. One of the four walls was lined with wooden book-shelves, with more shelves taking up the longest wall flanking a large brick fireplace. Every last inch of the shelves was full of books, weird-looking objects (*was that a skull?*), and neat stacks of old newspapers. There were more books piled on the floor near the shelves. A large window on the third wall was covered with heavy cur-tains. The furniture, from what Jason could tell in his limited experience with such things, was old, quite probably very expensive, and well-worn. The whole place looked like a cross between an old-fashioned library and an antique shop specializing in international oddities. Hesitating a moment, he opened the indicated cabinet, examined the contents, and pulled out a bottle three-quarters full of whiskey. He waved it at the man questioningly.

"Good choice. Dose me up, there's a good chap. And sit down before you fall down. You look more done for than I feel."

Jason again did as requested, pouring a healthy measure of the whiskey into the man's teacup and another into his own. He put the bottle down on one of the small tables scattered around the room, then finally allowed himself to slump down on the overstuffed sofa in front of the window. It was strange, but now that he was (at least supposedly) safe and at last free to start asking questions, it was as if something had shifted his brain into neutral. He didn't even know where to begin. Every time a question occurred to him, another even better one flitted by and knocked it out of the way. It was like trying to catch fish in a fast-running stream.

The stranger regarded him for a few moments over steepled fingers, and then when it became obvious he wasn't going to speak, he smiled ruefully. "This is all a bit much to take, isn't it? Believe me, you have my sympathy. Why don't I start, shall I? Introductions are a good place to do that, I think. I'm Alastair Stone. And you are—?"

"Uh...Jason Thayer."

The man gave him a sideways, searching look, but did not comment. "Jason Thayer. Excellent. Now we can stop calling each other 'hey you.'" Alastair Stone took a sip of his tea and set the cup down on a side table. "Now that we've got that out of the way, I'm sure you have a lot of questions. I've a few of my own, but those can wait. Or, if you'd rather—" he pulled a pocket watch from his front pocket, consulted it, and returned it to its place. "—it's getting rather late and I'm sure you're quite tired. You're welcome to stay here until morning, of course. You can—"

"No." Jason shook his head violently. "No...I'll never be able to sleep. I can't—"

"Quite understandable," Alastair Stone said sympathetically. "You've seen rather a lot of new and baffling things tonight, haven't you? I'll wager you don't even know where to start with your questions. I'll do my best to answer what I can. Just pick somewhere and start, and we'll go from there. And if you need more tea, just let me know."

Jason took a deep breath, gathered his thoughts for a few seconds, and plunged his mental hand into the stream. He blurted out the first thing that popped into his mind: "What—what happened to Charles?"

"Charles." Stone raised an eyebrow. "Is that your friend, the man who died? Terribly sorry, by the way. If I'd arrived sooner, I might have been able to prevent that. Dreadful waste." He shook his head sadly, staring down into his teacup.

"Yeah...What happened to him? He was running away, and then—" He could feel himself starting to shake a little as the images flooded back into his mind. "They didn't shoot him—I didn't hear a shot—but...there was blood—everywhere—"

Stone nodded. "Hmm," he said after a moment. "I might have to alter my approach, now that I give it a bit more thought. This is going to be hard enough for you to digest without giving it to you in scattershot bits and pieces. Let's try this: tell me what you saw tonight."

For several seconds Jason contemplated that in silence, still trying to organize his thoughts. He poured another healthy shot of whiskey into his teacup (there was more whiskey than tea in there now by a good margin) and took a large swig. "Do you — know me?" he asked at last. "Do you know who I am?"

"Let's just assume for the moment that I don't," Stone said with a raised eyebrow. "Start at the beginning — or at least the beginning of when you got to that warehouse, and why you were there in the first place."

"I was — looking for my sister. Verity. She's seventeen, and has...mental issues. She ran away from her halfway house, and I'm up here trying to find her. Charles — he worked at the halfway house, and he thought she took off because she was scared of something. He was trying to help me find her."

An odd look crossed Stone's face, but it was quickly gone. He nodded. "Go on. Why the warehouse? Did you think she was there?"

"Yeah. She was supposed to be staying with one of Charles's friends, but when we got there the friend was dead and my sister had taken off with somebody else. We found that out from another woman who'd been at the house. She was hurt but not dead."

Again Stone nodded, expressionless. "And this other woman told you they might be at this warehouse? That seems an odd place for them to go, wouldn't you say?"

"I thought so, but the woman in the hospital told us the other woman was homeless, and her group was squatting there. We went inside and found evidence that somebody'd been there, but nobody was there when we were. It looked like maybe they'd left in a hurry."

"Any idea why?"

This was all sounding so utterly normal that Jason had almost managed to fool himself into believing that it wasn't all going to take a left turn into the Twilight Zone any minute now. He hung onto these last moments of sanity like a drowning man clutches at a life preserver. "Well, it wasn't long before the DMW showed up. They were the gangers," he added. "Dead Men Walking, Charles told me. I guess they're big around here."

"I'm familiar with them," Stone said with a small, wry smile. "So what did you do when they got there?"

"We were inside—we thought we were done for, since neither of us had a gun, but we had to do something. We left through the back—there was a secret way in. When they came around the back, we went around the front. We thought we'd make it, but—" he spread his hands as if to say, *Well, you saw most of the rest.*

Stone nodded. "Go on..."

"That was about when you showed up," Jason said. His gaze, which had been roaming around the room without really registering anything, locked suddenly on Stone. He leaned forward. "What did I see back there? What the hell happened to Charles? What happened to that kid? What did you do to them? Because I know what I thought I saw, and I know there's no way that could have been what I really saw. Not unless I'm going as delusional as my sister."

Stone's expression didn't change. "What did you think you saw?"

Nearly a minute passed in silence. Something in the back of Jason's mind was telling him that if he put it into words—if he let it out into the real world—then he *was* going to go insane. Normal sane people couldn't even afford to pretend to believe stuff like what he'd seen.

"Jason," Stone said, his voice gentle. "I know it's difficult for you. I'm not going to lie to you—there's nothing I can do about the fact that none of this is going to be easy.

Might as well have it out, though. I can see it's not sitting well in there."

Jason could feel his breathing picking up, his heart starting to beat faster. At that moment, finding Verity was the farthest thing from his mind. "He—" he said at last "—the ganger... he...grabbed the kid...then he pointed at Charles..." His voice was shaking as he pictured it again. He suspected that particular image was going to be the main attraction in his nightmare theater for quite some time to come.

Stone said nothing, waiting.

"—he...his...Blood came out of his head. Out of his *eyes*." His own eyes bored into Stone's, begging the other man to give him some explanation that made sense. Spontaneous catastrophic stroke, long range sniper—he would have accepted anything that sounded even vaguely plausible. When Stone still didn't reply, he forced himself to go on: "...and he screamed. And...and..." This time he didn't even make a pretense of putting scotch in the tea. He picked up the bottle with shaking hands and took a swig straight from it.

"And what?"

"And...the kid...The kid screamed too, at the same time. I—I was watching Charles, but...I looked back at the ganger and...the kid just...disappeared. He screamed, and then there was a flare of light and he was gone."

Stone's expression grew grimmer. "Indeed. You're sure about this?"

"I'm not sure about anything anymore!" Jason's voice rose and pitched higher than his normal tone as he tried to stem his instinct to just get up and run from the room. He didn't want to hear any more. He didn't want to *think* anymore. By sheer act of will, he pushed the instinct down. "I...I'm pretty sure that's what I saw," he said dully.

"Okay," Stone said. "All right. Go on. I think that was about the time I arrived on the scene."

Jason nodded. He stared at his hands in his lap; they were still shaking. "They—the gangers, I mean—I looked at them. They were all..." He took a deep breath and swallowed. "Their faces...they all looked like they'd just—" his eyes flicked up for a second and then back down "—like they'd just had some kind of—freaky orgasm." He glanced up again, gauging how Stone would react to that.

He didn't, except to nod. "And then—?"

"And then you showed up. I got in the car. They were gonna throw one of those grenade things at us. I yelled, and then—" He took a deep breath and stepped the rest of the way over the abyss "—and then you—pointed your hand at them and the grenade hit something and bounced back."

"Right," Stone said, nodding again.

"And we got out of there." Jason shrugged, thinking a moment, then added, "Oh—and there was the shimmery thing."

For the first time, a flicker of an expression crossed Stone's eyes. "Shimmery thing?"

Jason nodded. "Didn't you see it? After the grenade bounced back and blew up in their faces, I saw the air kind of—shimmer—over them. Something flew up out of them." He stared at Stone. All this time the man had seemed to have everything under control and failed to be shocked or even affected by anything Jason had said, which had been strangely comforting. But now— "You didn't see it?"

Stone shook his head. "No. But by that point I was more than a bit incapacitated. Interesting..." He sat back and his gaze went to a thousand-yard stare for several seconds. Then he switched back on. "Interesting indeed."

"What's it mean?"

"No idea," Stone said cheerfully, shrugging. "P'raps nothing. Might have just been a trick of the light." He finished the last of his tea and set the cup down. "All right, then. We've had the what. Now I guess you'd better hit me with the why, and the how. I'm sure you've got questions. Though I'm not sure you might not be better off without hearing the answers. It's up to you."

Jason stared at Stone, realizing he was giving him an out. If he so chose, he could just get up, thank Stone for getting him out of a bad situation, and walk out into the night. He could just pretend none of this had happened. Of course, that still meant he had no idea where Verity was. And the DMW were after him now for sure, so whatever weirdness he'd experienced tonight wasn't likely to be an isolated incident unless he just gave up on Verity and took the next bus back home to Ventura. He sensed that he was looking at an open door in front of him, and he had no idea what was on the other side. If he stepped through, it would slam shut behind him and there would be no going back.

He did allow himself to feel a few seconds of regret before he made the only choice that was really available to him. "I want to know," he said at last.

Again, a flicker of something—was it satisfaction? Approval?—flitted across Stone's face. "Ask away, then."

The "blurt now, think later" style of questioning had worked before, so Jason saw no reason to change it now. "What—happened to Charles? How did that guy kill him?"

"Magic," said Stone.

Jason stared at him, momentarily rendered speechless. If he'd said "pancakes," or "universal joints," or "Martian death rays," the sentence wouldn't have sounded any more outlandish to him. "Magic," he said, glaring. "You're screwin' with me, aren't you? A nice round of 'let's taunt the crazy person'?"

Stone's own gaze was quite steady. "Do I look like I'm screwing with you, Jason?"

Watching his last chance to hang on to sanity slipping away, Jason shook his head. "No. You don't. And that's what scares the shit out of me." He let the silence hang for a long time, then looked back up. "So — you're saying that Charles was killed by magic. That the ganger — cast a spell at him. Like in the movies. Merlin the Magician and all that."

Stone chuckled. "Not much like that, no. But I assure you, magic is entirely real, and entirely dangerous."

"And you know this how — ?" Jason wasn't sure he wanted Stone to answer, and very much afraid he already knew what he was going to say.

"I think you've already figured it out, haven't you?" Stone said softly, leaning forward a little in his chair.

"You're one of them too, aren't you? A — wizard or something."

That got another chuckle. "I prefer to call myself a mage, but yes. I am."

Oh, shit. Yeah, Jason was firmly entrenched in the Twilight Zone now, and sinking fast. "So — you can — kill people by making blood come out their eyes?" He knew even as he said it that it shouldn't even make the first page of questions that were busily poking him on the inside of the skull, but he spit it out anyway.

Stone's expression grew serious. "I daresay I could if I had to — but that's not the sort of thing I make a habit of doing. I'm not that kind of mage."

"There are different kinds? What kind *are* you, then? What *do* you do?"

"Slow down, slow down. I said I'd answer your questions, but this isn't going to be easy, or fast. Are you sure you don't want to get some sleep, and we can —"

"No. I couldn't sleep now if my life depended on it. I want to know what's going on."

Stone nodded as if he expected nothing else, but had felt it was only polite to ask. "All right, then. Fair enough. Yes, there are different kinds. I'm not going to go into the esoteric details right now — I'd probably bore the stuffing out of you; I've been told I can have that effect when I get going — but the long and short of it is that magic has different manifestations, and different ways to approach its control. The most simplistic way to say it is to say that it's split between so-called 'good' or 'white' magic, and 'evil' or 'black' magic."

Jason took this in for a brief moment, then almost laughed like an idiot. It was all so absurd. He managed to quell the compulsion with difficulty, but he couldn't help grinning. "So — are you a good witch, or a bad witch?"

That actually got a reaction out of Stone. He laughed, shaking his head in amusement. "I, my dear boy, am a good witch. Or at least I try to be most of the time. As for what I do — research, mostly. And teaching."

"Teaching? Wait a minute — you teach magic? There are schools for magic?" Jason had thought things were so weird before, but he was starting to realize that he hadn't even scratched the surface yet.

"No. Not per se. I teach at Stanford, actually. I'm a visiting professor of Occult Studies."

"Occult Studies? What's that? Like...Ouija boards and tarot cards and stuff like that?"

"Not exactly." Stone chuckled. "But I can't begin to imagine that's really the sort of thing you want to ask me right now, is it? I'm not going anywhere — we can talk more in the morning about things like that, if you still want to. Let's hit the highlights now, shall we?"

Jason took a deep breath. "Okay. But much as I want to know this stuff, I really do need to get back to trying to find my sister. I don't know what she's tangled herself up in, but there's no way she's got the street smarts to survive out there very long."

"I might be able to help you with that," Stone said. "But it will have to wait until morning. There's no way I can attempt any kind of magic as wiped out as I am right now. So we might as well have our chat now and then get a few hours' sleep and start fresh in the morning."

"Wait—" Jason stared at him. "You can help me find her? Why would you do that? You don't know me from some bum on the street. I don't know you. I don't even know why you came by there tonight. That whole area was deserted. We didn't see another car the whole time we were there. How did you know what was going on?"

"Hrm," Stone said. "I'll leave that one for now, I think. Suffice it to say that I was in the area on some business and decided to investigate. It's really not important why at the moment. It's just fortunate that I did happen to drive by."

"Damn fortunate," Jason agreed. "Okay, then, you don't want to tell me that, I guess I'll have to deal with that. As long as you don't plan to blow me up or make my brains leak out my ears, we're cool."

"No plans of either type," Stone assured him.

Jason leaned back on the couch, debating whether or not to take another swig of the scotch. He decided against it—the last thing he needed to go with all the rest of the night's insanity was a raging hangover. "What happened to the kid?" he asked suddenly. At Stone's raised eyebrow, he added, "The one that got—torched."

"Ah." Stone nodded. He sighed, looking troubled. "What you witnessed there, my friend, is the primary difference between so-called black and white magic."

Jason's eyes widened. "You mean you have to kill people to do black magic?" That didn't seem logical— you'd either be limited in a hurry in the amount of magic you'd be able to do, or you'd end up being hunted down as a serial killer in pretty short order.

Stone shook his head. "Not always. You see, the fundamental difference between white and black magic is philosophy, and mindset. It all comes from the same source, but the way it's accessed is different. Practitioners of white magic draw their power from within themselves, and from carefully constructed rituals and objects designed to channel the power safely. Black magicians wrest the power from others. Depending on the immediacy and power level of the spell, and its potency, this can either kill the 'battery' or drain him of energy for a time. Some powerful dark mages keep people around for this very purpose, compelling them with the sheer force of their personalities." He shook his head in what was almost a shudder. "It's a very dangerous path to take, though not without its allure. From what I'm to understand from my research, there's a definite 'rush' associated with casting black magic. It's immediate, visceral, and very powerful in the short term. Many black magic spells are combat oriented, designed to injure or kill the victim."

"So—" Jason's words came out slowly as he thought it through, "—that guy, the ganger—he drained that kid for the power to cast a spell?" He thought he might be sick as the implications hit him. "He killed a *kid* just because he wanted to use magic to blow somebody away?"

Stone nodded soberly. "Most of them aren't that blatant about it. From what I've heard, there are a few minor talents in the DMW—and all of them are dangerously unstable. You must have run into one of them tonight."

"So they're not all like that? Please tell me I'm not gonna be running into that on every streetcorner. How many of you guys *are* there, anyway?" Deciding that he needed the booze now more than he cared about the hangover later, he took another swig.

"Mages?" At Jason's nod, Stone offered him a gentle smile. "Not that many overall, though they do tend to concentrate more in some areas than others. You'll find more in large urban centers than smaller towns, for instance. Don't worry—you're unlikely to encounter another for a long time, even around here and even if you go out looking for one. We're generally a pretty secretive lot. For obvious reasons we don't flaunt our talents, because being found out would cause us a great deal of difficulty. Even the black magicians, most of them, keep quiet. They go about their business and—as they say—fly under the radar of mainstream society."

"So—why are you telling me all this? How do you know you can trust me? How do you know I won't go straight to—I dunno—the police? The media? and blab your secret all over the six o'clock news?"

Stone chuckled. "First of all, I do consider myself a fairly good judge of character, and I don't see you as the sort who'd do something like that. Second, I *did* get you out of a pretty sticky situation back there, and I'd like to think you owe me at least not causing me a large amount of inconvenience. And thirdly and most importantly: who would believe you? Let's think: 'Mr. Reporter, I know this chap and he's a magician—a real one—and he can cast real spells.' Or 'Mr. Policeman, I want you to go arrest this guy I met. His crime? He's a wizard!' They'd lock you up or laugh you out of their lobby before you were able to get half of that out of your mouth."

Jason had to admit that he had a point. "Well, it's not like I'm gonna do that anyway. Believe me, I'm grateful for all the help I can get right now. I'm feeling pretty much out of my league and have been for awhile." He spread his hands. "I mean, I'm just a guy. I fight pretty well, I can fix things, I did okay in school. But this—" He shook his head, letting a breath out in a loud hiss through his teeth. "This is fuckin' weird. And it scares the hell out of me—especially to think that Verity's tied up with it somehow." He paused a moment, then looked back at Stone. "So you say that black magicians pull the power from other people, and white ones take it from themselves. Is that why you messed yourself up so bad when you cast that spell?"

Stone nodded. "White magic doesn't lend itself well to fast, active spells like the ones I cast back there. They require an enormous expenditure of energy. As I said, white mages generally are more focused on rituals and longer-term or permanent spells. White magic is ultimately more powerful than black—for instance, we can imbue objects with magical power and use them as batteries if we need to, but they have to be specially prepared. Since the last time I cast a damaging spell was—" he thought about it "—a little over two years ago, I don't generally keep those kinds of items around."

"You said the black mages don't necessarily kill people when they use them—can you use willing batteries? People who know what they're getting into?"

Stone stared at him, looking startled and a little disturbed. "Short answer: yes. It's possible. But any white mage who would contemplate it wouldn't be a white mage for long. I told you about the rush that comes from casting black-style magic. From what I understand, it's almost like a drug. I know we're getting a little philosophical here, but bear with me. Think of casting spells as affecting your inner core...your soul, if you will. Every time you draw power from another human, especially an unwilling one, it—diminishes your soul somewhat. If you diminish it too much, it essentially makes it impossible for you to cast anything *but* black-style spells. You're so addicted to the sensation of it that you can't do anything else."

"So..." Jason ventured, "It's sort of like guys who spend so much time looking at porn that eventually they can't do it with a real-live girl?"

Stone tilted his head, then nodded. "I'd never thought about it that way, but the comparison is valid."

"Can you recover from this—blot on your soul?" In the back of his mind Jason was wondering why he was wasting time asking all these questions that had nothing to do with finding Verity, but part of him was finding the explanation interesting and he couldn't help forging on. "If you—I dunno—didn't cast black magic for awhile, would it—grow back? Kind of like detoxing off drugs?"

"You know," Stone said with a wry smile, "You'd make a very good magic student. You're quite adept at homing in on the right questions. And the answer is—yes, eventually. But it takes a long time, and any backsliding will put you right back where you started. It's the reason why, even though there aren't that many mages in the world, most of them are of the black—or at least gray—variety. It's very hard to resist the temptation."

Jason nodded. That made sense to him. Growing up as a cop's son he had encountered, at least peripherally, a lot of the bad things that happened behind closed doors in his own home town, and he doubted it was much different anywhere else. "Okay. One more question about that, and then I gotta start thinking about what I need to do next to find V. So—do black mages *need* to use other people to power their magic? You said they can't cast white spells after awhile, but does that mean they have to drag a little group of people around with them or they can't do anything? That doesn't seem very practical."

"No," Stone said. "They don't need other people. They can cast their spells under their own power just like I did back there—but with the same results. They end up depleting their own energy to the point where they have to withdraw and rest. Needless to say, this isn't something they're in a hurry to do. As I said, the more powerful ones have 'willing' minions who will share their power, but it's a dangerous thing and requires either a lot of trust or a lot of compulsion. They have no guarantee that the mage will stop with just taking some of their power."

Jason wondered why anyone would ever want to do such a thing, but didn't ask. He knew there were some very twisted people out there in the world. Unconsciously he yawned, then tried hard to suppress it.

Stone wasn't fooled. "Listen," he said, standing up. "It's almost 3:30 a.m., and I don't know about you, but I'm going to be useless tomorrow if I don't get at least a few hours' sleep. Let me show you the guest room, and we can continue this tomorrow."

Jason was torn. He was exhausted both mentally and physically—no sense trying to pretend he wasn't. But allowing himself to rest when his sister was still out there somewhere—"I can't," he said. "Verity—"

"—sounds like she's probably with some people who can keep her safe for the night," Stone pointed out. "From what you were telling me, they managed to get out of that warehouse before the DMW showed up. They're probably holed up someplace getting some sleep too. You'll be no use to her if you're so tired you can't see straight. Come on." He motioned out of the room ahead of him.

Jason sighed and rose. As he started toward the door, another random thought popped into his head. "Hey."

R. L. KING

"What?" Stone turned back, eyebrow raised.

Jason reached in his pocket and pulled out the small piece of notepaper that Willow had written on. "Have you ever seen this symbol before?"

Stone took the paper and examined it in silence for a few seconds, then looked up at Jason. "Where did you get this?"

"From Willow, the lady at the hospital. The one who told us where to look for Verity. She said to look for that symbol, or to show it to anyone I saw around there. I found one chalked on the back wall of the warehouse, near the concealed entrance."

"Interesting..." Stone murmured, as if his thoughts were far away.

"There's another one, too." Jason took the paper back, dug his stubby pencil out, and drew the other symbol, the one he'd seen at the rest stop and the motel. "According to somebody else I talked to, this one means 'bad place' or 'don't stay here.' I think the two of them are related somehow. It seems too weird for them not to be."

Stone took a deep breath and let it out slowly. "And who told you about the other one?"

"A couple of bums I ran into on the way up here, at a rest stop. I gave them something to eat, and they pointed it out on the side of the john and said I shouldn't stay there. They said that sign meant it wasn't safe. And then I saw it again, up here, on the curb in front of a motel I almost stopped at. I decided not to. I felt pretty stupid about it, but—"

"—but best not to take chances," Stone said, nodding. "One moment. May I see that again?" When Jason handed it over, he rummaged in a drawer and pulled out a notebook and pen. He copied both symbols, jotted notes next to them, and then handed the original back. "Let me think about this a bit," he said at last. "Tomorrow."

Jason knew better than to argue or press for more details. Besides, now that the possibility of sleep was near, he was finding he could barely keep his eyes open anymore. He didn't think he'd sleep with his mind whirling this hard, but at least he could rest for a bit.

8.

Jason awoke to filtered sunlight coming in through the room's open curtains and the sound of a knock on the door. "Going to sleep the day away?" came Stone's cheerful voice from the other side.

Quickly he glanced at the clock on the nightstand: a little after 9 a.m. He hadn't expected to sleep nearly that long—and he couldn't remember dreaming anything, either. "Uh...coming," he called, his mind trying to remind him of everything that had happened in the last several hours.

He was downstairs in ten minutes, after grabbing a fast shower (hardly seemed worth it, since he didn't have a change of clothes with him and he imagined his current outfit was getting pretty rank by now). "In here," Stone called from down the hall, the opposite direction from the room they'd occupied the previous night.

Jason followed the voice into a dining room dominated by a large rectangular table. Stone was seated at one end, a bunch of books, papers, and notebooks spread out in front of him. "Sit down," he said without looking up. "Hope you're hungry. Mrs. Olivera seems to think it's her calling in life to put weight on me, so—"

At that moment, a stout woman of about fifty-five bustled into the room pushing a wheeled cart full of steaming dishes. "Oh, good," she said. "Your guest is finally awake. Good morning," she added to Jason. "I hope you're hungry." She set the tray down and began offloading plates, bowls, and glasses: eggs, bacon, a carafe of orange juice, a pot of coffee, and a plate stacked with English muffins. She glared at Stone and his array of papers in mock exasperation. "Can't you wait until after breakfast, Dr. Stone? I've got no place to put your plate."

"Sorry, sorry," Stone said with a lopsided smile. He shoved everything off to the side and waited while she put down plates, silver and glasses in front of each of them. "Thank you, Mrs. Olivera. It all looks lovely, as usual."

Mrs. Olivera smiled her thanks, then made herself scarce with a "Call me if you need anything else!" over her shoulder.

Stone smiled at Jason. "My one luxury indulgence," he said. "I'd likely starve or exist on delivered pizzas and live in squalor if I didn't have someone to look after the place for me."

"Uh...yeah."

"Eat up before it gets cold," Stone told him, pouring a cup of coffee and dragging his papers back over in front of him. "We've got a lot to do today."

"We—er—do?"

"Well, we do if you still want me to help you look for your sister." Stone raised an eyebrow in question.

"Uh—yeah. Yeah, I do. I still don't get why, though."

"Let's just say it's because I like mysteries," Stone said. "And it's always nice to get some real-world opportunity to put my magic to good use. That'll do for now. Fortunately I don't have many classes this week and I was able to find a colleague to take them for me, so we can get started right away."

Again, Jason got the impression that there was something Stone wasn't telling him, but once again he didn't ask. There would be time for that later. He decided for now that he'd just keep an eye on the man—he still didn't completely trust him—but his gut was telling him that he wasn't a threat. He hoped it was right—he could use somebody on his side right about now. "Er...I'm gonna need to go back to my motel room today," he said. "My stuff's there, and I at least need a change of clothes."

Stone nodded. "You're welcome to stay here if you like. We can stop by and pick up your stuff today. I've got the guest room, and I'm going to guess you're not exactly swimming in cash right now. Safer, too, if the DMW are looking for you."

Jason had almost forgotten about that. "What, they can't find me here?"

"I didn't say that. But there are certain magical protections around the place that will make it more difficult to find than your hotel room or wherever else you decide to stay."

Jason hooked a thumb over his shoulder in the direction of the kitchen. "Does she — Mrs. Olivera — know about you —?"

Stone chuckled. "As far as dear Mrs. Olivera is concerned, I'm a slightly eccentric college professor with some very strange possessions that she'd prefer not to dust. Now then," he said briskly, becoming all business. "You said the last place you knew your sister to be was in that warehouse?"

"Well...I'm not certain she was there," Jason admitted. "Willow said that the woman she left with was hanging out with a homeless group that were squatting there. They —" he stopped suddenly as his eyes fell across one of the newspaper sections in front of Stone. He stared at the headline:

Three dead at Redwood City warehouse; fire razes building

He snatched up the paper and quickly scanned the article. "Holy shit," he breathed. "All they found were charred bodies. I guess the gangers burned the place after we left, or else the fire they started by tossing that thing at my bike did it and they took off." He continued skimming to the end. "They say they don't know who the bodies are, but gang involvement is suspected."

Stone nodded. "Nasty business. I doubt anyone saw us leave, though, or they'd be calling for the public's help in locating my car."

"Yeah..." Jason couldn't help thinking about Charles. Here was this guy who'd befriended Verity and was just trying to help her out, and now he was dead.

"Jason..." Stone's voice cut gently into his thoughts. "There's nothing we can do about what happened now. We need to concentrate on finding your sister. Now — you said you're not sure she was at the warehouse. Where *are* you sure she was?"

"At Melody's house, I think. That's Charles's friend who took her in."

"But you said something tipped her off that danger was coming, and she left with this other person, right? And her name was — ?"

"Susanna. Melody was the one killed, and Willow is the one in the hospital who told me to show that symbol when I got to the warehouse."

Stone nodded and sighed. He took the paper from Jason, turned a couple of pages, folded it over and handed it back. "I'd hoped we might question Willow, but it appears that's not to be."

Jason looked at the folded paper. Another headline:

Woman killed in EPA home invasion; second victim dies in hospital

Again, he skimmed it for details. "Willow died shortly after Charles and I talked to her," he said dully. They don't say they're looking for anybody else for questioning, and they don't have anybody in custody." He tossed the paper down in frustration. "It seems like we've got dead ends everywhere we go!"

"Not quite," Stone pointed out. "We can try to track down this Susanna woman, and hope that your sister is still with her."

"But where do we start? Willow said she's homeless. There are homeless people all over the place around here. Do we just start driving around looking for random bums to question? I kinda doubt that they have the Bum Network where they all keep up with each other's business, don't you?"

Stone shrugged. "You may be right. But unfamiliar as I am with their culture, I do believe that they quite possibly communicate more than you might think. It's a dangerous world out there—it always has been for the disenfranchised, and these days that's true more than ever. Keeping each other up to date on potential dangers and news in general would be a valuable thing."

His words triggered something in Jason's mind: he'd almost forgotten about the group of vagrants he'd spoken with at the library yesterday—that seemed like about a hundred years ago after everything that had happened in the last few hours. "Wait a minute..."

Stone glanced up from his eggs, which he'd finally noticed. "What?"

"Hang on...let me think this through a sec." Jason's mind was spinning again, trying to make connections that kept flitting away from him. "You said something about communications... Yesterday I was at a library near where I'm staying, just looking through some old newspapers for stories about missing persons. There were some of those transients there, sitting at a table. Librarian said they come in almost every day."

"Yes, and—?"

"And I went over to talk to them for a few minutes, figuring since they must spend a lot of time on the street I could ask them to keep an eye out for Verity, and I'd check back at the library to see if they saw her."

"Did they agree to do that?"

"Yeah, kinda. It was weird—they didn't really seem to want to talk to me, but then one of 'em asked me what my sister looked like. Only I hadn't told them it was my sister I was lookin' for."

"Indeed?" Stone's eyebrow rose as he once again forgot about his eggs.

Jason nodded. "Yeah. Freaked me out a little. And one of the others—this spacy girl who wasn't much older than Verity, said I was a good one, that I was okay. And after that it was like their whole attitude toward me changed. They told me they'd keep an eye out and let me know if they saw anybody who looked like V."

"Interesting..." Stone said.

"That's not all, though." Jason's voice was becoming more animated—he was sure he was on to something. "One of them didn't talk the whole time I was there. This old guy—he just sat at the table and scribbled around on a piece of paper. I barely noticed him at the time. I thought he was crazier than the rest of them. But when I left it dawned on me that what he was scribbling was a bunch of symbols that looked like they could have gone with the ones I showed you."

Stone's gaze sharpened. "Did you see either of the two we have here?" he asked, pulling his own copy of the two symbols Jason had showed him out of one of the notebooks in front of him.

"Definitely not the first one—I'd have noticed that right away, since I was still a little weirded out by seeing it in two different places within less than a day. Not sure about the other one. Remember, I didn't see it for the first time until later on that night, so I wasn't looking for it."

"Very...interesting..." Stone murmured as if to himself. He dug around in the pile and came up with another notebook. "Take a look at this," he said, riffling through it until he found what he was looking for, then opening it to a page near the middle and shoving it across the table toward Jason.

Jason looked at it, his polite interest quickly morphing into a stare of wide-eyed amazement. Across the two open notebook pages were a whole series of symbols very much like the two with which he was already familiar, arrayed in neatly written rows. All in all there looked to be between twenty and thirty of them, and the two Jason already knew about were included. Most of them had notes jotted below them, but Jason couldn't make out more than a word here or there—they seemed to refer to locations, and included dates. Several of them, including Jason's two, had tally marks beneath them and multiple notes.

"What—what is this?" he asked, unable to hide his astonishment. "Where did these come from?"

"I've been collecting them," Stone said. "For the past four or five years, ever since I saw the same one twice and made the same inference you did—that they must mean something. I haven't done anything with them other than jot them down along with where and when I saw them. I showed them to a couple of colleagues in the department but they had no idea what they might mean." He took the notebook back and examined the symbols. "All I know for sure is that they're not magical sigils—at least not in any magical system I'm familiar with, and I daresay I'm at least passingly familiar with most of them." He pointed at Jason's two. "These two are fairly common and widespread—I've seen them in several locations, over a long period of time. These, though—" he pointed at several others, one after the other "—are rarer. And a couple of these seem to be regional variations of each other: similar, but not quite identical." Finally, he pointed at one near the bottom of the page: "And this one I actually noticed on the curb in front of my own house once or twice. The rain washes it away, but it occasionally turns up again."

"So—you just drive around looking for these things? There are that many of them around?"

Stone shrugged. "I don't look for them specifically, but I've gotten better at spotting them. If you know what to look for, they're fairly common. I've seen them on business buildings, on residential mailboxes, grocery stores, abandoned buildings, schools—" He spread his hands. "The only thing that they seem to have in common is that they have nothing in common. The one there, that you say means 'bad place,' I've seen on some pretty frightening looking abandoned buildings, but I also spotted it on a perfectly innocent-looking children's daycare center in San Luis Obispo once when I spent a week down there on holiday last year."

Jason took a slow deep breath. "So—what's it all mean? Where do they come from? Who makes them? And what's this got to do with Verity?"

"I don't know. Perhaps nothing. But I like to keep my mind open. Possibilities can occur in the oddest places when you let yourself consider them."

"Yeah, I hear you on that," Jason agreed. "Hey, listen—after we go get my stuff from the motel, can we go by that library and see if they're there? Maybe they've heard something. And maybe stop by the police station on the off chance that somebody there might have gotten a line on her."

Stone shrugged. "Sure, why not? Let's get going."

"Oh—one other thing." Jason hesitated, wondering how Stone would react to what he was about to say. "I don't suppose you know where I can get—a gun, do you?"

Stone raised an eyebrow. "I trust you don't refer to going down to the local sporting goods store and picking one up?"

"Er...no. I'd prefer something — a little faster. And a little less registered. I felt way too vulnerable the other night when those gangers jumped me and Charles. If I'd had a gun, I might have been able to get us out of there."

"Sorry," Stone said. "Not really my area of expertise." He glanced sideways at Jason. "Do you even know how to *use* a gun, or is this simply the effect of watching too many police shows in your misspent youth?"

Jason grinned. "No, I know what I'm doing. My dad was a cop — he first took me to a range when I was about 9, and I've kept up on it. I've got one at home, but — well — I'm here and it's there."

Stone nodded, but he didn't offer any helpful suggestions. "Shall we, then?" he said instead, indicating the door to the garage.

9.

Picking up Jason's gear from the motel room was quick and easy (he was beginning to fear that nothing would ever be quick and easy again, so it was nice to be pleasantly surprised). He stayed long enough to change into fresh clothes, then headed up to settle his bill with the front desk and bribe the clerk to pass along any messages that might be left for him.

As they drove toward the library he leaned back against the passenger side window and watched the scenery as it went by. In the few miles they traveled on mostly commercial city streets, he spotted three of the strange symbols and pointed them out to Stone. "Yes, they're quite ubiquitous around this area," the mage said, nodding. "I occasionally have reason to leave the Bay Area on business or for holidays, and I've noticed that they occur much less frequently outside larger cities. Though I've seen a couple in and near some fairly tiny towns, so who knows? It's definitely a mystery, and I'd love to know what the hell it all means."

By the time they reached their destination it was getting close to noon. "I hope they're here now," Jason said. "It was later in the day when I saw them the last time. But the librarian did say they spent a lot of time here, so I guess there's a decent chance."

"Indeed, since apparently this is a good place," Stone said, pointing.

Jason followed the line of his finger. The symbol was quite discreet this time, chalked at ground level off to the side of the library's double glass front doors. He let his breath out slowly. He couldn't afford to get himself caught up chasing mysteries if they didn't help him find Verity, but he had to admit this one was damned compelling.

R. L. KING

The homeless group wasn't sitting around the same table where Jason had seen them before. He went up to the front desk and smiled at the librarian in what he hoped was a friendly manner. "Morning. I was in here yesterday — remember?"

She nodded. "I do. You're the one who wanted all those newspapers. Back for more? If you want to go back too much further I'll have to dig out the microfiches."

"No, no thanks. I think I got what I was looking for with them. But you know that group of homeless people who come in here?"

"How can I forget them?" she asked, wrinkling her nose in distaste.

"Do you know when they usually come in? I need to ask them something."

"Oh, they're here now," she said. "In the back. When they came in this morning I watched them mill around and point at the front window, and they seemed to get into a little disagreement. Then they all trooped back toward the study room at the back of the library." She sighed. "It's not a very big room, and it doesn't have any exterior windows. It's going to take me weeks to get the smell out if they decide that's where they want to stay. It's odd too, because they've been coming in for weeks and they always sit at that same table, or near it."

"Thanks," he said, and motioned for Stone to follow. Stone put down the magazine he'd been leafing through and together they headed for the rear of the library. "Wonder why they changed their spot," Jason mused.

"No idea. Does seem odd, though. P'raps you should ask them."

Jason couldn't tell if he was kidding, so he didn't reply.

The back room was a small brick enclosure with a single door. It had half-height display windows on either side of the door on the wall facing into the rest of the library; Jason and Stone could see a large table and several chairs; the vagrant group was seated around the table in the same configuration as they had been yesterday. All three of the lucid ones looked up almost simultaneously as the two newcomers approached; the spacey girl looked bored and troubled, and the Scribbler was still scribbling away. He'd gotten hold of a lined notepad and several pencils of varying lengths were spread out in front of him.

Jason wasn't quite sure what to do, so he knocked on the door. He felt a little stupid doing it, but apparently it was the right thing to do because the leathery middle-aged man nodded and motioned them inside. "Thought you might be back," he said, his voice as gruff and gravelly as before. The smell in here was overwhelming, but Jason did his best not to react as he stepped inside. Stone followed.

Meanwhile, the old woman with the watery eyes and the multitude of mismatched tote bags seemed to be fumbling with one of them on the floor. She made a sudden lunge as a small fast-moving *something* leaped from the bag, but she missed. It darted toward Jason and Stone, who were standing near the still-open door.

Jason was startled, but Stone leaned down and deftly scooped it up before it could escape. He held it up—a tiny black kitten with wide, frightened eyes. "Now, little one," he murmured, stroking its head with two fingers. "Trust me, you don't want to go out there."

The kitten immediately ceased its struggling and started to purr loudly, snuggling into the crook of the mage's arm. He smiled, raising an eyebrow at the old woman. "I believe you lost this?"

"She likes you," the woman said in a shy, quavery voice. "You can hold her for awhile if you like. But—" she glanced at the window looking out over the library " — she's not really supposed to be in here, so if — "

Stone nodded sympathetically. "Of course," he said, opening his overcoat and allowing the kitten to burrow inside. "No one will be the wiser, I promise."

The middle aged man had apparently had enough of all this small talk. He fixed his squinty gaze on Jason and said, "What are you doing back here? What do you want?"

"I just wanted to ask you all a couple of questions," Jason said.

"We ain't seen your sister," the man told him flatly.

"Okay, that was the first question." He was disappointed, but not surprised.

"Who's that guy?" the man asked, pointing at Stone and glaring at him rather rudely.

"He's a friend. I met him yesterday — he helped me out of some trouble."

"He's a magic man..." the spacey girl said in a sing-song voice. "Got magic hands..."

Stone looked startled, then quirked a questioning eyebrow at Jason, who shook his head and shrugged as if to say, *I didn't tell them anything!*

The middle-aged vagrant ignored them all. "So what's the second question?" His tone was confrontational.

"I wanted to know if any of you knew a homeless woman named Susanna."

"Nope," the man said, too quickly.

"Are you sure?" Jason asked. "I really need to find her — I think she's with my sister. I don't know if you heard, but she and a friend of hers were visiting a house last night and — well — some bad stuff happened."

"They died," the old woman quavered. "They were killed. It was in the paper today. We always read the paper, first thing."

Jason nodded. "Yeah. They did. I think something dangerous is going on, and I want to help. I want to get my sister out of it, and if Susanna is with her then we can try to help her too. But I need to know where they are." On a hunch, he pulled the little paper bearing the symbol out of his pocket and put it down on the table where they could see it. "Susanna's friend Willow gave me this last night, at the hospital. She said I should show it to Susanna if I saw her. Do you recognize it?"

That definitely got their attention — they didn't even try to hide it. Even the spacey girl and the Scribbler paused in their pursuits momentarily to look at it. Then as one all five of them looked up at Jason like they'd never seen him before. "You say Susanna's friend gave you that?" the middle-aged man demanded.

"Yeah. Last night. We snuck into the emergency room so we could talk to her, and she told us to show it to Susanna. Why? Do you know what it means?"

Benny, the young dark-skinned man, nodded. He glanced at the middle-aged man; when he didn't react, he continued: "We know Susanna. We knew Willow." Tears shone in the corners of his dark eyes.

Jason leaned over the table. "Do you know where Susanna is? Willow told us that her group was squatting at a fruit packing plant in Redwood City, but when we got there—"

"—they'd already left," the middle-aged man said. "Yeah."

"Do you know why they left? Did they somehow know that the DMW—the gang—were coming?"

The middle-aged man shrugged. "Maybe. Don't know." He glanced up at Jason, his eyes going a little glassy. "Hey, man, you got any weed?"

"Uh—sorry, no," he replied, taken aback by this shift in topic.

The old woman put a hand on the middle-aged man's arm. "It's all right, Hector," she said softly. "Lissy says he's all right—you're all right, too. Everything's going to be fine." Her voice took on a somewhat hypnotic cadence, like a chant. She looked up apologetically at Jason and Stone. "He has—episodes sometimes. They don't last too long." She smiled. "If Willow trusted you enough to give you that, she must have thought you meant Susanna no harm."

"We don't mean anyone any harm," Stone said, stepping forward, his tone soothing. "We simply want to find Susanna and ask her a few questions, and with any luck find Jason's sister before she gets herself into something she can't handle."

Jason nodded. "I don't know how to ask this without sounding rude, so I hope you'll understand I don't mean to. But you seem to be based down here, and Susanna was up in East Palo Alto. How do you even know about each other? You don't travel far, do you?"

"We don't travel too much," the old woman said. "But we can get around when we need to. All of us can." She paused, watching the spacey girl, Lissy, as she stared out the window at the library patrons wandering around out in the main area. "Susanna—if your sister's with her, she's safe. I can promise you that."

"How can you promise that?" Jason asked. "No offense, but you guys don't look like you'd be much good in a fight, and if they run into somebody like the DMW—"

"—if they do, there might be trouble," the old woman agreed. "That's why it's best not to run into them at all, isn't that so?"

Jason turned to look at Stone, his expression exasperated. Talking to these vagrants was like having a conversation with a group of mentally unstable seven-year-olds. They couldn't be counted on to stay on topic for more than a few minutes at a time, and when they did, half the time they didn't make sense. "So," he said, turning back, "Do you know where I can find her? Do you even know where I should start looking? Can you contact her and tell her I want to talk to her?"

"We might be able to do that," Benny said. "World's getting more dangerous. Things are going on. Not safe to be out and about, you know?"

"Yeah, I'm getting that impression," Jason agreed.

"Magic man can find her," Lissy singsonged. "Magic man can make the magic happen, if he knows how to do it. Show him, Frank. Help him make the magic..."

All of them, even Hector and Lissy, stared at the Scribbler. For a moment, nothing happened: he continued drawing random figures and patterns on his piece of paper. Then he tore it off the pad with a flourish, tossed it aside, glanced up at Stone, and began attacking the next sheet with feverish intensity.

Jason turned to Stone again and rolled his eyes, thinking that it might be best to just get out of here and carry on their search without assistance from the local chapter of the Lunatic Fringe. But Stone was not rolling his eyes or looking exasperated. His gaze was locked on the piece of paper in front of Frank. "Fascinating..." he murmured under his breath.

"What?" Jason hissed out of the corner of his mouth.

Stone didn't answer, though. He was still watching Frank intently as he worked. Jason tried to do the same, but as far as he was concerned, the man was producing nothing more than a page full of random scribbles, even less intelligible than the symbols he'd been drawing before. Everyone watched silently until at last he slapped the pencil down on the table with a *thunk*, ripped the page off, and tossed it toward Stone without looking at him.

"What is that?" Jason asked, looking back and forth between the vagrants and Stone. "How is that supposed to—"

"Shh!" The harsh sibilant hiss cut through Jason's words. For a moment he didn't realize where it had come from, and then he saw that Lissy was staring at the window, looking frightened.

"What's going on?" Jason demanded, getting frustrated.

"Coming," Lissy said. She sounded very scared. "In here. Somewhere. Coming."

10.

"Who?" Stone was looking out the window now too—nothing looked out of the ordinary. "Who is coming?"

"Did you see somebody? The DMW?" Jason couldn't decide whether he should pay attention to this delusional girl or just leave now.

"Sit down," Benny ordered, scooting to the side and motioning for Jason and Stone to take two of the empty chairs at the table. "Do it quick. And whatever you see or hear, stay quiet."

Jason looked skeptical. "But—"

"Do as he says!" the old woman said, sounding a lot less quavery than usual, though very nervous. She was twisted around in her seat and was also looking out the window into the library. All five of them looked tense, even Frank the Scribbler. "Please. Hurry!"

Stone was oddly tense too. "Come on," he said under his breath to Jason, nudging him toward the chairs and stashing the scribbled paper Frank had given him in one of his overcoat pockets. "Do what they say. Something's going on here, and I want to see how it plays out."

Jason sighed and did what he was told. He dropped down into the chair next to Hector, and Stone sat down between him and Benny. "Just be quiet and don't look at anybody," Benny told them, his voice tight. "If anybody asks you questions, pretend you don't understand."

Lissy let out a long, agonized moan and began rocking back and forth in her chair, her eyes clamped shut. "They're coming," the old woman said, turning back around. She pulled an old tattered magazine out of one of her tote bags and opened it to a random page.

A couple of seconds later, two men came around one of the shelves. They were both dressed in police uniforms. "It's just the cops," Jason said, relieved. "They're—"

"No!" Benny cut him off, eyes blazing. "You don't know anything. Be quiet."

The two cops headed straight for the door to the little conference room, and pushed it open without knocking. They were both young, both looked quite formidable, and their expressions were identically cold and devoid of any kind of compassion or humanity. The swept the room with their gazes; oddly, they didn't seem to notice or care that there were two people in the group who didn't look like the rest of them. "Stand up, all of you," the older of the two cops said. "Hands where we can see them."

The vagrants shuffled to their feet slowly. The old woman helped Frank up. Lissy remained in her seat, rocking and moaning. After a moment and a furtive gaze from the old woman, Stone and Jason rose as well.

"We got a complaint about you people," the cop said, his voice dripping with contempt. "I can see why. You're stinkin' the place to high heaven. You can't just squat here all day and drive off all the regular citizens."

"Sorry, Officer," Hector said meekly. He appeared to have recovered from his 'episode.' "We'll clear out. Don't want to cause anybody any trouble."

"Smart man," the other cop said. His voice was as cold and uncaring as his partner's. He laid a hand on his nightstick. "We don't like bums around here. We find you hanging out in this place again, it's not gonna go so nice for you, you know?"

The first cop was examining each of the vagrants' faces in turn. "One more thing—we're looking for a guy. You guys squat on the street—maybe you seen him. Maybe you tell us where you seen him, we might look the other way and you can stink up the library till tomorrow."

"What—what does he look like?" the old woman asked.

"White, mid 20s, dirty-blond hair in a ponytail, athletic build, jeans and T-shirt and brown leather jacket," the cop said. "No picture, but if you know of somebody like that, tell us now. He's wanted."

Jason's eyes came up for a second in a frank stare of amazement, but he quickly quelled it and looked back at his hands. The cop's description — the one he'd uttered while staring straight at him — could have described his twin. Or himself. *What the – ?*

Next to him, Stone shifted his weight and nudged him imperceptibly. When Jason glanced at him, he shook his head once, his eyes still downcast.

"What's he wanted for?" Benny asked.

"Murder," said the cop. "You seen him?"

The vagrants looked at each other, each one shaking his or her head. "Sorry, but we haven't," Hector said in his slow, gravelly voice. "We'll keep an eye out, though. We see him, we'll tell the nearest policeman. It's dangerous enough for folks like us out there without having murderers running around free."

That seemed to satisfy the first cop, though the second one still looked like he'd like nothing better than to have an excuse to clout some heads with his nightstick. He pointed at Lissy. "What's with the nutcase chick there?"

"She doesn't know anything, Officer," the old woman said. "She's — not right in the head. We look after her."

The cop sneered. "Might as well just drop her off at the nearest booby hatch." He started to say something else, but his partner touched his arm and motioned him out. Reluctantly he moved toward the door.

"I want to see you bums out of here by tonight," the first cop said. "And I don't want to see you back here anymore. The good citizens of this area deserve to be able to read in peace without being stunk up and creeped out by you loonies. Got it?"

"We'll be out, sir," Hector assured him.

The cop glared at him for a moment as if trying to decide if he was giving any lip, then nodded once, turned on his heel, and followed his partner out. He tried to slam the door but the pneumatic return prevented that. Instead, it closed with a soft *click*.

For a long time, nobody moved. They barely breathed, except for Lissy and her moaning. Nearly two minutes passed in silence. Then, slowly, Lissy's moaning began to cease, along with her rocking. She hunched over the table, sobbing quietly into her folded arms. As if that were some kind of signal, the vagrant group dropped back down into their chairs. Jason let his breath out. "What—the hell —is going *on* here?" he demanded, spacing his words out carefully. "What was that about?"

Hector shrugged. "Cops aren't safe. Never figure they are. Some of 'em are all right, but can't never be sure."

Jason pointed at Lissy. "She *knew*. She knew they were coming and she knew they were bad. What the hell *are* you people?" His gaze darted wildly around between them like a loose pinball. "How did they not see us? That's—me they're looking for. They described me perfectly. And they didn't see me! I was standing *right under their noses* and they didn't see me!" In the back of his mind he was thinking, *I finally started getting my head around the fact that I'm hanging around with a guy who can shoot magic beams out of his hands, and now I've got to accept weird psychic bums too? Where is all this going to end?*

"You better get out of here," Benny said, ignoring his words. "Not safe for you either. I'd stay away from cops if I was you."

Jason was in danger of imminent mental overload again, and Stone must have noticed because he put a bracing hand on his shoulder. "He's right, Jason. We'd best be on our way." He reached inside his overcoat and withdrew the black kitten, who mewed sleepily in protest at being disturbed. He handed her back to the old woman. "I'm not sure exactly what you did," he said softly. "I'd like very much to have a chance to discuss it with you, but I doubt you'd be amenable to that. Besides, I think it would be prudent for *all* of us to be on our way."

The old woman nodded, tucking the kitten back into a nest of blankets in one of her bags. She was gathering them all up and arranging them on the table. Around her, the others were also rising and picking up their meager belongings.

Jason had apparently decided that he wasn't going to get any straight answers, so he gave up trying. "Are you guys gonna be all right?" he asked. He realized, watching them, just how vulnerable they all looked. Even Hector, who still had the vestiges of a military bearing and a military physique, looked broken down and world-weary.

"We'll be all right," the old woman said, smiling gently as she helped Lissy into her ragged coat. "We've been here too long anyway—I think we got a little settled, and that's never good. Time to be moving on." Behind her, Benny nodded.

"Listen," Stone said. "I have no idea what you did or how you did it, but I suspect strongly that if you *hadn't* done it, Jason and I would be in a world of difficulty right about now. Whatever it was, we're grateful. I hope you won't think me rude or presumptuous, but—" He pulled out his wallet, withdrew several bills, and offered them to the old woman. "A bit of help for your travels," he said. "Or—if you prefer—something to help keep your little friend in the bag there warm and fed."

Her watery blue eyes sparkled with tears as she accepted the bills. "Thank you," she whispered, holding Stone's hand in both of her wrinkled ones. She looked earnestly into his eyes, and then into Jason's. "Please—be very careful who you trust. There are dangers everywhere these days, sometimes where you least expect them."

"Where you least expect them..." Lissy echoed dreamily, reaching out to pet the kitten, who was poking her head up out of the bag.

"Thanks," Jason said. "Thanks a lot, you guys. Listen, if there's anything I can ever do for you—"

"Yeah, yeah," said Hector gruffly. "Heard it all before. Come on, crew. Let's clear out before those guys come back. You two take care and stay safe."

Jason and Stone decided to take their leave as well. They gave the vagrant group a couple minutes' head start, then left via the front door. Jason glanced at the librarian at the front desk as they went by, wondering if it was she who'd reported them. Seemed odd that she would after allowing them in here for all this time, but he didn't stop to ask. He didn't want her remembering too closely what he looked like, in case those cops came back.

Back in the car and heading toward Palo Alto, Jason was agitated. "Okay, so not only are we back at square one in our search, but things just got a lot worse. Apparently I'm wanted for murder, the only link we have to Susanna is heading away to who knows where, and what the hell was going on back there with those guys? What did they do?" He glared at Stone. "You said there weren't very many mages around. But it sure seemed to me like they hid us or something. Those cops didn't notice us, I'm damn sure of that."

"That wasn't magic," Stone said. "At least not any kind I've ever had experience with."

"What was it, then?"

"I don't know." Stone didn't look at him; he was busy watching the road. "But I'd give a hell of a lot of money to find out. It's obvious that they—or at least one of them—

did something to conceal us. And another one, the young girl, seemed to know that those policemen were coming before they arrived. How did she know that? Did you notice that she became more agitated as they got closer, and by the time they arrived she was nearly catatonic?"

"And don't forget the other dude with the pencils," Jason said. He'd decided that there was no upper bound to the amount of things that were going to freak him out today—he just had to roll with it. "What was that thing he gave you? You looked like you thought it was more than a page of scribbles."

Stone rummaged in the pocket of his overcoat, took out the page, and handed it over. Jason smoothed it out and looked at it, perplexed. "It looks like Picasso exploded and started writing in Norse runes, or Chinese or something. Weird little pictures and a lot writing I can't read. Can you?"

"Not specifically," Stone said. "But I don't think it's Norse or Chinese. It's more the intent I can sense, rather than actually reading the content. As strange as it might sound—and I'll have to give it a bit more study to be sure—it looks like our artistic friend has given us—how do I put it?—the essence of Susanna."

"The hell?" Jason turned the paper in his hands, looking at it from different orientations. "I don't see anything here that looks like a woman, or a name, or anything. That might be an eye right there," he said, pointing. "Damned if I can tell." He glanced at Stone. "So let's assume you're right for a minute. What good is having the 'essence of Susanna'? Does that mean you can—I dunno—talk to her or something? Magically?"

Stone shook his head. "No. But it might mean I can find her."

That perked Jason up; he'd thought that avenue was pretty much lost with the exit of the vagrant group from the scene. "How?"

Stone took a deep breath and let it out slowly. "I'll explain, but it's going to take some time. First I need to go pick up a few things. I trust you've lost your desire to go to the police station to look for news?"

Jason's eyes widened. He hadn't thought about that. "If I'm wanted...yeah, walking in there might not be the best idea."

"I rather wonder if you are, though," Stone mused.

"Huh? That cop said I was, didn't he?"

"Yes, but..." Stone shook his head as if trying to clear it. "For now, we'll be prudent and avoid the police. In fact, it probably wouldn't be a bad idea to ask Mrs. Olivera to give you a haircut and lend you some of her hair coloring, but that's probably overkill." He paused, thinking. "I suppose if they're looking for you for murder, they must think that you killed those gangers at the warehouse."

Jason nodded. "The newspaper said all they found was charred bodies, though, and it's not like they could find shell casings or anything. How would they even know? I doubt they've even identified the bodies yet. That kind of thing can take weeks, depending on how badly burned the corpses are."

"You sound like you speak from experience," Stone said. "Ah, right. You said your father was a policeman, didn't you?"

"Yeah..." Something had been nagging at the back of Jason's mind, and Stone's words finally triggered it. "You know, I think there was something wrong with those cops."

"Oh? How so?"

Jason thought about it for a moment. "Well...this area's pretty decent, right? Even with things as crappy as they are now?"

Stone shrugged. "I suppose so, yes."

"I've seen some bad cops in my time. It sometimes happens, especially for low-level ones who don't make that much money, that they'll go on the take or fall a little too much in love with their power. You know, hassle the citizens, scare teenagers, that kind of thing."

Stone nodded. "Yes, and? I'd say those two were throwing their weight around quite effectively."

"Yeah, but that's the thing. They were *too* nasty. Especially since there were two of them. Bad cops, especially the ones who really like to bully the citizenry — you don't usually see them partnered up like that. Like I said, they're around but they're not *that* common, and the chance of two of them being together is pretty low. Most police departments will look the other way for a certain amount of that kind of thing, but if they get too many reports of police brutality against the same guys, they have to investigate it. And that's especially true in areas like this. Poor people don't tend to report cops for brutality, but middle-aged rich white people? Hell, yeah. Some of 'em do it if cops look at 'em funny."

Stone thought about that. "You might have a point," he conceded. "But I don't see what it—"

"I don't either," Jason said. "I'm just thinking out loud. And I'm not about to call up the department and file a complaint or anything. But it just kind of reminded me of something Charles said. He told me it didn't used to be like this when he was younger. That the whole area has just gotten meaner in the past few years. I guess that could apply to cops too."

"I guess it could," Stone agreed.

"Where are we going, by the way?"

"Stanford," he said. "I need to pick up a couple of things from my office, and then we're off to a little shop near downtown for a few more things."

"What kind of things? I mean, no offense, but your dry cleaning can probably wait."

Stone chuckled. "No dry cleaning," he assured him. "Just keep your head down and try not to look like a potential murderer, all right?"

"I'll do my best," Jason grumbled.

11.

Stone's office at Stanford was in an old, vine-covered building far off the beaten track. It was even more cluttered than his living room, filled from floor to ceiling with stacks of musty old books, strange looking items (in the few minutes they were there, Jason spotted some sort of mummified animal paw, three skulls including one that appeared human, something that looked like a wooden wand with a purple crystal on the end, several art prints illustrating bizarre rituals, a stack of parchment scrolls tied up with a black ribbon, and a whole collection of half-burned candles), and drifts of papers that nearly obscured the wooden desk beneath them. Stone rummaged around in a desk drawer, grabbed a bag from a nearby shelf, and started tossing items into it. There seemed to be some method to what he was doing, but Jason sure as hell didn't see it. He kept quiet, contenting himself with trying to take in as much of the place as he could. It wasn't every day you got to see the office of an Occult Studies professor, after all, even one that *wasn't* a real mage in his spare time.

"Done," Stone said after five minutes. "Come on, I want to get going on this before dinnertime. It's not going to be quick in any case."

"What's not going to be quick?" Jason demanded, hurrying to follow him as he took the mostly deserted corridor leading to the exit door in long, fast strides.

He didn't answer, just got back in the car. Jason resolutely joined him, and they were on their way again.

This time, he drove into downtown Palo Alto. "Never easy to park here," he remarked as he negotiated the tight traffic and looked around for a space. "Sometimes I find myself wishing that magic could help me find a spot, but sadly it doesn't work that way."

"Uh...yeah." Jason was getting hungry, but Stone hadn't mentioned anything about lunch so he didn't either. "So where *are* we going, anyway?"

"Little shop near here," Stone said. "Let me pick up what I'm after, then we can grab a quick late lunch — there's a lovely noodle house next door — and then back home. I should be able to get everything set up in a couple of hours."

Jason wasn't sure if Stone was being deliberately cryptic or if his mind was just moving so fast that he'd forgotten that not everybody had boarded his train of thought. Either way, he decided he'd see soon enough. At least things were relatively normal for the moment.

They found a parking spot after a few more minutes of cruising, and Stone led him up a block and then down another one to a row of shops that looked like they'd been around for a very long time. Jason looked at them, perplexed: there was the noodle house he'd referred to, a dry cleaner, an insurance agent's office, and a clothing store that looked like it catered to ladies older than the old vagrant woman, whose fashion sense had stopped evolving thirty years ago. "Uh..." he said.

Stone didn't answer, but headed for an unmarked door between the insurance agent and the noodle house. Motioning for Jason to follow, he disappeared through it and descended a steep flight of stairs to another door. Carefully lettered on it was "Huan's Antiquities," along with some Chinese script below it. When he opened it, a soft bell tinkled somewhere off in the distance.

"What is this place?" Jason whispered, looking around. They were standing in a large, dimly lit room stuffed to the ceiling with...things. He suspected that this was where Stone shopped for all the weird junk he had in his living room and his office. He couldn't begin to take it all in at once, but it was easy to tell that there was no order or apparent arrangement to the objects haphazardly scattered around. The place looked like the attic of someone who spent a lot of time at upscale garage sales.

"This," Stone whispered back, "is the premier magical supply store for this part of the Bay Area. You won't find a finer one outside San Francisco. But don't tell Madame Huan I told you that, or she'll raise her prices."

Jason looked skeptical as he peered around, trying to make sense out of some of the eclectic items. Broken furniture was stacked haphazardly next to dusty old lamps, toys from bygone days, books, sculpture, ancient rusting appliances — everywhere he looked was something different. "Uh — this stuff is magical? It looks like junk to me."

Stone grinned. "Ah, but this isn't where the good stuff is. Just wait — she should be out soon. You don't rush Madame Huan."

Jason busied himself wandering up and down the narrow aisles, and after a couple of minutes he heard the melodious tinkle of a beaded curtain being swished aside. He hurried back to Stone in time to see a tiny Asian woman of indeterminate age moving quickly toward him. "Well, well," she said, smiling. She didn't have a trace of an Asian accent. "Alastair Stone. I haven't seen *you* in a while."

"Too long, Madame Huan," Stone said, returning her smile and allowing her to grasp his hand warmly in both of hers.

"What brings you to my humble store? And who's your friend? You haven't taken an apprentice, have you?"

Stone chuckled. "Hardly. No, he's a friend I met recently — he's caught up in some rather interesting business, part of which is that he's trying to locate his missing sister. I've agreed to help him, which means I'm going to need a few items I don't normally keep 'round the house."

"I see," she said. "Well, come along then, and we'll see what we can find." She glanced at Jason. "I'm afraid your friend will have to wait here, though."

Stone nodded. "I'll be back in a few minutes, Jason. I'm sorry, but—" he spread his hands apologetically. "Store policy."

"Uh, sure," Jason said. He was a little disappointed that he wouldn't get to see "the good stuff," but a few minutes of just wandering aimlessly (and not encountering bins of Eye of Newt or a cauldron full of "Bats—Buy One, Get One Free" or something) might be good for him. Stone nodded, and he and Madame Huan departed through the beaded curtain.

They were back in ten minutes, Stone carrying a large tote bag stuffed full of various lumpy items. "Ready?"

"That was quick."

"I knew what I was looking for. Come on—let's get some lunch and then get back. The sooner we get started, the sooner we can find Susanna. At least I hope we can." He bid Madame Huan farewell and exited the store.

They grabbed a quick bite at the noodle house. Jason was nervous—Stone was right, the food was very good, but he couldn't shake the feeling that they were being watched, or followed. He insisted on sitting facing the door and kept looking out the window, wolfing down his lunch so quickly that he barely had time to enjoy it.

He didn't say much until they were back in the car, driving toward Stone's house. "So, is she a mage too?"

"Madame Huan?" At Jason's nod, he too nodded. "She is, but she specializes in more indirect, passive magic like divination and psychometry. And, of course, she both creates and imports magical items. She makes a very good living at that, so much so that she doesn't really need to do anything else."

"So what have you got in the bag there?" He pointed to the back seat, where Stone had stashed it.

"Some items to help with the location spell, and also a few other items that I can fashion into magical batteries, in case I need to cast some of the more tiring spells."

"You mean like spells that hurt people?"

"Yes. It's not the sort of thing I prefer to do, but it's obvious that something dangerous is afoot, and I'd like to be in a bit better position to defend us if we encounter it again."

"I'd still rather have a gun," Jason grumbled. He was still trying to figure out how to get hold of one, even if he had to go to the black market to do it. Trouble was, he didn't know anything about the black market up here. Down in Ventura he knew half a dozen local miscreants who'd get him what he needed for a reasonable price and keep their mouths shut, but he also knew it was dangerous to delve into an unfamiliar underworld scene without a guide—especially when the police were looking for him. Much as he hated it, for now he'd have to depend on his knife, his fists, and Stone's magical punch to keep them out of trouble.

They got back to the house without incident. Mrs. Olivera, who was puttering around in the kitchen, waved a greeting. "You've had lunch, I assume?" she called.

"Got it covered," Stone assured her. "You can go on home if you like—we're going to be busy with some work for the rest of the afternoon. We'll call out for pizza if we get hungry later."

"Unless you get so caught up in what you're working on that you forget to do it," she said cheerfully.

Stone didn't answer except to chuckle—obviously it was an old topic with them. "Stay here," he told Jason. "I need to grab a few more things from upstairs, and then we'll get started on this."

He was back in less than five minutes carrying both the bag of items he'd bought from Madame Huan and another bag that looked about half as full. Motioning for Jason to follow him, he moved off down a hallway and unlocked a nondescript door. He opened it to reveal a staircase leading downward into darkness. "Basement?" Jason asked. "You do magic in the *basement?*"

Stone shrugged, flicking a light switch. "Magic takes room, and a lot of setup. It's easier to keep things cleared out and set up down here. And since Mrs. Olivera doesn't have the key, she's not tempted to come down here and see what's going on — or worse yet, to tidy up."

At the foot of the stairs was another door. Stone opened it and waved Jason inside. On the other side was a large empty space featuring a bare concrete floor scattered with small rugs, and unpainted gray walls. Jason stared at it. "I — kinda expected something a bit more...magical?" he said, grinning. "This place looks like where you'd stash kidnap victims."

"Aha, and you've walked right into my trap, haven't you?" Stone returned his grin. "No, seriously, I can't really make permanent modifications, since I'm renting this place. I've got access to some much nicer setups back home in England, but that won't help us much right now. And in any case, this will do fine. The magic doesn't give a damn about one's skill at interior decorating." He waved toward a chair by the wall that was one of only a few pieces of furniture in the room. "Might as well sit down — this is going to take awhile, and you can't really help me with it."

"Wish you'd told me that before we came down here," Jason grumbled. "I'd have brought something to read."

Stone grinned again. "Watch and learn," he said. "Patience is a virtue. Or something like that." Putting the two bags down on a small table and draping his overcoat over another chair, he opened the first one and began spreading the items around. Jason watched as he set down a series of candles in different sizes and colors, a small but elaborate incense burner, several sticks of strange-smelling incense, a compact brazier, a handful of multi-hued chalk, and a pocket-sized box of matches. Then he reached for the second and withdrew three large leatherbound books.

"What are you going to do with all that stuff?" Jason asked, curious in spite of himself. This whole business was so far outside the realm of his experience that he didn't even have a frame of reference for it. As a child, his reading had tended more toward sports, adventure, and gory true-crime stories than anything about magic or fantasy.

Stone picked up a piece of light blue chalk and one of the leatherbound tomes and moved to the center of the room. He replied as he opened the book, consulted it, and then crouched and began to draw something on the floor, shoving the rugs out of the way. "Rituals, as I told you before, generally require setup before they can be implemented. This part is called "casting a circle" — you create a space to contain the energy that you're going to summon."

"And that works?"

"Quite effectively. Though you have to make sure you get it right, which is why I need to be careful. Nasty things can happen if you get them wrong."

"Nasty things like what? Big evil bug-eyed monsters come through from the great beyond, rampaging through the countryside killing women and having their way with people's housepets?" Jason couldn't help it — it all just sounded so *crazy.*

"Possibly," Stone said, dead serious. "Well, not the housepets bit, of course. But the whole thing is highly unlikely, especially in our case since this ritual isn't designed to summon anything. Summoning rituals are notoriously tricky and most mages who have any sense don't even attempt them anymore. That, and they require a large number of participants to get them right, and trying to get enough mages to actually agree on summoning something is next to impossible. Getting that many mages to agree on *anything* is next to impossible. So no, you needn't worry about rampaging extradimensional beasties." He turned back to what he was doing, continuing to draw the large circle with the blue chalk.

Jason decided not to push his luck. He sat back to watch, keeping his mouth shut.

It took Stone about an hour to draw the chalk circle, moving with slow precision and pausing to consult the book twice in the process. It wasn't just a circle — when it was finished it was actually one circle within another, with other shapes or cryptic sigils holding the two sections together at several points. He stepped back for a moment to examine his handiwork, then put the book down and carefully crossed out of the circle without touching any of the chalk lines. Still, Jason didn't say anything.

Next, he moved back inside and placed the candles at four points around the circle, though he didn't light them yet. He examined the brazier and the incense burner, chose the brazier, and placed it in the center where there were no chalk lines or figures. Then he stepped out again, grabbed a different book, and compared a page in the book to what he'd created. "That looks about right," he said, swiping his hair off his forehead. "Close as I'm going to get, I think."

Jason examined it with interest. The whole thing was pretty elaborate now that it was done. "I guess mages who can't draw don't get very far, huh?"

Stone didn't favor that with an answer. "Now comes the interesting part," he said instead. "The actual ritual." He crossed the room again (it was harder now not to step on the chalk lines, and he almost had to jump to get out of the circle) and pulled out the sheet of paper Frank the Scribbler had given them, looking it over.

Jason looked back and forth between Stone and the circle. "So let me get this straight," he said. "You're going to do something with that paper inside that circle and it's going to help you figure out where Susanna is, and hopefully Verity too?"

"Hopefully," Stone said. "I won't get Verity, of course, since I don't have a tether object for her. You don't happen to have any personal belongings of hers, do you? I probably should have asked you that before."

Jason shook his head. "Nope. I haven't seen her for years, unfortunately." He was regretting now that he hadn't snitched something from her room at the halfway house, but it was too late now.

"Right, then. We'll work with what we have." He stepped back into the circle with the paper and leaned down to place the incense in the brazier. "I have no idea how long this is going to take. It should be fairly quick, but don't be surprised if it takes longer. And whatever you do, whatever you see, don't enter the circle. And don't break it. I doubt anything horrible will happen, but if you break it while I'm in the middle of the ritual, the backlash will give me a headache for a week. So don't do it, all right?"

"Got it. Don't step on the pretty chalk outline while the mage is casting spells inside it." Jason sighed. "You know, none of this is easy for me to swallow."

Stone chuckled. "Hang around me long enough and you'll be encountering a lot stranger things than a magical circle. My colleagues have accused me of being a—what did they call it?—a 'magnet for weird shit,' I think it was."

"I believe that," Jason said, nodding emphatically.

Stone turned away and lit the incense. Soon the room was filled with a strange, albeit not unpleasant, mixture of odors Jason had never smelled before. As the small wisps of smoke rose and began to dissipate through the room, he was reminded of his teen years when his stoner buddies would sit in their rec rooms passing joints around and listening to progressive rock. The intermingling of the odors and the smoke made him feel oddly detached, like he was watching the proceedings from somewhere above his body. It felt good, though, so he didn't fight it.

Stone stood inside of the circle, behind the brazier. His lips were moving; he seemed to be reciting something under his breath, but Jason couldn't make it out. Currently, he was facing the candle that he'd placed at the circle's north side. Jason watched as he continued his soft chant, lulled into a relaxed, soporific state. This was so cool...

He nearly fell out of his chair when the candle's flame suddenly flared bright blue, the same color as its candle, and grew to about three inches high. It continued to burn thusly as Stone turned, now facing the south candle. It too flared up after a time, its flame glowing red. Jason, the spacey feeling driven out of his head now, leaned forward and stared.

Stone did this twice more—first east, then west. The east side candle's flame turned green, and the west side's flared bright yellow. For several moments he just stood in there, focused on the candles and chanting. Then he took out the paper full of scribblings, spread it out, and laid it inside the brazier. His voice rose a little louder; Jason could now tell for sure that whatever he was saying, it wasn't in English. Taking the matches from his pocket, Stone lit one and touched it to the paper, the chant rising louder. Flames—normal ones for the moment—flared around the paper. Stone watched them for a couple more moments, then barked out one sharp word that Jason couldn't understand but that sounded like it didn't have any vowels.

Instantly, nimbuses of golden light formed around the four candles, shooting beams across the circle to meet in the center—North to South, East to West—making a glowing golden cross through the circle converging on the brazier. Stone had already stepped aside as if he'd expected it to be there. There was a soft *whump!* sound as the paper was consumed by the flames, and then a shaft of bright white light spiked up from the brazier, up through the basement's low ceiling. Stone reached out, no longer chanting, and cupped his hands around the light shaft without touching it. As Jason watched, forgetting to blink, forgetting to breathe, it looked to him like the mage was struggling—like he was trying to grasp something in the light but it kept eluding him. His eyes closed, his face taking on a tight look of concentration as he fought to do—what? Jason didn't know.

And then, like someone flicked off a light switch, it was over. The candle flames went out, the little fire in the brazier went out, and the golden and white light beams extinguished. For a moment Jason just sat there, aware that his mouth was hanging open but not caring. "Holy...*shit*," he whispered at last.

Stone didn't answer—or even appear to notice he was there—for several seconds. He was breathing hard as if he'd just run a couple of blocks at top speed, but it wasn't anywhere near the level of exhaustion Jason had seen in the car the previous night. "You okay?" Jason asked, getting up.

"Fine," Stone said. His breathing was already returning to normal. He stepped out of the circle, not worrying now that he was smudging anything. It was clear even to a complete magical imbecile like Jason that the circle at this point was dead and inert.

"So—did you find her? Do you know where she is?"

Stone sighed, looking defeated. "No."

"No?" Jason demanded. "But wasn't that the whole point of—"

"I touched her mind. I know she's out there somewhere, and I think she's still in the area. But she—fought me. I've never seen anything quite like it. It was as if—every time I got a bead on her, she slipped away into a fog." Stone looked utterly perplexed. He ran a hand back through his hair again and began gathering up the spent candles. "This is getting more and more interesting by the hour."

"I'd say it's getting more *frustrating* by the hour," Jason grumbled. "How can she hide from you? Can people do that? I thought only other mages—"

"I thought so too," Stone said. "That's why it's so fascinating. Our elusive Susanna is either a mage—which I highly doubt—or else she's got some sort of magic-like abilities similar to those of our vagrant friends back at the library. And if you'll forgive me a little professional curiosity, encountering at least four homeless people with pseudo-magical abilities in less than a day is interesting enough that I'd like to get to the bottom of it."

Jason sighed. "That's all great, but it still doesn't get me any closer to finding Verity." He was feeling the old familiar impatience rising in him again: he wanted to run outside and go *do* something. *Anything.* Just so he didn't have to feel like he was sitting here on his ass while his little sister was out there on the streets dealing with God knew what. "I wish I could call Arrelli," he said.

"Who?"

"The detective assigned to Verity's case. Maybe he's found out something. But I'd be an idiot to call the police department if they're just gonna pick me up if they get wind of me. Those two cops at the library—" He stopped as something clicked in his head. "Wait a minute... Wait...a...minute..."

"You're on to something, aren't you?" Stone asked, his gaze sharpening.

"Maybe. I want to test it out, but it could be dangerous. Is there a pay phone around here? I need to make a call, and I don't want to do it from here in case they trace it."

"There might be one a couple of blocks away at the park. I'm not sure I've ever noticed."

"Come on—let's go find it. I think I'm right, and if I am then things are about to get even more interesting."

Stone was right—there were two pay phones near the edge of a small grassy park a few blocks from his house. "Wish me luck," Jason said as he jumped out of the car and fumbled in his pocket for change. "And get ready to get us out of here fast if I don't have it."

He glanced around to make sure nobody was watching him, then dropped a coin in the slot and punched in the number from the business card Arrelli had given him. It rang twice, then picked up. "Mountain View PD, Arrelli," said a gruff voice.

Jason hesitated so long that the voice spoke again, more suspiciously this time. "Who is this? Who's on the line?"

"Lt. Arrelli? This is—Jason Thayer. Remember me? I talked to you about my missing sister." He didn't dare to breathe—Arrelli's next words would tell him whether his wild hunch had been correct, or whether he'd have to go on the run again.

"Ah, right, Thayer." Arrelli sounded completely normal and mundane. Jason allowed himself to relax just a bit. He wasn't out of the woods yet.

"Yeah. I'm—just checking in to see if you have any news about Verity."

"Nothing, I'm sorry to report. Like I said when we talked before—I can't devote a lot of time to the case unless I have reason to believe she's in danger. So far, that hasn't been true, at least as far as I've heard. I'll give you a call if I know anything. I told you that before."

"Yeah. Yeah, I know. But you can't blame me for being a little impatient. I haven't had any luck either and I'm really starting to worry about her."

"Understandable. We're doing everything we realistically can, Mr. Thayer. If I find out anything else, I'll let you know. Are you still at—" he paused, and Jason could hear him scrabbling papers "—the Ocean Breeze Motel?"

"No, not there anymore. Hold on a sec." He put the phone down and went over to where Stone was waiting in the car. "Can I give him your number so he can call if he finds out anything?"

Stone shrugged. "Why not? In for a penny, in for a pound, I guess." He raised a questioning eyebrow at Jason, but he'd already turned and headed back for the phone.

Jason passed along the phone number. "I'm staying with—a friend. You can reach me there."

"Got it. Like I said, though—don't hold your breath. And make sure you don't cause any trouble if you're out looking for her yourself, okay?"

"Yeah. I'll remember that. Thanks."

When he came back to the car again, he was looking contemplative. "All right, out with it," Stone ordered, starting the engine. "You obviously figured something out and took a chance on it—what was it?"

"Those cops at the library," Jason told him. "I've had it in the back of my mind ever since we saw them that there was something wrong about them, but I couldn't put my finger on it. It finally came to me—they weren't wearing name badges."

Stone looked confused. "What?"

"Name badges. You know, the little gold pins cops wear on the front of their uniforms, with their last name on it? They had their police badges, but no name badges."

"Couldn't they have just—forgotten to put them on?"

Jason shook his head. "No way. Cops have inspection every morning. Their commanding officer would have noticed it instantly. Citizens don't like it when they can't see the name of the cop that's hassling them. They want to be able to report 'em, write letters to the editor, all that good stuff."

"So the fact that they didn't have them means—?"

"I'd bet a lot of money it means they weren't real cops." Jason blew air through his teeth. "It also explains why they were so nasty."

"I still don't get it," Stone said. "Why would they impersonate policemen in order to kick a group of vagrants out of a library?"

"I don't know. I don't think that's what they were doing—that was just a side effect. Maybe my paranoia is in high gear right now—not without reason, I might add—but I think they were looking for us. Or at least me."

Stone contemplated that, then finally nodded. "You could well be right. It did appear that they were looking for someone—and they did have your description."

Jason put his face in his hands, kneading his temples wearily. "I dunno what the hell is going on anymore. It's like we've got a bunch of pieces but we haven't got a fucking clue about how they go together—or even *if* they go together." He sighed. "I don't know what to do next. It

R. L. KING

seems like all our leads have dried up. You can't find Susanna, Arrelli's got nothin', and we don't even know where the magic bums went since they got punted out of the library."

Stone echoed his sigh. He looked troubled. "I'm sorry, Jason, but I'm afraid I must concur. I can't think of any other avenues to take at this point. Unless—" He looked up. "Do you have any way to get hold of anything personal of your sister's? Clothing, a keepsake...even a photo?"

"Uh...I'm not sure. Why?"

"Well..." Stone mused, "We could always try the ritual again, only using an object of hers as the tether instead."

Jason thought about that. "It's worth a try," he said. "Although if she's with this Susanna person and she can block you, would she be able to do it to keep you from getting at Verity too?"

"We won't know until we try. But it's all moot if we don't have something to use. While it's possible to do a ritual without a tether, it's extremely difficult, has a much higher chance of failure, and I would have to know the target personally and fairly extensively."

They were pulling into Stone's driveway now, and Jason was thinking. "When I went to the halfway house they showed me her room. There were a few of her things in there, but I don't know if they're still there. And since I'm still not convinced that all this shit with the fake cops and the fake murder rap aren't somehow connected to whatever's going on there, I'd be an idiot to show my face there even if they *did* agree to let me in."

"Probably true," Stone agreed. "But p'raps I can manage it."

Jason stared at him. "You? How?"

"Leave that to me." He led Jason back into the house and sat down at the breakfast bar. "Tell me about the place, and especially where your sister's room is. Please be precise. I wouldn't want to barge into the wrong room and get arrested if they catch me."

Jason had no idea what he was up to, but he was willing to give it a try. He told Stone everything he knew about the halfway house—the layout, the location of Verity's room, a description of Pompous Delancie and his henchman Tony, and the address. Stone nodded when he finished. He hadn't written anything down. "All right, then. You'd best stay here and let me take care of this one. I'll be back soon, with any luck bearing our prize."

Jason didn't like the idea of staying home, but he didn't want to argue and he knew it was best that he not be seen anywhere near New Horizons. "I gotta find some wheels," he muttered.

"Hmm?"

"I need a car, or a bike, or something. I hate feeling dependent. Know anywhere I can pick up a good used car? I can work on it if it needs it. I'll probably have to—I don't have a lot of money right now. If I stay up here much longer I'm gonna have to find a job."

"I'll see what I can turn up," Stone assured him. "I do have to go up to Stanford tomorrow for a couple of hours—unavoidable meeting—so I'll check the notice boards. There are always students trying to make some quick cash by selling vehicles. Or check the paper." He motioned toward the day's paper, still with a rubber band around it, sitting on the breakfast bar. "If you see anything you like, let me know and I'll give you a ride to check it out. But right now I'd best be going. I doubt they want me showing up at bedtime."

He was back in an hour. Jason, who was sitting in the living room leafing through the classifieds, tossed the paper aside. "Did you get it?"

Stone grinned. "My natural charm, coupled with a bit of persuasive magic, carried the day," he said, pulling something from his overcoat and tossing it at him.

Jason caught it and his eyes widened. It was the small teddy bear that he'd seen in Verity's room. "How did you — ?"

"Easiest thing ever. I played the role of a worried — and wealthy — father who was looking for a good place for his emotionally disturbed son to live, where they could look after him and know how to deal with his bouts of extreme depression. I assured them I'd heard nothing but glowing reviews of the place and asked them for a tour. Dr. Delancie — you're weren't kidding: he is a pompous prat — didn't want to give me one, said it was late and I should come back, but that was where the persuasive magic came in. I made sure to cause a small disturbance just as we were passing Verity's door, and was able to slip in, grab the bear, and slip back out before anyone caught on." He chuckled. "I even got to pretend to be American," he said, in a quite passable California accent.

"And they just — fell for it?"

"Like I said, I can be persuasive. I think I was helped a little by the fact that they seemed a bit off their game today. I heard that Tony chap talking to one of the kids, who was asking where Charles was. He said he didn't know, and he actually looked quite concerned, as did the kid. Apparently Charles was popular around there."

Jason sobered. He'd almost forgotten about Charles. "So — now that we have it, what now? Are you going to do another ritual tonight?"

Stone shook his head. "Can't. I'd need to pick up some more supplies tomorrow, and I have that meeting I need to attend." He hooked a thumb at the paper spread out over the couch. "Find any likely prospects?"

"What? Oh—yeah, actually I did find a couple in my price range." He picked up the classified section and waved vaguely at it. "I called a couple of these guys and they sound likely. One's in Sunnyvale and one's in Mountain View."

"Might as well go do that now, then," Stone said. "We can grab something for dinner and that way if one of them suits your fancy, you won't be stuck in the house tomorrow while I'm gone."

Jason got another of his rare strokes of luck on his search—the first car he looked at, a 15-year-old Ford Galaxie with a dented fender and an interior that smelled of smoke and fast food, fit his criteria. He insisted on taking it for a test drive, then popped the hood and spent twenty minutes checking out the major systems, driving the overweight middle-aged owner half crazy by insisting that he keep starting it up and hitting the gas while Jason listened and evaluated. "Hey, buddy, it's an old cheap car," the guy protested. "It's a damn good deal for what I'm asking."

Jason allowed that it was an okay deal, but even so he managed to talk the guy down fifty dollars on the final price, which he could just barely afford. "It's gonna take some work," he told Stone, who'd hung back and stayed out of the proceedings, "but it runs and it's not likely to break down this week, which is good enough for now. I'd rather have a bike, but after what's been happening lately I'd prefer to be a little more protected—and a little more anonymous."

"I call that prudent," Stone agreed. He followed Jason back to the house in the Jaguar, and they made it without any incidents. "I must admit I half expected I'd have to be dodging loose parts most of the way home," he teased when they arrived.

"Yeah, well, I'll change that when I can. Right now all I care about is that it runs."

Next morning Jason came downstairs to find Stone wearing a tweed sport jacket, sitting at the breakfast bar sipping coffee and reading the paper. "Any plans for today?" the mage asked.

"Not really. I guess I should start seeing about finding a way to make some money. I can't stay here forever, and even if you do let me stay awhile I want to pay my way."

Stone shrugged. "You're a guest. I don't mind the company. This place is pretty quiet when I'm not working and Mrs. Olivera isn't around."

"I know, but it feels weird. I'm not a mooch."

"Think nothing of it. You're providing me with a fascinating puzzle. If you knew any of my colleagues, they'd tell you that I consider that far more interesting payment than mere money." He glanced at his watch. "Must be off soon, though. The meetings go from ten until around one, after which I'll pop by Madame Huan's again and pick up some more materials. We should have our ritual going by three at the latest, so don't go too far. Good thing I left the circle—a few modifications and it should adapt nicely, especially since it's likely our last subject and our current one are together."

Jason nodded. He hoped fervently that this would pan out, because if it didn't then they'd truly lost their last lead. He didn't have the funds to hire a private investigator to hunt Verity down, or to bribe various street people to let him know if they saw her. Hell, he didn't even know what she *looked* like these days. A spear of guilt poked at him—if he hadn't been such a lousy brother and actually made the effort to keep up on what was going on with her, maybe none of this would have happened. It was embarrassing that somebody who was almost a stranger had had to tell him that Verity liked girls. That's the sort of thing brothers are supposed to know about their sisters because they actually spent time with them and made the effort to be involved with their lives.

Stone was gathering up a stack of papers and stuffing them into a battered leather briefcase. "Have fun, then. And be sure to lock up if you go out. Ah!" He rummaged in a cabinet and came up with a key, which he handed to Jason. "This will get you in through the back door."

Jason grinned, pocketing the key. "You sure are trusting. For all you know, I could rob you blind and be out of here and halfway to southern California before you get home."

"True," Stone admitted, returning the grin. "But remember—you've no idea if I've nicked some small insignificant personal item of yours that I can use to track you down wherever you try to hide."

"Good point," Jason admitted. "I guess your bat skulls and old musty books are safe."

Stone chuckled. "See you in a few hours. Do try to stay out of trouble."

"Famous last words."

Jason decided not to go out right away. He didn't really have anything pressing to do other than trying to find a job, and that would be better served by spending some quality time with the classified ads again. He took a long shower, dressed in clean clothes, found the laundry room and put his dirty ones in to wash, and perched at the breakfast bar with the paper spread out in front of him.

There were a lot of jobs listed, but most of them he either wasn't qualified for or required a far larger commitment of time than he was willing to devote until he found Verity. Ideally he'd have liked to find a part-time or occasional gig fixing cars or bikes, or something else where he could use his mechanical skills. He made a mental note to ask Stone—maybe he could check the job board up at Stanford next time he was there and see if he could find anything.

After he finished looking through the employment ads he leafed through the rest of the paper, scanning the articles to make sure no headlines like "Body of teenage girl found" jumped out at him. They didn't, though there were plenty of stories of murders, traffic fatalities, rapes, muggings, and other violent crimes. There were also a few horrific and inexplicable ones, like another man flinging himself in front of a train in full view of his wife and three school-age children, two teenagers who freaked out in the middle of their journalism class and decapitated the teacher with the blade from a paper cutter, and an eight-year-old girl who had poked a pencil into her sleeping mother's eye, then blacked out and claimed to remember nothing of what had happened when she awakened. The whole local section read like the police blotter from some blighted inner city—or in some cases, from hell—not from a relatively upscale collection of sleepy bedroom communities. Jason wondered what things must be like in places like San Francisco and Oakland if it was this bad here.

Once again, Charles's words came back to him: "It's like people just got *meaner*." After being here only a few days, he could definitely see that was true. Hell, it seemed like it had gotten worse since he'd arrived. If this was a movie, the hero and his plucky reporter girlfriend would probably discover that an evil mastermind had put something in the water, or hit the whole area with a "mean ray." Jason couldn't help chuckling at that, even though the real-life situation was anything but funny. He knew that a lot of tempers had been frayed for years after the economy had tanked a few years back, but it was nothing like this in Ventura.

The phone rang when he was taking a break from the unending misery of the local-news section by glancing over the sports page. He listened as it rang three times, then the machine picked up. The voice spoke after the beep: "This is Sgt. Yansky of the Mountain View Police Department. I'm trying to reach Jason Thayer. It's—"

Jason had already vaulted across the kitchen and snatched up the receiver. "This is Jason Thayer," he said in a rush, hardly daring to breathe.

"Ah, Mr. Thayer. I'm glad I caught you," the voice said. It sounded tired and subdued. "I'm afraid we've found something."

"Found what?" Jason yelled, unable to keep his voice level.

"Well—we're not absolutely sure, but we think we might have found your sister. We need you to—to come and help with the identification."

Jason's entire body froze. For several seconds he just stared at the phone, utterly numb. "You—found her?" he finally stammered. "Where?"

"Please, Mr. Thayer. I know this is terrible news, but as I said, we're not completely sure that it's your sister. We need your help with that. Can you come?"

"Yes, yes! Of course I can come! Where?"

Yansky gave him an address. "It's outside South San Jose—an old junkyard." The cop sighed. "We've—found bodies there before. How long do you think it will take you to get there?"

"I'll leave right now." Jason could barely force the words out of his mouth as the reality began to sink in. "I'll meet you there. Where's Lt. Arrelli? Is he going to be there too?"

"He's already out there," Yansky said. "Just check in at the front gate and they'll let you in."

R. L. KING

"All right. Leaving now," he said again, and hung up. For several moments he just gripped the counter, his knotted knuckles turning white. *Can't lose it now,* he told himself sternly. *This ain't the time. Just get out there and hope to God they're wrong and it isn't her.*

12.

Jason was on the road five minutes later, heading south after checking the route on his map. It was several miles before he realized he hadn't left Stone a note telling him where he'd gone, but he was too numb to care. He was too numb even to remember that the freeways usually weren't safe, but this time of day there was quite a bit of traffic and thankfully he didn't run into any trouble.

He drove on autopilot, his brain spinning with questions. If it was Verity out there, what had happened to her? Who had killed her? Had she been killed at the junkyard, or had her body been transported there and dumped? Where was Susanna? Was she dead too, maybe stashed somewhere at the same junkyard and not yet found? He could barely afford a corner of his mind to pay attention to his driving, too busy tossing out question after question with no answers. He was amazed that nobody pulled him over, but he supposed with all the shit going around nowadays a speeding car that actually looked like its driver knew what he was doing was pretty low on the Highway Patrol's priority list.

"Aw, man, V..." he whispered aloud. "How could I let you get yourself into this?" His hands were practically thrumming on the steering wheel, trying to make the old car go faster by sheer force of will. He couldn't shake the vision of his sister, the little tomboy sister who used to keep him company while he worked on cars in their dad's garage so many years ago, laid out among the junked cars, bloody or burned or hacked up...his sister covered by a white sheet on a slab in the morgue, her face gray, her eyes lifeless —

— on a slab —
— in the morgue —
Wait a minute...

R. L. KING

Holy shit!

The realization hit Jason so hard that he had to physically restrain himself from slamming on the brakes and stopping the car right there in the middle of the freeway. "Idiot!" he yelled, smacking the steering wheel hard with his right hand. "I am a *moron!*"

He whipped the Ford off at the next exit and pulled to the shoulder, his entire body shaking. They'd almost gotten him that time. They'd counted on his fear and emotional turmoil to drive out any rational thought, and it had almost worked. He'd almost driven full-speed, both eyes open, into what was almost certainly a death trap.

He leaned back in his seat, willing his breath to return to normal. How had he not realized it before? He was a cop's son, for fuck's sake! He'd grown up with this kind of thing all his life! How many times had he heard his dad's subdued voice on the phone, arranging to meet with a distraught parent or spouse or adult child to identify the body of their loved one who had met with some fatal misadventure—

—at the *morgue*.

It was *always* at the morgue. They would never call up somebody and bring them to the crime scene to see their loved one in the kind of state in which they usually found dead bodies. Especially dead bodies that had been dumped somewhere. What purpose could it possibly serve, other than to add to the person's emotional agony and possibly compromise the crime scene? If at all possible, they always waited until after the body had been cleaned, prepared, and wrapped in the white sheet. It was hard enough to look when someone you loved was being rolled out on a slab, but at least they'd do their best so you didn't have to see the worst of it—the bloody wounds, hacked limbs, missing eyes. Jason couldn't even imagine a police department that would call someone to the actual crime scene.

And he had fallen for it — or almost had.

So, the question was — what did he do now? He could find a pay phone and try to call Stone, though he doubted the mage would be home yet. He could turn around and drive back to Palo Alto, letting whatever ambush they had waiting for him down there at the junkyard stand around with their thumbs up their asses, waiting for a patsy who'd never show. The thought gave him some satisfaction, true. And it was probably the smartest course of action he could choose.

However...

The smallest of thoughts scratched at the back of his mind: *what if you're wrong?*

What if they do *do it that way up here? What if it has something to do with the fact that they're strapped for cash and people? It would be easier to just call the relative to look at the body at the scene. Maybe they can't afford to care about things like compassion and niceties these days.*

And if he *were* wrong, Verity *was* lying dead down at that junkyard, and he just turned around and left — what did that say about him? He'd already turned his back on her too many times in her short life. Sure, he'd never meant to. It had never been on purpose. Their lives just — didn't intersect. But that wasn't an excuse.

He had to know.

He knew he was probably making a big mistake, but he didn't care. He had to know for sure.

But he didn't have to be stupid about it, and he didn't have to be a patsy. He'd find out, but on his own terms. He only hoped that whoever was waiting for him down there hadn't planned for that contingency.

Starting the car again, he got back on the freeway and continued south. It was another five miles to the exit he wanted, and he spent them thinking, planning, trying to anticipate potential problems. He'd only get one chance at this—if he blew it, he'd be lucky if his body ended up dumped at a junkyard. More likely, he'd probably never be found, and Stone would be left wondering if he'd made good on his joking threat to take off for southern California.

Maybe he can look in the dryer and use my clean laundry to track down my charred remains. The thought almost made him grin even in spite of it all—the thought of Stone, all serious and chanting incantations in the middle of a magic circle with candles, shafts of golden light, and a pair of plaid boxer shorts spread out in front of him like a sacred object.

There was the exit. He was south of the southernmost part of San Jose now, in an area where the terrain looked more like dusty abandoned farmland than urban sprawl. He left the freeway and turned on a smaller road, occasionally glancing at the map spread out on the passenger seat to make sure he was still going the right way, but mostly keeping his eyes constantly scanning both in front of him and behind him, always on the watch for anyone who looked suspicious. He half expected to see a flock of DMW bikers approaching fast, but aside from a few clapped-out trucks and the occasional tractor, the place looked pretty deserted.

The address that Yansky had given him (he paused to wonder if there even *was* a Sgt. Yansky on the force, and kicked himself mentally again for not checking) was several miles off the freeway, at the end of a winding road that led off into the hills. It seemed an odd place for a junkyard, but he was moving back into a more urban area now with old warehouses, truckyards, and farm machinery sales lots, so he supposed it wasn't that strange.

About a mile from where the map showed the junk-yard to be, he pulled off the road again and evaluated his situation. He was now almost certain that he'd been duped—even in these days of grisly murders happening frequently, he would still be seeing cars in the area: black and white cop cars with lightbars, unmarked nondescript late-model sedans, crime-scene investigators, nosy report-ers in news vans—they'd all be milling around, moving in and out of the perimeter of the scene as they went about their business. He remembered the scene at Melody's house: three police cars and an ambulance, and that was East Palo Alto, which Charles had told him was a very poor community that certainly didn't have cash to spare for extraneous police presence.

Still, though, the need to know drove him to investi-gate. He had to be sure. He couldn't trust any of his assumptions anymore.

Examining the map, he saw that the junkyard was ac-tually bounded by four different streets: the one that served as its actual physical address and three more on the other three sides. Though the junkyard itself wasn't marked on the map, it looked to Jason like it took up a fairly large block's worth of space all on its own.

That was good, especially since it was the middle of the day and he wouldn't have any darkness to hide him. He consulted the map again and decided the best way to do this was to go a few streets over and approach the place from the back. He wasn't sure he could sneak in if the junkyard had a perimeter fence, but maybe he could climb over or maybe the view would be clear enough to know for sure whether anybody was there.

He fired up the Ford and matched action to plan. He drove about half a mile down a road parallel to the one the junkyard's address was on, then hung a left and con-tinued on until he hit the street that ran along its back wall. He was pretty sure the DMW (if it were in fact they who were behind this — he didn't really want to contemplate quite yet that somebody *else* might be after him too) didn't know what he was driving these days, and the Ford certainly blended in with the scenery around here. He decided to risk parking close by in case he had to make a quick getaway.

As he pulled into visual range of the block where the junkyard was, he could see its contents rising up in large untidy piles above the chain-link fence that bounded it. *Damn,* he thought as he got closer. *Razor wire. Not going over the top here. I'll have to find an opening somewhere.* After spending a couple of minutes scanning the vicinity to make sure nobody obvious was lying in wait for him, he got out of the car and, leaving it unlocked, moved across the street until he was standing next to the fence. He still felt very vulnerable, as there was no real place to hide. It helped that it was an overcast and rather chilly day — at least the sun wasn't blazing over his head.

As he'd noticed when approaching in the car, the junkyard was full to brimming with stacks of metal — mostly old crushed cars. There were rows between them, but most of them were now impassable, blocked by some of the stacks that had toppled, spilling their debris into the open spaces. Jason had been to many junkyards before, and he'd never seen a working one that allowed its stock to get into this state. Even though to the layman they looked like nothing more than big piles of undifferentiated scrap, he knew a good junkman could tell you exactly where to find nearly anything in his yard. This place had been severely neglected. Odd that so much of the stock was here, but the place looked and felt abandoned.

Creeping down the fence he looked for an opening large enough to wriggle through, encouraged by the continued lack of any signs of people, hostile or otherwise. He found what he was looking for almost at the end of the block: a spot where somebody had snipped through the bottom part of the fence, probably with some kind of metal shears. It was a neat cut, neatly put back together so it was difficult for the oblivious passerby to notice. For someone like Jason, though, who was actively looking, it was as good as a doorway.

With a glance back to make sure nobody was bothering the Ford, he quickly pulled aside the loose part of the fence and wriggled in, coming up behind a tall and still intact pile of crushed cars. Crouching low, he crept forward until he came to the next intersection and chanced a peek around the corner. This aisle was still unblocked and accessible, and it was deserted.

Where would they be if they were here? The more he thought about it, the more he thought that a junkyard would be an odd place to dump a body. It was much more common to dump them in landfills, where the smell of decay would be masked by the olfactory cacophony of thousands of tons of garbage. If she were here, it would either be because they'd found her in one of the crushed cars, or else they simply had put her here for convenience.

If she were here at all, of course. His doubts were growing. It was very quiet here, and so far he hadn't heard any sounds at all. No sirens, no crackles or electronically tinny voices coming from police radios, no crunch of tires as vehicles entered or exited the scene. It was as quiet as a —

No, let's not think that. It's creepy enough out here as it is.

He moved off again, still keeping low and occasionally glancing not only behind him, but upward. Charles had said that the DMW didn't use guns, but now he knew at least some of them used magic and that was even worse. He wondered if they could magically tell he was here somehow, then angrily reminded himself that he could completely scare the shit out of himself if he kept making up things that magic could "possibly" do. Being able to kill people by making blood come out of all their head-holes was quite freaky enough, thank you very much.

Reaching another junction, he stopped once more and just listened. Still nothing broke the silence but the occasional squawk of a crow overhead, or the far-off creak of metal on metal as one of the piles of scrap shifted. He didn't even hear the normal sounds of trucks or men calling to each other that would indicate that this was still a going concern. The little hairs on the back of his neck were edging their way to upright positions again.

She's not here, you idiot. Get out of here while you still can.

Good advice, he decided. There was no way the cops were here. Even from where he was, the place wasn't big enough that he wouldn't be able to hear the regular hubbub of a police presence anywhere inside. Better to get back in the car and get back to Palo Alto. Stone should be back home soon and maybe they could finally locate Verity and get this whole business over with.

Coming up from his crouch, he turned with the intention of sneaking back the way he came as fast as he could. He wasn't going to feel safe until he was back on the freeway, driving toward—

Someone was standing behind him, not six feet away.

He yelped—he couldn't help it—and leaped back, eyes wide, crashing into a pile of scrap that teetered alarmingly but didn't fall, although he himself nearly did.

Scrambling to get his balance back, he stared wildly at the person who had so silently sneaked up on him. It was a teenage boy, maybe fourteen at the most, and he had not moved. He returned Jason's stare, his eyes unblinking, his mouth stretched into a wide and very unnerving grin. Fishbelly pale under a layer of grime, he wore a tattered navy-blue coat, a stocking cap pulled down low over his stringy hair, and dirty jeans. His hands hung limply at his sides.

While he struggled to stop his heart from pounding, Jason swung his gaze left and right to make sure that nobody else was sneaking up on him too. So far, it was just him and the boy. The kid didn't look like the DMW, but that didn't mean he wasn't a threat. That smile was enough to haunt his nightmares all on its own.

And then the kid spoke. "Hi," he said. He was still smiling, and still hadn't blinked. His voice was high — the voice of a boy, not of a young man past puberty.

"Uh — hi," Jason replied, mentally calculating how easy it would be for him to vault past the kid and make a run for it before his inevitable buddies showed up.

"It's dangerous to play here," the kid said.

"Um...yeah, I'm getting that feeling."

"You should go."

Jason took a deep breath. "That's what I'm trying to do. You — uh — scared me."

"People say that a lot, that I scare them," the kid agreed. "I don't mean to."

"Er — I'm sure you don't." Jason's Weird-O-Meter was pegging again, and he could not get any kind of read on this very strange boy. He glanced left and right again — still no sign of anybody else. He decided to take a chance. "Um...I'm going to go now, okay? But can you tell me if you've seen any policemen here?"

"I'm scared of policemen," the kid said.

Jason nodded. "But have you seen any? Today?"

The kid shook his head. "No policemen. You should go, though. They're waiting for you."

Jason's blood chilled. "They're — who's waiting for me?"

"You should go," the kid said again. "I think they might have heard you yell. I have to go now too. Bye!" And he stepped backward—and disappeared into a pile of junk.

Jason blinked twice. He had *not* seen what he thought he'd just seen. It wasn't possible. Even after all the weird shit he'd witnessed in the last couple of days, this was simply the last straw. Freaky grinning teenagers did *not* just disappear into piles of junk.

They're waiting for you...

He clutched his head for a moment as if squeezing it would pop all of this insanity out of his brain. It didn't work, so he did the next most logical thing that came to mind.

He ran for it.

13.

He was still amazed, fifteen minutes later when he was back on the freeway and forcing himself to stick to the speed limit on his way back to Palo Alto, that he'd gotten away. Whoever the creepy kid had been, he'd never know whether anybody really *had* been lying in wait for him, because he never saw anybody else. He'd made it back though the hole in the fence and to the car without as much as a sound from behind him to indicate that anyone knew their quarry had flown the coop.

What he did know for sure now, though, was that Verity had not been at the junkyard. And he was pretty damned sure that he'd better stop trusting Arrelli. It could be that the cop knew nothing about this Yansky character and the phone call, but he could no longer take that chance. He hated giving in to paranoia, but until this whole mess was over he was going to have to be very careful who he trusted.

He didn't calm down until he was back at Stone's place. The area was parked up pretty good so he had to find a space a few houses down (he hoped the neighbors in the tony little enclave didn't have a problem with this junky interloper in the midst of their solidly upper-middle-class vehicles, but at this point that was the least of his problems).

He let himself in through the back door. Mrs. Olivera was there in the kitchen, puttering around cleaning the counters. She didn't look up from her work as Jason came in. Glancing at the kitchen clock, he noted that it was getting close to time when Stone would be due back, so he was surprised to hear the mage's voice from upstairs: "Is that you, Jason?"

"Yeah," he called.

There was a moment's pause, then Jason could hear the sound of someone coming down. He moved out of the kitchen to the hall to meet him. He must have been home for awhile—he'd swapped his tweed sport jacket for a gray Stanford sweatshirt and jeans. "You're home early," Jason said.

Stone nodded. "Meeting ran short, for the first time in recorded history. Out job hunting? Any luck?"

Jason took a deep breath, trying to decide where to start, and then without any warning or preamble he was pouring out the whole story of his morning as Stone listened with growing alarm. When he finished, Stone stared at him. "You're saying that they—tried to lure you out there by telling you they'd found your sister dead?" he asked, incredulous.

"Yeah. And they nearly succeeded. If I hadn't realized in time what a moron I was being, we probably wouldn't be having this conversation now." He was surprised that he was shaking a little now—even the retelling was spooking him. "Hey, you mind if I have something to drink? This hasn't been one of my best days."

"Go for it," Stone said, shooing him out. He followed him to the sitting room and continued to pepper him with questions as he rummaged in the liquor cabinet and poured himself a generous measure of whatever he got his hands on first. "And this boy you said you saw—"

"Fucking *creepy* boy," Jason corrected. "*Nightmare fuel* creepy."

"Yes, creepy," Stone agreed, nodding. "But you say he warned you away—and then disappeared into a solid wall?"

"Yeah." Jason nodded emphatically. "He just stepped back and—*poof!*—he was gone!" He met Stone's gaze earnestly. "Do you think I'm going crazy? Do you think I've started seeing things? Because people don't *do* that in real life." He paused. "They don't, right? Can mages—?"

Stone shook his head. "No. We can't walk through solid objects."

"So you're sayin'—what? That I was seeing things? That he was a ghost?" His gaze sharpened. "*Are* there ghosts? Do you know?"

"No idea," Stone said, shrugging. "I've never seen one personally, but not believing that things are impossible rather goes with the job description in my line of work, so I'm not going to tell you that they don't exist."

Jason tossed back his drink, set the glass down, and began kneading his forehead again. "I don't know how much more of this I can take. Every time I think I've got my mind around it, something *else* weird—weird and *different*—happens."

"Indeed," Stone said, sitting down in his ratty leather armchair. "As I said, this is all very interesting, and obviously more than a little frightening. And it's bringing all sorts of questions to mind."

"Such as—?" Jason took a seat on the overstuffed couch and decided not to pour another drink. It wasn't even helping this time—he still felt nervous and keyed up.

"Such as: Who is it that's after you? Are they after you, specifically? If so, why? Is there something about your sister that whoever this is, they don't want you to find her?"

"The DMW—" Jason started.

"The DMW are a gang," Stone said. "A very dangerous and powerful gang to be sure, but I'll wager quite a large sum that they don't often instigate these sorts of things on their own. Yes," he added before Jason could speak again, "I'm sure they've got whatever drug or prostitution or other illegal endeavors they run, but why would a gang be interested in chasing down a rather nondescript young man from southern California? I could see why they bothered you that first time—just for fun, most likely, since they bother everybody who wanders into their line of fire. But it seems now like they're actively stalking you. And that troubles me."

Jason stared at him. "You think there's something about Verity—?"

"I've no idea. I don't know her—I only know what you've told me about her, which hasn't been much. You said she's seventeen, and that she's mentally or emotionally disturbed. Has she always been this way?"

"No," Jason said, shaking his head. "She was fine when she was a kid. Something happened a few years back, and she just—kinda—" he spread his arms "—got strange."

"Strange in what way? How did this disturbance manifest?"

Jason thought about that, taking a deep breath and letting it out slowly. His brain didn't really want to delve into the past right now—it was still busy chewing over the events of the last couple of hours. "She—sometimes she'd just sit in the room and not say anything. She'd stare out the window and talk to herself. Sometimes she'd be afraid—she'd say that things were after her. She'd drink or smoke dope when she could get away with it—she said it 'made them go away.'" Jason shrugged. "None of us knew what to do with her. Dad really didn't want to put her in the hospital, but he couldn't handle her. I know the guilt about it ate him up."

"Did she ever have any lucid moments? If so, did she remember anything she spoke about? Did you ever ask her what she thought was after her?"

"No. Sure, she'd have lucid moments. But she never remembered any of what she said. When we'd ask her about it, she'd look at us like *we* were the crazy ones."

Stone nodded slowly. "And...remember back to the time when she first started showing these symptoms. Do you recall if it came on over time or all at once?"

"What do you mean?"

"I mean, did she seem to grow stranger over a period of a few weeks or months — perhaps having occasional episodes but mostly fine, or did she wake up one morning with this problem?"

Jason thought back. "I'm...not sure," he said. "It wasn't overnight, but I'm pretty sure it came on fast. I was in the Academy at the time, so I was away from home a lot."

"Academy? You were in the military?"

"Police academy," Jason corrected. He looked away, unable to meet Stone's eyes. "I — got expelled a year later. I — uh — sort of let my temper get the better of me and got into a fight with one of the instructors."

Stone raised an eyebrow. "I see. But getting back to Verity — so this came on fairly quickly, a few years back, you said. Do you remember how many years?"

"Around five. She was twelve at the time. The doctors told Dad it might have something to do with puberty. We never really knew for sure, though." He looked up at Stone. "Is there some reason you're asking me all these questions? Do you have some idea in mind?"

"No, not really. I'm just gathering data. I have some thoughts, but nothing concrete and certainly nothing with enough backing to bring it to light yet. Let me mull it over for a bit, and do some research. That's for later, though. Right now, I think it's best that we locate your wayward sister and bring her back here before one of you gets in over your head." He looked Jason up and down. "You look, quite understandably, I might add, like a man who's just been scared out of his wits. Tell you what—why don't you go upstairs and lie down for a bit, and I'll put the circle together and call you when it's ready? There's really no point in your sitting down there watching. It's not going to be any different from what you saw yesterday—in fact, it will likely be even less exciting, since most of it's already in place. Shouldn't take more than an hour or so to get it sorted the rest of the way."

Jason was all ready to protest, but he realized that he *did* feel pretty bad, and a chance to calm down a little wouldn't be such a bad thing. He nodded. "Okay, I'll do that." He took a deep breath. "I sure hope this is the end of it. We've had so many false alarms..."

"Amen to that," Stone agreed.

Jason went upstairs to the guest room, switched on the small portable TV for a healthy dose of one hundred percent mundane background noise, and lay down on the bed. Staring up at the ceiling, he didn't know if he'd actually get any rest—he certainly wouldn't sleep, with his mind going a mile a minute—but maybe he could at least get himself calmed down enough that his fight or flight reactions weren't ready to launch him out the nearest window at the first unidentifiable sound.

The TV was playing a football game. Idly, he rolled on his side so he could watch it for a few minutes. It seemed like it had been years since he'd done anything as normal as watching a football game, and it felt good to do it now even if he was only halfway paying attention to what was going on. He wondered if Stone *would* be able to find Verity with the ritual. He hadn't been able to find Susanna, even with that page of scribblings that he'd claimed represented her "essence." Did the teddy bear contain Verity's essence? It was a strange concept—but magic in general, at least so far, was pretty damn strange. Every time he got away from Stone, it became harder for him to convince himself that he'd actually experienced it at all.

Sighing, he resumed looking at the ceiling. This wasn't working at all. "Lying on the bed" did not equate to "resting," no matter how much he wanted it to. He gave it his best try for five more minutes, half-listening as commercials droned on for a local Chevrolet dealership and one of former talk-show host Gordon Lucas's local charity shindigs, but all he could do was keep thinking about was how much he hoped the ritual would work this time, and wonder how far along Stone was in getting things set up so they could start. Finally he gave it up as a bad job. He decided he'd just go downstairs, grab a beer or a soda or something, and head on down to the basement. It might be boring, but it couldn't be any worse than this and at least he'd have somebody to talk to.

He left the bedroom and descended the stairs. Rounding the corner to the kitchen, the first thing he was greeted by was the sight of Mrs. Olivera's not insignificant posterior shining up at him like a polyester-clad full moon. He stared at her for a moment, confused. She appeared to be rummaging around under the stove with a broom handle. "Uh—hi?" he ventured.

She started, turning her head to look at him without getting up. "Oh. Hello," she said, smiling. "I'm sorry—this must look strange. I dropped something behind the stove and I was just getting it back."

"O...kay," he said, still uncertain. "Need some help?"

"No, I'm fine," she said cheerfully. "I've got it already."

Jason nodded, his mind still on the proceedings downstairs. He crossed to the refrigerator, quickly examined the contents and decided on a soda (Stone's beer preferences were a bit too dark and British for his tastes). He grabbed it and headed out, waving. "See you."

She didn't answer, but he didn't notice. He was already halfway down the stairs to the basement.

Stone's filtered voice answered his knock. "Jason?"

"Yeah, it's me."

"Give me a minute, I'm almost done with this part." It was actually somewhat closer to five minutes before the door clicked open.

"How's it going?" Jason asked, coming in.

"Fine, fine. I figure another fifteen minutes or so to get everything perfect. I don't want this to fail because I placed a candle wrong." Stone glanced over at Jason, who by now had sat down with his soda in the same chair he'd used yesterday. "Couldn't sleep?"

Jason shook his head. "Mind's going too fast. I even tried watching TV, but no dice. I just want to get this over with."

"Quite understandable." He glanced at the soda can. "Ah, good idea. I wish I'd known you were bringing that—I'd have asked you to bring me one too. It can get a bit warm down here."

Jason got up, glad to have something to do. "I'll get you one," he said. "Better than sitting here waiting." He hurried across the room and out the door.

Mrs. Olivera was nowhere to be seen when he got to the kitchen. That was a bit odd, since he hadn't been gone more than a few minutes. He'd reached the fridge and opened it when it occurred to him that there was something else odd about her behavior: she'd responded to his offer of help by telling him that she'd already retrieved whatever she'd dropped behind the stove. But if she'd already retrieved it, why was she still poking around under there with the broom handle? Had she found something else back there?

Curiosity getting the better of him, Jason closed the fridge and grabbed a flashlight from its charger on the wall. He got down on all fours, ducking his head down low so he could look under the stove. It was a nice one, massive and gas-powered, the kind of thing owned by people who really enjoyed cooking. There was only about a four-inch gap from the bottom of the stove to the floor, so Jason practically had to put his cheek flush with the floor to be able to see underneath. He switched on the flashlight and shined its beam into the gap.

The first thing he noticed was that it was very neat under there: no sign of dust bunnies or grease stains or any of the other things people often had under their stoves for lack of cleaning. He started looking on the left side, but almost immediately noticed something else out of the corner of his eye on the right. He moved the beam over and it illuminated a small object, mostly cylindrical and about two or three inches in diameter. It appeared to have some kind of wire sticking out of one end that snaked around behind it, and a tiny red light flashed rhythmically at the other end.

The thing was humming.

14.

To his credit, Jason's brain only seized up and refused to act for a grand total of about five seconds. That was probably quite a bit better reaction time than the average civilian would experience when confronted with a similar situation. Then he was on his feet in one motion, flinging the flashlight aside and pelting toward the basement barely touching the stairs on the way down. "DOC!!" he screamed at the top of his lungs, pounding on the door with his fists so hard that if it had been a normal interior door it would have buckled. "DOC!!! GET OUT HERE *NOW!!!*"

There was a pause that seemed like it took about twenty years, and then the door swung open. Stone stood there, looking confused and a little freaked out. "Jason? What is—?"

Jason seized his arm. "We gotta get outta here! Now! Right now!" He was practically babbling.

"Jason, what's going on?" Stone pulled back as Jason tried to drag him bodily up the stairs.

"Come *on!*" Wild-eyed with terror, he met Stone's eyes before resuming his efforts to pull him up. *"There's a bomb in the kitchen!"*

Stone stared at him, dumbfounded. "A—?"

Jason wasn't talking anymore. He redoubled his efforts and had succeeded in getting Stone about halfway up the stairs before the mage's brain finally locked on to what he'd said and he began moving under his own power. At the top of the stairs he stopped. "Wait—my books—my research—"

"*Fuck* your research!" Jason yelled. He was definitely a long way from rational now. "I don't know how long it's set to go before it blows. If you don't want them picking what's left of us up with a spoon, let's get our asses *out* of here!"

"Go on!" Stone yelled, wrenching his arm away from Jason. "Get out. I'll follow you."

"No way!" Jason lunged at him again, but missed. Glaring, he followed the mage into the sitting room, where he snatched up the notebook full of strange symbols he'd shown Jason and stuffed it into the waistband of his jeans.

"All right, let's go," Stone said grimly. Together they hurried to the front door. Stone flung it open. Then he stopped in the open doorway. "Wait! Mrs. Olivera!" He made as if to turn and run back into the house, but Jason grabbed him hard and restrained him, plucking up his leather jacket from the chair by the door.

"Doc," he said, practically sobbing with frustration now. "I think she's gone. I'm pretty sure she's the one who set the bomb!"

"What the hell—?" Stone glared at him like he'd suddenly announced that sentient rabbits had taken over the world's governments and were scheduling mass executions. "How—?"

"Never *mind!*" Jason tightened his grip on Stone's arms and frog-marched him across the yard out toward the street.

The bomb went off as they made it halfway across the yard toward the street. There was a far off *whoomp!* sound followed by a massive explosion a couple of seconds later as the heat and flame from the small device contacted the gas from the line its initial detonation had ruptured. The force of the blast blew Jason and Stone forward, tumbling them over a parked car. Jason saw something bright flare into existence around them just before they hit, then wink out. They rolled and came to rest in the middle of the street, where a passing pickup truck had to swerve to miss them and smashed into another parked car on the other side. All around them car alarms were going off, each one adding its individual note of warning to the general cacophony.

Jason must have blacked out briefly; when he came to, somebody was trying to drag him out of the street. He could hear screams now: people were coming out of nearby houses and running into the street. He struggled out of his rescuer's grasp—it was a chubby middle aged man in a Rolling Stones T-shirt and sweat pants. "I'm—okay," he breathed. Taking quick inventory of his major systems, he discovered that his head hurt a little, he was bleeding from several minor cuts, and in general his body felt like he'd gone another round with the bar gorilla back in Ventura. Nothing broken as far as he could tell. He looked around. "Where's Dr. Stone?"

The man pointed. "He's over there. You sure you're all right?"

Jason struggled to his feet, picking up his jacket from where it had landed next to him and shrugging into it. "Yeah. Thanks." And then he was gone, heading over to where Stone lay on the grass in a neighbor's yard two houses down, surrounded by a small knot of worried neighbors. Already the car alarms were stopping; Jason could hear the far-off sound of sirens getting closer.

Pushing his way past the neighbors he dropped down next to Stone. The mage was awake, though he looked somewhat out of it. He was covered in the same collection of cuts and scrapes that Jason was. Jason touched his shoulder. "You okay?" He looked past Stone to his former home, appalled and shaking to see the towering orange flames and black smoke rising from it. *We were almost in that when it went off,* he told himself. *Down in that basement we wouldn't have stood a chance.*

Stone nodded wearily. "Yes...I—think so." He fumbled at his middle and pulled the notebook from his waistband. "Here—take this. Put it—in your pocket."

Jason did as he was told, stashing the leatherbound notebook in the inner pocket of his leather jacket. The neighbors, most of whom had gone back to staring at the fire now that it was clear Stone wasn't badly hurt, didn't notice. Jason leaned down close so he wouldn't be overheard. "I saw—some kind of bright thing show up around us right as the explosion went off. You—shielded us somehow, didn't you?"

Stone nodded again. "Not very effectively, I'm afraid," he said. "But at least we're still alive." He moved to sit up, and Jason helped him. He stared at the burning house, letting out a long, slow breath. "Well, that's the house done for, then." Sadness flashed across his face. "I've been in that place for nearly four years now. I'd gotten rather attached to it, not to mention my library, the artifacts—" A pause, and then he looked around. "But none of that is important now. Was anyone else hurt?"

"I don't think so." The fire trucks—three of them—were rolling up now, along with several police cars and a couple of ambulances. "Though I wouldn't be surprised if some of the nearby houses had their windows blown out, so I guess they'll probably be checking."

Stone stared at him. "You got us out of there," he said, as if he couldn't quite believe it. "If you hadn't—"

Jason nodded, still shaking. Despite the heat radiating out from the house fire, he felt cold. "Yeah," he breathed. "If I hadn't gone up to get that soda—"

That seemed to trigger something in Stone's mind. "Wait a minute—you said something about—Mrs. Olivera? Did I hit my head, or did you say that she—set the bomb?"

Jason was about to answer, but he noticed a couple of policemen and a pair of EMTs approaching the little crowd standing in front of them watching the fire. "We can talk about this later, okay? I don't think I really want to talk to the cops right now."

Stone nodded. "I—understand. I'll talk to them—I'll see if I can distract them long enough for you to slip off into the crowd and disappear. Your car's still all right, yes?"

"Yeah. I had to park down the street. I guess yours is history."

"Sadly, I fear so." Stone got to his feet with a little help from Jason. "I'll tell you what—I'll deal with this as best I can, and I'll meet you at the Fifth Quarter. It's a bar over on El Camino, near Page Mill. Just sit in the back and watch the games and no one will bother you. Don't be surprised if it takes awhile—I suspect this sort of bureaucracy moves slowly." He pulled out his wallet and handed Jason a couple of twenty dollar bills. "Go to a gas station and get yourself cleaned up as well as you can. I'll be there as soon as I can get away. And don't lose that notebook."

Jason nodded. Stone moved forward, swaying a little unsteadily at first but recovering quickly. He moved through the crowd and intercepted the knot of police and EMTs before they reached it. By this time an even bigger crowd had gathered, so it wasn't too hard for Jason to mingle his way to the edge and then saunter to his car and get away before the whole street was blocked in. *Score another tiny victory for dumb luck, I guess*. As lucky as you could be when you had just been nearly blown to bits by your friend's cleaning lady, anyway.

15.

It was a little over two hours before Stone turned up at the Fifth Quarter. Jason was sitting in the dimly lit back room as the mage had instructed. There were several TV sets stationed in various corners of the room, showing everything from football to cricket to auto racing. He'd parked himself in a booth in the far back corner where he could watch all the entrances and was now working on his second beer. Fortunately his leather jacket coupled with Stone's shield spell had taken the brunt of the impact from the bomb, so most of his superficial cuts had been confined to his face and hands. He'd easily been able to clean them up at a nearby gas station bathroom. There were still a few bloodstains on his jeans, but he rubbed some dirt over them and hadn't thought they'd draw much attention in a bar. He was right. So now all he had to do was sit here feeling all the various aches and pains throughout his body, watch sports he didn't care about, and wait. By the time Stone walked in, he was beginning to feel like he should instigate a bar fight just to have something to do.

The mage was still looking pale and shellshocked. He'd gotten an overcoat from somewhere, but he was still wearing his shredded and bloodspattered Stanford sweatshirt and jeans and his hair was disarrayed. He dropped down into the seat across from Jason and for a moment he just sat there, silent and staring at nothing.

"You—uh—got away okay, I see," Jason ventured. "Gimme a sec and I'll get you a beer. You look like you could use one."

Stone nodded. "Guinness, please." he said. His voice sounded numb.

Jason went off and returned a few minutes later with Stone's order. He set the glass in front of the mage and

R. L. KING

resumed his seat. He didn't speak either, willing to wait for Stone. He himself had had two hours to sit and contemplate what had happened—Stone had likely had no such luxury.

"I—think I'm done with the police," the mage said at last, taking a sip. A long pause, and then: "I told them that I smelled gas inside, and I'd left the house to go to a neighbor's and call the gas company when the explosion went off. They seemed to believe me."

Jason nodded. "Did anybody else get hurt?"

"Unfortunately yes," Stone said. "The explosion blew out a plate-glass window in the house behind mine, and the shards hit two young children playing in their family room." He sighed, staring down into his glass. "They think they'll recover, but they were both badly injured. One of them might lose an eye."

Jason closed his eyes for a second. "Did they make you go to the hospital?"

Stone shook his head. "They tried, but I declined treatment. Oh, and I also called the University and arranged to take some leave. I had quite a bit of it saved up, and under the circumstances they had no objection."

Jason nodded and glanced up again, not sure how to ask the next question. "Did you—tell the police about Mrs. Olivera?"

"No. I wanted to talk to you about that a bit more, since you told me practically nothing. As far as I know she was still in the house and died in the explosion." His gaze sharpened. "I sincerely hope you have something to back your claim. I might have been able to save her. Though I did notice when I left that her car wasn't where I saw it parked when I got home."

"I don't think she was there," Jason said. He told Stone about what he'd seen in the kitchen.

Stone stared at him, jolted out of his numbness. "So she was poking under the stove with a broom handle *after* she said she'd retrieved whatever she dropped?"

"Yeah. That's what finally registered to me as strange when I went back up. When I got down there to look myself, there was nothing there but the bomb. I don't know what else to think. If she saw something that weird under there and hadn't put it there herself, wouldn't she have said something about it? And why would she leave so soon afterward? I was only downstairs for five minutes or so before I went back up. It seems like she was getting out of there in a hurry."

"So if that's true," Stone said slowly, his gaze returning to his glass, "then it means my housekeeper — the woman who's worked for me for the better part of three years — just tried to murder me." He sighed again. "You'll pardon me if that's a little hard to take — whether it's true or not."

Jason didn't say anything. There wasn't much he *could* say at that point. He concentrated on his beer for awhile, and the two of them just sat in an uneasy silence. Finally, he looked up. "What are we gonna do now?"

"I need to give that some thought," Stone said after a long time. "If it were ever in doubt that some very dangerous and powerful people want you, me, or both of us dead, I think that's been quite effectively removed by the latest events. I don't know about you, but I'm getting tired of running, and of not having a bloody idea what the hell is going on. I've always been much more comfortable on the offensive than the defensive."

Jason stared at him. "What are you saying — that you want to go after them? We don't even know who they are. We don't know what they want, other than to snuff us out. And we don't know *why* they want that. So where can we even start?"

"Let me work on that," Stone said. "Right now I'm still shaking, and my concentration is buggered to hell. Our first priority is to find a place to stay temporarily, and set up an answering service so the police can reach me without having to know where I am. After that—" He spread his arms. " I don't know yet. I have some ideas, but give me a little time."

"Yeah," Jason agreed with a sigh, nodding. "Guess it's all we can do." He looked up. "You—didn't happen to save the teddy bear, did you?"

Stone shook his head. "Sorry, no."

"So you couldn't do another ritual to find V even if you found a place where you could do it."

"I'm sorry, Jason. I'm afraid not."

Jason nodded. He'd suspected as much, but he had to ask anyway.

"Oh—" Stone said. "That reminds me. Do you still have my notebook?"

"Oh, yeah." He pulled it out of his pocket and handed it over. "What's so important about this thing, anyway? It's the one that has all those symbols in it, right? But you don't even know what they mean."

"That's not all it has in it by a long way," Stone said, stowing it away in an inner pocket. "I take it you didn't succumb to temptation and have a look?"

Jason shook his head. "Honestly it didn't even occur to me. I forgot that I had it. I was—a little freaked out, you know?"

Stone chuckled, but it was a mirthless sound. "You wouldn't have understood it anyway. Even if you *could* manage to decipher my chicken scratches." He stood, finishing the last of his Guinness. "We should get going, though. I'd like to have a place to stay before it gets dark, and we should pick up a few changes of clothes. Fortunately, unless whatever evil force is stalking us has access to my bank account, cash shouldn't be a problem for awhile. I don't fancy holing up in a dump."

16.

By six o'clock that evening things were looking a little more sane. They'd stopped at the Stanford Mall and gotten some spare clothes and a quick early dinner, then Stone used a pay phone to call up one of his professor colleagues at the University who had some cabins near campus that he rented out by the week to parents visiting their children. Fortunately one was available, and after a quick stop at a nearby grocery store for a few food staples and some toiletries, they were settling into a small but well-stocked house a block from Stanford with two bedrooms, a tiny kitchen, a bath and a combination living/dining room. "I'll owe Professor Boothby one," Stone said as he tossed some bags containing their purchases on the sofa. "It's not exactly prime season for these, and he was happy to accommodate me. Remember, don't let anybody in — that means don't even call out for pizza delivery. I don't want to get *another* place blown up."

"Don't worry about that," Jason said. "At this point I wouldn't tell my own mother where I'm staying."

Stone went off to his room to set up his answering service, so Jason switched on the TV to watch the news. The explosion was one of the top stories — the talking-head reporter was saying that authorities suspected a leaky gas line as the culprit, but they were still investigating. "The occupant, a professor at Stanford, got out with only minor injuries because he left the home to report a gas leak," the reporter said, "but unfortunately we've just gotten word that one of the two young children in a neighboring home who were hit by flying glass has died of his injuries. The other child is in serious but stable condition."

"Damn," Jason whispered under his breath. There was another casualty to whatever sickos were after them — and another innocent one. So far at least five people had died because of whatever was going on: Charles, the unnamed kid who'd powered the ganger's spell, Melody Barnes and her friend Willow, and now this innocent child whose only crime was that he'd been playing in what should have been his safe living room at the wrong time.

He switched off the TV and picked up the evening newspaper instead. The explosion story was there too, on the front page along with a story about a hostage situation in a San Jose bank that had ended with four people dead, a small puff piece on Gordon Lucas's upcoming charity gala, a gloomy article about the rising unemployment rate, and another one detailing the recent uptick in gang activity all over the Bay Area. Jason sighed, leafing half-heartedly through the rest of the front section. *They sure don't report much good news these days.* He was about to toss it down in disgust when his eyes fell on a small clip on the back page.

Local woman dies in single vehicle accident

A San Jose woman died today after the vehicle she was driving veered off the road and struck a light pole. The accident occurred at 1:30 p.m. near the intersection of Middlefield and San Antonio Road in Mountain View. The victim's identity was withheld pending notification of next of kin, but an unnamed source has tentatively identified her as Isabel Olivera, 54, a housekeeper. Witnesses claim that there appeared to be no cause for the sudden swerve. An autopsy will be conducted to determine if a medical condition was responsible.

Jason just stared at the article, scanning it over again to make sure that he hadn't read it wrong. When Stone came back out a couple of minutes later, he held up the paper. "Look at this."

The mage read it over, eyes widening. "I'm very sorry to hear that," he said at last. "I would very much have liked to have a chance to talk to her about her involvement in what happened. And if she wasn't involved, then I've lost a good friend."

Jason nodded. "Look at the time, though. If the explosion happened at 1:00 and the accident happened at 1:30 in Mountain View, then she didn't have much time to get away." He paused, thinking. "Kinda makes you wonder if she didn't have help veering off the road, doesn't it?"

"I wouldn't be at all surprised at this point," Stone agreed. "That's one mystery we'll likely never solve, though, unless the autopsy results show that she had a sudden heart attack or something."

"Add it to the list," Jason said sourly. He leaned back on the sofa with a loud sigh of frustration. "So what do we do now? You said you might have some ideas. Now's the time to spill 'em if you do, because I'm fresh out."

Stone looked troubled. "I do," he said. "But give me until morning. I still need to do a bit more thinking about it."

"Why?" Jason glared at him. "If you've got something that might work, spit it out. You said you wanted to go on the offensive. So let's do it. I'm as tired as you are of sitting on my ass waiting for somebody to try to kill us again."

"It's not that simple." Stone didn't meet his eyes. "The idea I've got in mind requires some—rather extreme action. And in all honesty, I'm not sure I'm ready to take it yet." Jason opened his mouth to speak, but Stone held up his hand to stop him. "I'm sorry, Jason, but this one's my show. As I said, I'll give it some thought and let you know in the morning. That's the best I'll do."

Jason started to protest, but he got a look at Stone's eyes and stopped in mid-word. "Okay. I guess I'm stuck with it, since you're the only game in town at the moment."

"Thank you," Stone said softly. He did genuinely look troubled — more so than he had following the explosion. "I promise, whatever I decide you'll know in the morning."

The morning couldn't come soon enough for Jason. He had gone to bed early since there wasn't much else to do; he'd tried to read one of the books left on the shelf but stopped after a few pages — he couldn't get into the classics when he was a kid in school, and *Moby-Dick* wasn't any more interesting now that he had a few more years on him. When he got up to use the bathroom around midnight, he saw the light still glowing in the front room. Stone was sitting there in silence, staring into the flames of the fire he'd started in the fireplace. He looked like his mind was a thousand miles away wrestling with a very difficult problem. Jason didn't disturb him.

It was nearly ten a.m. when Jason came back out the next morning — he was surprised when he looked at the clock next to the bed, but he couldn't deny that the several extra hours of sleep had been good for him. Stone was still sitting in the same chair, and the fire had burned itself into ashes. "Did you even sleep at all?" he asked.

"Not much," the mage admitted. "Had a lot to think about."

"And —? Did you come to a decision about whatever this idea is?"

Stone nodded slowly. "I did."

"Are you...going to tell me what it is?" Normally this kind of evasiveness would have made Jason frustrated and impatient (two emotions he was never good at hiding), but right now he almost felt sorry for Stone. He looked like a man contemplating an impossible decision.

Again, Stone nodded without meeting Jason's eyes. "Yes. God help us, I don't see another option."

"So—you've decided—whatever it is, you're going to do it?"

"I am." He stood up, and his expression changed to one more determined than troubled. "We need to go to England."

17.

Jason stared at him, convinced he couldn't possibly have heard him correctly. "What did you say? Because I thought I heard you say we had to go to England."

Stone nodded. "There's something there—at my home—that I need in order to do this."

"Wait a sec. We don't have *time* for this. You know how hard it is to get a flight these days, and even if we left now and turned around to immediately come back after we get whatever this thing is, it'll take a minimum of two days. That's not even counting things like jet lag and delays getting tickets. Verity could be dead by then, if she's not already. And besides," he added, "I know this sounds a little crazy, but I don't like flying under the best of conditions. With these mystery wackos trying to kill us, I'd rather not be shut up in a metal tube with no exits for ten or eleven hours, thanks."

Stone took a deep breath. He appeared for a moment to be sizing Jason up, gauging his potential response to his next words. "We won't be flying," he said at last.

Jason took a moment to let that sink in. "We're—not flying. Well, we sure as hell can't *drive*. We—" He stopped. "Wait a minute. This is some other magic thing you haven't told me about yet, isn't it?"

"Yes."

"What, you just— sprinkle some pixie dust around, click your heels together three times, and say 'There's no place like London'?"

Stone didn't smile. "This is serious business, Jason, and it can be very dangerous. That's part of what I was trying to come to terms with last night. Because I don't think it's safe for you to stay here while I go, so you'll have to come with me."

"Okay," Jason said, glaring at him. "Why don't we start at the beginning? I know how much you like your cryptic little reveals, but right now I think we're pretty much past that. Tell me what the hell is going on."

"It's very simple, really." Stone still wasn't rising to the bait. His voice was even, making him sound like he was lecturing to one of his classes on some mundane — well, as mundane as things can get when you teach Occult Studies — topic. "It's possible — though potentially quite dangerous — to travel great distances in a short time. It requires a high degree of magical skill and a specially prepared portal or gateway at both ends. Not all mages can do it by any means — for one thing, very few of them even know of the existence of the gateways."

"But you do." Jason took a deep breath, feeling like he was once again taking one of his frequent detours into the Twilight Zone.

"Yes. As it happens, I've one of my own back at home. It's one of the few active ones in England, and only a few people there know of its existence."

"You — built this thing?"

"No. It's been around since many years before I was born. I come from a long line of mages."

"O — kay," Jason said dubiously. "So you've got one of these gateway things in England. And you know where one is around here?"

"Yes."

"And where is that? Up at Stanford? At some — I dunno — super secret mage clubhouse somewhere?"

"No. Actually, it's in the basement of a local restaurant."

Why do I even bother asking? "A restaurant."

"Yes. But listen — that's not the important part." Stone moved closer, his own bright blue gaze boring into Jason's eyes as if attempting to read his mind.

Jason shifted uncomfortably, by no means sure that wasn't exactly what he *was* trying to do. "Okay, what is, then?"

"The method by which we'll be traveling." Stone said. He began pacing around the room restlessly as he continued. "You see, the gateways connect to their destinations by means of an—extradimensional space we call the Overworld."

"Extra...dimensional space?" Jason's eyebrows both went up. *Holy crap, it is the Twilight Zone!*

"It's hard to explain without a lot of theory that will no doubt bore you senseless, even if I had the time to explain it to you. Here's what you need to know if you're going to come with me: the reason it's dangerous to travel this way, especially with those who aren't familiar with it, is that the Overworld has its own—population."

"Population of—what?" Jason was almost afraid to ask.

Stone shrugged. "Nobody's hung about up there long enough to study them. But here's the thing—they're drawn to any kind of strong emotion, especially negative emotion. When traveling in the Overworld, it's absolutely imperative that a person keep himself completely under control. No fear, no anger, no disagreements with one's companions—even excessive happiness or curiosity can draw them out to investigate."

"And—what happens if you draw them out?"

"They attack you. And more often than not, they kill you. Or if you're lucky, they just drive you mad."

Jason stared at him. "You're kidding, right?"

"I told you it was dangerous. You can see why I'm reluctant to do it. Especially with someone with your—shall we say—previously demonstrated self-control issues."

Jason stood there for a long time, contemplating this. Finally, he ventured, "So you want me to travel though this—Tunnel of Freak-Outs—with you, keep myself from getting scared or angry, and eventually we'll pop out on the other side in England. And then once you get whatever it is you're after, we have to do it *again.*"

"That's about the size of it," Stone said, nodding. "Believe me, if there were any other choice, I'd take it. I'd leave you here if I thought you'd be here when I got back."

"What makes you think I won't?" he demanded, even though he wasn't at all sure he wanted to take this particular trip. He wasn't by nature a fearful guy, but this was just off the rails when it came to weird shit.

"Because I know you," Stone said. "Tell me—if I left you here, would you sit quietly in the house and wait for me to come back? Or would you be bored or frustrated or guilty enough in a few hours that you'd set out in search of your sister on your own, just so you could tell yourself you were doing something?"

Jason sighed. He didn't answer, but he didn't have to. His silence was all the answer either of them needed. Changing the subject, he asked, "So what is this thing that's so important that you have to get it in England? Can't you just have somebody get it and ship it to you, whatever it is?"

"No, that's not possible. It's a book, which is all I'll tell you at the moment. I did say this plan had more than one danger associated with it—the trip to retrieve it is only the first. But I wouldn't trust anyone to ship it, even if anyone could get at it. Even my caretaker back home doesn't know about it. It's carefully hidden under magical lock and key in an area of the house he doesn't know exists."

"Of course it is." Jason tried not to sound sarcastic, but his capacity for accepting weirdness had been just about pegged for the day. This concerned him, because he expected things were going to get a hell of a lot stranger before tomorrow. He sighed. He knew how much was at stake here, and every day they hadn't located Verity was another day when the DMW or whoever was directing them or some other random danger could find her. But he had to be honest, too. "I don't know if I can do it."

Surprisingly, Stone nodded. He even looked sympathetic. "I know. It's not easy, even if you know what to expect. My first time through — on a lot shorter trip than the one we'll be taking — I was so frightened that the two other mages I was traveling with had to knock me out to keep us from being attacked. Even then they had to run like hell because I attracted unwelcome attention."

"Then how do you expect me to be able to do this? I'm pretty sure I can keep from getting angry, but I can't stop myself from being scared, can I?"

"You can," Stone said. "Let me ask you this — do you love your sister?"

Jason glared. "What kind of stupid question is that? Of course I love her!"

"And naturally you want to see her home safe, right? Otherwise, why are we doing all of this at all?"

"Yeah, of course I do. I'd give anything to have her back right now. I can't stand the thought of her being out there and me not knowing where she is."

"All right then," Stone said, his tone gentle. "That's your talisman. If you're tempted to be frightened, just use that as something to hold on to. You're doing this to help your sister. Her only hope of getting home safely is if you can manage this without letting your fear get the better of you." He paused a moment to let that sink in, then continued: "I promise you, Jason. I give you my word — it's only dangerous if you let it be. If you can keep your feelings under control, it's safe as houses. Considerably more unnerving, I'll admit — nothing that can be done about that, sad to say — but completely safe."

Jason took a deep breath. "How long will it take? The trip through, I mean."

"It varies, but for that distance, I'd say perhaps two or three minutes."

"That's all? You made it sound like it would be a lot longer."

"Believe me, it will *seem* longer. Time works differently there — it will feel like you've been up there a long time. But once you're through, you'll see that it wasn't that long at all."

Jason nodded. As was often the case lately, he knew that ultimately there was only one answer. He might have washed out of the Academy for pasting an instructor a good one in the chin, but at least the "to protect" part of the police motto "to protect and serve" was wired pretty deeply into his DNA. "Let's do it, then," he said. "Before I lose my nerve."

18.

The restaurant Stone had referred to turned out to be in Sunnyvale and was called, amusingly enough, "A Passage to India." It was a hole-in-the-wall place in a decently upscale cluster of eateries of various ethnicities on Murphy Street. The sign outside showed its name in stylized letters that were apparently supposed to look Indian. "You're kidding, right?" Jason said when he saw it. "This is all a big joke and you're about to drop the punch line on me."

Stone chuckled. "There are more jokes at work here than you might suspect. For instance, the owners are actually British, though they did spend some time in India in their youth."

"And one of them is a mage?"

He nodded. "His partner knows all about it, though — when you run a restaurant together it's pretty difficult to hide a teleportation portal in your basement without your partner getting wise at some point that something dodgy is up."

"So we're not going to end up in India by accident?" Jason pulled the Ford into a nearby space and shut off the ignition.

"I certainly hope not, since I don't know of any gateways there. Come on — we're in time for the lunch special. The food here is quite good, and we'd best have something to eat before we do this. No idea when we'll get to again."

It was a bit early for the lunch rush but the restaurant was fairly well populated even at this hour. A waitress waved Stone and Jason toward a table, dropped menus in front of them, and immediately scurried off to help other customers. Stone studied the menu while Jason looked around. They didn't have many Indian restaurants where he came from, and his dad had always been more of a steakhouse kind of guy. The decor was suitably exotic, done in shades of gold, orange, and red with flamboyant flocked wallpaper featuring images of tigers, sultry looking women in Indian garb, and some sort of multi-armed creature with the head of an elephant. When Stone caught him looking at it, he said, "That's Ganesha. He's one of the more popular Hindu deities."

Jason nodded. "I'll take your word for it."

"Might want to offer him a little prayer while you're sitting here taking in the scenery. He's supposed to be the creator and remover of obstacles. We could certainly do with having a few obstacles removed right about now, wouldn't you say?"

Unsure whether Stone was serious or not, Jason just nodded noncommittally.

The waitress showed up again; Stone ordered the special and recommended that Jason do the same. When the woman had finished jotting down their orders, Stone motioned her to move closer. "I'd like very much to speak to Marta or David if they're around. Please tell them Alastair Stone is here."

She looked a little confused, but nodded and disappeared toward the back of the restaurant. After about five minutes a short, balding and cheerful-looking man about ten years older than Stone came out of the kitchen and made a beeline for their table. "Alastair!" he said, smiling broadly. "I haven't seen you in ages!"

"Morning, David." Stone shook his hand, then indicated Jason. "This is my friend Jason Thayer."

"A pleasure, I'm sure." David bustled over and pumped Jason's hand with great enthusiasm. "Are you a student of Alastair's?"

"Er—" Jason began, but before he could say more, Stone shook his head. "No, I'm helping him with a spot of difficulty he's gotten himself into. Which is actually the reason for our visit. That and enjoying your excellent chicken tikka masala, of course. We need to take a little trip."

"I see, I see." David's smiling expression didn't change, but something in his eyes did. He glanced at Jason. "Both—of you will be traveling?"

Stone nodded. "Yes, both of us. I'll vouch for Mr. Thayer—you have my word that he won't cause you any trouble."

David regarded Jason for a long moment, sizing him up and considering Stone's words. "All right, then," he said at last. "We'll see to that right away. You just sit here and enjoy your meals—they're on the house this time, naturally—and I'll be off to assist you with your travel plans." He waved goodbye to them and hurried back toward the kitchen.

Jason watched him go. "So—how does this work, anyway? Do you have to pay to use the gateway? Are you on some kind of timeshare where you all get a certain number of uses every year and everybody fights over Christmas?"

Stone chuckled, shaking his head. "No, it doesn't work like that. It's more professional courtesy—I use their gateway on occasion, and in return I help them out when they need a favor. Technically it doesn't belong to them in a conventional sense—several other mages helped to set it up, so there are a few of us who have access to it."

"Are there others around here?"

"Not many in the country. I believe there's one some-place in San Francisco, but the closest one otherwise is in New Mexico, of all places. I'd estimate there are fewer than a dozen permanent gateways in the United States. Most of them are back East."

"I...see." Jason only half jokingly wondered if he should be taking notes on all this stuff. "You said 'permanent' gateways. Are there temporary ones too?"

Stone nodded. "There are. It's possible to set one up that's only intended to last for a few hours at most—but they're extremely difficult and expensive to construct, and frightfully dangerous to use. You'd only ever want to set one up if you absolutely had to get somewhere in a hurry and you didn't have access to one of the permanent ones."

The waitress chose that moment to show up with their food, so he waited until she had placed the dishes before continuing. "I once had a colleague who was part of a group that was trying to discover a way to make the temporary gateways safer."

"I take it he didn't succeed?"

"She. And I've no idea. We lost touch, and I never heard anything more about it, so I'd guess not."

Jason nodded. "Can you do it? Set up a temporary one, I mean?"

"I can, but I wouldn't. I can't think of anywhere I'd ever need to be so quickly that I couldn't just use this one here, or mine at home if I'm back there. Or—you know—just take a plane," he added with a raised eyebrow.

Jason let it go at that, concentrating on finishing his lunch. The chicken dish was tart and spicy and he'd never had anything like it before, but he enjoyed it. He just wished the butterflies in his stomach would enjoy it too and stop clamoring around in there. He forced himself to think of Verity. He owed her this, and he would do his best to make sure that he didn't mess things up.

All too soon they'd finished, and as if on cue David came out again, this time accompanied by a woman who was taller and thinner than he was. "I hope everything was to your liking," David said, smiling.

"Excellent as usual," Stone replied. "My compliments to the chef."

"Good, good." David made a motion toward the kitchen door. "Perhaps you'd like to compliment him yourself, and take a small tour of the kitchen?"

"We'd be delighted." Stone rose and indicated for Jason to do so as well. When he started to protest, the mage gave him the barest of head-shakes followed by a "come-along" gesture.

Jason sighed and followed, trying hard to contain his impatience. Perhaps this was the first test to see if he could control his emotions. But to his surprise, they walked right past the kitchen and out the other side, into a dingy, dimly lit hallway containing two doors. The one at the end was labeled "EXIT" and the other one said "MAINTENANCE." David went to a blank space on the wall halfway between the two and stopped. He remained there for a few moments and Jason thought he could hear him mumbling something under his breath. When he finished speaking, the wall shimmered for a second and then a third door appeared in the blank wall. This one wasn't labeled at all. He pulled it open and motioned them in. Jason, eyes wide, allowed himself to be herded through in front of Stone.

A wooden stairway led downward, lit only by a single bulb hanging overhead. There were boxes of nonperishable restaurant supplies piled up on one side, and the foot of it was shrouded in darkness. The dusty odor of a disused space hung in the air. David and the woman plunged into it without a second glance, and Jason reluctantly followed.

They followed a long narrow hallway for a fair distance. Jason could see, far ahead, something glowing strangely—flickering and phosphorescent like some kind of weird swamp lights. Deciding that this would be a good time to start getting control over his fear, he caught up with the two restaurant owners as they stepped into an open room. David reached around the corner and flipped on a light switch.

Jason wasn't sure what he expected to see, but this was definitely not it. The room, approximately fifteen feet on a side, was empty of furniture; its only decorations were a few rugs with Indian patterns spread on the floor. "What *is* it with you people and doing magic in basements?" he asked nobody in particular. "Somebody'd think you were all a bunch of vampires or something."

David laughed. "I assure you, my young friend, it's purely coincidental. This odd basement is part of why we chose this location for the restaurant. As you can see from the door upstairs, it would be very difficult for anyone to get in — or even to find it — without our knowledge."

Jason nodded, but he wasn't really listening. Instead, he was staring at the —*thing*— in the center of the room. About seven feet tall and roughly as wide with no physical frame or boundary, the magical gateway hung there in the air like some sort of flickering movie screen without the screen. As he watched, transfixed, it cycled through a series of colors: blue, red, green, yellow, purple, white. The colors blended and ran together like watercolors, then flowed away from each other and skittered around the gateway's perimeter. It wasn't quite the most beautiful thing Jason had ever seen in person (a certain young lady he'd known rather intimately a few years ago took that distinction) but it was certainly near the top of the list. Every once in awhile he thought he saw images flickering over the colors, but every time he tried to focus in on them they would shift maddeningly away. It was like trying to watch a color television in the process of being washed out by a flood.

"Jason—" A hand touched his shoulder and startled him out of his reverie. Stone was standing there, looking very much like he understood what Jason was experiencing. "We need to get going."

"Yeah..." He tore himself away from the beautiful colors and looked at the mage, the reason they were here returning instantly to his mind. "What do I need to do?"

"We'll leave you two to it, then," David said. "Must get back to the customers, or the staff will start wondering where we've gone."

Marta gave him a wicked little grin. "I'm sure they have their ideas."

David chuckled. "No doubt, but no point in arousing their suspicions. You'll be all right, Alastair?"

"Oh, yes. We'll be fine. Thanks again. We shouldn't be gone long."

They waited until the two restaurant owners had gone, and then Stone turned back to Jason. "All right, are you ready?"

"No," Jason admitted. "But that's okay. I don't really see how I could *get* ready for this. Let's just do it before I lose my courage. Maybe I should have had a nice stiff drink first," he added, wondering if perhaps he should go back to the restaurant and do just that. Plenty of people got good and drunk before taking flights to keep them from being scared—why would it be any different for this?

"Bad idea," Stone said, shaking his head. "I need you controlling your inhibitions, not losing them."

Jason shrugged. "Can't blame a guy for trying."

Stone faced the gateway. "All right—be quiet for a few minutes and let me do the spells to focus this properly, so we don't end up coming out in the wrong place. Then we'll step through together. Just stay close to me, and remember what I told you: it's only dangerous if you want to make it so."

"Okay. I guess I have to take your word for it." He stepped back and did his best to stay out of the way.

Stone only took about five minutes to adjust the gateway, which to Jason looked like he simply stood in front of it and stared hard into its colorful depths. Nothing changed as far as he could tell—the colors were still the same, the strange watercolor effect still danced around, and the flickering images were as elusive as ever. But Stone seemed satisfied, because he turned back with a nod. "Ready to go," he said. "Let's do this. Stay close."

"I don't have to hold your hand, do I?" The absurd thought almost made him laugh aloud: *Be sure to hold tight to Dad's hand while crossing the interdimensional space portal against the light.*

"Not necessary, but it wouldn't be a bad idea to keep hold of my shoulder or something. In any case, just make sure you don't stray far away. I can mask us a little bit if we're close, but if you get out of my range all bets are off."

Jason couldn't think of any other ways to stall, so he nodded. "Let's go." He was surprised to hear his voice shaking a little.

Together, they stepped through the gateway. The feeling was one of the strangest Jason ever experienced: it was like stepping through a cool waterfall laced with an electrical field. His whole body felt energized; he half expected to look down at his hand and see it sparking. He looked over to make sure Stone was still there—he was—and then took in his surroundings.

He was standing in what looked like a foggy tunnel. Most of the space ahead of him was featureless and gray, broken up by occasional dark shapes flitting back and forth, or flashes of, for lack of a better term, dark lightning arcing from one side to the other. The tunnel itself was a little larger in diameter than the gateway itself had been; Jason thought that perhaps three or four people could walk it abreast if they squeezed close. Tentatively he tried out his voice: "So—we just go forward now?" It sounded dead and mechanical, the fog producing some kind of damping effect that removed all nuance.

Stone nodded. Jason noted that the mage's expression was unreadable, but there was a definite tightness in his jaw that suggested this trip was not a walk in the park for him either. "Yes," he said. "There's really no way to get lost. Just follow the passage." He moved forward, and Jason hastened to follow.

There were sounds here too, but nothing that was possible to distinguish. Vague growls, mechanical rumbles, far-off dissonant cries—all of them were soft and almost subsonic. And all of them were making Jason's skin crawl. "Doc..." he muttered, deciding that grabbing Stone's shoulder might not be such a bad idea after all.

"Hold it together, Jason," the mage said evenly. "Just keep moving forward. Slow and steady, that's the way. Try to just look straight ahead if you can. And remember Verity."

One step. Two. Three. Was the tunnel getting darker? Was it getting bigger? He wasn't sure, but he thought so.

Four steps. Five.

The vague subsonic sounds were speaking to him. He knew it. He couldn't understand them, but nonetheless he was convinced they were focused on him. He took a deep breath. "Something's—here," he whispered.

Stone nodded. "I can feel it. That's normal. It won't notice us. Just keep moving."

"It's *looking* for me..." His hand tightened on Stone's shoulder. The sounds were seeping into his brain now, into his body, into his soul. The tunnel was definitely widening out and getting darker. He could barely see

Stone next to him anymore; he was just a dim figure moving along through the fog. He could have been anybody.

What if it *wasn't* Stone? What if one of those — *things* — had taken his place when Jason wasn't looking? What if it was even now leading him off the path into darkness, into madness —

"Jason!" Stone's sharp voice managed to fight its way out of sounding dead and mechanical. Something poked Jason's hand, and he yelped.

"What the —?" he demanded, but then stopped. The voices had receded. Stone was right there next to him, solid as ever. He let his breath out slowly. "Thanks," he said, voice still shaking. "I — think I needed that."

"It's all right." The voice was even again. "Just focus on Verity. Remember that we're doing this to help her. We're almost there now. We —" His head snapped around to look at something behind them. "Oh, bugger —"

"What?" Jason demanded, but by the time he got the word out he needn't have bothered because the reason for Stone's exclamation was obvious.

About twenty feet behind them (or whatever passed for that distance in here) a dark *something* was detaching itself from the fog and moving in their direction. It didn't have a shape — in fact, it looked like nothing more than a darker piece of the rest of the tunnel. But as it broke free it grew more solid, hovering a few feet off the "ground" and then proceeding slowly and deliberately toward where they stood.

"Holy shit," Jason breathed, catching a glimpse behind it. More of the dark things, further away and still attached to the fog, were converging on the first one's location. His breath quickened; it was all he could do to not let go of Stone and take off running. Instinctively he knew that if any of those dark things reached him, that would be all she wrote. "What do we do?" he whispered urgently.

"Just keep moving. Faster now." Stone's voice was tight and clipped. "My masking is holding, I think — they only got a glimpse when your fear flared back there. Just stay close and keep moving. Go now." He stepped forward, moving at a brisk pace that wasn't quite a jog but threatened to become one any second. "If I say the word, run straight ahead. You'll see a light in the distance — it will look like the portal we went through. Head for it and don't stop. It's vitally important that you don't stop. Got it?"

Jason nodded several times, feeling each nod as a jerk of his head. "Run when you say. Got it." *Think of Verity. I'm doing this for Verity. It's safe unless we attract attention...Must get through so I can help Verity.*

He dared not look behind to see if the things were getting closer, but he was convinced he could hear them breathing on his neck, feel them nipping at his heels. Any minute now they'd catch up —

Think of Verity. You're doing this for Verity.

"See the portal up ahead?" came Stone's soft even voice to his right.

Jason looked. Far ahead, so far that it looked like the tiny beam of a flashlight shining toward them, he could see faintly shifting lights. He nodded. "Y-yeah, I see it." An unbidden thought popped into his head, reminding him of a poster he'd seen once in a head shop: *What if the light at the end of the tunnel is coming from the oncoming train?*

"All right. When I say the word, we're going to run for it." The mage's tone was completely flat — he sounded like a frightened air-traffic controller trying to talk down an 8-year-old piloting a jumbo jet. "Ready now?"

"Ready." *Ohgodohgodohgod they're right* here —

"GO!" Stone's voice boomed out, echoing from one side of the tunnel to the other. Jason felt the mage's shoulder tense as he flung himself forward. Jason barely gave him a one-step head start before he was at his heels. He dared a glance behind him and wished he hadn't—there were more of the things now, milling around in great agitation. As the two of them began to run, the things seemed to catch their scent.

"Run! Run! Run!" Jason yelled. Younger and faster than Stone, fueled by a panic that he couldn't begin to articulate, he was soon overtaking the mage. He grabbed Stone's arm in a death grip and pulled him forward, his eyes fixed on the ever-growing, ever-shifting portal up ahead.

The things were all around them now. Stone waved a hand and a shimmering shield formed to enclose them. A couple of the dark shapes dived for them, but bounced off it. The places where they hit flared bright, while the overall brightness of the shield dimmed correspondingly. Jason was pretty sure it wouldn't take more than a couple of hits. The portal was just ahead. Desperate now and running on animal flight-instinct, he grabbed Stone bodily and just about threw him through the glowing space, then flung himself through behind him. Just before he went through, one of the things cruised up next to him and he got a good close look at it, but then he was through the electric waterfall and sailing forward, his momentum crashing him hard into a gray stone wall. That was all he remembered.

19.

When he opened his eyes he was lying on a stone floor. Gingerly he sat up a little — his muscles ached, and for a moment he couldn't remember why. Then he saw the wall only a couple of feet in front of him and realized what had happened.

Another figure lay on the floor a few feet away from him: Stone. He wasn't moving. Jason scrabbled over to him and turned him over, checking to see if he was still breathing. He was, but he was showing no signs of awakening. Jason took a deep breath, let it out slowly, and let his mind drift back over to what had just happened. His whole body was still shaking. As his mind lit on the image of the *thing* he'd seen right before they'd exited the portal, a sudden overwhelming wave of nausea swept over him. He looked wildly around and spotted a trash can next to a table; he barely made it there before his entire Passage to India lunch special made a violent and spectacular return appearance.

For awhile he just knelt there clutching the trash can, his hair hanging limply down over his eyes, and tried to get his breathing under control. Holy crap, what had that been? He'd never been more frightened in his life. Those things — it was as if they had contained the essence of everything that was wrong with the world. And they had *wanted* him. He had no doubt about that. If this was how mages traveled, then he'd take a bus, thank you very much. He was going to have nightmares about that trip for the rest of his life. Again, an absurd thought popped into his mind (that was happening a lot lately, he noticed): he'd never done drugs with his friends back in high school, but he was pretty sure he had just won the distinction of having the worst "bad trip" ever. Too bad he couldn't tell anybody about it.

The nausea abating now (which was good, because he didn't think he had anything else to offer if it hit him again), he slowly dragged himself to his feet and took in the room around him. It was entirely made of gray stone — walls, ceiling, and floor. A closed, old-fashioned wooden door was on the far side, and the only furniture was the table he'd spotted before, a couple of wooden chairs, his trash can, and a bookshelf containing several leatherbound tomes. Lighting was provided by a couple of sconces on the walls (electric, not the actual torches he would have expected given the rest of the decor). The whole place looked very medieval, like a secret room in a castle somewhere.

Oh, and of course there was the shimmering portal in the middle of the room. Mustn't forget about *that*. Jason eyed it warily, not wanting to get too close for fear one of those *things* would reach a hand or a claw or a tentacle or whatever else it had through and yank him, screaming for dear life, back through to the other side. Yeah, it was irrational. He didn't care. He thought he was entitled to a little irrationality right about now.

He thought about checking to see what was on the other side of the door, but decided against it. It might be nothing more than a mundane hallway, but he was learning fast to never make such assumptions around Alastair Stone. Staying close to the wall and skirting the portal as far away as he could get, he moved back over to Stone and shook him. "Doc? You there?"

The mage groaned. "Mm?"

"Wake up. I think we're — wherever we were trying to get to." His mouth tasted horrible, and he wished that guys still carried handkerchiefs — or better yet, that he could get his hands on a large quantity of water.

Stone put a hand to his head and winced. "You — chucked me into a wall."

"Yeah, well—sorry about that. I hit the same one myself. I wasn't exactly thinking straight at the time, y'know?"

"Yes—that didn't go so well, did it?" He gingerly pushed himself up on an elbow and looked around at his surroundings. "At least we made it to the right place." Wrinkling his nose, he added, "—and what's that smell?"

"Don't ask. Trust me." Jason took hold of his arm and helped him to his feet. "So what now? I'm gonna go out on a limb and guess that whatever book you came here to get, it's not on that shelf over there."

Stone glanced over. "What? Oh. No, of course it isn't. Come on. We've got a bit of a hike up to the house. I don't want to stay here long, but I could definitely use a drink and I think you could too."

"Yeah, definitely. But first a nice bottle of mouthwash and a big glass of water." He paused. "What the hell happened in there? You said it was safe if I kept it under control."

Stone moved over and opened the heavy wooden door, motioning Jason out. "You didn't."

"I did!" he protested. "I was fine until they started— *talking* to me."

That stopped him. "Talking to you?" he asked with a raised eyebrow, fixing that intense 'I may or may not be reading your mind' gaze on him. "What do you mean? They actually *spoke* to you? Intelligibly?"

Jason shook his head. "No. I couldn't understand them, if that's what you mean. Not the words. There weren't really words. But I could tell they—wanted me. They were making me feel strange. It's hard to explain. Like at one point—" he shuddered with the memory "—I was convinced that you weren't really you. Like they'd taken your place and were leading me off the path."

"Fascinating," Stone said, almost to himself. Then, louder: "I've never experienced anything like that before—but then again, I've never made the trip with a nonmagical companion."

"Might have told me that *before* we left, Doc," Jason protested.

"Slipped my mind," Stone said. "And would you mind terribly if I asked you to stop calling me 'Doc'? Just Alastair is fine."

"Sorry, man. Too many syllables. You know how lazy we Americans are. How about I just call you Al?"

Stone looked practically stricken. "No. Just—no."

Jason grinned. "Al it is, then."

Stone sighed loudly, but he didn't push it. He opened the door and motioned Jason out, then closed it behind them. Then he waved his hand at it and muttered something under his breath, and it became just another part of the solid stone wall.

There was a stairway outside the door, leading up. "Oh, look. More basements! I'm proving my theory, you know," Jason said with a grin.

"I think not," Stone said, heading up. "You'll see."

At the top of the stairway was a long, narrow trap door, about the size of a standard interior door but set into the ceiling. It had a rope attached to one end. Stone pulled it and the door swung smoothly down to reveal a short stairway of its own, like the kind people sometimes used to get into their attics. "Hold on," he said. He went up first and Jason could hear him fumbling around with something that sounded rather heavy. Then whatever it was slid aside and a patch of dim light appeared above them.

"Where the hell are we?" he demanded.

"Come on up." Stone was already scrambling further upward and seemed to be climbing over something. Jason followed him to the top of the dropped staircase and dis-covered that he was standing on a narrow ledge inside an enclosure that was around seven feet long and three feet wide. There was a stone cover that had been shoved aside—that must have been what Stone was fumbling with. The rest of the room was empty. The whole thing looked vaguely familiar to Jason—and then he realized what it was.

Leaping out quickly, he stared at Stone with wide eyes. "This is a *crypt!*"

"I told you it wasn't a basement," Stone reminded him with a quirked eyebrow and a grin, pulling a false bottom over the trap door and settling it into place. "Now budge over so I can put the cover back on."

Jason helped him move the lid back onto the sarcoph-agus—it wasn't nearly as heavy as it looked, he discovered—and then looked back at Stone. "Why do you have the entrance to your portal inside a crypt?"

Stone shrugged. "You have to admit, it's not a place that your random passerby is likely to investigate." He crossed to the exit and muttered something at the door, which made a small *click* and swung minimally open. "Come on."

Outside, it was dark. Jason was confused until he re-membered that if Stone was telling the truth, they were in England now. If they'd left at lunchtime then it was even-ing already here. As he expected, they were standing in the middle of a graveyard. "What is this place?" he asked, looking around. It didn't look large—perhaps a grand to-tal of forty to fifty graves with headstones scattered haphazardly around, along with the crypt that dominated the space. The whole area was surrounded by trees, mak-ing it seem very intimate and more than a little creepy.

"It's my family's plot," Stone told him, heading toward an opening in the trees.

"Your family has a private cemetery?" Jason hastened to keep up, beginning to wonder just how much more there was to his strange new friend. It was okay, though—getting the subject of conversation back to mundane things—even mundane creepy things—was helping him get his bearings again.

"Not exactly grand enough to call it a cemetery," Stone said. "It's been here for centuries. Nobody left but me now, so—" He didn't finish that, but kept going. Jason saw that he was now heading up a small path through the trees.

After a hundred feet or so the path broke free of the trees onto a large empty field. Far off in the distance, Jason could see the dark bulk of what looked like a very large house rising up. It was toward this that Stone seemed to be headed.

"Is that your house?" Jason asked, hurrying to catch up again. "What—you live in a castle?"

"Yes, that is my house, and no, it's not a castle. It's a dump, mostly, to be honest. You'll see. Come on—it's cold out here, and I'd really like to get inside and have that drink."

They'd made it about halfway across the field when Jason spotted a small light bobbing toward them. He stiffened. "What's that?"

"Ah, good." Stone didn't sound the least bit disturbed—in fact, he sounded pleased. "It's about bloody time." Picking up his pace, he hurried off in the direction of the bobbing light. Again Jason had to speed up to catch him.

"Aubrey!" Stone called. "Where have you been?"

The light drew up to him, revealing itself to be a stocky old man in a flat cap, heavy coat, and plaid scarf carrying an old-fashioned lantern. "I'm sorry sir," he puffed. "Unavoidably detained. Come on—let's get you inside. I've laid the fire and I've got the teapot on."

"Excellent, excellent." Stone motioned behind him. "Aubrey, this is Jason Thayer. Jason, Aubrey Townes—he looks after the place when I'm not around, and generally looks after me when I am."

The old man held up the lantern and squinted at Jason, looking him over. He had the severe, craggy face of a man who'd spent a lot of his life doing physical work out in the sun, but it lit up in a pleasant smile after a moment. "It's a pleasure to meet you, Mr. Thayer."

"Same," Jason said. He had decided again that he wasn't going to ask questions for awhile—just watch and roll with whatever happened.

Jason and Stone followed Aubrey back toward the house. As they drew close, Jason could see that Stone was right—it was not a castle at all. Instead it was one of those huge, dark, gothic mansions that you saw on TV adaptations of novels about rich girls who died of consumption, or creepy old men who kept children prisoner in the basement. It had a central core flanked by two smaller wings, and the whole place presided over a circular, graveled driveway like some sort of malevolent spirit. Jason half expected to see gargoyles on the edges of the roof, but all he saw as they passed by were a couple of wayward crows and a whole lot of missing shingles. "This place must be great at Halloween," he muttered loud enough for Stone, but not Aubrey, to hear.

"It's a little grim," Stone agreed. "Needs far more work than I can afford—the trust fund barely covers basic maintenance and repairs and Aubrey's salary, and even so we have to close off one of the wings because we can't afford to heat it. It does look a bit better in the daytime. You'll have to take my word for that, though—we'll be long gone by then."

Aubrey opened one of the heavy double front doors and motioned them inside. They moved through an entryway into a large open greatroom with a soaring shadowy ceiling and an enormous fireplace dominating the left wall. Arranged around this were some comfortable looking old couches and chairs around a low table, and it was to this area that Aubrey motioned for them to head. "Please," he said, "Sit down. I'll bring you refreshments. You both look tired."

"What I really need, if it's okay," Jason said, "is a bathroom."

"And a stiff drink or two," Stone added. He pointed off at a hallway leading from the other side of the room. "Loo's over there, Jason. And Aubrey—don't spare the alcohol."

When Jason returned, feeling much more human after rinsing his mouth out several times and drinking a large quantity of water, Stone was still seated on the couch in front of the fire. Aubrey must have returned, because on the table was a plate of small cakes, a teapot and cups, two glasses, and a large bottle of something amber and alcoholic. Jason threw himself down at the other end of the couch with a loud sigh.

"Feeling better?" Stone inquired.

"Yeah. As good as I can feel after having the crap scared out of me."

"Good. Why don't you sit here and have a drink—please don't get yourself drunk, though. We're heading back soon, and I think you see now what I meant."

Jason froze. "Doc—Al—I can't do that," he said seriously. "There's no way you're gonna get me through that thing again."

Stone gave him a rueful smile. "Jason, I'm afraid there really isn't any other option. If you want to help Verity, we need to get back home."

"I'll take a plane." Jason leaned over and poured a healthy dose of liquor—he didn't even care what kind it was—into his glass.

"That could take days—especially if we have to explain to the authorities how you got here in the first place without a passport. And I can't get on with what I need to do without you."

"You take the plane too." Jason was aware that he was being completely irrational, but he still felt like he'd earned the right after what he'd experienced.

"Jason, you know I can't do that even if I wanted to. There's no way I'm taking what I came here for on a commercial flight."

"I'm sorry. I can't do it."

"You can, and you will. Verity's depending on you. And besides, now that I know what happened to you, I can do something about it."

Jason looked up, not daring to let any flicker of hope reach his face. "What do you mean? You're just saying that to get me in there again."

"No. Believe me, Jason, I've no more desire than you do to have a repeat performance of what happened today. That frightened me almost as much as it did you. We had a very narrow escape there."

"No shit?" He paused and took another drink. "So—assuming that you really *can* do something—what can you do?"

"I can put a block on your mind so they can't reach it."

"What the hell does *that* mean?"

"It's hard to explain—think of it as being a bit like hypnosis. I'd forgotten that most mages' mental protections are more highly developed than the average person's. You're one of the most stubborn non-mages I've ever met, though, which will help. You've got the raw materials—I just need to tweak them a bit so those things won't be able to get in."

Jason thought about that. "What—will it feel like?"

Stone shrugged. "Nothing, really. You won't even notice it."

"Then how will I know you succeeded?"

"You'll just have to trust me on that. And once we've successfully made the trip back, you'll know for sure."

Jason took a deep breath and considered. As always, he knew there was one answer, and as always it was the one he didn't like. "Okay," he said at last. "For Verity, I'll do it. But no more after this. You want me to do any more traveling, I'm taking a plane."

"Fair enough," Stone said, nodding. He got up. "All right, then. You sit here and enjoy your post-flight snack, and I'll be off to retrieve what I came here for. We should be back on our way in less than half an hour. If you want anything else to eat, the kitchen's through there." He pointed to a doorway across the large hall. "Aubrey's out there—just ask him for whatever you need."

Stone returned about fifteen minutes later carrying a leather briefcase. Jason was still on the couch, staring moodily into the fire. He'd finished off the whole plate of cakes and most of the tea, but hadn't touched the rest of the liquor. He rolled his head over the back of the couch as he heard Stone approach. "Find what you were after?"

"I did." The mage dropped down on the couch next to him and put the briefcase down between them.

"That's it? Can I see it?"

Stone pondered a moment, then opened the briefcase and pulled out a book. It was a little larger than a standard hardback, bound in cracked dark brown leather with metal straps holding it together. In the center of the front cover was a dull red gem set into the leather. The book had no obvious title or any other markings. Even Jason, whose experience with books leaned more toward school textbooks and the occasional paperback bestseller, could tell that it was very, very old.

"So—are you going to tell me what it is now?"

"Not yet. Let's get back to California. All I'll say for now is that the reason I need it is because it contains the instructions for some techniques that might help us locate Verity."

Jason looked a little surprised. "So we're leaving already?"

"Don't see why not. I've nothing more I need to do here. Do you?" He put the book back in the briefcase, snapped it shut, and stood. After a moment Jason did too.

They bade goodbye to Aubrey, who seemed disappointed to hear that Stone was leaving so soon, and trooped back out across the field toward the little graveyard. Far sooner than he wanted to be, Jason was face to face with that flickering portal again. "So..." he asked, hesitant, "you're sure whatever this 'block my mind' thing is that you want to do will work? Because I'm not kidding — if what happened before happens again, you might as well just drop me off at the nuthouse."

"Have a little faith," Stone said. "Just sit down here in the chair and be quiet."

Jason did as he was told. Stone took the other chair, pulling it around so the two of them were facing each other, knees only an inch or two apart. Leaning forward, Stone reached out and put three fingers on Jason's forehead. "Watch my eyes," he said in a low voice. "Just keep watching, and try to keep your mind as clear as possible."

"You're not gonna—you know—read my mind, are you?" Jason couldn't help sounding a little alarmed—there were more than a few thoughts in there that he'd rather not have Stone—or anybody else, for that matter—mucking around in. And naturally, not thinking about those would be very much like the old child's game of 'don't think about a zebra.'

"I'll give away one of my secrets, Jason," Stone said with a raised eyebrow. "Mages can't read minds. If anyone ever tells you we can, they're lying."

"You could be lying telling me you *can't*," Jason pointed out.

"Quite true," Stone admitted. "Now be quiet and just watch my eyes so we can get on with this."

Jason sighed. "Yes, master," he said in his best Igor the Hunchback imitation. He leaned back and focused on Stone, humming over a mindless tune in his head to try to keep it clear. The mage's eyes were bright blue and currently very steady, focusing on Jason's own eyes without a blink.

"That's it..." he murmured softly. "Just keep doing whatever you're doing...you're doing very well." His fingers moved a bit as if probing for a particular spot, then settled. A few seconds passed in silence, and then he pulled back. "There," he said. "All done."

"That's it?" Jason reached up and touched his forehead. He didn't feel the slightest bit different. There wasn't even a tingle.

"I did say that you wouldn't feel anything," Stone reminded him. "Now come on." He picked up the briefcase and motioned toward the portal. "No need to set it this time—it's already good to go."

It was the hardest thing Jason had ever done in his life to step into that portal again, but he knew if he didn't do it, he'd never be able to look at himself in the mirror. *They don't let you have mirrors in the crazy house,* he told himself, and stepped forward into the flickering light.

The trip back through was as uneventful as the previous trip had been horrific. The tunnel of fog was still there, as were the black flitting shapes and the occasional flash of black lightning. But the voices that had plagued Jason on the trip out were absent now. He walked briskly next to Stone, keeping a loose grip on the mage's shoulder, and before he had time to be afraid they were stepping out into the storeroom of A Passage To India. He realized that he had been holding his breath almost the whole time, and let it out in a rush. "We made it."

"See? I told you that you could trust me." Stone gave him a wicked grin. "Come on. Unless you want something else to eat, I'd really like to get started on this as soon as possible. Let me just tweak the settings here so the next user doesn't show up in my graveyard and we'll be off."

They exited the portal room and went back up to the restaurant, retracing their steps through the kitchen and out into the dining room. David was there, standing near the kitchen door overseeing some waitresses. "How did it go?" he asked when he saw them come out.

"Just fine," Stone assured him. "Jason here has earned his — er — wings."

David laughed. "Well, good. I do hope we'll be seeing you again soon, Alastair. It's been far too long."

Stone and Jason bade David goodbye and soon they were back in the Ford heading north toward Palo Alto. For a long time they drove in silence, just watching the mid-afternoon traffic and almost subliminally keeping an eye out for DMW or other potential threats. Jason's mind kept going over everything that had happened in the past couple of days; he was getting better at accepting weirdness, but it still all seemed sort of like a dream. He wouldn't have been surprised if he woke up in Ventura and realized that all of this had been a result of a bad batch of chili and too much beer. Would he regret it if it was? He wasn't sure at this point, if he had to be honest with himself. "Hey, Al?" he asked suddenly.

Stone winced a little. "Yes?"

"Can I ask you something?"

"I suppose you can."

"Why are you doing all this? Awhile ago I asked you if you knew me from somewhere, and you said something like 'let's assume for the moment that I don't.' What did you mean by that?"

For a long time the mage didn't answer. "I don't know you, per se. But I knew your mother."

20.

Jason nearly veered the Ford off the road. *"What?"*

"Jason! Drive the car!" Stone sounded alarmed. "Honestly—I'd rather not survive a trip through extradimensional space only to be wrapped around the back end of an eighteen wheeler."

"Sorry," Jason muttered, righting the Ford and getting it settled back on course again. "I just—you knew my *mother?* My mother died eighteen years ago."

"I know."

"So how could you know her, then?"

Stone watched the traffic out the front window. "I'm not sure I should say any more right now."

"Why not?"

"Well, driving properly and surprising news don't seem to play well together with you."

Jason glared at him. "Out with it, Al. I won't drive off the road. It's not like you're going to tell me my mom was a mage or anything like that, right?"

Stone was silent.

"Right?" *Oh, holy crap...*

"I met her when I was almost eighteen," Stone said softly. "I had taken my first trip through the gateway—I told you about that before—to visit America and attend a meeting of a group of mages. She was there. She was ill—I don't believe at that point she had much time left. But I had the opportunity to talk with her for a while, and she took a liking to me in a mentor sort of way. She told me about her family—her husband and young son and baby daughter, and how much she regretted that magic couldn't do anything about what was killing her."

Jason did as he promised—he didn't run the car off the road. In fact, he was driving even more carefully than usual, hands knotted around the steering wheel as if letting go would plunge them instantly off a cliff. "Did—did my dad know?" His voice came out dead—almost as mechanical as it had sounded in the Overworld.

"I don't think so." Stone's tone was gentle. "She said it was better that way—there would have been too many questions to answer. At that point she didn't really practice magic much, being more focused on raising her family and dealing with her illness. But she did keep up on the latest developments, and attended get-togethers when she could."

Jason swallowed hard. A lump was rising in his throat and he struggled to keep it under control. He didn't remember a lot about his mother—she'd died when he was still a young boy—but he did remember her as being very kind, with a wicked sense of humor that leaned a little toward the macabre, and much more flighty and spontaneous than his steady, reliable father. "What—what was she like?"

"I only met her the one time, and it was a long time ago. But I do know that she made quite an impression on me. I think I might have had a bit of a schoolboy crush on her, truth be told," he said, chuckling. "She teased me unmercifully about my difficulties coming through the gateway. And I do remember that she was quite practiced in the Art, though that was obviously dimmed by her illness."

"Wow..." There wasn't really much else he could say at the moment. Of all the shocking things he'd heard and seen and experienced in the past few days, to find out that his own mother— "Just...wow." He glanced over at Stone. "So—were you ever gonna tell me this, if I hadn't asked?"

Stone nodded. "Eventually, yes. After this whole business was sorted and we had Verity back. I didn't want to fragment your concentration with it until then."

Jason nodded slowly. Well, he'd been right about that—it was definitely fragmenting his concentration. "So—is that how you found me?"

"What?"

"You know, back when you first got me away from the DMW. Were you keeping some sort of magical tabs on Mom's kids after all these years? Does your—I dunno—magic bat signal go off when we're in trouble?"

Stone chuckled. "Hardly. If it did, then don't you think I'd be able to take you straight to Verity? No, the encounter itself was pure coincidence. I was driving back from a meeting with a couple of other mages in the area and I happened upon that little scene and figured I might be able to make myself useful. But when you told me who you were, and mentioned your sister's name—I was almost as surprised as you were just now when I told you about your mum."

"So that's why you decided to help me instead of just getting me out of there and dropping me off somewhere?"

"Exactly."

Jason pondered. Well, at least that sort of made sense. On more than one occasion he'd wondered why this guy who'd essentially been a stranger had put his life on the line numerous times to help out some random dude he'd met in a bad neighborhood. "I'd really like to talk to you more about this," he said. "We can later, right? I have so many things I want to ask you. But right now we should probably be focusing on getting V back."

Stone nodded. "Don't worry—if I haven't forgotten her after all these years, I won't do it in the next few days."

They'd exited the freeway now and were heading back toward Stanford. Jason spotted a little knot of vagrants huddled together in a doorway, and it reminded him of the group at the library. "I wonder where those bums ended up," he said.

"The ones at the library?"

"Yeah. It's still freaking me out a little bit, what they did. You know, hiding us from those fake cops and all. Are you sure they weren't mages of some kind?"

"If they were, it was of a type I've never seen before. I can't say it's not possible—as I told you, I'm reluctant to say *anything* isn't possible—but it's unlikely. It's fairly uncommon for mages to fall into those kind of circumstances, to begin with. It happens—occasionally the power just overwhelms someone, or they become addicted to alcohol or drugs and lose control of it—but not that often. And we do try to help each other as much as we can if we see something like that occurring. There aren't that many of us around, so we do keep up with each other as much as is practical."

Jason nodded, then remembered something else. "The two bums I saw at the rest stop—I don't know if they had any kind of powers or abilities or whatever, but now I'm kind of wondering if those weird symbols are somehow connected to the weird abilities."

"I've wondered that myself," Stone admitted. "About the symbols, anyway. The weird powers are something I never knew about until we saw them in action the other day. It's one of those projects I've got on my list, to try investigating that further, perhaps even by tracking down some of them and talking to them, assuming they'd even give me the time of day. But between work and all the other things I've got on my plate, hunting down groups of hobos, magical or otherwise, has had to take a back seat."

Hobos...why was that word tickling something in Jason's mind, where "bums" or "vagrants" hadn't? Something he'd read a long time ago, when he was a kid—and then he had it. "Hobos!" he yelled suddenly.

Stone jumped. "Don't *do* that!" he said, irritated.

"Hobos!" Jason yelled again, ignoring him. "That's it!"

"That's *what?*"

"Hobo code!" So overwhelmed with his revelation that he couldn't hold it in anymore, Jason pulled the car off the road and turned to Stone, his eyes blazing. "That's what it is! Hobo code!"

"Jason..." Stone was eyeing Jason nervously, as if expecting his head to start spinning around on his neck, or bats to fly out of his mouth. "What the *hell* are you on about?"

Jason took several deep breaths, forcing himself to calm down enough to explain. "When I was a kid, I read this book from the library about hobos — you know, bums who travel around the country by hopping trains. One of the things that interested me the most about it was Hobo Code — this group of symbols that hobos used to let each other know things like which towns were safe to stop in, which houses had dogs, where nice ladies lived who'd give them food if they told a good sob story — that kind of thing. A couple friends and I even used it for a couple of weeks, leaving messages around the neighborhood until somebody read a book about something else and we forgot about it."

Stone raised an eyebrow. "I've never heard of such a thing."

"You wouldn't have, I'll bet, if you haven't been here that long — I think it's pretty much an American thing, and it was mostly from a long time ago, back when a lot of hobos used to ride the rails. But — man, I wish I still had the book — those symbols in your notebook look a lot like it."

"Do you think it's important enough to research?" Stone asked. "Should we go to a library and try to find another book with samples of this hobo code?"

Jason shook his head. "I doubt it would help. I do remember enough to know that the symbols aren't the same—but I'll bet a lot of money that the bums use these new ones in the same way: to pass on information, warn each other about dangers, things like that."

"That—would imply some sort of organization," Stone said slowly, thinking. "Remember I told you I've seen those in other parts of California too? I wonder how far-reaching they are? And if they're only used by vagrants who have these odd powers—"

"—does that mean there are a lot of them?" Jason finished, eyes widening. "That's crazy. How could there be that many magic bums and nobody knows about them?

Stone didn't answer. They'd almost reached the cottage now, and he didn't say anything else until they'd arrived and were back inside. He pulled out the old book he'd brought back from England. "You might as well find something to do for awhile," he told Jason. "I'm going to need time to study what we're going to be doing. Believe me, this is not something I want to get wrong because I read it through too fast and missed a step."

"You still aren't going to tell me what you're planning to do, are you?"

"I will, but not yet." He was looking very serious again.

Jason decided not to push it. He grabbed a stack of magazines off the coffee table in the living room and took them back to his bedroom, where he lay down on the bed and began leafing through them. They were all at least three months out of date, but that was okay because he couldn't focus enough to read them anyway.

After about an hour had passed, Stone appeared in his doorway and knocked once. He glanced up and looked startled: Stone looked like a man who'd spent the last hour contemplating his own mortality, instead of looking at pictures of football players and crusty old political leaders. "You okay? You don't look so good."

Stone sighed. "I'm all right. Come on. We need to go a couple of places. And I need to find a place to do this."

"You can't do it here?" Jason noticed that he was holding the briefcase containing the book.

"Not enough room. And not safe."

Jason stared at him. "Not safe? For who?"

"For anyone."

"Al—"

"Just bear with me, all right? Let me get what we need, and then I'll explain everything to you. You'll still have the opportunity to back out after you've heard the details."

"Back out? You mean I need to be part of this too?"

"Yes."

"How? I don't know any magic—" Jason tossed the magazines aside and swung his legs off the bed.

"Jason, please. All will be revealed. Just come with me."

Jason followed him. "Do you mind if I drive?" the mage asked. "It will be easier than trying to give you directions."

"Uh—sure, that's fine."

The first place Stone stopped was his office on campus. Asking Jason to wait in the car, he went inside and returned less than five minutes later carrying something in a leather satchel. Next he went back to Madame Huan's. Again he asked Jason to wait (there was a parking spot right in front of the place this time). This visit took a bit longer—it was nearly twenty minutes before he came out, and this time he wasn't carrying anything. Jason looked puzzled. "If you're going to do a ritual, don't you need all those candles and other doohickeys you got before?"

"It's not that kind of ritual," he said, and started up the car again. "The few things I need, Madame Huan can't supply. But she did convince a friend of hers to allow us to use a location she knows."

The final stop made Jason very nervous. It was a tiny unmarked store in a very bad East Palo Alto neighborhood, where most of the other store windows were broken or boarded up, with faded "FOR LEASE" signs hanging from them. "Uh..." Jason said, looking around. "I don't like this." He didn't see any DMW or other immediate threats, but he knew they could appear from around any corner at any time. He did spot what he was pretty sure was an example of the modern hobo code, chalked on the side of the building next to the one to which Stone was headed. He didn't recognize the symbol, though.

"I know. I don't like it either, but we've no choice. Just wait here—I'll put a small enchantment on the car so anyone happening by won't notice it. I won't be long."

By the time Stone returned ten minutes later, Jason had been swiveling his neck around so much trying to watch everywhere at once that it was starting to ache. A couple of people, including one guy Jason was almost certain was DMW, had walked by but hadn't stopped or appeared to even notice the car. Stone dropped back into the driver's seat and tossed another bag into the backseat next to the leather satchel. "So what was that place?" Jason asked as they pulled back out into traffic.

"Another magical supply store."

"Like Madame Huan's?"

"In name only. This one caters to a—slightly more nefarious clientele."

Jason stared at him. "It's a—black magic shop?"

Stone nodded. "Right in one."

"And you went there, and they let you get away?" He looked around nervously again as if expecting to find someone following them.

"Not all black magicians are evil *per se*," Stone told him. "Some of them simply prefer—more expedient methods of getting things done, and have a somewhat more malleable moral core. The proprietor of that shop and I go back a long way. I wouldn't call us friends, exactly, but we're not enemies. Occasionally we compare notes on research problems."

"Did you have to tell him what we were doing?" In Jason's mind, the fewer unnecessary people who knew about their search for Verity, the better.

Stone shook his head. "No. The items I purchased were fairly generic." He chuckled a little. "If old Stefan knew about what I was preparing to do and how I'd learned to do it, he'd have been practically salivating to get his hands on my book. I can't let that happen. I have a lot of respect for his abilities, but I would never trust him with that sort of thing."

"Wait a sec," Jason said, twisting in his seat to face Stone. "You're going to do black magic? I thought you said that was a bad idea. That it—what did you say? Corrupts your soul or something?"

"Not corrupts. Not something this small and simple. Blots a bit, yes. But it has to be done, and it's not like this is the first time I've done magic that's not strictly white." He smiled a little, but his eyes were still serious. "I guess you could say I'm a white magician with a few streaks of gray here and there."

Jason wasn't sure how to reply to that, so he didn't. It did make him nervous, though. Did he have the right to let Stone do something that might cause him permanent harm in order to find his missing sister? On the one hand, the mage was a big boy and knew what he was getting into, but now that Jason knew the connection between him and his mother—

He wrestled with that question for awhile, until he realized they weren't heading back to the cottage near Stanford. "We're not going home?" he asked, surprised.

Stone shook his head. "I'd like to get moving on this as soon as possible so we can find Verity. It will be dark soon—no helping that—but if we succeed, I'd rather not be out tracking her down at midnight."

"So where *are* we going?"

"Madame Huan has a friend who lives in the Los Gatos hills. He's got an outbuilding he's willing to let us use."

"How far is that?"

"We should be there in half an hour or so."

Jason sighed and settled back. He could feel his old impatience resurfacing again—not that he knew anything about magic beyond what he'd learned so far from Stone, but it was frustrating that it required this much traveling. He noticed that Stone had taken the car back on the freeway. "Are you doing your masking thing again? Because I really don't want to run into DMW right now."

"I am."

That at least was comforting. Jason allowed himself to relax a bit, reaching out to flip on the car's radio. He'd never even checked to see if it worked. The slightly tinny sounds of something by Pink Floyd wafted through the speakers. He reached out to change the station but Stone put a hand up to stop him. "Wait, I like this."

"A mage who likes Pink Floyd." For some reason Jason found that amusing. He left the station where it was and leaned back again.

21.

They switched freeways once and shortly after that Stone took an exit. Jason could tell right away that this was a much more upscale end of the Bay Area than most of those they'd been visiting—even nicer than the part of Palo Alto where Stone's place had been. "Madame Huan's friend must have money."

"No doubt," Stone agreed. In only about five minutes he left the main drag and made a right onto a tree-lined two-lane road. It meandered past some expensive looking homes for a couple of miles, then began to gain elevation and grew more twisty. The streetlights were infrequent but all worked up here, and Jason could see the closed gates along the road and the twinkling lights far back from them indicating the locations of homes at the ends of long driveways.

Stone appeared to be watching for house numbers now, so Jason didn't say anything else. They drove another mile or so up the twisty road, and then Stone slowed. "That's it," he said. "Madame Huan said her friend wasn't home but that he'd given permission for us to use the building in the back." He pulled up next to an intercom with a keypad on it, punched in a code, and the gates swung silently open, then closed again behind them as they drove in.

The main house was at the end of a sweeping driveway, but Stone drove around the back to where a smaller and far less impressive building sat at the end of a path about fifty feet away. "What is this, some kind of barn or something?" Jason asked.

Stone didn't answer, just got out of the car, gathered up the items in the backseat, and motioned for Jason to follow him. They crossed to the building, the door of which also had a keypad lock. Stone opened it and reached around to flick on the light.

Jason wasn't sure what he'd expected to see, but if he'd been given twenty guesses he wouldn't have come close. Looking over Stone's shoulder, he saw a large empty room with a smooth wooden floor, track ceiling lighting, and a full-length mirror along the entire opposite wall. At about waist height along the mirror was a wooden bar attached to the wall and running its full length. Aside from this there was nothing else in the room except for a couple of small tables, three folding chairs, and a stack of cardboard boxes labeled "XMAS STUFF" piled against the far right wall. The room had no windows. "What—is this?" Jason asked again, stepping inside. His footsteps echoed ominously.

Stone closed the door behind them and put his various bags and cases down on the smaller of the tables. "Madame Huan's friend's daughter was quite serious about the ballet, so he built her this studio so she would have a place to practice. She's at university back East now, though, and he hasn't gotten 'round to repurposing it for other uses."

"So—we're gonna do magic in a ballet studio." Jason sounded dubious. "I guess it's better than a barn."

"Much better than a barn, since one of my main requirements was a large mirror." Stone grabbed hold of the larger table and began dragging it across the room. "Give me a hand here, will you?"

Jason picked up the other end of the table and, under Stone's direction, helped him carry it over and place it directly in front of the mirror halfway along the wall. Stone retrieved the items from the other table and brought them over. Opening the leather satchel first, he pulled out a wooden book stand with a small flexible attached light and put it in the center of the table. Then he removed two red candles (Jason was starting to surmise that it was impossible to do magical rituals without at least one candle) and placed them on either side of the book stand. Finally, he took out a purple silk cloth and laid it out lengthwise in front of the stand, and a black leather sheath from which he drew a black-bladed knife almost long enough to qualify as a shortsword. He placed that on top of the cloth. Jason continued to watch with interest.

Stone put the satchel aside and took up the bag. From this he took a shallow copper chalice and put it down behind the book stand, between the two candles. Then he removed a smaller bag. Crouching down near the wall, he carefully poured reddish sand in a thin line, making a semicircle that surrounded the table and about three feet of space around it. It looked like he was using icing to decorate some kind of weird cake; when he finished, the two ends of the semicircle met up with the mirror on the wall, making the whole thing appear like a full circle. Then he stepped back and examined the whole scene. Nodding as if satisfied, he picked up the briefcase, withdrew the book, opened it to a particular page and placed it on the stand, taking care not to smudge the sand.

Jason moved in closer and looked at the open book. The pages themselves seemed to be made of some sort of heavy parchment or even thin cured leather. The text written on them was in rust-colored ink in a language he didn't understand. There were several diagrams on the two pages, including a small depiction of a chalice like the one Stone had placed, and another that looked very similar to the knife currently resting on the purple cloth. "Okay," he said. "Looks like you're all set up here. You mind filling me in on what we're doing?"

Stone nodded. Before he spoke, though, he lit the two red candles, flicked on the book stand's light, and then moved over to switch off the overhead lights. The result was a very eerie flickering glow around the table, illuminating the items and about three feet of mirror on either side of the table. The book stand's light was not harsh, but it was bright enough that they could see the open pages. "First of all," he said at last, "I have to tell you that I've lied to you about something."

Jason stared at him, startled and a little nervous. "You—did?"

"Yes. I told you that it's not possible to do summoning spells with only one mage."

"Uh...okay. Yeah, I do remember you saying something like that."

"I also told you it wasn't possible to use magic to locate someone without a tether object, which was why we couldn't try again after your sister's stuffed bear was destroyed in the explosion."

"So—it *is* possible, then?"

Stone nodded. "It is. The things I told you before assumed that the only magical techniques available were of the white variety."

Jason eyed the items arrayed on the table. "You're going to use some black magic technique to summon something?"

"Exactly." Stone's eyes picked up the flickering flames of the two candles, giving him an uncomfortably demonic look. "We are going to summon a spirit and, using you as our tether object, send it off to search for your sister. If all goes well it will find her and return to us with her location."

"Using me? What do you mean?"

Stone looked him up and down. "This is the part where you get to back out if you want to. I will tell you that this particular technique does involve a certain amount of danger—to me more than to you, but there is still a chance that something could go terribly awry and you could sustain serious injury — or worse. Consider that a disclaimer."

"What is it I have to do?" Jason was trying to keep his fear under control, reminding himself that he was doing this — all of it — for Verity. "And how big a chance is there that something will go wrong?"

"In order for a living person to serve as a tether for a location spell, two things must occur. First, he or she must have some strong connection to the person sought. The stronger, the better. Blood ties work best, though strong feelings will do in a pinch, especially if there's a sexual connection. You, as her sibling, are nearly ideal. The only better choice would be a parent or child."

"That makes sense," Jason said, nodding. "And since both our parents are dead and she doesn't have any kids, that pretty much makes me the best you got. But what do I have to do? What's the second thing?"

"The second thing," Stone told him, "is that the tether must provide his or her life essence to fuel the casting."

"Life essence?"

"Blood."

"Blood," Jason repeated. He had the wild urge to laugh along with his inner twelve-year-old: *Oh, that's a relief. I thought you meant the* other *life essence. I'm not really feeling up to providing any of* that *right about now.* But still — "Uh — how *much* blood?"

"Not much. A few drops, into the chalice there. That's what the knife is for. I'll have to provide some as well, since I'll be doing the actual summoning."

Jason was still confused. "Okay, I have to cut my finger and bleed into a cup. That doesn't really sound that hard, or that dangerous. I don't get it."

Stone's expression was very sober. "Jason, first of all, the sacrifice of life essence to fuel a spell is extraordinarily powerful, even in such a symbolic fashion as just a few drops of blood. I've never done anything like this before. This summoning is fairly minor — I'd never attempt it if it weren't — but nonetheless this is uncharted territory for me. I think I know what I'm doing, but if I'm wrong —" He shook his head. "If the spirit breaks free from my control, I have no way of knowing what it will do. Spirits don't like to be controlled or ordered about. That's why it normally takes so many mages to do a summoning — it requires that level of willpower to keep the summoned spirit confined and to ensure that someone doesn't become tempted to use it for his or her own purposes. By doing this ritual," he pointed at the open book "we're circumventing those safeguards. The only thing keeping us safe is my ability to keep the spirit under control, and to not allow it to tempt me."

"And if it breaks your control..." Jason started.

" — If it breaks my control that likely means it's killed me. And since you're the only other living being in the area, you will likely be its next target, for having the audacity to participate in its summoning. After that, it will almost certainly return to its home plane. But there's always the chance it will decide it likes it here and run wild for awhile before returning."

"But we won't care at that point, since we'll both be dead," Jason pointed out, only half sarcastically.

"True," Stone admitted. "But it's also possible that it might go after Verity, since she's the one it was meant to go find in the first place. And if it does find her, I can guarantee it will do more than simply point, shout 'Found her!' and nip off for home."

Jason pondered that. "So that's the choice, then. You don't have any other way of finding her."

Stone shrugged. "We can always continue looking by more conventional means. But you can see how well that's worked out so far. It's up to you, Jason. I won't think any less of you if you decide you don't want to do it. This is dangerous stuff. To be honest, a small part of me will be *relieved* if you decide not to do it. But even in this short time we've known each other, I think I know you well enough to guess that's not going to happen, is it?"

"No," Jason said. He sounded resigned, and he didn't look at Stone when he said it. "If you're willing to do it, I'm willing to do whatever I can to help. I owe V that much."

"All right, then." He pointed to a spot to the left side of the table. "Stand there, inside the circle but be careful not to touch it or smudge it. Remember before how I told you not to do that because it would give me a wicked headache if you broke it while I was inside? Well, this time it's a bit more serious. Once we've got the spirit here, breaking the circle will almost certainly mean both our deaths. No pressure," he added with a quirky smile and a raised eyebrow.

Jason did as instructed, fearful that for the one time in his life his natural dexterity would desert him and he'd stumble right onto the sand line. But that didn't happen, and after a moment he was standing in front of the table. He could feel his heart beating a little faster than normal, but he wasn't as nervous now as he had been prior to stepping through the teleportation gateway. Either he was beginning to trust Stone more, or evil blood rituals bothered him less than traveling through other dimensions.

Stone nodded and stepped in next to him, standing to the right side. He took a couple of deep breaths, squared his shoulders, and picked up the knife. "Ready? Last chance to back out."

"Let's do it," Jason said. He held out his hand.

Stone took hold of his wrist and guided his hand over the chalice. Jason glanced at him—his face was utterly expressionless, his eyes focused fully on what he was doing.

He raised the knife and quickly made a slice across Jason's finger. Jason winced a little but held steady, allowing Stone to turn his hand over so the drops of blood fell into the copper chalice.

The mage reached out and turned the page of the book. Jason, now sucking on his sliced finger, examined it but could make no sense out of it. These pages didn't even have illustrations, just densely packed text in the same weird language. Stone began to recite something in low tones. He waved a hand over the chalice and a faint glow began to emanate from it. "That's you," he murmured. "Now we'll add a bit of me and see what happens." He held out his own hand over the chalice and made another slice, allowing his blood to drip down and mingle with Jason's. The glow got brighter, taking on a reddish hue. Stone set the knife back down on the cloth, all the while still reciting words in the odd language that sounded to Jason just vaguely like Latin but not quite. Not that he knew any Latin, but he was pretty sure this wasn't it.

"All right," Stone said in the low murmuring tone, barely moving his lips. "Now comes the fun part, where we get to find out if we succeeded. Remember, whatever you do, whatever you see, don't step out of the circle or break it."

Jason could see that the mage's jaw was tight, his forehead dotted with beads of sweat. He alternated between watching Stone's face and his hands moving hypnotically over the chalice. There was no doubt about it: the glow was brighter now. Something — it looked like a wisp of fog — was forming there under his hands. He continued reciting the incantation, his voice growing louder, his hands moving as if he were a sculptor bringing form to the shapeless mass of fog.

After a few moments of watching, Jason realized that was exactly what he *was* doing. The little reddish mass was taking on a vaguely humanoid shape, and growing larger. It was rising up out of the chalice like a genie emerging from a lamp. Stone watched it without blinking, his hands never still. A couple of times Jason thought he saw a jerky motion as he appeared to lose control for a split-second, but then he got it back and the little figure continued to roil and grow.

This went on for awhile—Jason had no idea how long and he wasn't about to take his eyes off the proceedings to check his watch. The figure coming up out of the chalice was about half human size now, and Stone seemed to be having a harder time controlling it. His incantation picked up in speed and Jason could hear his voice shaking a bit, but he was afraid to say anything and disrupt the mage's concentration.

Expecting that the figure would continue to grow larger until it reached man-size and then step out of the chalice, Jason was startled when it suddenly disappeared. "What—?" he couldn't help demanding, sure that something had gone wrong.

Stone's shoulders slumped a little, but he didn't look disturbed. "Watch the mirror," he said softly, raising his head to do the same. "Any minute now—"

And then a—*form*—was shimmering in the mirror. It started out insubstantial, but slowly solidified into a bare-chested, reddish-skinned humanoid a little taller than Stone. It appeared to be standing directly behind the two of them, its head rising in the space between them. Jason whipped his head around—he couldn't help it—but there was nothing there. The room behind them was completely empty.

He turned back and there it was in the mirror, solid as the two of them. Its body writhed as if it were fighting invisible bonds. Its expression was cold, malevolent—and it was glaring at Stone. It said something, its voice the sound of old bones rubbing against ancient parchment. Jason couldn't make out a word of it—or even that there *were* words. All he could tell was that the thing looked pissed.

Then it made a lunge at Stone, its muscular arm actually reaching out *through* the mirror and going for his real-world throat. It took all of Jason's willpower not to leap backward, but Stone stood firm. He raised his hand and barked out a command in a booming voice. The figure recoiled as if it had touched a hot stove. Its hand and arm receded back into the mirror and it was left glaring once more at the mage from the other side. *If looks could kill,* Jason thought, *Al would be a fine red mist right about now.*

"I think I've got it now," Stone said under his breath. His voice was still shaking, more than a little now. "I'm going to send it out."

Jason nodded quickly. He'd be glad to be rid of it. To his uninitiated eyes, the thing looked like nothing more than a demon straight up from Hell. He was a little worried now that it might not just settle for finding Verity and bringing back news, but he knew he'd come way too far now not to trust Stone.

The mage reached out and put his hands directly on the mirror, one on either side of the spirit's "body." He met its eyes, still unblinking, and uttered a short, sharp sentence that sounded like a command.

The spirit glared at him for several seconds, but then it made a noise that could have been a resigned grumble, executed the most infinitesimal of all possible bows, and then winked out.

"There," Stone said on a rush of breath, finally allowing himself to focus on Jason.

"Did it work?" Jason moved to step back out of the circle, but Stone grabbed his arm and shook his head emphatically.

"Don't do that," he said, panting. "We can't leave the circle until the spirit's returned and been dismissed. And as for your question: I don't know. We won't know until it comes back. But it didn't rip us limb from limb, and my commands seem to have worked on it, so at least it appears that I performed the summoning correctly." He reached up and used his sleeve to wipe sweat off his forehead.

Jason let his breath out. "You're—sure that thing won't hurt Verity?"

"I'm not sure of anything," Stone told him. "If it follows my orders, it won't, but there's no way to know that right now. Might as well get as comfortable as you can in here. I don't expect it will be long before it's back, if it's had success."

There wasn't really any way to get comfortable within the tiny confines of the circle: there wasn't room to sit down, and Jason didn't want to lean against the table for fear of knocking over the book or one of the candles. So he just stood there, shifting nervously from foot to foot and trying to keep himself occupied by glancing at the strange characters on the open page of the book. Every few seconds he'd glance up at the mirror to make sure it hadn't sprouted any extra reflections, but so far the two of them were alone in the room. Stone, meanwhile, stood without moving, staring moodily into the mirror without appearing to see it.

A minute passed, then five, then ten. Jason looked at his watch. "You said this would be quick if it worked, right?"

"I said I thought so," Stone reminded him. "Remember, this is as new to me as it is to you. Be patient." Jason noticed that he was starting to look a little restless himself, though.

Fifteen minutes. Twenty. Still no sign of the spirit. Jason let out a loud sigh, his natural tendency to want to *move* nearly overwhelming in its compulsion now. "How do we know if it doesn't work? Do we have to stand in here forever?"

Stone was about to answer when he stiffened, startled. "It's back," he said, pointing at the mirror.

Jason spun around. Sure enough, the reddish figure had reappeared behind them in the mirror, looking as angry as ever. It said something to Stone in its bones-and-parchment voice, punctuated by many growls and other sounds of displeasure. The mage nodded. "She's there now, then?" he asked.

The figure snarled and glared at Stone. It appeared to be contemplating another lunge out into the real world, but eyed the mage warily and decided against it. Instead, it spat at him. The spittle flew out, contacted its own side of the mirror, and ran down toward the table with a sizzle. Then it reached out with a ropy, muscular arm and attempted to sweep all the objects off the table on its side of the mirror. The candles, knife, and chalice went, careening silently over the edge and out of sight. The book remained, and the creature screamed in agony as its arm contacted it.

"It's fighting me—" Stone said under his breath. "I'm going to release it now." He reached up with both hands and put them on the mirror again. Loudly and clearly, he uttered a long sentence in the strange Latin-like language, then pulled his hands back abruptly and clapped them together in a sudden sharp sound that made Jason jump. He stumbled, reeling back, realizing with horror even as he did so that he had no way of stopping himself. He was going to fall over backwards, taking out a good chunk of the circle when he landed.

As he went over, he got a last look at the creature's face. Instead of looking angry, it looked suddenly surprised and triumphant. That lasted for about two seconds. It flung itself forward again, its hands grasping eagerly in front of it, reaching for Stone, for Jason —

— and it winked out, its scream of frustration and agony abruptly cut off as it was sent back to whatever dimension it called home.

A second after that, Jason crashed to the floor and, just as he thought he would, smudged a significant portion of the circle. He had an instant to see a look of terror on Stone's face before the mage realized the spirit had already departed. Stone leaned over, clutching the table and breathing like he'd just run a marathon. "Good lord, Jason," he got out between breaths. "If you'd fallen only five seconds sooner —"

Jason was already rolling back up to his feet, shaking as what had almost happened hit him full force. He couldn't even say anything, so he just nodded.

"Remind me if we ever have to do this again to make a bigger circle. Or find a companion with smaller feet." The mage had recovered himself sufficiently to stand up, and he was already blowing out the candles. "Switch on the light, will you? And bring those bags back over here. We have to hurry."

Jason did as he was told. "Did it — find her? It sounds like it did."

"It told me where she is now," Stone said, gathering up the candles and chalice and stuffing them into a bag. "I'll clean this stuff up later — we can't just leave it here." He put the knife back in the sheath and put that in the satchel along with the book stand, then carefully picked up the book, closed it, and slipped it into the briefcase. "Can't do anything about the sand — it'll take too long to clean up. Just smudge it around. With any luck we can get back here with a broom before Madame Huan's friend gets back from his trip."

"Where is she?" Jason moved the sand around with his feet until it no longer resembled a semicircle, then hustled the table back over where he'd found it while Stone finished arranging the rest of the gear in the bags.

"San Jose, in an area near downtown. There's some kind of encampment near the Guadalupe River—more than one, I think. But the spirit's given me enough information that I can find her. Come on—let's go. It won't take that long to get there from here, but the way things have been going, I want to be as fast as possible in case something spooks her and she moves again. Especially since we won't be able to drive the whole way."

Jason waited until Stone had shut off the lights, locked up, and stashed all the gear in the trunk before speaking again. "Encampment? You mean homeless encampment?"

"Probably." Stone started up the Ford and headed out through the gate and back down the winding road as fast as he dared.

Jason shivered. He knew about homeless encampments—they didn't have as many back in Ventura County, but one of his outings when he'd still been a police cadet had been helping to roust the vagrants out of places they weren't supposed to be. It was a dirty business—even when the homeless themselves didn't cause any trouble, the lack of sanitation facilities made the larger camps into smelly cesspools full of flies and scavengers. "You think she's hooked up with one of these groups of magic bums?"

"I'd be surprised if she hadn't," Stone said. "It makes sense—the woman we know she was with seems to be affiliated with them, and from what you tell me she doesn't have the street savvy to survive on her own. If

she's still alive, she must have joined with up with someone — or multiple someones, more likely — for protection."

Jason leaned forward, willing the car to go faster. He
knew it wasn't safe for Stone to push the Ford any harder,
but that didn't stop every nerve in his body from being on
edge. They were close now — they had to be!

They were back to the freeway now. Jason looked at
his watch: it was almost eight o'clock now. At least it
wasn't raining, and there was enough of a moon out that
they'd have some visibility. Stone drove for a few miles,
then took another exit. A left turn and a few more blocks'
drive took them into the heart of downtown San Jose. Jason could see knots of homeless again, squatting under
overpasses and in abandoned parking lots. They eyed the
Ford as it went by, and when it stopped for lights a couple
of them approached carrying signs. Stone ignored them
and drove on when the light changed. Jason was looking
everywhere at once, always on the watch for potential
danger. "Pretty quiet down here, really."

"San Jose is fairly dead at night from what I hear,"
Stone told him. "Unless there's something going on at the
Arena, which there doesn't appear to be tonight." He
pointed up ahead. "There's the Guadalupe River Bridge."

"She's down there?" Jason looked out the passenger
window as they drove over it as if he might be able to see
Verity standing there waving at him.

"Close by." Stone took the next right and drove down
another quarter-mile or so, then pulled off and parked. He
looked grim. "I hate to leave this stuff in the car, but I
think it's safer than taking it with us. I'll do what I can to
mask it."

"Hurry up," Jason said, impatient. He was already out
of the car, and it was all he could do not to just take off
running, calling his sister's name.

"No offense, my friend," Stone said, moving around to the trunk. "But I'm going to make sure no one gets hold of this book. Just keep yourself together for another minute or two and we'll be off."

Jason grumbled but didn't argue. He spent the two minutes looking around, keeping watch for anyone approaching them. "There," Stone said at last, coming up alongside him. "Let's go."

Stone had parked the car near a large open area that Jason could see was a park as they got closer. He could identify a volleyball court, a couple of barbecue pits, and several picnic tables in their vicinity, and the park itself seemed to stretch out a fair distance on both sides. "They're in a park?" he asked. Instinctively he kept his voice down, not wanting to attract unwanted attention even though it didn't look like anyone was nearby.

Stone shook his head and pointed ahead of them. "The river's up there, and the encampment is near it. As I said, there are quite a few of them—under overpasses, under the branches of large trees, hidden in bushes—they're all along the river. The police don't bother them much because they don't have the manpower, and as soon as they break up one camp, another one forms. I see stories about them in the newspapers sometimes."

Jason was looking around nervously as they moved forward. "This whole place is pretty creepy."

Stone nodded. "Keep your wits about you. Do you have any sort of weapon?"

Jason pulled his knife out of his pocket and flipped it open. "Never did find a gun." He wished now that he'd tried harder.

They were moving out of the park area now, down into thicker underbrush. Jason could see evidence of human habitation: discarded food wrappers, a mangled old shoe, some newspapers, a shredded sleeping bag. He was reminded of the story he'd read what seemed like an eternity ago, about the group of homeless who'd been discovered murdered around the remains of their campfire, and wondered if it was near here. He couldn't recall if the article had contained any details. He glanced over at Stone; the mage was still looking grim. "You okay?" he whispered.

"Fine," Stone replied. "Just—this sort of terrain isn't exactly my forte."

Jason grinned. "Guess they didn't have Boy Scouts in England, eh?"

"Not really my thing." They continued to move forward; the ground sloped downward now, and Jason could see trees and bushes stretching out ahead of them on either side, hiding the river mostly from view. Stone touched his arm and pointed to the left, then started to move in that direction.

They walked in silence for another five minutes or so, Jason getting more and more impatient. Every once in awhile they could hear or see indications that they weren't alone: the far-off glow of a campfire, the sudden sound of a laugh or a raised voice, a snatch of music from somebody's portable radio—but they all sounded far away. "Are we getting close?"

Stone nodded. "Yes. This looks like the area the spirit showed me. Spirits are notoriously bad about giving directions—they don't understand North or South or 'three hundred yards past the rock shaped like a bird's head.' They're more about impressions. I've been looking around trying to match the vision it gave me with the landscape, and this looks about right. Come on—let's go down closer to the trees."

Jason followed him. "Did the spirit show you the camp? Is it under an overpass, or under a tree, or what?"

"Hard to say. It couldn't really show me the camp itself. It tried, but the vision was—fuzzy. I can't explain it better than that. It might just have been the spirit exerting its will any way it could. As you might have noticed, it wasn't exactly ecstatic to be doing my bidding."

"But it couldn't have—I dunno—shown you the wrong place, right?" Suddenly Jason was even more nervous than he had been before. He wished his mind would shut up and stop giving him ideas like that.

"I don't think so," Stone assured him. "If I had it under control, it had to follow my orders. If I hadn't had it under control, you saw what would have happened. I think the best it could do is try to circumvent my wishes as much as it could."

Jason nodded, hoping the mage knew what he was talking about. They were approaching the trees now, only about twenty yards away. He squinted into the dimness, looking for movement and wishing there was more illumination than that provided by the moon and the few functional lights in the park. "See anything?" he whispered.

"Not yet." He crept forward, moving more slowly now and trying to keep as quiet as he could, and Jason followed him. As they reached the trees and stepped under their canopy, even the dim light they'd had before was cut in half, leaving them with visibility of only a few feet. "If I'm interpreting the spirit's instructions correctly, they should be somewhere close on the other side of these trees."

Jason stayed level with him, his gaze never holding still. He spotted the symbol first, and grabbed Stone's arm.

The mage jumped a little. "What?" he asked irritably.

"Look." Jason pointed. On the large trunk of a nearby tree was the triangle-and-rays symbol, sprayed there in white paint.

Stone nodded, satisfied. "Then we are in the right place. Good. We—"

He didn't get to finish his sentence. Suddenly there was laughter—high, maniacal laughter—and it was all around them. Leather-jacketed figures were stepping out from behind three of the trees, including the one with the symbol on it. "Hey, assholes!" yelled one of them. "Nice ta see ya! Right on time, too!" The others laughed even louder, as if that were the funniest thing they ever heard.

Jason spun around. More figures were moving from behind trees behind them. All of them were holding knives, chains, or other close-fighting weapons "Shit!" he whispered under his breath to Stone. "DMW—we're surrounded!"

"Stay calm," Stone muttered. He didn't look calm, though. He looked scared. He remained facing forward while Jason, his back to him, watched the rear. They eyed the gangers warily.

So far they weren't moving, content to form a ring around their prey. The one who'd spoken before laughed again. "We thought you might be here. The boss told us about you, that you might be coming. Big mistake. And now you're gonna die. Any last words?"

"The boss?" Stone asked, sounding a lot more confident than Jason knew he was. "And who would that be? Who's telling you lot what to do?"

Another of the gangers snorted in contempt. The leader moved a little closer to Stone. "None of your business. But we know everything. We know you're a magic man, and we know you should keep closer track of your little friends so they don't talk to the wrong people." He laughed again. "'Cause, see, I think he liked us better than he liked you."

"What's he mean by that?" Jason hissed, barely moving his lips.

Stone didn't answer that. Instead, he whispered back: "Get ready. I'm going to try to take out the leader. If he drops, try to break through the line where he's standing now."

"Hey now!" the lead ganger yelled. "No talking, you two. You're here to die, not to chat. We're gonna make it nice and slow, so we can enjoy it. How do you like that?" He took a step forward, as did the other gangers.

Jason, back to back with Stone, could feel the mage tense up. He turned his head in time to see Stone raise his arms and cry out a command. Bright light formed around his hands, then flew out and hit the lead ganger and the one next to him. They screamed and staggered backward; the second ganger fell, and the leader dropped to his knees. "Get 'em!" the ganger screamed as behind Jason, Stone staggered, reeling.

Jason didn't hesitate. Grabbing Stone's arm, he vaulted forward into the space vacated by the fallen ganger. If they could get out of the circle so they weren't surrounded anymore, they might have a chance. He slashed at the lead ganger's arm as he went by and was rewarded by an angry grunt of pain. "Are we shielded at all?" he muttered in Stone's ear.

The mage nodded. "Not—much, though, so be careful."

The gangers were approaching now, trying to circle back around behind them. "Take 'em!" the leader yelled, clutching his arm and trying to struggle back to his feet. "Boss says they can't get to the girl! Just fuckin' kill 'em!"

Jason clutched his knife, dropping into a defensive stance as two of the gangers surged forward. He could feel Stone tensing up again next to him, preparing another spell. The mage was still on his feet, but Jason didn't think he'd be able to get off too much more magic before he was exhausted. He lunged at the ganger on the right, getting in under his wild swing and slicing through his leather jacket. Bright red blood sprayed out and the ganger roared in pain.

Meanwhile, Stone went after the other one. He ducked sideways and grabbed the kid's arm. Again his hands flared and a glowing nimbus formed around the ganger's entire upper body. He shrieked and dropped.

Stone was so busy dealing with the ganger in his face, though, that he didn't notice one of the others in the shadows. Before he could react—before Jason even saw what was happening—a knife flew across the clearing and buried itself in Stone's side. The mage, arm to arm with Jason, suddenly sagged, his face going dead white and his hands clutching at the hilt. He dropped to his knees, then fell over and curled up, writhing.

*Oh, holy crap...*Jason didn't know what to do next. Several of the gangers were still functional, and Stone was out of action now. He stood, legs spread wide, crouched low, trying to look in every direction at once, but he didn't see a way out of this one. There wouldn't be any eleventh-hour rescue this time: his rescuer was lying at his feet bleeding, possibly dying.

Oh, man, V – I'm sorry. I tried. He crouched lower and waited, planning to at least take out a couple of them before they took him down.

Then, suddenly, it seemed like the clearing was full of more people than it had been before. *More? I can't even handle these –*

A ganger leaped forward, swinging a chain at Jason's head. Before Jason could jump back, a voice—a female voice—yelled "Get—*out!*"

The ganger did something very strange then. He clutched his head and staggered back, dropping the chain. As Jason watched, wide-eyed, *something* – some sort of shimmering, barely visible ball of energy – flew up out of the ganger's head. It paused for a moment, then darted toward Jason. Jason yelled something inarticulate and held up his hands to block it, but it stopped before it reached him. For a second it hovered there, looking as confused as it was possible for a shimmering ball of energy to look. And then it dissipated, flying to shimmering pieces and then vanishing.

Jason was so confused by what happened that he wasn't paying attention to what was going on around him. But something was happening. All around him, the remaining gangers were turning tail and running. They didn't even stop to grab their injured colleagues – they simply ran for the hills, screaming. Jason could see other figures moving around the area now, figures in shapeless clothes – bums? How could it –

Something hit him hard on the back of the head and he pitched forward and didn't see anything else.

22.

When he awoke, he was lying on something soft that smelled bad. "Uh?" he grunted, opening his eyes. His head felt woozy but it didn't hurt. He remembered getting hit pretty hard—what had happened? And then the memories rushed back, all at once. Shoving himself up to a sitting position, he looked around quickly. "Al?"

"Shh," said a voice behind him. He spun around to find himself facing a young woman sitting Indian-style by a crackling fire next to the sleeping bag he'd been lying on. A slender, pale young woman with dark brown hair cut boy-short, a black leather biker jacket, and big dark eyes.

Jason's mouth dropped open, and he didn't even bother to close it. Instead he spun around so he could face her fully. "Verity?"

She smiled wickedly; it lit up her whole face, making her look like a goth pixie. "Hi, big brother. Long time no see."

He stared at her. He hadn't seen her in years, but even back then he had never seen her look this—*good.* Even with her face smudged with dirt and the lingering odor that told him she hadn't done laundry in quite some time, her face looked alive, engaged—*okay, let's just come out and say it*—she didn't look *crazy.* For a minute he could just look at her, drinking in the sight of her, not daring to believe that after all this time he'd finally caught up with her. When he did finally speak, all he could manage was: "Where—have you—*been*?"

Again, she smiled, reaching out to pat him on the shoulder. "Don't worry. I'll tell you everything. I knew you were looking for me, but I didn't know how to get hold of you."

"How did you—?" he started to ask, but then another thought poked the question violently out of the way. "Al! Where's Al? Is he—?" He scrambled to his feet, looking around.

He was standing in the middle of what looked like a hobo camp, with a couple of fires, some ragged-looking tents, and sleeping bags stretched out near the fires. Several huddled figures also sat around the fires, covered in tattered shapeless coats and hats. A shopping cart full of various bags was parked off to the side, and somewhere a dog barked. Jason didn't see anybody who looked like Stone, though. "You didn't leave him—?"

"Your friend?" Verity got up to join him. At his nod, she pointed over toward one of the tents. "He's in there. He was in a bad way—Lamar's working on him, though. He should be okay."

Jason's blood froze. That ganger had buried his knife—his no doubt far from sanitary knife—in Stone's side, and some bum was working on him inside a dirty tent in a camp that smelled, quite literally, like shit? Verity momentarily forgotten, he hurried across past the fire and flung open the tent flap.

Inside, by the light of the ancient lantern flickering in the corner, Jason took in the scene: A large middle-aged white woman in a garishly colored sweater and a slim black man with close-cropped gray hair and wire-rimmed glasses were crouched down on the tent's floor, leaning over the unconscious figure of Stone. The mage looked very pale; they had removed his overcoat and shirt, and Jason could see that they'd pressed some kind of compress onto his side. Blood was already beginning to seep through the compress.

"Hey!" Jason yelled, and the two crouching figures looked up, startled. "What the hell are you doing to him? He needs a hospital!"

"Hush," the woman said as if speaking to a young child. "Your friend is goin' to be fine."

"Look," Jason said, exasperated, dropping down next to them. "I'm grateful that you guys saved us from those gangers—I have no idea how you did it, but that's not important right now. I don't want to offend you or anything, but—it's not clean here. You're gonna kill him trying to help him. I'm gonna go call an ambulance, and—"

"It's all right," the black man said. His voice was soft and gentle and he didn't seem at all disturbed by the agitation in Jason's tone. "Look." He lifted up the bloody compress.

Jason glanced where he was indicating, then did a double-take and stared. "What the *hell*...?"

Stone's side was covered with blood; it had seeped down to stain the top part of his jeans and a larger stain flowered on the tattered sleeping bag on which he was lying. But there was no sign of a wound. His skin was whole, without any scar or mark or any indication that it had ever been broken. "How did you—?"

The old man shook his head and smiled at Jason. "He's lost a fair bit of blood, and I believe he was already weakened by the spells he cast. He'll probably be unconscious for awhile. But I promise you, he'll be fine. He's in no danger."

"Well, no more than any of the rest of us ever are," the woman said wryly. She picked up Stone's overcoat and gently covered him with it. The mage shifted slightly but didn't awaken.

"Wait," Jason said, looking back and forth between Stone and the black man. "You know about—magic?"

"Come on out, Jason," a new voice said. Jason turned around to see that Verity had poked her head unnoticed through the tent flap. "Let's go get something to eat and we can talk. It looks like your friend's gonna be out of it for awhile. Good time to catch each other up."

Jason took a last look at Stone; the mage's breathing appeared to be regular and he didn't look in any immediate danger, so he got up and followed Verity out of the tent. She led him over to one of the campfires, picked up a couple of old mismatched plates, and ladled something that looked like baked beans from a pot hanging over the fire onto both of them. She handed one to Jason along with a plastic fork. "Don't worry," she said, noticing the look of suspicion and distaste that he hadn't been quick enough to hide. "It's okay. I've been eating their cooking for awhile now and I haven't been sick yet." She took his arm and steered him over to a tree that no one was currently sitting under. "Have a seat. You took a pretty good thump on the head back there. They fixed you up but I'm betting you're still dizzy."

Jason was indeed still a little dizzy, but he had no idea how much of it was from the hit on the head and how much was from the shock of all that had happened to him. He sat down next to his sister and took an experimental taste of the beans. For bland spice-free beans, they weren't bad. He realized he *was* hungry—but he was more hungry for answers than food. "I don't know where to start," he said with a sigh. He looked Verity up and down. "So—you've been here this whole time?"

"Not here," she said. "We move around a lot—we have to. You saw the kind of thing they have to deal with. And that's just the start. Cops, people who just want to hassle them because it's fun—it really sucks."

Jason leaned back against the tree and rubbed his head. "Oh, God, Verity, I have so many questions. It seems like all I've been doing for the last several days is asking questions."

"We're safe here," she told him. "We're not going any-where for awhile, and it's way too early to go to bed. Just start somewhere. I don't know if I can answer 'em all, but I'll tell you what I can. And I'll ask you a few, too. Okay?"

Jason nodded wearily. "Okay." He ate a couple more bites of beans and thought over all the things he wanted to ask. Finally, he looked at her. "You seem—better," he ventured.

"You mean I don't seem like I'm crazy anymore?"

"Well—I wouldn't have said it that way, but—yeah."

"Lemme get back to that. That part's a little more complicated. But you're right—I'm not. At least for now. And hopefully not ever again."

"Okay, then...Why don't you start by telling me what happened at New Horizons? Why did you leave? What did you see? Where did you go after you left?"

"Slow down, slow down!" she said, laughing. Then her expression sobered. "I heard a rumor that Charles was dead. Do you know if that's true?"

Jason nodded, looking down at his plate. "Yeah." When he glanced up at her, he was surprised to see tears sparkling in the corners of her eyes. "I'm sorry, V."

"Yeah..." Roughly she swiped her sleeve across her face. "He was a good guy. He was the only one who even tried to make that hell of a place tolerable for me."

"V, I—"

"Yeah, yeah. I know. You're sorry you never visited, but you didn't know how to deal with your batshit sister. I get it. Why don't we just forget about that for now, okay? I'm not sure if I've forgiven you for it yet and I might still tell you what I think about it, but—later. Right now we have more important things to deal with." Her voice sounded bitter but surprisingly mature. *When had Verity grown up so much?* She was silent for almost a mi-nute, concentrating on eating. Then she looked at Jason.

"So—yeah. I woke up one night and thought I heard something, so I went downstairs to check it out. We weren't supposed to be downstairs after lights-out, so I was afraid I'd get caught, but I had to find out what it was."

"What did it sound like?"

"Like a kid. Screaming." She took a deep breath and shuddered a little as she pictured it. "When I got there, I noticed that the basement door was open—and it's never open. And I heard a voice, and somebody whimpering. So I snuck down there. I have no idea why I was brave enough to do that, but the kid seemed like he was in trouble, or hurt—and I kinda thought of you."

"Me?"

She nodded. "Yeah. How you always used to protect the little kids in the neighborhood, remember?"

Jason smiled. That had been a long time ago. "Yeah, I remember."

"So I opened the door and looked inside—and there was a guy in there towering over a kid. A boy, maybe nine or ten. The kid was scared to death, and the guy—I couldn't see his face 'cause his back was to me—he seemed to be getting off on the kid's fear."

Jason's eyes widened. "You mean he was—?"

Verity shook her head. "He wasn't molesting the kid, if that's what you meant. Everybody's clothes were on. But he was definitely getting something from scaring him. And then he reached out and touched his head, and—" She paused, as if gathering her courage to continue speaking. "—and then the kid screamed again, and he—he disappeared."

"Disappeared?" A cold chill ran down Jason's back at that. What she'd described sounded exactly like what he'd seen the night Charles died.

"Yeah. I know it sounds hard to believe, but—"

"No. I believe you. Go on."

She looked surprised by that, but didn't ask. "So after he did that, *I* screamed. I couldn't help it. I was scared to death. And the guy turned around, and his eyes were all freaky, and he came at me. And I—I—just sort of *pushed* at him. With my mind." She looked at him again. "This all sounds like I'm crazy again, doesn't it?"

"I'm not sure," Jason said honestly. "What do you mean, you 'pushed' at him?"

"I can't describe it. It was like I punched him with my mind. And then something flew out of him. It looked like some kind of shimmery thing. It flew at me, but I shoved it away, just like I'd done with the man. Then it flew away, and the guy fell over."

Jason was staring hard at Verity, riveted by her words. This was all sounding so familiar—well, all of it except the "pushing with her mind" part. He had no idea what she meant by that. "And then you ran away?"

She nodded. "I didn't even stay to see if the guy was dead or alive. I just ran back upstairs—and straight into Charles. He was in the kitchen. I almost knocked him down, I was going so fast. I thought I was busted for sure, but he saw my face, how scared I was, and asked me what was wrong. I told him I'd seen something terrible in the basement."

"Did he go check it out?"

She shook her head. "I think he'd thought there was bad stuff going on at New Horizons for a while. He told me I had to get out, and he'd help me. That's when I went to call you. But you didn't answer."

Jason sighed. If only he hadn't gotten into that bar fight and got tossed into jail overnight—if only he'd been there to take her call—how different the events of the last few days would have been. "I'm sorry about that. I—wasn't home when you called."

"Well, it's good at least that you weren't just ignoring me," she said, this time without bitterness. "I went back to find Charles, and he told me to pack up and get ready to go, fast. He said he had a friend I could stay with. After I got back with my stuff, he sent me down the block to the pay phone, and gave me his friend's address and cab fare to get there. Told me to lie low and he'd be in touch."

"This friend—it was Melody Barnes, right?"

Verity nodded. "Yeah. She's dead too, isn't she?"

"Yeah. She and her friend Willow are both dead."

"So many dead people..." Verity whispered, looking down at her lap. For a long time she didn't speak. Then, pulling herself together, she continued: "Anyway, Willow and her friend Susanna came to visit Melody. They were both strange—Melody did some fortune telling during the day, and Willow was another fortune teller friend of hers. Susanna was a friend of Willow's—she was homeless. But there was something weird about her. We were all just sitting in the living room talking when all of a sudden she looks up like a dog that smelled something. She told us somebody bad was coming, and we all needed to get out."

"But Melody didn't want to go," Jason said. "Right?"

"Yeah. She thought it was all a big joke. Susanna was getting really agitated, and Willow was trying to get Melody to go. She told her to take me out too. Susanna grabbed my arm and practically dragged me out the back door. Willow told us to go and she'd bring Melody. We never saw them again after that."

"Do you know who was after you guys?" Jason asked.

"I didn't at the time—I really had no clue what was going on. Remember, I was still pretty out of it back then. I know now, though—it was that gang. Dead Men Walking. The one that ambushed you and your friend tonight."

Jason nodded. "So where did Susanna take you? We talked to Willow at the hospital before she died—she told us to go to this abandoned fruit packing plant in Redwood City. Is that where you were?"

"Yeah. It was a safe place Susanna knew about—she and some of her group were squatting there. We took a bus over as far as we could, then walked the rest of the way. Her group was there, but we didn't stay very long. She was still freaked out that somebody was after us. The others—they seemed to really listen to what she said, so we all cleared out. That was when we headed down here. We met up with another group and they were the ones who told us you were looking for me. But by that time I couldn't contact you, because nobody knew where you were."

Jason leaned back against the tree, picking at the beans (they were cold by now) and mulling over everything she'd told him. "Okay, so...that explains where you'd been all this time. But it still doesn't explain *why* DMW and God knows who else is after you. Does it have something to do with the guy in the basement? Do you even know who he was?"

She shook her head. "I don't know who he was—but I'm sure that's what it had to do with."

"So it wasn't that Delaney guy?"

"Dr. Delancie?" She looked surprised. "No, it wasn't him. He was full of himself and could be a real ass sometimes, but I don't think he was part of this." Taking a deep breath, she continued, "Okay, now you know where I was. But I guess you need to know what's going on here. Why I'm hanging out with these people."

"I was wondering about that," Jason said, nodding. "It sounds like they kinda took you in and took care of you — that's a good thing. But—why homeless people? Al—my friend in the tent there, Alastair Stone—and I are getting more and more convinced that there's more to them than meets the eye. That's true, isn't it?"

R. L. KING

Verity looked off into the camp, watching the various residents moving around. "Yeah," she said. "Your friend's a mage, isn't he?"

"You know about mages?" Jason was surprised. For a bunch who were supposed to be as secretive as Stone had implied they were, a lot of people seemed to know about them.

"Only since recently," she said. "A lot of the Forgotten know about them."

"Forgotten?"

She nodded. "That's what they call themselves. The — special ones."

"The ones with powers, you mean."

"Yeah."

Jason leaned forward, searching her face. "What's with the powers?" he asked. "We've seen some of them in action, but I don't really get it. Do they all have them? Where did they come from? *Are* they mages? Al says they're not as far as he can tell, but it sure seems like magic to me."

Verity spread her hands in a *how should I know?* gesture. "I don't really know anything about mages except than that they exist. But — a lot of the Forgotten have the powers. They don't have a lot of control over them — they just kind of *happen,* you know? When they need them to, I mean."

Jason thought of the way one of the library group had concealed them from the fake cop. "You mean like hiding people."

She nodded. "Yeah, that's one of them. That one's fairly common — most groups have somebody who can do that."

"So what would other ones be?"

"Lots of things," she said, shrugging. "Lamar can heal — you saw that with your friend. That's pretty rare, from what I understand. We're lucky to have him. Some are like detectors — they can tell when something dangerous is around, or getting closer. Some of them can influence animals — you know, calming down mean dogs and that kind of thing. One lady — I think you met her, she's one of the group who told us they'd seen you — has a shopping cart with all these bags, and she always seems to be able to dig around and pull out whatever she needs at the time."

Jason remembered the old lady with all the tote bags at the library. "Yeah...I think I do know her."

"Another one some of them have — I thought this was kind of cool to find out — You know how you can drive by a building a bunch of times and never really see it?"

"Yeah." He knew exactly what she meant. Every town had them: those nondescript, faceless buildings, usually government offices or businesses that didn't cater to the public, that everybody missed unless they had some reason to be there. He called them "invisible buildings."

"Some of the Forgotten can do that — make a building hard to find like that. It's not like you *can't* find it, but if you're not sure where you're trying to go, or you're not looking for it specifically, you tend to just go right past it without seeing it."

Jason remembered how they'd passed the fruit-packing plant the first time and had to turn around and do another pass before they found it. "Where — do these powers come from? Does anyone know? Have they always had them?"

"They haven't told me everything, so I'm not sure about that part. But from what little I've been able to put together, I think the powers started showing up right around the time things started going bad around the country."

R. L. KING

"Five years ago?" Jason stared at her. His mind was spinning again, trying hard to put things together. "Wait a minute. Hasn't anybody thought this whole thing is too big a coincidence to be a coincidence?"

"What are you talking about?"

"You're telling me the bu—er, the Forgotten—started to get these powers five years ago. Which is about the same time you started having your—episodes. Which is around the same time a *lot* of people started having problems. You don't think this stuff is all connected?" He remembered again what Charles had said. "And—Charles was telling me this—around five years ago is when he said people around here started to get meaner. It might have happened around Ventura too, but maybe not as bad since there are fewer people down there."

Verity was looking contemplative. "Are you saying that—something happened five years ago to cause all of this? That's crazy, Jason! What could it have been? And how could it have happened without anybody knowing about it?"

"I dunno. I think I need to talk to Al about this when he's awake. It doesn't make any sense, but I can't shake the idea that there's something to this." He looked at her again. "Putting that aside for now, though—I got more questions. I don't think I'm gonna run out any time soon. So—what is it about these symbols I see all over the place? Is that a Forgotten thing too?"

Verity nodded. "They told me about that. They use them to communicate with other groups. It's dangerous to let the groups get too big—people squabble and it makes us more vulnerable to attacks. You have to remember, even though they have these weird powers, most of these people have some kind of mental stuff going on. They don't always play well together. But they use the symbols to let each other know things — what places are safe, what places are dangerous, where the Evil is — "

"The Evil?" Jason leaned forward, stiffening. "What's the Evil?"

"Oh, right. I didn't tell you about that. That's what they call it. Kind of a dumb name, I know, but — "

"What *is* it?"

"They don't know, exactly. It's the shimmery thing I saw coming out of that guy in the basement. It's some kind of — spirit, or being, or something — and it possesses people. Some of the Forgotten can see it in people — see when they're possessed. That's one of the reasons they stick together — it's trying to kill them, because they're the only ones who can, or almost the only ones. Nobody knows why."

"They — possess people?" *Holy crap. That explains a lot.* "How? Can they possess anybody? Do you *know* they've possessed you?" Jason considered it a mark of just how far he'd come in the past few days that he accepted this information without questioning it.

Verity shook her head, holding up her hands to ward off his questions. "Jason, stop. I don't *know* all this stuff. I've only been around them for a few days, and some of what I know, I only know from listening to them talk. You should really talk to Lamar, or to Marilee. They can tell you more. And they're — some of the more 'together' of the group."

Jason was barely hearing her. "Could — being possessed by these — Evil things — have been what caused your episodes? Caused you to — "

" — to go crazy? No. That much I do know. Forgotten can't be possessed. I think it has to do with the powers somehow, or with how their brains are mixed up."

"But wait. That means you're — ?" Jason's head was reeling again.

"Yeah, I guess I am, sorta. Though I don't think I have any powers."

"What about that 'mind push' thing you were talking about?"

Her eyes widened. For a moment she just looked at him. "Oh my God...Jason...I didn't even think of that. I didn't tell anybody about it, 'cause I didn't think they'd believe me. By that time I wasn't even sure myself that I'd really done it. I thought I was just remembering things wrong, like I used to do a lot. And I wasn't even sure I could do it again. But—I did it tonight. To get that guy off you. I saw him about to attack you, and I sort of went on instinct. And it worked."

"Good thing, too," Jason said wryly. "So—how are you not—having problems anymore? Did these guys stop it somehow?"

"Not stop it," She said. "I guess it's more like—suppress it. It's one of the things Susanna can do. It doesn't always work, though. She said it's only ever worked on three or four people she's tried it on, and if I get too far away from her, it'll probably stop working. Her main power is keeping us hidden so we don't get found, and sometimes knowing when bad stuff is coming. I guess it's kind of rare to have more than one power, too—she's the only one I know who does."

"The DMW—are they part of this—Evil?" That would make a lot of sense too. He remembered something else Charles had said: how they'd been a small-potatoes gang until a few years ago, then gotten a new leader and took several steps up the food chain in short order.

Verity nodded. "Yeah. They're kind of—the foot soldiers. That's another thing I think is true, but like I said, you really should talk to Lamar or Marilee. I think they have—like—levels. Some of them are more powerful than others. The more powerful ones use DMW — maybe other gangs, too — to do their dirty work."

"Mmm," Jason said, thinking that over. He looked up and saw that a shadowy figure was heading across the camp toward them. As it got closer, it resolved itself into a familiar form: Hector, the alcoholic ex-military man he and Stone had seen at the library. He stumped up and stood in front of them till they noticed him. "Hey there," Jason said. "Haven't seen you in awhile."

Hector nodded. The tang of marijuana mingled with his usual odor. "Your friend's awake. He wants to talk to you," he said in his gruff, abrupt tone.

Jason leaped to his feet. "Thanks." To Verity he said, "I'll be back soon, okay? I want to talk to you some more. I still have more questions, and you probably do too."

She nodded and rolled her eyes a little. "Not like I'm going anywhere. You might be a big dork sometimes, but you're kind of handy to keep around."

Jason grinned and hurried back to the tent, poking his head tentatively through the flap. The woman in the colorful sweater was gone now; Lamar waved him in. "I'll leave you two alone," he said, getting up slowly. Jason helped him up and waited until he'd left, then dropped down next to Stone.

The mage was still very pale and looked exhausted, but his eyes were open. "Hey," Jason said. "You okay? You gave me quite a scare out there."

Stone smiled faintly. "I gave *myself* quite a scare," he said. His voice had nearly no volume behind it; Jason had to lean in to hear him. "The kind chap who's been taking care of me tells me that I missed the big reunion."

Jason nodded. "Yeah, you did. She's here, Al. I've been talking to her. And I've got plenty to tell you."

R. L. KING

"Oh?" Stone tried to struggle up to a more elevated position, but failed and sank back, panting. "P'raps I'll wait a bit before I try that."

"Does it hurt?" Jason indicated Stone's side, covered now by his wool overcoat.

"Surprisingly, not at all. I'm not quite sure why. I distinctly remember seeing that ganger's knife sticking out of my side and quite a lot of blood before I blacked out. But all I feel is—ghastly. So tired I can barely move. But no pain." He glanced up at Jason. "I suppose that's one of the things you want to tell me about?"

"You sure you're up to this? It can wait, if you need to—"

Stone looked at him sternly. "Jason, if you have answers to any of our little puzzles, I want to hear them. Don't be cruel—I don't have the strength to zap you right now."

Jason grinned—same old Al. "Okay. I'll tell you what V's told me so far, but I think we're gonna have to talk to the others to get the rest." Trying not to forget anything or leave anything out, he told Stone the story of what had happened to Verity, and what she'd revealed about the Forgotten.

Stone's bright blue gaze, dimmed a little by exhaustion but still laser-sharp, focused in on Jason's face, barely blinking the entire time he spoke. The mage didn't ask any questions while Jason was telling the story, but he tensed when he got to the part about the Evil and the possessions. "So you're saying," he said when Jason finished, "that these so-called 'Evil'—this—force, or spirit—can possess people at will?"

"I'm not sure," Jason said, shifting position. The tent floor was uncomfortable, and even though he was getting acclimated to the smell of the camp, it was still pretty bad. "Verity said we need to talk to Lamar—I guess that's the guy who was in here—or Marilee. She said they know more."

Stone nodded, but didn't appear to be listening closely. His eyes were closed again. "Al? You okay?" Jason asked him, concerned.

The mage opened his eyes. "Just...thinking," he said. "There's something here I'm convinced I'm missing, but it's eluding me. Brain's a bit foggy right now. But this—this is fascinating. Somehow all of this seems to be connected to something that happened around five years ago—but what?"

"I was hoping you'd know," Jason admitted. "You're the expert on weird shit and magical phenomena around here. Five years ago? I was neck deep in Criminal Law classes and running obstacle courses and getting yelled at by guys with short haircuts and big ears."

Stone nodded vaguely. "Can you go find Lamar, or this Marilee person? I don't know how much longer I'm going to be awake for awhile, but this is important. I have questions for them."

"Yeah, give me a sec. You want anything to eat?"

"No. Just—find them."

Jason got up and hurried out of the tent, looking around. People seemed to be settling in for bed now, laying out sleeping bags and bedrolls around the two fires. He found Lamar eating a plate of beans under a tree. "My friend wants to talk to you if that's okay," he said. "Or, if you're busy—Marilee. I don't know who that is, though."

"Verity's been telling you about us," the old man said. It wasn't a question.

"Yeah. And Al—Dr. Stone—she said you knew he was a mage."

Lamar nodded. "We saw the spells he was casting when the DMW showed up. Those were no Forgotten abilities."

"He's a mage," Jason confirmed. "And he wants to ask you about some things—things Verity didn't know about. Are you willing?"

Again, Lamar nodded. He had a slow, methodical way about him that made him seem like a real doctor rather than merely a homeless man with healing powers. "I'm willing. You should ask Marilee to come as well. She's over there by the fire, near her cart. I'll meet you there."

Jason looked over to where he had pointed and was surprised to see the old woman from the library sitting next to an overflowing shopping cart. He realized he'd never known her name. Moving over to her, he saw that she was knitting something in her lap while the small black kitten batted at the ends of her needles. "Hi," he said, smiling. Cocking his head at the kitten, he added, "I see you and your friend are still doing fine."

The old woman, Marilee, looked up at him and returned his smile. "Well, hello," she said. "Didn't get a chance to talk to you before. It's good to see you, even in times like this."

"Same here," he said. "Hey, would you mind coming with me to the tent? Lamar's there, and my friend. He wants to talk to you."

"I thought he might," she said, nodding. She offered the kitten to Jason, carefully stowed her knitting in one of the bags hanging off the side of her cart, then used the cart to pull herself to a standing position. "Your friend is very lucky."

"Yeah. It's a good thing you guys were here, for sure." He followed her as she shuffled slowly toward the tent.

Lamar was already inside, seated next to Stone, who appeared to be asleep. He opened his eyes as Jason and Marilee came in, though. The two of them settled themselves into seated positions; it took a few moments because space was tight and they didn't want to jostle Stone too much. As soon as Jason had sat down, the kitten leaped out of his arms and settled herself in the crook of Stone's arm.

"She certainly does like you," Marilee said with approval. "Kitties always know. That's why I like them."

When they were all settled down, Stone looked at Lamar. "Thank you for coming," he said, still speaking very softly and more slowly than his usual tones. "And thank you for—whatever you did for me. I'm reasonably sure that I wouldn't be here talking to you now if it hadn't been for your efforts."

Lamar nodded solemnly but didn't speak. Marilee fussed around the mage a bit, pulling up his overcoat covers and mopping at his forehead.

"Jason's told me a bit about you—things he's learned from his sister. He's told me about your—abilities—and how you use them to help you keep yourselves safe from—the Evil, you call it?"

Again, Lamar nodded. "Yes."

"Can you tell me a bit more about it? About your abilities, and about this Evil? Do you know anything about its nature? Do you know where your abilities came from, or why you have them?"

"Dr. Stone," Lamar said, leaning forward to look into the mage's eyes. "You are a mage. I know this—and I know also how curious mages are. How they want to know everything, and study everything. That is your nature. I understand this. But what we have—we haven't studied it. It simply—is."

Stone sighed. "It can't simply *be*. Jason tells me that it started appearing five years or so ago. But no one knows why? Is it a cause, or an effect? Did it affect people who were already—mentally unstable—or did it cause them to become so?"

"Nobody knows," Marilee said. "Maybe both. Take your sister, for example. She said she was fine until she just started—seeing things. Thinking things were seeking her, trying to kill her. But others—" she shrugged. "Hector—you met him—he had problems with drugs and alcohol before any of this happened, and something about the war...did something to him."

"So this—whatever it is—took hold of people, drove them mad—or madder—and caused them to develop these odd abilities? Do all of you have these abilities?"

Lamar shook his head. "No. And there are degrees of them as well. Some of them are useless. Some are common—like the ability to shield one or more people or a location, or the ability to sense when the Evil is nearby—while others are much less so, like my particular gift. No one knows what determines a person's ability."

"Verity said you can't control them," Jason pointed out. "That they—just sort of happen when you need them."

"Yes," Marilee said. "It's instinctual. It's more a sense of—we see someone we want to help, or we pick up on something in our heads without realizing it. And it just—flows out of us."

"And—one of you healed my wound?" Stone asked. He weakly lifted up his overcoat to inspect the bloody aftermath of his knife wound.

"I did," Lamar said.

"You healed it—completely? It doesn't hurt...I don't feel feverish—which means that you likely haven't left any of whatever was on that knife inside of me. That's—amazing. I can do a bit of healing magic, but nothing like this." He shivered a bit and let the overcoat drop back down. "So—about this 'Evil.' What is it, exactly?"

Lamar shook his head. "Nobody knows that. Not exactly. We try to avoid it when we can—it's dangerous and unpredictable. But it seems to be some kind of—" he struggled for the right words "—disembodied life force that seeks out humans to possess."

"Why, though? What does it get from this possession? Does it just want a physical body?" Stone turned a little toward Lamar and paled again. He seemed frustrated with the limitations of his own physical body right now—Jason could tell his mind was trying to go a mile a minute, but his body was failing him.

Marilee pushed him gently back down. "It seems to want—emotions."

Stone looked startled. "Emotions?"

"Strong ones," Lamar clarified. "And particularly strong negative ones. It seems to feed best off of despair, depression, anger, fear—"

"—so that's what it tries to cause," Marilee finished. "It wants to cause trouble, to make people scared or unhappy because it seems to grow stronger when it's near that."

"Wait a minute—" Jason said, leaning forward. "You're saying it—gets off on this negative emotion?"

Lamar nodded. "Yes. That's what we think, at least, and so far everything we've seen has supported it."

"Verity said she heard you talking about—levels—of this Evil. She said she wasn't sure what you meant, and that we should ask you about it."

"That much we do know," Lamar said. "Just as the power levels of our abilities vary, the power levels of the Evil vary as well. We think there are one or two very powerful ones that direct activities in this entire area, with lesser minions doing their bidding."

"Do you know where it is? Is it possessing somebody too?" Jason asked.

"Is it possible for these things to act independently of a host body?" Stone added. His voice was taking on more power now—clearly this whole business had piqued his not inconsiderable curiosity, and he was doing his best to fight his exhaustion to find out as much as he could.

Lamar and Marilee were looking a little overwhelmed under their two-pronged onslaught of questions, but they did their best to keep up. "We don't think they can operate without bodies," Lamar said. "You understand this is all based on observation, and not just from our own group. The various Forgotten groups compare notes when they encounter each other, but as you well know, we all—have our limitations. So some of the stories might be nothing more than the fanciful guesses of a disturbed mind."

Stone nodded with a "go on" gesture.

Lamar shrugged. "Like I said, we don't think they can operate without a body. What we think is that the more powerful the Evil, the longer it can exist without one. We're not sure if it's even possible for the weakest ones to find another body once the one they're in is destroyed. But the strong ones—they might be able to go awhile. Days, or maybe longer. But they can't do anything when they don't have one."

"Where do they go if they can't find a body? Are they destroyed?"

Marilee looked rueful. "We don't know. We're not even sure if it's different depending on how powerful they are. Maybe the weak ones just go poof, and the strong ones go back to wherever they came from. Or maybe they all just die if they don't."

"How do you get them out of a body? Do you have to kill the body?"

Lamar nodded. "Yes. Knocking them unconscious isn't enough to do it, at least as far as we've seen. Some of us are able to see them leaving a body when it's killed. In fact, we think that the more powerful Evil sometimes uses the weak ones as pawns—they send them off to do something suicidal, like walk in front of a train, just to generate the strong emotions that the rest of them need to thrive."

"Or maybe to draw out its enemies," Marilee added.

"What about what Verity can do?" Jason asked.

All three of the others looked at him oddly. "What can Verity do?" Lamar asked.

"Oh, that's right, she didn't tell you. But she said — she can make them leave."

"What?" Lamar's eyes were wide.

Jason nodded. "She said she's done it twice now — once at the halfway house, and once tonight, when one of those gangers was attacking me. She said she can't control it — it just...happens."

"She can make the Evil leave its host body without killing it?" The old man was staring at him now, and so was Marilee.

"That's what she said." Jason looked back and forth between them. "I take it — that's odd?"

"I've never even heard of anyone who can do it," Lamar told him.

"Bloody hell, I'm an idiot," Stone said, looking disgusted.

"Huh?" Jason turned back to him, confused. "Why?"

"That's it. You told me about it before. It was all right there in front of me, and it went right over my head."

"Told you about—"

"—about your sister's encounter with the man in the basement. How she drove the spirit out of him by 'pushing' with her mind."

"Yeah, and — ?"

Stone sighed. "Don't you see? All of these people — they have these abilities with regard to the Evil. They can hide from it, detect it, do useful things that help them stay one step ahead of it. But none of the Forgotten seem to be able to *fight* it. Until now."

When Jason still looked confused, Stone fixed him with a withering stare. "Honestly, Jason, I'm the one who's supposed to be operating at diminished capacity right now. Let me spell it out for you: your sister can fight them. She can destroy them. Therefore, she's a threat."

"But she can't control it," Jason protested.

"But she has the *potential* to be able to control it," Stone reminded him. "And if she does ever get that ability under control, she actually represents several kinds of threats."

"How so? I get that she can drive them out, but—"

Stone took a deep breath. "Look around you. Look at these people. No offense intended," he added, glancing at Lamar and Marilee. "But they're disaffected. They're marginalized. Most of them have mental issues that make them difficult for the general public to deal with. They have very little contact, by choice, with the authorities. I'm correct, aren't I?" he asked Lamar.

The old man nodded. "You are, yes. We avoid the authorities. The police and other similar agencies are prime hunting grounds for the Evil. They prefer to possess people in authority when they can, because that allows them to get away with causing more trouble without being caught."

Stone nodded. "Exactly. So the fact that the Forgotten know about the Evil make them a threat, but not a large one. Certainly it sounds like they would like nothing better than to be rid of you, but they don't consider you an imminent threat because you can't tell anyone about them. No one would believe you. You've no way to prove it, and it sounds so farfetched that it comes out like the ravings of a deranged mind."

"You're right," Marilee said, nodding sadly. "Every once in awhile one of the younger or more idealistic Forgotten tries to tell someone about what's happening, but it never works. We talk to each other—we know. Eventually we just stopped trying, and we concentrate on our own safety and dealing with the Evil when we're forced to."

"Right," Stone said. He struggled up to a slightly more seated position, and Jason stuffed a couple more tattered pillows under him to help. "But Verity—though she is by all appearances one of the Forgotten, she's not only lucid, but she's got friends who *will* believe her about the Evil—and who have the capacity to do something about them. Jason here presumably still has contacts in the law enforcement community, and I, as they say, have quite a lot of experience with believing six impossible things before breakfast. So suddenly instead of a bunch of mentally unhinged homeless people, they're dealing with a young girl who has the capacity to destroy them one at a time, her highly motivated brother, and a fully trained mage. That's going to tip their odds in a direction they aren't going to like one bit." Exhausted from getting all that out, Stone sank back, going pale again.

Jason was finally catching on. "So—" he said, "That's why they were after her—and after us! They didn't want us all to meet up, because as long as they kept us separated—or better yet, made sure we were dead—then all they'd have to deal with would be the mage and the brother who were confused as hell about what was going on, and the girl who didn't have any support system."

"Gold star for the man with the leather jacket," Stone said faintly, nodding.

"But the question is, how did they know all of this?" Jason asked.

"I have a theory about that," Stone said. "It's conjecture, but it fits."

"Do tell."

"Remember the story you said Verity told about driving the Evil out of the man in the basement?"

"Yeah."

"I don't think that one was destroyed. Lamar here said that the Forgotten think that the more powerful Evil can survive outside a host body for a longer time—perhaps even days. I think the man Verity found in the basement was not one of the minions, but one of the more powerful version. If it was able to escape and find itself a new host body while retaining its knowledge of what went before, then it would have very good reason to want to track her down."

"That makes sense," Jason admitted. "It even fits—if it took it awhile to find another body, then it couldn't be tracking V. That would have given her time to get away, and by the time it found one, she'd disappeared and hooked up with the Forgotten, who could hide her."

"Exactly," Stone said, nodding.

"But—" Jason's eyes widened. "That still doesn't answer another question."

"And what's that?"

"Remember what Verity said she found the guy doing? Draining that kid for power like that ganger did the night Charles died. But I thought you said that was something mages did. Black mages. Not this—Evil thing."

Stone just stared at Jason for several long silent seconds. "Bloody hell..." he whispered.

"What?"

Stone raised up on his elbow again, heedless of what the exertion was doing to him. "Jason—you're right. You're—right. And that changes everything."

Jason didn't even think Stone was aware that Lamar and Marilee were there any longer. "I—I don't get it. Why?"

"Because," Stone said as if talking to a slow toddler, "It means that these things can co-exist with mages. It means they can possess us. Do you realize what kind of danger that could represent?" He turned his laserlike gaze on

Lamar. "When the Evil possess people—does it submerge their personality?"

"I—I don't think so," he said. "Not entirely, anyway."

"And how do you come to this conclusion?"

"We believe it's that way because we don't know where these things came from, but they're obviously alien. And we've seen that they prefer people in positions of power. They would never be able to perform the sorts of jobs that they do—we think some of the stronger ones have possessed high-level police administrators, politicians, businessmen—with nothing but their own knowledge."

"They couldn't pass," Stone said, nodding. His arm was shaking, but he didn't even seem to notice it. "They can't go to work every day and convince their colleagues that they're police captains or senators or what have you without the knowledge and memories of the actual person making a contribution—willing or otherwise."

"So are you saying," Jason put in, "that they *allow* these things to possess them? That's pretty farfetched."

"I agree," Lamar said. "I don't think they *allow* it, exactly. But I do think, and others agree with me, that some people are more receptive to them than others are."

"What kind of people?"

The old man shrugged. "People who might be more willing to do the kinds of things that the Evil want them to do. I think they seek out those kinds of people."

"So-called 'evil' people," Stone said. "Or at the very least, people whose moral compasses are a bit more shaky than the average citizen's."

"So you think black mages would be more receptive because they don't mind causing pain?" Jason asked.

"Hard to say," Stone said, finally allowing himself to sink back down again. "Mages in general have very strong minds—we're trained for it from the time we're apprentices. It's very difficult to compel us to do anything against our will. I'm not sure what this Evil could offer a mage that would make him or her willing to let it in. Mental possession—" he shivered a bit "—to have one's mind taken over by another being—that's something I can't imagine any mage would ever allow. So either it's an isolated incident and somehow they got through to an individual mage, or I'm incorrect and there's more going on here than I've begun to understand."

"Or some of them are powerful enough that they can force their way in without permission," Jason suggested.

"Or that," Stone agreed.

Jason could see that despite his best efforts to continue with the discussion, the mage's strength was failing. "Listen," he said, "You look like you could use a good night's sleep. Why don't we clear out of here and let you rest, and we can talk about this some more in the morning."

His suspicions were confirmed when Stone nodded without protest. "I hate to admit it, but you're right. You could probably do with a bit yourself."

"Yeah, probably. I think I'll go talk to V some more, and then find a place to catch a few hours at least." He nodded to Lamar and Marilee as he got up.

The two of them got slowly to their feet as well. Marilee smiled down at the kitten who was still snuggled up next to Stone. "She can stay with you if you like. I think she likes you more than she likes me."

Stone didn't answer; his eyes were already closed. Jason exited the tent and waited for the two old Forgotten to follow him. "He's gonna be okay, right? I don't need to take him to a hospital or anything?"

Lamar shook his head. "He should be fine. He's just tired from the magical exertion and the blood loss."

"What about my sister? She was saying that somebody here was keeping her from—having her crazy thing. If she leaves here she'll go back to the way she was, won't she?"

"I fear so," the old man told him. "As I told Dr. Stone, we have no idea what causes these symptoms. There just seem to be some people who are susceptible to them, and your sister seems to be one of them. Unless we can somehow cut off the source of the symptoms rather than simply blocking it, then leaving the one who can do the blocking will have predictable results."

Jason looked him up and down. "Can I ask you something?"

"Of course."

"Don't take this wrong—you know I'm grateful for what you did for Al, and I'm sure he is too. But—you don't seem like the rest of the people here."

"What do you mean?"

"You look like them," he said, taking in Lamar's thin stooped frame, ragged clothes, and unshaven face. "But you don't act like them. What were you before you were—here?"

Lamar smiled gently. "I was a doctor, a long time ago."

"Seriously?"

He nodded. "A good one, too. But I had some issues in my life, and my various coping mechanisms became addictions that I could never completely recover from." He patted Jason on the arm. "I like it here, Mr. Thayer. I can take care of people, but the pressure that drove me away from my 'good life' doesn't exist here."

"Just having to wonder where your next meal is coming from, and being stalked by some weird disembodied alien bodysnatcher who wants to kill you because you know too much."

Lamar chuckled. "Yes, there's that. But we have each other, and we've adapted. The Forgotten are very resilient. We have to be—we're all each other have. The rest of the world pretty much ignores us—hence the name we've chosen for ourselves."

Jason nodded, realizing uncomfortably how much truth there was to the old man's words. How many times had he himself walked right by homeless people without even noticing them? It was just too much trouble to stop and talk to them, to give them some change—to even recognize their humanity. "Why—do you stay out here? There are places you can go—shelters—"

"No, that's not possible." Lamar gave him the kind of look you give a beloved small child who had just made an amusing grammatical error. "Don't you remember—the Evil are hunting us. They want as many of us dead as they can manage. Wouldn't you think homeless shelters would be the best place for them to hunt?"

"I—guess I didn't think of that," Jason mumbled.

Lamar smiled. "Don't worry about it, Mr. Thayer."

"Jason."

"Jason, then. You needn't worry about us, really. We do what we can to survive. It's best to just avoid them, since none of us enjoy the alternative. Perhaps if we can find more of us who have your sister's gift, we'll never have to kill anyone again."

"You actually care about killing them?"

"Of course we do. Not the Evil, of course. If I could kill every last one of those things by saying the word, I'd do it in an instant. But the people they possess—they're just people like you or me. Maybe they've made some bad choices in their lives, but that doesn't give us the right to pass final judgment on them."

Jason nodded. He supposed that was right. He'd never been a religious man, but his instincts were to protect people, not to kill them. Even homicidal gangers deserved trials, or society would degenerate even further than it already had.

Again, Lamar patted his arm. "Go find your sister, Jason. Get some sleep."

"Yeah, I should do that. I'll see you in the morning."

Lamar moved off back toward the fire, and Jason went in search of Verity. By now most of the Forgotten were asleep, huddled around the two fires or wrapped in heavy old blankets. He thought he spotted Frank the Scribbler a distance away, but he didn't move over to check.

"Hey, Jason—over here." He looked up and saw Verity still sitting leaned against the same tree where he'd left her. Hurrying over, he sat down across from her. "So, is your friend okay?"

"Yeah. He'll be fine. I'm just glad you guys had somebody who could help him."

Verity nodded. "Lamar hasn't been here long, but everybody respects him. He's kind of the leader of our little group, and sometimes he helps out settling disputes when other groups get together. These guys squabble a lot when everybody gets their different kind of crazy going at once. You ever watch somebody with germophobic OCD trying to deal with somebody who never takes a bath even when they get the chance?"

In spite of himself, Jason chuckled. "It must be interesting to watch."

"I guess it is—I feel bad for some of them, though. There's this one little boy about 9 who never says a word—he just sits and rocks and goes along wherever somebody leads him. He mutters to himself in some kind of weird gibberish language, and seems to get really agitated when the Evil's nearby. They use him kind of like a canary in a coal mine, but up until a day or two ago nobody could talk to him. Then this other guy showed up and seemed to hit it off with the kid right away. He couldn't figure out why nobody else could understand what he was saying."

"Wow," Jason said, shaking his head. "This is all just so—overwhelming. A few days ago I was back home playing poker and getting in bar fights, and now look at me. My crazy sister's a magic bum, my new friend is a mage who moonlights as a college professor and travels by teleport gateway, I've seen more people get killed than I have the whole rest of my life, and I've found out some weird spirit things from Dimension X are out to take us all over and make us miserable so it can get its jollies." He shrugged, flashing her a lopsided grin. "What's next? Talking cats? We're all just living in somebody's fishbowl? I wake up to find out this was all the world's most elaborate dream?"

Verity chuckled. "Don't call us 'magic bums,' Jason. That's not cool."

"Sorry. Just—realizing how freaked out I really am, and how much I've had to keep hold of it so I don't just start running around like I'm as crazy as some of these folks are."

"Think of how *I* feel," she reminded him. "Meeting Susanna—having her be able to block whatever it is that was causing me to have problems—it was like coming up from being underwater. I know you don't know it or realize it, but there were lots of times during the last five years when I was perfectly okay. It was weird—it was like waking up from a dream, having no idea where I was or what I was doing, and knowing that there was nothing I could do to prevent it happening again. You know how hard that is? There toward the end it got better—I'm glad, or I never would have gotten out of that place alive. I hope you're not mad at me for all those times I yelled and screamed. I hope Dad wasn't."

"You know — Dad's gone, right?" Jason asked gently.

She nodded, her eyes sparkling a bit with unshed tears. "Yeah, I know. They told me once, during one of my lucid periods." She looked up at him. "Jason, what are you going to do now?"

The question startled him. "What do you mean?"

"Well, tomorrow you're going to wake up, and your friend's going to wake up, and there's no reason at all why you need to stay here. You have lives, jobs, things to do. You're not crazy — and you won't go crazy if you get away from the people who are keeping you sane. So what will you do?"

For a long time he didn't answer. "I don't know," he said at last. "I don't know what I *can* do. I don't want to leave you here, but it sounds like you don't want to go."

"I *can't* go," she said. "I want to go home with you — or maybe just get a place around here and start having a normal life. But until we figure out why I'm like I am, I can't do it." She sighed. "I like these people a lot, but — I can't help feeling that I've given up one prison for another one, you know?"

Jason nodded. "Yeah, I can see that. I'll think about it — see if I can come up with anything. Or maybe Al can. He's good with that kind of thing. I'll ask him tomorrow."

"How did you meet him, anyway?" she asked. "You two don't exactly seem like you run in the same circles."

Should I tell her? Will it just make things more complicated? But as usual, he knew the answer. "V...he...he knew Mom."

"What?" Her eyes went wide. "How could he — "

"Long story. I'll tell you the whole thing later. The meeting was kind of a coincidence, but after he found out who I was, that's why he agreed to help me. To help us," he added, nodding toward her.

R. L. KING

"This I gotta hear," she agreed. "But you're right—tomorrow, unless you're planning on leaving right away. You really should get some sleep. You look tired."

"We're not going anywhere for awhile. Too much we still need to talk about with these guys. They seem to have the other piece of the puzzle we've been trying to solve, which means I won't be able to pry Al away with a crowbar. Maybe between us all we can come up with something." He dragged himself to his feet. "Where do you sleep, anyway?"

"There's a tent on the other side of the fire. I share it with Susanna and Lissy."

Jason remembered the spacey girl from the library, and nodded. "Okay. I'll see you in the morning. And V?"

"Yeah?"

Impulsively, he pulled her into a hard quick hug. "It's good to have you back."

She kissed his cheek. "Yeah. It's good to be back. Thanks for not giving up on me."

23.

Jason didn't sleep that well; the ground was hard and his mind was too busy to let him get much rest. That, and he still wasn't convinced that the DMW weren't going to show up and kill them all while they slept. That didn't happen—he wasn't sure if it was because one or more of the Forgotten were masking them from view or if the gang had simply decided to call it a night and lick their wounds. Either way, by the time the filtered light of the sunrise woke him up he'd only gotten about three hours of sleep. He was surprised when he sat up to discover that some of the Forgotten were already awake, including Marilee. The old lady was cooking something in a pot over the near fire, occasionally seasoning it with various things she pulled from the bags hanging off her shopping cart. "Morning," Jason said, coming over.

"Oh, good morning. I didn't expect you to be awake yet. Would you like something to eat?" She motioned toward the pot. "I'm making some oatmeal."

"No, thanks. I'm gonna go check on Al."

"I checked on him a little while ago. He's still asleep, but he looks fine. I'd leave him alone until he wakes up, though: he can use all the rest he can get."

"You need help with anything?"

"Oh, no, I'm fine. But thanks for asking."

He wished she did have something for him to do, since he hadn't brought any of his gear and he didn't feel comfortable wandering off. He was lucky, though: apparently these people weren't much for sleeping in. By the time the sun was up so were most of them, gathering their things and rolling up their bedrolls. Some of them filtered off in groups of two or three; Jason didn't ask where they were going. He figured by that time it was safe to go check on Stone, though, and then he'd go find Verity.

The mage was awake when Jason poked his head through the tent flap. He did look better—still tired but not nearly as pale as he had last night. The black kitten was still curled up next to him, fast asleep. "I was wondering when you were going to show up," he said, a little irritably.

"Sorry. Marilee said you weren't awake yet and I shouldn't bother you."

"Just woke up a bit ago."

"How do you feel?"

"Still ghastly. My back hurts from sleeping on the ground, I'm starving, and I'd like very much to get out of this tent but I'm not sure whether I should chance it yet."

"Why don't I bring you something to eat? Marilee's making oatmeal. Then we can talk for a bit and figure out what we want to do next."

"Excellent idea."

Jason got up and went back outside. He'd collected a largish bowl of oatmeal and a plastic spoon from Marilee and was heading back to the tent when Verity intercepted him. "Morning," she said, falling into step. "Where you going?"

"Taking this to Al," he said, indicating the bowl.

"Ah. Can I come with you? I want to talk to you guys some more."

"Uh, sure."

Soon they were back inside the tent, seated on either side of Stone's makeshift bed. He accepted the oatmeal gratefully and made a tentative attempt to prop himself up to a mostly sitting position. He evaluated that for a few seconds, then nodded and began eating.

"So..." Jason said. "Verity wants to know what we're planning to do. She can't leave here because she'll lose it again if she gets away from Susanna, but we can't stay here forever."

"No," Stone said, "we can't." He looked at Verity. "Pleasure to meet you, by the way. Forgive my lack of manners." He set the bowl and spoon carefully down and offered her his hand. "Alastair Stone. And I've heard a great deal about you."

Verity shook his hand, looking amused. "I've heard quite a bit about you too, last night," she told him.

"All of it lies, I'm sure," Stone said with a raised eyebrow. "So — Jason here tells me that this lucidity you're enjoying at present is as a result of some sort of power that one of these people has to block out whatever is causing your mental issues."

Verity nodded. "Susanna. She can do that, sometimes. I'm not sure it's not permanent because I'm afraid to get too far away from her and find out, but she says I'll probably go back to the way I was if I do."

"I see. I wonder if there might be something I can do about that."

"What do you mean?"

Stone shrugged. "I'm not certain unless I examine you, but I have some expertise with this sort of thing. There's a chance that I might be able to put a more permanent block in place."

Her eyes widened, her expression warring between hope and cynicism. "You can do that?" she asked, leaning forward.

"As I said, I don't know. And I'm not really in a position to check now. But it's possible. I'm assuming that you don't really want to remain here."

"No. It's like I was telling Jason last night — I'm really grateful for what these people have done for me. I wouldn't be alive if they hadn't taken me in and hidden me from those gangers. But — " she sighed. "I don't want to spend the rest of my life in a homeless camp because that's the only way I can avoid going back to the halfway house — or somewhere worse, once I'm 18."

"Quite understandable," Stone said, nodding. Then he looked at Jason. "We need to figure out our next move."

"Do we even *have* a next move? I mean — we've found V. That's what we were trying to do. If you can do something that will block the crazy rays so she won't go right back to the way she was before, then — that's it, isn't it? She can come home with me, or — " he shrugged " — I don't really have much dragging me back down to Ventura. If she'd rather stay up here, I can find odd jobs here as easily as I could there."

"Well," Stone mused, "It *can* be it, if you want it to. It's up to you."

Jason cocked his head like a confused dog. "I don't get it. What else would there be?"

"We could go after it at its source."

"What?" He stared. "Al, are *you* getting hit by the crazy rays? We don't even know what the source *is*. Even if we wanted to, how would we find it?"

"I think he's right," Verity said suddenly.

Jason swung around to face her. "What? Why? I'd think you'd have had your fill of whatever these things are by now."

She spread her hands in an encompassing gesture. "Look around you. All these people are always scared, always hiding, because whatever this thing is, it's looking for them. It wants to kill them. They don't really have any way to stop it."

"And you think we do?"

She looked at Stone. "I don't know. Do we?"

"No idea," the mage said, but the wheels in his mind were obviously turning. "It would take a fair bit of research. Not only to figure out where the one in charge is — assuming that Lamar and the others are correct and there even *is* one in charge — but in order to go on the offensive against such a thing we'd need to prepare."

Jason sighed. Clearly his friend and his sister hadn't realized that it was safe to step *out* of the Twilight Zone now and come back to the real world. "Can we talk about this later? I think right now our priority is getting V straightened out so she can leave, then getting back to civilization. And a shower," he added, sniffing at his leather jacket and wrinkling his nose in distaste.

Verity glared at him. "Don't you get it, Jason? You're part of the problem. You use words like 'civilization' — the Forgotten are plenty civilized. Just because some of them are a little strange and they have to live like this doesn't make them any less human."

"You're quite right," Stone said softly. "This past night has been quite an eye-opener for me. It fascinates me that this whole subculture — this whole *society* — has existed right under our noses, and I never noticed it. I don't think anybody has."

"And you," she said, turning her glare on Stone, "You sound like you just want to *study* them. They're not some kind of — science experiment. They're *people.* Believe me, I spent enough time like them to know. Do you know how much it sucks to have people ignore you, or be scared of you, because you don't act 'normal'? What *is* normal, anyway?"

Stone raised his hands to ward off her words. "Calm down," he said. "I make no secret of the fact that, yes, I would like to know more about this society — and especially about these unusual powers many of them possess. As a mage, that interests me professionally. But in case you've forgotten, they've also saved my life. I owe them something for that. If there's anything I can do to help rid them — and the rest of us, as it happens — of this threat, I'm willing to do what I can."

R. L. KING

Verity turned back to Jason. "Jason? What about you?"

He shrugged, looking resigned. "Looks like I'm outvoted, so I guess I'm in. But I still don't think this is a great idea." He paused a moment, and then: "So what now?"

"Now," Stone said, "You hand me my shirt and help me up. I think I'm feeling brave enough to venture out, and we need to discuss some things with the Forgotten."

Jason did as requested, helping the mage shrug into his shirt and overcoat. The kitten, unceremoniously evicted from her warm sleeping spot, mewed a protest and began looking for new one. Verity scooped her up. "I'll take her back to Marilee," she said. "You guys come out when you're ready."

Stone, once Jason hauled him up to his feet, was alarmingly unsteady at first. His face paled and he looked like he was going to keel right back over any second, but things seemed to improve the longer he remained upright. "You gonna make it?" Jason asked, concerned and hovering nearby ready to grab him.

"I think so," he said. "As I said before—nothing hurts except my stiff back, which is hardly short of amazing. Just feeling a bit dizzy."

Jason nodded. "We need to get you more to eat than a bowl of oatmeal." His stomach rumbled sympathetically at the thought. "And me too, it sounds like."

The camp was fully awake now, split between people sitting around eating and those who were continuing to clean up the area: striking tents, putting out fires, gathering trash. They found Lamar sitting under his favorite tree with Verity and a couple of other Forgotten that they didn't recognize. "You guys look like you're getting ready to leave," Jason said, helping Stone sit down and then doing so himself.

Lamar nodded. "We are. We can't afford to remain in the same place for too long. Our concealment abilities are not foolproof, so we like to move around every few days at least."

"Where are you going?"

"One of our scouts found an abandoned building in Mountain View. We'll probably head there. We prefer buildings to open parks — they're more defensible, and obviously warmer this time of year."

"How do you guys — operate?" Jason asked. "How do you get food, move around — it seems like you're pretty mobile."

Lamar shrugged. "We do what we can do. Sometimes we take the bus, though for obvious reasons we can't do that as a large group so it can be dangerous. Some of us do odd jobs to earn money, some beg, and some know the places to go where they can find things that others have discarded. There are people who help us — sympathetic restaurant owners and such. Sometimes we'll deal with charities that we know to be safe — there are a few around here, including that old talk-show host Gordon Lucas's events when they come around — they're one of the few outfits where we've never sensed any Evil involvement. Forgotten groups don't really have any formal organization, but generally each small group takes care of its own — pooling resources, using our talents to help us when we can."

"How many groups are there around here?"

"No way to know, really. We cross paths occasionally and compare notes. Aside from our symbols — I believe Verity has told you about them — that's the only way we have to communicate with each other. Sometimes we leave notes in specific places in public buildings -- libraries are popular, naturally."

"And you pretty much stay in this general area?"

"As much as we can. Sometimes a group is forced to move completely out of its area, but that's quite a drastic choice and not made lightly. Our group moves around from a little north of Palo Alto to the south part of San Jose. It's safer when we know the area, the safe places, the places to avoid."

Stone, who'd been silent thus far, nodded and then said, "May I ask you a few questions?"

"Of course. You're looking much better this morning, by the way. I'm glad."

"Thank you — and thanks to you," the mage said. "You said before that you believe that there are 'levels' of Evil. That there are more powerful ones directing the activities of lower-level ones."

Lamar nodded. "Yes."

"Do you have any idea how this hierarchy works? Is it a formal structure? Do they literally report up a chain of command? Or is it a more informal thing, where the powerful entities have an agenda and they communicate it to their minions and leave it up to the minions to implement it?"

"I don't know that, Dr. Stone," Lamar said. "I don't think any of us have any desire to get close enough to the more powerful Evil to be able to figure that out. If I had to make an educated guess, I'd say that the powerful ones confine their influence to more high-level issues — trying to infiltrate government, business, law enforcement — while the lower ones are more concerned with simple mayhem to feed their need for emotion."

"So —" Stone appeared to be working things out as he went on " — the more powerful entities can gain their sustenance by more abstract methods?"

"I'm not sure I understand what you mean."

"I mean, if what you say is true then whatever they seek, or need, can be supplied in different ways. The weaker ones cause mayhem and misery to individuals or small groups and then drink it up, while the more powerful ones incite their mayhem on a more subtle but larger scale. Perhaps it's an issue of concentration—if you're causing pain in one person you need to cause a great deal of it to get the same effect as you would from causing a large number of people a smaller amount of pain." He shook his head as if clearing it. "I'm just tossing out ideas now—I'm likely completely off track."

"It's as good a theory as any," Lamar admitted. "As I said, we don't really have any way to check, even if that were something that we wanted to do. Generally any of us who come into contact with the Evil's higher echelons don't come back to tell the tale."

"Let's leave that for a moment, then," Stone said. "Do these—Evil—have any powers? Do they have abilities like the Forgotten's, or like a mage's? Or is their power simply derived from the person they choose to possess? For example, if they possess a ganger then they would acquire his strength, his knowledge of the streets, and so forth, while if one possessed a police chief, its power would be largely in the chief's influence and his ability to direct the actions of numerous other people."

Lamar thought about that for a couple of minutes, staring off into nothingness in a way that reminded Jason very much of Stone in one of his contemplative moods. "I don't think I've ever heard of them exhibiting any abilities beyond what they get from possessing someone," he said at last.

"Unless they possess a mage," Jason reminded them. "And we know they can do that."

"We know they've done that once," Stone corrected. "As I told you before, I doubt there are many mages who would allow it."

"And like *I* said, maybe they don't have a choice," Jason said stubbornly. "And anyway, it's not once—it's twice. That we know of."

Stone raised an eyebrow. "Twice?"

"Yeah. Don't you remember the DMW ganger who torched that kid to kill Charles? You said that there were a few minor talents in DMW."

"I did, but there's no proof that the ganger was possessed—or even that the majority of DMW are possessed." He gave Lamar a questioning look.

"We don't think they are," Lamar confirmed. "I wasn't aware that there were mages in the gang—if there are, there aren't many. But if there were enough Evil around to possess every member of the DMW along with all the others we've encountered—" he shuddered. "I doubt any of the Forgotten would still be alive."

Marilee came over along with Lissy, who was humming to herself. "Mind if we join you?" the old lady asked. When Lamar waved her to a seat, both of them settled down next to the tree.

Stone nodded politely to them but kept going. "Which brings up another question—do they reproduce?"

Marilee's eyes widened. "The Evil?"

"Dr. Stone has many questions about the Evil," Lamar told her. "I'm trying to answer them as best I can." To Stone he said, "That's another question we don't know anything about. Given that they essentially showed up five years ago, we have no idea where they came from, or whether more are able to come from that place. Nor do we have any idea if they're reproducing."

Stone nodded. "It rather makes sense that they do—as sinister as they are, from what I understand they operate like any other living entity: they seek out sustenance and they seek to further their own agenda. It only makes sense that they have some way to reproduce, even if it's simply to split themselves in two."

"I never thought about that," Lamar said. "I guess we've got enough to worry about with the ones that are already here, without thinking about them producing more." He tilted his head. "Do you mind if I ask *you* a question, Dr. Stone?"

"Not at all. And please, call me Alastair."

Lamar nodded. "Why are you so interested in the inner workings of the Evil? I understand that as a mage, curiosity is unavoidable, and this kind of phenomenon must be very interesting to you. But I sense that there's more to it than that."

Lissy, unnoticed until now, giggled. "Magic man wants to kill 'em," she said matter-of-factly, waving a long blade of grass for Marilee's kitten to bat at.

Lamar and Marilee both stared at him as that sunk in. "Is that true?" the old man asked in a near-whisper. He had a very strange expression: not quite fear and not quite hope.

Stone looked troubled. "I don't know. The thought had crossed my mind — that if we can track down the ones in charge, p'raps if we can destroy them, or at least force them to go back to wherever they came from, it might put the rest of them into such disarray that they'd be a reduced threat and easier to deal with individually. But there are many problems with this approach. For example, we don't know where these so-called leaders keep themselves. And if driving the Evil out of a person requires killing that person, then what I'm proposing essentially amounts to mass murder. I'm not really up for that, I'm afraid."

"But it doesn't," Verity reminded him. "Remember — I can drive them out without killing the person."

"True," Stone said. "But you've said yourself that you have no conscious control over your ability. And you're only one person. Lamar here says he's never heard of anyone else having your ability. Even if you were willing to do it, the danger would be immense."

Verity shrugged. "I don't care about danger. I'm pissed at these things for taking away a third of my life. If there's a way to kick their asses, I'm in."

Jason started to say something, then got a look at his sister's face and decided not to.

Stone sighed. "Well, in any case, it's not something we could do overnight, even if we decided to give it a go. It will require thought and planning—and probably more than a bit of help on the part of the Forgotten, if they're willing. I don't see any way this can work unless we can identify where the leader—at least the one who's taken over our area—is located, and I don't see how Jason or I would be much help there." He looked at Lamar. "Your group—the other groups you talk to—you see things. You hear things. You communicate with each other. That's what we would need. But perhaps you don't even want to get involved, and I certainly don't blame you. It could be dangerous for you as well, and I wouldn't want to put you and your people in danger." When Lamar started to say something, he held up his hand. "Please. Don't make any decisions now. I'm not going to either. Just—talk it over with your group, and any others you happen to encounter in your travels. If you all decide you're willing, then I'll do what I can to help you."

"Me too," Verity said, nodding. She looked at Jason.

He took a deep breath. After a long pause, he nodded. "Back to the Twilight Zone," he muttered, just loudly enough for Stone to hear.

"Good," Stone said briskly. "Now, then. I'm going to have to head back home for awhile, and I think Jason wants to come along as well. The question is, will it be safe to bring Verity along with us, if we get her back to Susanna's care by tonight when you've arrived at your new location?"

"I think it'll be okay," Verity said. "A couple of days ago she left for a few hours and I was fine. I could feel something trying to touch my mind a couple of times, but I think it has to—I don't know—kind of build up a bit before it really takes hold."

"A few hours should be plenty of time," Stone said. Slowly and carefully he got up, and made a little bow to Lamar. "Thank you again, my good sir, for all you've done for me—for all of us. Believe me, although there's no way I can adequately repay you for saving my life, I'll do my best to help you if we decide to go through with this mad plan."

Lissy giggled again. "He talks funny," she announced.

Jason and Verity got up too. "Yeah," Jason said. "Thanks for everything. I don't even want to think about what might have happened to V out there on the streets if she hadn't found you guys."

Verity went over and gave Lamar a hug, then Marilee. "You guys rock," she said. "We'll be back. I promise. If they try to keep me away, I'll sneak out and hitchhike." She looked back at Jason and Stone. "I'm gonna go get my stuff and say goodbye to the others, and tell Susanna I'll be back soon."

Jason and Stone waited for her to return, getting the group's proposed new location and directions from Lamar. "We'll be back later today," Stone told him. "Just need to take care of a few loose ends and see if p'raps I can't do something a bit more permanent to help Verity."

"So she doesn't have to stay," Marilee said a little sadly. When Stone started to speak up, she shook her head. "No, don't worry about it. Of course she shouldn't have to stay here. This is no life for a young girl—or anyone—if they have any other choice. Maybe if your plan— whatever it turns out to be—works out, then some of the others of us will be able to go back to their 'other' lives." She sounded very wistful.

Stone leaned down and patted her shoulder. "We'll do what we can to help you all." He raised an eyebrow toward the kitten, who was now playing with the hem of Lissy's dress. "After all, I've taken a liking to that little one there. I can't let anything happen to her friends."

Verity was coming back across the camp now, carrying a small backpack. "Okay," she said, "I'm ready. Susanna says she thinks I'll be okay for six or eight hours."

"Well, then, we'd best get moving," Stone said.

24.

Amazingly, the Ford was still where they'd left it, and as far as any of them could tell nobody had messed with it or was currently watching it. Stone held his breath and let it out in a rush of relief as he opened the trunk and discovered that the leatherbound book was still there, safely stored in its briefcase. "I'm glad I was too out of it to think about this last night," he said. "I would have been frantic worrying about it." Leaving it where it was, he climbed into the passenger seat and motioned for Jason to drive.

Verity got in the back. "Nice ride," she told Jason, grinning. "Very attractive. Never thought I'd see you in something with four wheels. Especially something that old ladies would turn down for being too uncool."

"Yeah, well, Al doesn't like to ride on the back of my bike," he told her. "That, and the DMW blew it up." He turned to Stone. "Where are we going?"

"Back to Palo Alto," he said. "Ideally I'd like to stop at the nearest restaurant and order one of everything on the menu, but given how we look—and doubtless smell—I think a stop at home for showers all around should be our first destination. Then I want to go to my bank and put that—" he hooked his thumb over his shoulder toward the trunk "—in my safe deposit box. Then food."

It took them a little over an hour to get back to their temporary home near campus, take showers, change clothes and take the book to the bank. They did most of this in comparative silence, each of them content for awhile to just sit back and catch up with his or her own thoughts. It was only after they were all seated around a table in the back of a little diner off El Camino and polishing off pancakes, eggs, and the rest of the large late breakfast they'd ordered that they started to discuss their plans. "So," Jason said around a large mouthful of sausage, "You're saying that you might be able to help V with her problem."

"I might," Stone said. "Once we get back to the house I'll see. I don't really understand how these Forgotten powers work — they've got to be some sort of magic, but as I said before, it's no type I've ever seen. Nor do I understand the way the Evil — or whatever it is that's causing these widespread issues — operates. So it might take a bit of effort to figure out how to block it."

"I hope you can do it," Verity said. She looked like she was hardly daring to hope that it might be possible. "I want my life back."

"Too bad she's not a mage too," Jason said offhand, offloading more eggs onto his plate. "You have to admit, it would make things easier."

Verity rolled her eyes at him. "Yeah, and while I'm at it, I've always wanted a unicorn." She started to laugh, then caught a glimpse at the way Stone was suddenly looking at her. "Uh — why are you staring at me like that?"

At Jason's words, Stone had stiffened in his chair, fixing his probing gaze on Verity. "Al?" Jason was looking at the mage now too. "Did I say something wrong?"

"I'm a fool," Stone whispered, looking disgusted with himself. "I seem to be making a habit out of that lately."

"What's going on?" Verity demanded.

Stone didn't answer. He continued staring at Verity, unblinking, until she started to shift uncomfortably in her chair. "Jason, tell your friend to stop looking at me like that. It's creepy."

"Al, what the hell is going on?" Jason asked, looking angry.

The mage forced himself to break his gaze away from Verity, shaking his head as if clearing a vision. "I'm not certain," he said. "I'd need to do more checking. Finish up—we need to get back home." There was a certain urgency in his tone now.

"Is something wrong?" Verity asked, looking back and forth between them.

"Al, damn it, stop being cryptic!" Jason's voice raised a little now, causing an elderly couple two tables down to glance over at them nervously.

Stone fixed his focus on Jason. "I didn't tell you something before," he said evenly. It was very clear he was trying to keep something tightly under control.

"What?"

"Remember when we were in England and you were asking about my gateway? I told you it was many years old, and that I came from a long line of mages?"

Jason nodded. "Yeah, and—?"

Stone sighed. "Magical talent, my dear boy, is hereditary. It doesn't always show up—I don't think anyone's ever studied the genetics of it, but it's fairly uncommon even if both parents are mages. But it's much more likely to follow the same-sex line, for whatever reason. Fathers tend to produce magical sons—and *mothers tend to produce magical daughters.*" He emphasized those last words, driving them into Jason's brain like bright nails.

Sometimes it took Jason a little while to catch on to things—particularly things in the realm of the strange and unbelievable—but when Stone's words finally sunk in he just sat there, eyes wide, mouth open, looking like somebody had just punched him hard in the soul. "*Oh, holy crap—*"

"*What?*" Verity practically yelled. "Look—I hate to sound like a little kid butting into the grownup conversation here, but it sounds like you two are talking about me. I'd kinda like to be in on the joke."

"I assure you, there's no joke," Stone said. He looked deadly serious.

"V —" Jason turned to face her, forcing himself to be calm. "Al told me before — the reason he agreed to help me find you after we ran into each other. Remember, I told you last night: he knew Mom, a long time ago."

She stared at him, then turned to stare at Stone. "I forgot about that. You really knew our mother?"

Stone nodded. "I did."

"But that's not all he told me —" Jason continued, dragging her attention back to him. "V —He says that Mom — was a mage."

Only the fact that the diner had gotten much busier over the time they'd been there masked the loud clatter of Verity dropping her fork onto her nearly empty plate. "Mom was —?"

Jason patted her shoulder. "It's okay. I understand how you're feeling. I've spent the last few days in a perpetual state of 'what the hell is the *next* weird thing going to be?' You get used to it after awhile, but it's a little hard at first."

Verity looked like she wasn't sure who she should be paying attention to. She darted her eyes back and forth between them and finally settled on Stone. "You're saying that — our mom — was a mage? Like you?"

Again, Stone nodded. "A quite accomplished one, too."

"I — never knew her. She died when I was a baby." She stared down at her plate, then back up again. When she spoke again, she sounded very uncertain. "Am I understanding you right? You said magic can get passed down? And that mothers pass it to daughters, usually?"

"Yes."

"So — there's a chance —?"

"There is. And from the look of my very preliminary once-over, a good one. But I wouldn't be sure until I've had a chance to give you a proper examination."

She cocked her head at him and gave him a sideways look. "Examination?"

"Don't worry. It's quite painless. It mostly involves you sitting in a chair and me running a few tests."

She didn't answer for a long time. Then she said, "And if it's true? If you find out I am one — then what?"

Stone shrugged. "Then it's up to you. Being a mage isn't something you simply wake up one day and discover. Even having the talent doesn't give you the ability to cast spells or perform any other sort of magical rituals. It takes years of study to be any good. I've been at it for over twenty years now and I still have a lot to learn."

"Where — do you study?"

"Generally you apprentice yourself to another mage. As I told Jason before, there are no 'magic schools' per se. But let's not get ahead of ourselves. I don't want to get your hopes up and then find out that you don't have the talent. But I will say this — if it turns out that you do, it will make things somewhat easier on us."

"Why is that?" Jason asked. He was still looking like he was recovering from being gut-punched.

"Because it means I'll be able to teach her to do her own blocking. She won't need to depend on me, or Susanna, or anyone else to keep her mind safe. She'll have control over it on her own."

Verity was getting that 'I'm not even daring to hope' look again. "I — will?" she asked in a near-whisper. "You mean — whatever it is that's messing me up won't be able to do it anymore, and I'll control that?"

"If you have magical talent and apply yourself, yes." Stone motioned to the waitress for the check. "If it turns out that you don't, then I'll do my best to put up the blocks myself. You'll probably have to come back to me to have them renewed every once in awhile, but either way, you should be able to live a normal life."

Verity's shoulders slumped a little and tears shone in her eyes. She swiped them away in frustration. "I can't believe it," she said softly. "Finally, after all this time..."

They paid the check and got out of the diner. Stone walked fast toward the car and seemed to be lost in thought, so Jason hung back to walk with Verity. "Do you really think he can do it?" she asked him.

"I think so," he said. "I've seen him do a lot of fairly amazing things. And some damn weird ones, too. He's an odd guy, but so far everything he's claimed to be able to do, he's done." He reached over to ruffle her hair. "A mage." He shook his head. "That's gonna be pretty freaky if it turns out to be true. It's hard enough having a mage for a friend—now I'm gonna have one for a sister?"

"You'd better treat me right," she said, laughing. "Or I'll turn you into a frog!" Then she got serious. "I don't know, Jason. This is all too weird. Why can't things just be normal, like they used to be when we were back home?"

"I've been asking myself that a lot in the last few days," he admitted. "I think we might be done with normal for awhile, though, so we might as well get used to it."

"Pick up the pace, you two!" Stone called. He'd already reached the car and was waiting impatiently for them to catch up.

"Yes, master," Jason replied in his 'Igor' voice.

"If I end up being a mage and studying with him, I don't have to call him 'Master,' do I?" Verity asked, wrinkling her nose. "'Cause that would be creepy."

"He'll probably make you do his laundry, too," he told her, keeping his face deadpan and ducking as she aimed a punch at his shoulder.

25.

They arrived back at the house and Stone motioned Verity toward a chair in the living room. "We'd best get this sorted now, because it will affect some of the things we do going forward."

Nervously, Verity took the indicated seat. "So — I don't have to do anything?"

"Not a thing," Stone assured her. He pulled up a stool in front of her and sat down on it, facing her and about as close as he'd been to Jason when he'd shielded his mind before they went into the Overworld.

"And it won't hurt? Or feel weird?"

Stone shook his head. "No. And I won't have to touch you in any way, if that concerned you."

She looked relieved, and Jason could see from her expression that it *had* concerned her. "You — uh — want me to clear out?" he asked.

"No need. This won't take long."

Jason nodded and took a seat on the couch. "Uh — Al?"

He didn't look up from what he was doing. "Yes?"

"Is there any chance that I — ?"

He did look away then, facing Jason with a gentle, rueful smile as he shook his head. "I'm sorry, Jason. No. I checked when I did the shielding before our — return trip. You're 100% nonmagical."

Jason sighed, not sure whether he was happy or kind of disappointed to hear that. He supposed it didn't matter, since it wasn't going to happen either way. "Okay. Thanks for checking, I guess."

"I'd have told you if I'd found something, but I saw no point in disappointing you." He turned back to Verity. "All right, then, let's get this over with, shall we? I'll go ahead and put up the block if I can — even if you have the

R. L. KING

talent you'll need a bit of study and practice before you can do it on your own."

She nodded. "Okay. Let's do it."

The process took only about five minutes, during which Jason could see nothing happening other than Stone staring in that laserlike way of his into Verity's eyes. Once he held up a hand and slowly passed it across Verity's face from a distance of several inches away. For her part, Verity tried to sit as still as she could even though it was obvious that this whole process was freaking her out more than she wanted to admit. When Stone finally switched off the stare and leaned back on the stool, she asked jokingly, "So, Doc, am I gonna live?"

Stone didn't answer for several seconds; he appeared to be deep in thought. "Well," he said softly, getting up. "This is a first for me. I'm honored, honestly. I've never had the privilege of identifying a new mage before."

Verity's eyes widened. "Then—I am—?"

"You are," he said. "And if I'm any judge at all, you've got the potential for some pretty impressive ability, once you're trained. It doesn't surprise me, though, really—as I said, your mother was quite talented."

She seemed stunned. Looking back and forth between Stone and Jason, she slowly got up out of the chair and rubbed her hand across her eyes. "Wow..." was all she could get out.

"Did you do the shielding?" Jason asked Stone. "Is she gonna be okay away from Susanna?"

He nodded. "I think so. It was very strange—that's most of why it took so long to do it. The identification itself was actually quite fast. But—there's definitely something trying to get into her head."

"Something?" Verity asked. "You mean like—one of those Evil things?"

"I don't think so. It's not that specific. It seems more like a—force, or an aura, rather than an individual. Mind you this is just wild fancy on my part, but if I had to qualify it I would say that it's something that just exists in the world that you're susceptible to."

"I don't get it," Jason said. "How could that be? You're saying there's something just floating around out there, and it makes some people crazy but not others?"

"Essentially, yes. That's my impression anyway—I could be dead wrong."

"But whatever this is—it just showed up five years ago? Could it have been around before? Did it show up and affect her, or did something happen with her—like maybe that doctor was right about puberty—that made her more vulnerable to it?"

Stone spread his hands in an 'I don't know' gesture. "I couldn't tell you. I couldn't get a handle on what it was. The best I could do was make an estimate of its magical—frequency, as it were—and put up some protections to block it from getting into her head."

"So this is the thing you meant that I'd have to renew every once in awhile?" Verity asked.

"Yes. But with any luck you'll be well enough along in your training before that happens that you'll be able to take over the blocking yourself. Assuming," he added, turning back to face her, "that you even want to be trained. There's no requirement that you are. I'll warn you—the training isn't easy. At the beginning you're likely to be bored senseless by some of it, and as it goes on, you'll be doing things that could potentially be dangerous as you stretch your abilities and learn your limitations."

"If I did—decide to go ahead with the training," she said after a long pause, "How would it work? Would—you be the one doing it?"

"I could be, if that's what you wanted," Stone said, nodding. "That decision is up to you. Let's not talk about that now, though. It's something that neither of us want to decide quickly—you'll need time to examine your other options. Right now, if we're going to help the Forgotten and deal with the Evil, we'll have to concentrate on that. There's no way we could split our focus by beginning any sort of training now."

She nodded, looking a little reluctant but knowing he was right.

"What do we have to do?" Jason asked. "Where do we start?"

Stone sighed, sitting back down on the other end of the couch. "The way I see it, there are several problems we need to solve. The first, as I said before, is that we need to figure out somehow where our quarry is located—and how many of them there are. If there's one top-level Evil running the entire area like some sort of district manager, then we'll need to find out whom that one has possessed and where he or she is. Obviously if what Lamar said is true and the more powerful ones seek out more powerful hosts, then likely this one will have protections in place that we'll have to circumvent."

"That's problem number one," Jason said. "What about the others?"

"Well...I would say the second one is that even if Verity here can drive it out of its body, we have to figure out how either to destroy it, or to contain it until it is simply destroyed or sent home because it can't secure another host."

"Or we can kill the host," Jason pointed out.

"That won't work," Stone said, shaking his head. "Don't you remember what Lamar said? They think the powerful ones are able to remain without a body for as long as a few days. If we kill the host, all we'll be left with is a dead person—quite likely a dead person of considerable power and influence—and the need to resume our search again when the Evil finds a new host. That is, of course," he added with a raised eyebrow, "if they haven't tossed the lot of us in jail because we've murdered the Mayor or the Chief of Police or some such."

"Okay," Jason said. "So is that something you can do? Contain it, I mean?"

"I don't know. It would require some experimentation, most likely with the lower level specimens."

"Wait—you mean we're gonna have to grab a DMW guy or something, and try to catch the thing that flies out of his head when Verity boots it out?"

"Crude, but accurate. And this will also give Verity some practice to determine whether she can control her power enough that she can use it at will. If she can't learn to do that, then we might be in trouble—at the very least we'll have to explore other options."

Verity nodded. "I don't know if I can do it when I want to. I've actually never tried. Like I said, I thought the first time was a fluke, and the second time I was doing it to save Jason."

"Our third problem, though this one is easy to solve, relatively speaking," Stone went on, "is that battling the hosts of these Evil is likely to require the sort of magic that I'm not used to performing."

"Combat stuff, you mean," Jason said.

"Exactly. I won't be much use if I'm keeling over from exhaustion every time I cast a spell. Which means I'm going to have to work on building some magical items that will help me to channel energy more efficiently when casting these sorts of spells."

"You can do that?"

"I can, but it will take some time. Remember I told you before that white magic was ultimately more powerful than black, because we can cast spells that are permanent, or imbue objects with power and then use them later, rather than having to draw our power from either ourselves or others."

Jason nodded. "I remember you did say that, yeah."

"So," Stone said, "I suppose the first item on my agenda at least is to get started working on those."

"And what are we doing, in the meantime?" Verity asked. "We're going back to the Forgotten later today, right?"

"Yes," Stone said, nodding. "We need to talk to them — find out if they're willing to help out with this. If they're not — and I certainly wouldn't blame them — then things will be a great deal more difficult." He sighed. "Actually, I think my first step before anything else is to secure better lodgings. Especially if Verity is going to remain with us for awhile, this place with its two bedrooms isn't going to work. It's also not practical to do magic here — not enough room. Tell you what: I'm sure you two have a lot of catching up to do — why don't you do that for the next couple of hours, and I'll make some calls and see if I can't locate a better place, at least temporarily. I wouldn't leave the house if I were you, though — too much risk that someone will spot you. I think for the duration of this little adventure it would be best if we remained together as much as is practical."

Jason nodded. He didn't like feeling like he couldn't go where he wanted to, but Stone's words made a lot of sense. Now that he had Verity back, he really didn't want to take her out to the mall and get ambushed by a DMW hit squad.

"All right, then," Stone said briskly. "I'll be off to my room to make those calls. If I can find a place quickly we'll go there and set up our base of operations. If not, we'll head back to the Forgotten a bit early."

This left Jason and Verity sitting alone in the front room. She leaned back in her chair with a loud sigh. "Well, I guess nobody promised us a normal life, huh?"

"You got that right," he agreed.

"So I'm gonna get to do magic," she said, her big dark eyes wide with wonder. She looked up at her brother. "What do you think? Should I do it? Should I ask him to train me? This is all sounding so weird that I'm even *saying* it. 'Do I want to let somebody train me in how to do magic'?"

Jason grinned. "Yeah, I've had a head start on you for getting used to weirdness. The funny part is how soon it all starts sounding normal. At first I thought the only thing I wanted to do was find you and head back to our boring normal life in Ventura. But now—" He shrugged. "I dunno. This is all—kind of interesting, in a way. Freaky as hell, sure, but it's a nice change of pace from fixing old motorcycles and getting tossed in jail for starting bar fights."

"So what do you think of him?" she asked, hooking a thumb toward the back room where Stone had disappeared. "Should I ask him to train me? You don't think he'll hit on me, do you? 'Cuz he's kind of cute and all, but he's *old.* That would be—"

Jason laughed. "If that's all you're worried about, I don't think you need to worry. He's okay. He's a magic nerd. Seems like magic's all he's interested in. That, and puzzles. If you showed up in front of him wearing a string bikini while he was in the middle of running some magical experiment, he wouldn't even notice you except to ask you to bring him a candle or a dead frog or something."

"Is he gay?"

"You know, I have no idea. Oh, wait—no, I don't think so. He told me he had a 'schoolboy crush' on Mom back when he knew her." He looked up at her. "By the way, speaking of that—when were you going to tell me?"

"Tell you—Oh." She smiled, shrugging. "I dunno. You didn't exactly come to see me, you know. I couldn't really tell you much of anything, could I?" Her expression grew more serious. "You don't—have a problem with that, do you?"

"Why does everybody keep *asking* me that?" he said, rolling his eyes. "V, I'm just glad to have you back safe—and having you safe and non-crazy is a huge bonus. At this point I wouldn't care if you were into Russian circus midgets, if it meant you had a shot at a regular normal life."

She giggled. "Oh, good. Because I was really worried about how you'd react to the circus midgets. Maybe you'd better tell your friend to get a place with more rooms, so I can tell them it's safe to come home now. Sergei and Natasha will be *so* happy to get out of that refrigerator box."

Jason laughed again. It felt so good to be laughing, after the last few days of fear and death and nonstop weirdness. "I'd forgotten what a goofball you used to be, V."

"And I'd forgotten what a dork *you* used to be," she said, grinning. "I guess some things never change, huh?"

26.

When Stone returned an hour later, he found the two of them sitting on the couch together, an old black and white movie on the television that they were cheerfully making fun of. "Well," he said, smiling. "Looks like the reunion went well."

"Did you find anything?" Jason asked, turning down the volume.

"I did. Fortunately for us, I found another colleague who has a furnished rental property that will fit our needs nicely. Once I assured him that I'll do my best to ensure that this one won't be blown up by a faulty gas main, he agreed to let me take it on a month-to-month basis. I'm still on the lookout for something more permanent, but this will do nicely for now."

"Blown up?" Verity asked, alarmed.

"Does it have a basement?" Jason asked at the same time, with a wicked glint in his eyes.

"I also took care of making some arrangements with my insurance company to cover some of the items I lost in the explosion," Stone continued, ignoring them both, "And located us a rental vehicle until I can replace the Jaguar."

"What, you don't like my car?" Jason asked innocently.

"Explosion?" Verity asked again.

"Tell you later," Jason told her. "His housekeeper tried to murder us a few days ago by blowing up his last house."

She stared at him, then at Stone, wide-eyed and obviously not sure if they were pulling her leg. "Your—housekeeper—?"

Suddenly, something clicked in Jason's mind. His joking expression went dead serious. "Al—Mrs. Olivera—"

Stone nodded, looking equally serious. "I just had the same thought." He sighed. "Really the only way they could have gotten in without setting off my defenses."

"What the hell are you two talking about?" Verity demanded. "This is gonna get old in a hurry if you keep talking like I'm not even here."

"Sorry," Jason muttered. "We're thinking now that one of the Evil must have possessed Mrs. Olivera and made her set that bomb. Remember how Lamar said sometimes they sacrifice the weak ones to do things they need done, or just to cause people to commit suicide so they can feed off the emotion?"

"And then when it finished with her," Stone said sadly, "it simply caused her to have a single-car accident that killed her. Perhaps it was even able to secure another body if there was one close enough." He sighed, looking down. "What a waste..."

"Just a sec, though," Jason said. "Didn't Lamar say that the Forgotten don't think that the Evil takes over people completely when it possesses them? Remember, he said that it couldn't, or else they wouldn't be able to do their jobs?"

"Yes, but he also said that no one knows for sure," Stone pointed out. "P'raps they're capable of doing it either way. I really don't know—it would definitely be something to study at some point. But for now I think we'll need to go on the assumption that they *can* choose to take people—at least some people—over completely if they need to. Possibly only for a limited amount of time, which is why the more powerful Evil use the weakest ones for their suicide missions."

"That makes sense, I guess," Jason said. "Just makes this whole thing scarier, though."

"Come on," Stone said, grabbing his coat. "Get your stuff together and let's take a look at the new place and pick up the car. I want to be as settled in as we can before we head back to Mountain View."

The new house was near the border between Mountain View and Palo Alto. It was a nondescript tan single-story place in the ubiquitous California ranch style, with a two-car garage and a large patch of green lawn. The neighborhood looked quiet and respectable. "How...suburban," Jason said.

"Yes, well, beggars can't be choosers, and at least it has three bedrooms and a large family room I can use for doing magic," Stone reminded him. "It will do until I can find something more to my liking, and the two-car garage means we don't have to keep our cars visible in case anyone happens by who might recognize them."

The inside of the house was as nondescript as the outside, furnished in Early Middle-American Boring. "The two bedrooms at the end of the hall are yours," Stone told them. "You can fight over who gets which one, but make it quick. I want to be out of here in fifteen minutes at most."

They beat that by nearly ten minutes — they had very little gear to stow. When they came back out front, Stone was installing their meager food stores in the refrigerator and cabinets. "Ready?"

Their next stop was the rental agency, where Stone revealed the "car" to be a beige van with tinted windows in the back. "Seriously, Al?" Jason asked, amused. "This one doesn't look like your style either."

"Right now, style isn't nearly as important as blending in," Stone reminded him. "These things are all over the place, so likely we won't be noticed. I'll get something more interesting again once we've sorted out our little problems."

Jason, with Verity riding shotgun, followed Stone back to the house in the Ford and stashed it in the garage. Then they all piled into the van. "Where to now?"

"I want to stop back at Madame Huan's, and we should probably go back to her friend's house and clean up the sand we left in his studio. And it's early enough we probably have time to stop by the mall again—I'm guessing Verity might like to pick up a few more clothes."

"I can do that?" she asked. She looked like she hadn't really thought about it, but now that she had, she was quickly warming to the idea. "I don't have any money—"

"Don't worry about that," Stone said. "We're not buying you fur coats or ostrich-hide boots or anything. Just a few things to get you by until you can decide what you want to do."

These stops ended up taking almost two hours between them, but by the time they finished Stone had a bag full of items he planned to use to make magical batteries and focusing objects, the ballet studio in Los Gatos was cleaned up and put back to the state in which they'd found it, and Verity had picked out several new pairs of jeans, a few subversive black T-shirts, and a pair of black leather Dr. Martens that Stone caught her staring at longingly and insisted she have despite her protests that they were too expensive. "This feels weird," she told him as the salesperson rang up the purchases. "It's like you're my—sugar daddy or something."

He chuckled. "It's not a hardship, believe me. And if you and your brother feel that you must do something, you can always take care of the chores 'round the house. I'm abysmal at housekeeping."

"See?" Jason said, grinning. "He *is* gonna make you do his laundry."

"*You* do the laundry," she protested. "I'll mow the lawn or cook or something." They were heading out now, and she looked back at Stone. "Are we going back to the Forgotten now?"

"Right you are. We'll drop this stuff off at the house and be on our way. We're not actually far from their new location."

"Can we get some food first?" Jason asked. Despite the big breakfast they'd had only a few hours ago, his stomach was rumbling again.

"I wish we could take something to them too," Verity said.

Stone raised an eyebrow. "Excellent idea," he agreed. "One more stop, then."

When they arrived at the address Lamar had given them for the Forgotten's new base, they found it to be an old auto-repair shop in the back of another of the area's numerous abandoned industrial parks. It was built like a warehouse but only about half as large. As they pulled around the back of the building, they immediately spotted the triangle-and-rays "good place" symbol chalked on the asphalt near the door. The door opened, framing Lamar and Marilee in the doorway. They both looked surprised as Stone, Jason, and Verity all got out of the van, each one bearing a large cardboard box. "What—?" he asked.

"Lunch is catered today," Stone announced, handing his box to Lamar.

The old man looked inside and his eyes widened. Stacked up inside were a large number of wrapped sandwiches from a local fast-food sub shop, the mingling scents of meats, vegetables and condiments wafting up enticingly. "I—"

"Coming through," Jason said. He was carrying another box full of two-liter bottles of soda along with plastic cups, forks, and napkins. Verity brought up the rear with a second box of sandwiches.

Inside, the building was one large open space. About fifteen of the Forgotten were sitting around inside, but most of them got up and began to filter over when they smelled the food. "I don't know what to say," Lamar said. "Except—thank you. Your kindness is appreciated."

"Think nothing of it," Stone said. "We were going to pick up some lunch before we came over here, and Verity quite rightly pointed out that you all might like to join us." He watched as Jason and Verity started setting out bottles and cups on the makeshift table the Forgotten had fashioned out of a door and two empty cardboard boxes, and soon everyone had grabbed a sandwich and a drink and had found a spot to eat. Stone sat down near the back wall with a small group consisting of Lamar, Marilee, Verity, Jason, and the gruff military man Hector. For awhile none of them spoke, intent on eating. But then Stone addressed Lamar. "Have you given any thought to what we discussed this morning?"

He nodded. "I've been thinking about it all day," he admitted. He looked troubled. "I've talked it over with Marilee and a couple of the others, and—we want to help. Some of our group are fearful, though."

"I'd be surprised if they weren't," Stone said. "Whatever we decide to do, I doubt it will be safe. But the risk to you and your group is minimal if we do this correctly. All I really need you to do is to help us figure out where the leading Evil of the area keeps itself. I need you to communicate with other Forgotten groups and try to figure out where its base is. Because if we strike, it only makes sense to strike there."

Lamar nodded. "That does make sense," he agreed. "I warn you, though—such a thing will take time. We don't encounter other groups that often. Of course we do have a few places where we can meet or leave messages for each other if we need to, but it's not as simple as calling them on the phone or putting out the call for a group meeting. We're not that organized, partially by necessity. Our groups are large enough for protection, but not so large as to attract the Evil's attention."

"Well," Stone said, "if you can do the best you can, that's all we can ask. I have some things I need to do in the meantime, to prepare. But all of this hinges on knowing where to look. We can be ready when we find out, but until we know—"

"I understand," the old man said.

Stone pulled out a small notebook and jotted down the phone number at the new house. He tore off the page and handed it to Lamar along with a few bills. "This is where you'll find us," he said. "Since we may not know where you've moved on any given day, it's probably best if you contact us when you find out something—or if you need anything."

"We can't accept—" Lamar protested, trying to give back the money.

Stone shook his head. "As I said, what I'm asking you to do could be dangerous. The least I can do is try to help a bit so you don't have to worry so much about your livelihood for the next few days. Don't worry," he added as Lamar still didn't look convinced. "I've got a fair bit of money squirreled away, and it's nice to have something helpful to spend it on."

Lamar nodded. "All right, then. Thank you. We do appreciate everything that all of you have done for us."

"That's mutual, I assure you," Stone said, patting his formerly wounded side for emphasis. "And if all goes according to plan, then I'm hoping that you'll all be in better circumstances soon."

Lamar looked philosophical. "I'm not going to think that far ahead, Dr. Stone. Around here, we pretty much take things one day at a time." He stowed the phone number and the bills away in his coat. "But I promise you—as soon as we know anything, we'll find a way to contact you."

For the next several days they heard nothing from the Forgotten, and Jason and Verity were both starting to get restless. Jason had a serious problem with being confined anywhere for any length of time and was starting to go stir-crazy inside the house despite their daily trips out for food and general shopping, while Verity was worried that something had happened to her friends. They kept busy by watching television and doing the chores around the house—Verity, it turned out, was actually a fairly decent cook and enjoyed experimenting with different recipes, while Jason put his mechanical aptitude to work on various small projects both inside and outside, and spent every spare moment doing what he could to make the old Ford run better.

Stone, meanwhile, was spending most of his time either holed up in his room doing research, or puttering around in the large family room which he had commandeered and was in the process of turning into a place to perform magical rituals. A couple of times he called Verity in to help him with some mundane task, but most of the time he kept to himself. "It's a good thing I've a lot of practice doing this sort of thing," he said at one point, annoyed. "Losing the better part of my research collection in the explosion is making things more difficult than they have to be."

When he wasn't doing research or filling the house with the smell of incense and burning candles while building the various magical devices he would need to help him combat the Evil, Stone did take a bit of time out to begin explaining the way magic worked to Verity. It was the same lecture he'd given Jason, about the difference between black and white magic and how they operated. "You'll need to know this stuff no matter who you decide to apprentice with," he told her, "so might as well give you a head start and not have you get it secondhand from your brother." For her part, she proved a quick study and very interested in the topic, asking many of the same questions that Jason had asked. Toward the end of the week when she wasn't attempting to whip up some new exotic dish, she found excuses to spend more and more time in the family room watching Stone do his thing and asking more questions.

One evening as they sat around the dining table eating Verity's latest experiment (like most of them, this one had turned out to be quite tasty, though a few of her failures had required herculean feats of diplomacy on Stone's and Jason's parts so as not to hurt her feelings), Stone said, "So, I think I've got all my items sorted, so now it's time to move to Phase 2 of our mad little plan."

"And that is—?" Jason asked. "I thought we had to wait for Lamar and his people to get back to us before we can go further."

"Not necessarily—there is something else we can do. Though we will likely have to hunt down the Forgotten to help us with this part, so I do hope they've left us some way to contact them."

"What do we need to do?" Verity asked.

"Find one of the Evil, so we can have you practice and see if you can control your power to drive it out of people without harming them."

"You want to find somebody who's possessed and experiment on them?" Jason looked dubious. "I still say that doesn't sound safe. What if they do communicate somehow, telepathically or something? That could bring them all down on us at once."

"Well, I wasn't proposing to do it *here*," Stone said with a raised eyebrow. "And in any case, I don't think that's how they operate. It's a theory again so I could be wrong, but we've seen no indication yet that they're in constant communication with each other—at least not when they're possessing a body. I don't think we're dealing with a hive mind here."

Jason was still looking apprehensive. "So you want to find somebody who's possessed, lock him up somewhere and let Verity play with him until she figures out how to kick the hitchhiker out of his body—and then what?"

"And then we need to figure out how to capture it," Stone said, "and confine it."

"Al, if you want a pet, why don't you just ask Marilee if you can have her kitten?" Jason's tone was light, but his nervousness was evident. "Seriously, you mentioned this before, but you didn't seem like you had any ideas how to do it. Do you have any now?"

Stone shook his head. "Not really. Hence the experiment. Not only do we need to determine whether Verity can drive it out at will, but I also need to study it so I can construct some sort of magical prison capable of holding it long enough that it will die or dissipate before it can locate a new host."

"How do you think you're gonna do that, though?" Jason asked.

"That's where the study comes in. My working theory is that if I can do something similar to what I did to block Verity's mind against the influence of whatever is causing her mental issues—find the 'magical frequency' these things operate on when they're incorporeal—then I can create a magical containment field that will cancel out that frequency and prevent it from seeking out another body to possess."

"Theory," Jason said. "That seems like a big stretch to me. If V can get the thing out of the guy we grab and you *can't* contain it, what's to stop it from flying off and phoning home?"

"Because the one we grab to experiment on will be one of the weak ones," Stone reminded him. "And we'll make sure to do it where there aren't any other humans in the vicinity, so when it vacates the premises, as it were, it won't have anywhere to go and will simply be destroyed."

"And what makes you think that the little ones operate on the same frequency as the big ones?" Jason persisted.

"That's why I keep you around, Jason," Stone said approvingly. "Because you ask all the good questions." He glanced up at Verity. "These are the kinds of questions you should be asking, by the way. Whomever you end up apprenticing with is going to expect you to keep your mind sharp at all times, and open to possibilities. Questioning and critical thinking are key to magic."

"Uh...sorry," she said. "I'll do better next time."

"See that you do," he said, his smile and quirked eyebrow taking the edge off his words. Then he turned his attention back to Jason. "The answer to this particular question is: I have no idea. As I said, it's a theory. I think in this case it's a pretty decent one, though. We've no reason to believe that the powerful ones and the weak ones aren't the same 'species,' so it follows that they'd operate on the same magical frequency, albeit no doubt at different potency levels. So all I have to do, theoretically, is figure out what that is and extrapolate from the housecat to build a cage that will hold the tiger."

"I hope you're right," Jason said. "Because I'm not in any hurry at all to have that tiger come flying out of your little cage and decide to hitch a ride in one of us." He paused to dish up some more potatoes. "So you said we have to find the Forgotten for this part. How come?"

"Oh, and you were doing so well asking the good questions, too," Stone said, chuckling. "Because, my dear boy, unless you've developed some way of detecting the presence of people possessed by the Evil, then we're going to need someone who has one."

"I get it," Verity said. "You're going to see if you can get one of their folks who are sensitive to the Evil to come around with you until they find somebody."

"Exactly."

"I see two big problems with that," Jason said. "First thing, the only one of those I've seen is a girl who can barely function under normal circumstance, and who freaks out and goes all catatonic when the bad stuff is around. And second, what are you going to do: just drive around at random until she goes off? That could take weeks."

"There's more than one of them," Verity told him. "I've heard of at least one other one—remember, Jason, I told you about him? The young boy?"

Jason thought back. "Oh, yeah. The canary. The one you said the guy finally showed up who could talk to him. I never saw him around, though."

"He travels with a different group, but Lamar's group could probably find him if they had to."

Stone was sitting back thinking while the two of them discussed this. "As for your other problem," he said when there was a pause, "No, I wasn't planning to drive around randomly. We've established that these things are attracted to strong emotions, particularly negative ones, yes?"

Jason nodded. "Yeah. Everybody seems to agree on that."

"Well, then, we need to locate someplace where they might find them in high concentration. Operating on the assumption that they would prefer to take the path of least resistance, if they could find a way to be in the vicinity of strong emotions without having to do anything themselves to cause them, then they can simply sit by and—"

"—get their emotional rocks off without risking getting arrested or discovered," Jason finished.

"You've such a way with words, Jason," Stone said with an amused sigh. "But essentially, yes."

"So we just need to come up with a place like that and go look there," Verity said. "That doesn't sound too hard."

"It might be harder than you think," Stone cautioned. "Because remember—the second part of this plan is that we have to be able to get hold of a test subject. That means that places like hospitals or prisons are right out: too much security. We'd never manage it, even using magic."

"If you don't mind, I'd really rather not show up at a DMW meeting or anything like that," Jason said.

"No. That wouldn't do at all. Let's think for a moment: they prefer negative emotions. Fear, suffering, anger, despair, depression...Brainstorm with me: what kinds of places do those occur in concentrated form?"

Verity shrugged. "Mental institution?"

"Uh—boxing match?" Jason offered. "Or some kind of underground fight?"

"Hmm..." Stone considered. "Might be too hard to get into a mental institution even if they had one 'round here, and underground fights don't generally allow tourists."

"Horror movie?" Verity suggested.

"Good thought, but horror movies are strange things: yes, there's fear, but it's generally more excitement than fear. Most people don't go to horror movies against their will, so it's assumed that they *want* to be scared. Same reason I don't think an amusement park would work. That, and again it would be hard to get someone out of a theater and drag them out to the van without someone seeing them."

"Wait, I've got it!" Verity yelled suddenly, grinning.

Stone and Jason both looked at her, startled by her sudden outburst. "What?" Jason demanded.

Her eyes darted around the room until she spotted a newspaper on the kitchen counter. She hurried out, grabbed it, and brought it back out to the table. Shoving the serving dishes out of the way, she spread it out and turned a few pages, then stabbed a triumphant finger at one of the ads. "There!"

The two men stared at the place she was pointing. "Fear Asylum — the Scariest Haunted House in the Bay Area," Jason read.

"Right!" she said, nodding. "I remember reading about these when I was in the halfway house — I wanted so much to go, but of course they never let us. Charles went once, though, and told me about it. He said it was plenty scary. They actually had people faint and have to leave because they couldn't get through the whole thing. They do it every year around this time."

"Oh, right," Jason agreed. "They have one down in Oxnard, too. All the teenagers go there." He looked at Stone. "You have no idea what we're talking about, do you?"

"Not a bit," Stone said. "Keep going, though — it sounds fascinating."

"It's at the fairgrounds," Verity said, pointing at the ad. "They take over some of the exhibit buildings, and sometimes they build mazes outside too."

"So why is this any different from a horror movie?" Stone asked.

"Oh, trust me, it is," Jason told him. "In a movie it's all on screen. It can make you jump, but you know in the back of your mind that it can't hurt you. These things are all based on that little fear everybody has: *what if these aren't all just employees who get paid to scare me? What if there's a real axe murderer hiding in here somewhere?*"

"Sounds like a pretty good hunting ground for the Evil," Verity said. "I'll bet some of them even had their hosts get jobs there, so they could get a steady diet of fear."

"They hire a lot of teenagers and people my age," Jason said, "and a lot of 'em don't ask too many questions, you know?"

"Excellent," Stone said. "Sounds like just the sort of place we're looking for. Now all we have to do is find Lamar's group and see if we can convince Lissy—and perhaps a minder for her—to come along with us."

Jason cocked his head at the mage. "Uh—Al—just doing a reality check here. You *do* realize we're talking about kidnapping, right?"

Stone nodded. "Quite so. But given the stakes, I think it's worth it to take the chance. We'll have to be careful, of course, and find another location to do our experiments, but—" He looked at Jason. "You're not backing out now, are you?"

"No, no," Jason said, shaking his head. "Just making sure we all know what we're getting into, is all."

"I'd say if you want to get down to it, what we're really doing is *stopping* a kidnapping," Stone pointed out. "Tell me—would you rather have yourself borrowed for a few hours' worth of harmless and painless magical experiments, or have some sort of alien hitchhiker riding around on your brain?"

"Well, when you put it that way..."

27.

As it turned out, it wasn't hard at all to locate Lamar's group. They simply drove around the Mountain View area until they spotted likely looking groups of vagrants, then showed them the triangle-and-rays symbol and asked if they'd seen anyone matching the description. The first few gave them blank looks, but finally they found a group in Sunnyvale who immediately recognized the symbol and suggested that they look in the back quadrant of a mostly abandoned mall not far from their current location. After that, it was a simple manner of going there and driving around until they spotted the symbol. They didn't even have to find a way in: Hector was just coming outside for a smoke as they were getting out of the van, and he led them through a maze of maintenance corridors to a large empty storeroom.

It was only Lamar's group now, which at some point seemed to have merged with Hector's: Lamar himself, Marilee, Benny, Lissy, Frank the Scribbler, Hector, Susanna, and a couple of others that Stone and Jason hadn't met yet. Marilee's cart was parked off to the side, and the kitten played among the bags. "Good to see you," Lamar said. "We didn't try to contact you yet because we're still working on getting the information you wanted. Things move slowly in our world, and some folks are understandably nervous about getting involved."

"That's all right," Stone assured him. "We're not quite ready for that step yet, so if it takes a while that's not an issue. We need to ask you something else, though."

"Go ahead."

Stone took him and Marilee off in a corner along with Jason and Verity, and together they explained their plan. Both of the Forgotten looked scared; Marilee glanced across at Lissy, who was, as usual, humming to herself with a vague happy smile. "I don't know," she said. "Lissy is—vulnerable, as you've seen. And she can be a bit hard to manage for anyone who doesn't know her well. We take care of her here. She'd never make it on the streets on her own."

Stone nodded understandingly. "I wouldn't even ask you to consider it if there were another option. You mentioned, Jason said, that there was another with a similar power—a young boy?"

Marilee shook her head. "No, that's Kody. He used to be with us for awhile, but he's moved on. He finally found someone who could communicate with him, and when he decided to move on, Kody decided to go with him. We haven't heard from either of them since they left."

"So you don't have anybody who can communicate with Lissy?" Jason asked.

"Susanna can a little. She seems to have a calming effect on her, unless the Evil are very close. You saw how she gets—"

"Would Susanna maybe come along too?" Verity asked. "This is really important, Lamar. And we won't let anything happen to her. You know we wouldn't."

"Wait a minute," Jason spoke up. "Wasn't Susanna the one who figured out the DMW was coming when you guys were at Melody's house? Isn't she the one who made you get out? Couldn't she just come with us and do that?"

"Sadly, no," Lamar said. "Susanna's ability is more general. She can detect the approach of danger—any danger, not just the Evil. And it's very spotty. Remember, most of the Forgotten's abilities aren't things we can turn on and off at will. They come when we need them, usually. But they aren't something we can put to use."

"Plus," Marilee added, "from what it sounds like you're describing, there wouldn't be any danger for her to detect. If one or more of the Evil have directed their hosts to work at this place in order to have access to the fear, they wouldn't need to do anything to cause it, beyond what their job needs, right?"

Stone nodded. "Very good point." He sighed. "So we're back to Lissy. If you have any other ideas, I'd be happy to hear them, but I'm fresh out at the moment."

"I'll ask her," Marilee said, looking troubled. "I'll ask her and Susanna if they'll go with you."

After she'd gone, Stone turned back to Lamar. "We need one other thing as well—a place to do what we need to do. Preferably one that's not far from this haunted house."

"That shouldn't be too hard," Lamar said. "That isn't the best area of San Jose—I'm sure there are abandoned buildings there. Let me talk with the others for a moment. I'm assuming you want to do this soon?"

"As soon as possible, I think, yes."

Lamar left, and after about five minutes both he and Marilee returned together, with Lissy and Susanna trailing behind them. Susanna turned out to be the large middle-aged woman in the multicolored sweater who had helped work on Stone when he was injured. Jason and Stone hadn't gotten a close look at her before; she bore more than a passing stylistic resemblance to Willow from the hospital. Both had frizzy hair, dramatic makeup, and a certain earth-mother look to them. She didn't look too pleased about the plans. "I'm not liking this at all," she said. "Taking Lissy out among reg'lar people. She gets real nervous doing that."

"It won't be for very long," Stone assured her. "And we'll make her safety—and yours—our top priority."

Lissy smiled a wide, vague smile and started humming a radio jingle under her breath.

"Plus," Susanna said, "I've seen these — these haunted house places. It'll scare the stuffing out of the poor little thing."

"She might not even have to go inside," Jason said. "Depends on how they've got it set up."

Susanna sighed. "I know there's no helpin' it. I know what you're tryin' to do, and if you can do it then things will be better for all of us. But it just don't seem right to — take advantage of her like this."

Lissy patted her hand. "Boo scary," she said, making a 'peek-a-boo' gesture.

"All right," Susanna conceded with a sigh, putting her ample arm around Lissy's thin shoulders. "If we're going to do it, though, let's get it over with."

Stone, Jason, and Verity came back the next night to implement their plan. They'd spent the remainder of the day going over strategies, trying to anticipate contingencies or possible things that could go wrong. "You know you can't do that, right?" Jason said as they got into the van. "No matter what kinds of things you plan for, something else always happens that you didn't expect. That's the way these things work."

"There's my good old optimist brother," Verity said, grinning. But she too looked nervous.

All three of them were dressed in dark, nondescript clothes that would blend in with the crowds of teens and twentysomethings that would be the attraction's largest clientele.

The Forgotten were waiting for them — not just Susanna and Lissy, but also Lamar, Marilee, and Hector were standing outside hidden in the shadows. To the new arrivals' relief, Susanna had exchanged her colorful sweater for one in a dull gray. Lissy's dress was covered with a shapeless dark coat, and she wore a jaunty knitted cap that actually, if you didn't get too close to her, might make passersby think that she was a normal high school or college girl. It was only when they got too close and saw her eyes that they would realize otherwise.

"Ready to go?" Stone asked briskly.

Lamar gave Stone the address of an abandoned gas station near the fairgrounds. "We won't be able to join you there — it's too far to travel in such a short time — but there shouldn't be anyone else around either. There's a Forgotten group over there, but you might not be able to find them. They know you'll be there, though."

Stone thanked him, waited until everyone was back in the van, and drove off. Next to him between the driver's and passenger's seat was a black leather shoulder bag containing some of the magical items he'd created; he also wore a couple of things he hadn't had before: a ring with a blocky purple stone on his right hand, and an odd-looking amulet pinned to his sport jacket underneath his overcoat.

Nobody spoke for awhile as they drove. Stone had the radio on and Lissy entertained them by humming along to most of the songs and many of the jingles — though it was soon obvious that while she was responding to the music, the tunes she hummed were of her own devising and had little resemblance to the ones actually playing. "What's the deal with Lissy?" Jason asked at last. He was pleased to note — but of course didn't say this — that both Lissy and Susanna appeared to have bathed recently and put on the closest they had to clean clothes. Aside from not making the van smelly, that also meant that they would be less likely to draw attention when they got where they were going.

"She's been with Hector's crew a long time," Susanna said. Lissy herself seemed oblivious that she was being talked about. "It's only recently that Hector's group and ours joined up, after we lost a couple, but we've helped each other out a lot over time. Nobody knows her history. We found her wanderin' around downtown San Jose one day, pickin' flowers in the park and dancin' around to the music in her head. When she tried to dance out into traffic a couple of times, Hector dragged her back and took her to Marilee. She seemed to take a likin' to the group, especially Marilee, and she's been there ever since."

Jason nodded. "So you don't know if she was — okay — before whatever happened?"

"No, no way to know that," Susanna said. "Hey, you mind if I smoke?" She'd already started fumbling in her shapeless handbag.

"Erm — " Stone said, uncomfortable. "Rental van. No-smoking policy. Sorry."

"Damn." She tossed the bag back on the seat in annoyance.

They spotted their destination from a couple of blocks down: it was one of the few parts of the area that was lit up. A large sign towered above the fairground's box office area, proclaiming "FEAR ASYLUM HAUNTED HOUSE" with appropriately gory artwork, surrounded by flashing orange and purple lights. Loud and spooky classical music in heavy-metal style boomed out over the area, and a large knot of people were gathered around outside in a rough line waiting to buy tickets. As they drove by on the way to the parking lot, Jason scanned the group as best he could. He didn't see any leather jackets with red and black logos on them, which was a good thing. Glancing back at Lissy, he noticed she was still humming to herself and didn't seem at all agitated. To the contrary, she appeared to be taking in the whole scene with wide-eyed wonder.

Nobody looked at them oddly as they waited in line to get tickets. Although the crowd was overwhelmingly teenagers and young adults, there were a few families and older couples there as well. The loud music made conversation difficult so they just drifted along together until they got to the front of the line, Susanna keeping tight hold of Lissy's hand. She still wasn't showing any signs of distress.

Once they handed their tickets to the attendant and went inside, they found themselves standing in a large open area full of milling people and little booths selling T-shirts, glow sticks, buttons, and other paraphernalia with the haunted house's logo on them, along with snacks. On a whim, Stone paused to buy everyone caramel popcorn balls, and a green glow stick for Lissy. She waved it around happily, her eyes shining. Susanna gave him an approving nod, though she still looked like she'd rather have a cigarette than a caramel popcorn ball.

When they'd entered the attendant had given each of them a little map showing the locations of the various different areas of the show. The largest of these was the Fear Asylum, which, by the images that went with it, appeared to be depicting a horrific mental institution. Other secondary attractions included the Haunted Forest, the Church of the Damned, and the Circus of Terror. "Where you want to start?" Jason muttered to Stone. "It could take us all night to go through all of these."

"Why don't we wander around outside each of them a bit," he said. "With any luck if any of the Evil are here, Lissy can give us a general idea as to their location and save us having to take a trip through every one of these no doubt fascinating places."

Jason nodded, and together the four of them began a slow circuit of the area. All but the Haunted Forest were inside exhibit buildings, while the Forest was set up in a large vacant area behind temporary fencing. They moved past the Fear Asylum and the Church of the Damned without any reaction from Lissy other than to continue happily waving her glow stick, but when they approached the Circus of Terror she began to move more slowly. Her eyes, big with excitement, grew fearful. "Wait," whispered Susanna.

The others stopped. "Is this it?" Stone asked. "In there?"

"I think so," she said. She had her arm around Lissy and was holding her close; the girl was clearly shaking now. "I'm not sure we're gonna be able to get her in there."

Stone contemplated that for a moment. She was obviously right: Lissy was growing more quietly disturbed by the minute. Instead of humming she was moaning; her glow stick dropped out of her hand and landed in the dirt. Verity picked it up and brushed it off, looking worried.

"Al," Jason said. "How about this: Susanna, you can hide the two of you, right? You can make that work here?"

Susanna nodded. "All I've got to do is worry about keepin' Lissy safe and it just works automatically. It's probably already workin'."

"Okay then—what if you stay here or maybe go sit somewhere away from here so she's not so scared, while Al and V and I go in and look for the guy."

"But Jason, how are we going to find him without Lissy to show us?" Verity asked.

Stone, however, had caught his line of reasoning and nodded. "Right," he said. "We just go in there and look for someone who's getting entirely too much—erm—personal pleasure from watching all these people being frightened."

"Yeah, exactly. It might take us a little while to find 'em, though. Will you guys be okay?"

"We'll be all right," Susanna said. "It'll give me a chance to have a smoke. Lemme have that back," she said, pointing to the glow stick Verity held. "It'll help keep her calmed down once we get away from here. We'll go sit by the food stands."

"We'll be back as soon as we can," Stone said as Verity handed it over.

As they once again approached the Circus of Terror, they noticed that the music had switched from heavy-metal classical to macabre minor-key calliope. The lurid painting on the outside of the building depicted a nightmarish clown with graying fangs and claws, blood dripping from his chalk-white face above a ripped clown suit in black, purple and gray polka dots. "Charming," Stone commented.

"I've always hated clowns," Verity said, shivering. "I probably saw something like this when I was a baby."

The crowd here wasn't as large as for the Fear Asylum, but they joined a little group of about fifteen people and moved past the attendant (dressed as a sinister ringmaster) into the darkness. The calliope music was getting louder as they moved in. The whole place smelled like sweat and sawdust and a hint of popcorn.

Inside, the large open space had been broken up into a maze of twisty corridors by portable barriers that occasionally opened up on one side or the other to reveal a tableau. The barriers were painted black, while the tableaus themselves were garishly colored and lit by ubiquitous black lights. "Just like the one back home," Jason said, bored. "This wouldn't scare a chihuahua."

It appeared that he was wrong, though. As they approached the first tableau, which depicted some sort of horrific clown-related torture session, they noticed that more than one member of the crowd did look agitated. When one of the clowns, who'd been hiding in the back of the group behind one of the black barriers opposite the tableau, lunged out with a roar waving a very realistic looking chainsaw, several people screamed and leaped backward and then giggled nervously as the clown sub-sided back into his hiding place to await the next group. One young boy started to cry. Stone, under cover of the milling crowd trying to reassure the boy as they started shuffling off toward the next tableau, peeked around the barrier at the clown. He was standing back there with a buddy, chainsaw leaned against a wall and both of them taking quick swigs from the beer cans they'd stashed. Stone quickly backed up and caught up with the rest of the group.

The next tableau was a sinister magic act, where the tuxedo-clad magician was sawing a curvaceous woman in a slinky red dress in half as two more evil clowns cavort-ed around off to the sides. The magician kept up his patter, looking relaxed, but then suddenly something went horribly wrong and the "blade" sliced through the woman's torso. She screamed so loudly that there had to be a microphone hidden around her somewhere, while blood shot out in all directions and her "guts" came spill-ing out of her body. The magician, meanwhile, was having hysterics, screaming and running around while the clowns tried to catch him.

"Wonder how long it takes her to stuff all that back in between groups," Jason muttered to Stone and Verity. His sister grinned appreciatively.

Stone wasn't listening, though. He was looking behind them — just in time to see another clown, this one wielding two large bloody machetes, leap out and begin screaming incoherently. He buried one of the machetes in the mid-section of one of the straggling group members, who screamed and fell to the sawdust-covered ground, writh-ing in agony and fountaining blood.

The crowd was going crazy, and even Jason wore a look of wide-eyed horror. "What the hell — ?"

Stone, however, was looking unimpressed. "I wonder how long it will take the rest of our group to realize that that unfortunate young man wasn't with us when we started?"

As if to punctuate his words, the "victim" got up, laughing, pulled out the "machete," and darted off behind the barrier. The clown was slower to follow. He waved his remaining machete a few more times, then moved off after his victim.

"Hang back," Stone muttered to the other two.

They did so, pretending to watch the magician for a moment, then used the crowd as a diversion while they slipped behind the clown's secret exit.

By the time they got back there, neither the clown nor the victim were anywhere to be seen. "Damn," Jason said under his breath, but then Stone touched his arm and pointed.

Barely visible in dark clothes and a dark stocking cap, a skinny boy around seventeen sat in a corner with his arms wrapped around his knees. A broom and dustpan were propped next to him. His eyes were closed, his face lit up in a transport of pleasure. "I think we've got our man," Stone whispered, motioning Jason forward.

It went just like they'd planned: Stone cast a spell that cause the boy to slump, his head dropping onto his knees. Jason picked him up, dragging him to his feet and supporting him as if helping a drunken friend. Verity pulled off his dark stocking cap and replaced it with a red and gold San Francisco 49ers one from her pocket. Together the three of them quickly made for the emergency exit, dragging the boy along with them. His eyes were open, but his head lolled alarmingly to one side.

Stationed outside the emergency exit was a burly man in a Fear Asylum T-shirt. He looked at them suspiciously when they came out, but Stone made a surreptitious hand movement that caused the boy to jerk in Jason's grip and vomit violently all over the ground in front of him. "Too much excitement," Jason said to the man. "My cousin couldn't take it. What a wuss," he added with contempt.

The man, staring in disgust at the splashes of vomit that had landed on his boots, waved them off. Jason doubted that he even looked at their faces, let alone registered them. Once they were safely away, Stone and Verity remained with the kid while Jason ran off to retrieve Susanna and Lissy. It was nearly ten minutes before they came back; Verity was pacing around getting nervous, and even Stone was starting to look apprehensive by the time the three arrived.

"Sorry," Jason said. "Susanna insisted on finishing her cigarette."

"Hey, you don't waste a good smoke," Susanna protested.

Lissy, meanwhile, was agitated again. It was very obvious that they'd managed to successfully grab an Evil-possessed individual, because the closer Lissy got to the boy, the less responsive she became. She sat down on the ground as far away from him as she could get and began to rock back and forth.

"Bugger," Stone muttered. Now they had two unresponsive people to deal with. He thought fast, then dug in his pocket and tossed the van keys to Jason. "Go get the van and bring it 'round to that side exit over there," he said, pointing. "I think that will be much more unobtrusive than trying to drag them through the front gate." Jason nodded and took off at a jog.

It seemed an eternity before Jason returned, but in actuality it was only about ten more minutes. "Hurry up," he said, glancing back over his shoulder. "I'm parked illegally." Quickly he grabbed the boy again, while Susannna and Verity helped Lissy up and hustled her out the exit.

Stone hurried ahead of both all of them, jumping into the driver's seat while the others arranged their passengers with Lissy as far as they could manage away from the boy.

Stone drove off quickly, careful not to draw attention to them. He pulled out a paper from his pocket and consulted it, then took a right out of the little side street where Jason had parked.

"How far is it?" Verity asked. She kept casting nervous glances at the kid as if she expected him to wake up any minute.

"Five minutes. Just sit tight—we'll be there soon."

Two more rights took them down a largely deserted commercial street lined with gas stations, small auto body and machine shops, and other similar light-industrial buildings. The gas station Lamar had told them about was right where it was supposed to be and did in fact appear abandoned. "Go check the left side roll-up door," Stone told Jason as he drove through the weed-choked parking lot up close to the building. "Lamar said it would be unlocked."

Jason leaped out of the van and ran over to tug on the door. It was indeed unlocked. He pushed it up the rest of the way, then pulled it back down again once Stone had driven the van inside. "Everybody out," Stone announced. "End of the line."

Jason hustled the kid out. When they looked back at Susanna, she shook her head. "I think we'll stay right here," she said. "I think Lissy will be okay once she's away from that boy." She started to fumble in her bag for a cigarette again, glanced at Stone, grumbled something under her breath, and settled back in the seat with a resigned sigh.

"I don't know how long this will take," the mage told her. "It might be a bit of a wait."

"That's fine. We'll just get us a little sleep. It'll be nice for a change to sleep without worryin' that something's comin' after us."

He nodded, grabbing his leather bag out of the front seat. "All right, then. With any luck we'll make this quick."

Taking the lead, he motioned for Jason and Verity to follow him out of the garage area and into the gas station's office. It was in the back of the building and didn't have any windows. Stone fished in the bag and came up with a flashlight, which he switched on and put down on an old desk. "Set him down in the chair there," he directed. "I'm hoping we can do this without ever having him wake up."

"How?" Verity asked.

"We don't need him. We need the thing inside him. And if he doesn't wake up, then there won't be any chance he'll see us. Safer that way." He opened the bag and started laying out items on the desk.

Jason set the skinny boy down in the chair, where he immediately tried to slump forward and fall out. Stone tossed him some light rope and he used it to tie the boy's hands behind him, more to keep him in the chair than to restrain him.

"So," Verity said, "How are we gonna do this? Do you just want me to stare at him and concentrate really hard on trying to get the thing out of him?"

"Not yet," Stone said, still fiddling with the various objects on the table. "First I want to see if I can determine anything about the nature of the Evil so I can try to get my cage right. We won't be able to contain this one since it's so weak, I suspect, but any readings I can get will be invaluable." Selecting something that looked like a short black wooden rod with a red crystal attached to one end, he moved closer to the boy.

"Is that a magic wand?" Jason asked, half joking.

"Not exactly," Stone sounded completely serious. "It's more a focusing object, to help me ignore outside astral influences while homing in on the one I'm trying to study."

"Of course it is," Jason said to Verity. She nodded and grinned.

"Oh, be quiet, you two." It was hard to tell if he was irritated or amused. He dragged another chair over, sat down, and held the crystal up near the boy's face. For a long time he neither moved nor spoke; he just did that weird unblinking-stare thing that Jason was learning to identify as 'doing something magic'. The boy twitched a bit and seemed uncomfortable, shifting back and forth in the chair, but he didn't wake. "You're in there, you bastard, aren't you?" Stone murmured. "I can feel you in there..."

"You can?" Jason whispered.

"Shh..." He moved the crystal again, this time touching it to the boy's forehead. Again he remained there, his arm shaking a little but otherwise unmoving, for nearly five minutes. Then he pulled back and let his breath out.

"Did you get anything?" Verity leaned in as if trying to see whatever it was for herself.

Stone seemed to be gathering his thoughts. "I — did. But I'm not sure *what* I got, exactly. I've got the maddening feeling that it's *familiar* somehow, but I can't figure out why, or how. It's fighting, though — it can't move the boy's body because he's unconscious, but it's trying. It's afraid — I think it suspects what we have planned for it. Best that we make this quick — I doubt this is good for its host's blood pressure."

"Did you get enough to make the cage?" Jason asked.

"I think so." Stone had already moved off and had pulled a notebook and pen out of the leather bag. He opened the notebook, moved over by the flashlight, and started writing rapid-fire notes. "Just—see if you can evict it now," he said to Verity without looking up. "I want to get this all down while it's still fresh."

Verity, looking thoroughly confused, cast a "What do I do now?" glance at Jason. When he shrugged, she moved closer to the boy and stared at him. She closed her eyes and screwed up her face—to Jason, it looked like she was either concentrating really hard or trying to lay a particularly troublesome egg. After about thirty seconds she opened her eyes and let her breath out. "I have no idea what I'm doing," she lamented.

"Um...maybe you have to tell it to get out," Jason suggested. "When you did it before, I heard you yell 'Get out!'" He glanced over at Stone for help, but the mage was still writing in his notebook, oblivious to their conversation.

"Guess it's worth a try," she said. Facing the boy again, she glared at him and yelled, "You! In there! Get out!" The boy shifted slightly in the chair, but nothing else happened. "I feel stupid," she complained.

"Al?" Jason called. "Little help here?"

Stone glanced up from his notebook. "What? Oh." He thought a moment, then said, "Erm—you told me before that you 'pushed' with your mind. Try that."

Verity rolled her eyes at him. "And I'm gonna maybe study magic with you? I can't wait for my first lesson: 'Okay—do magic!'"

Stone put the notebook away with a sigh and came over. "I can't really explain it, since I don't know exactly what you're doing. Remember, this sort of thing isn't the kind of magic I understand. It—" He stopped; his expression quickly went from confusion to revelation to disgust. He put his hand to his face, shaking his head. "Honestly, I don't know why you two bother to listen to me at all, given what an idiot I am. Again."

"What are you talking about?" Jason demanded.

"This...isn't...*magic*," Stone said, spacing the words out for effect. "Verity's ability to drive the Evil out of a host isn't a magical ability. It's a Forgotten one."

"So?" Jason was still confused.

"I get it!" Verity almost yelled in her excitement. "It's a Forgotten ability, so I can't use it because you did something to block my connection with whatever was causing me to be crazy."

Stone nodded, looking pleased with her. "Bright girl," he said. "Brighter than me, at any rate. If you end up studying with me, I won't be able to slack off at all if I want to stay ahead of you. But yes, exactly. It appears that there's some sort of connection between the energy that causes the mental problems and the Forgotten powers. Block one, you block the other one."

"So can you lift the block? Will that be safe?" Verity asked.

"Yes, and it should be, if what you tell me about it needing to 'build up' is accurate. This should only take a short time, and then we can put it back in place. But the first thing I'm going to have to teach you when this is over, even if you decide to go elsewhere, is how to control the block—to place it and remove it yourself. That's for later, though. Let's get this sorted before the kid wakes up and I have to put him under again."

Lifting Verity's block took less than a minute. "Now that it's established," Stone told her, "it's easier to manipulate. Once you learn to do it on your own, it will literally be like flipping a switch on and off."

She nodded. "Okay. Should I just try the same thing again?"

"It's a start. We might have to experiment a bit."

"If I can even do it at all," she muttered.

"I think you can. I have theory — since you're a potential mage, you should, even untrained, be able to have more control over a mentally-based power, even if you don't consciously know how to do it yet."

She looked dubious. "I hope you're right..." she said. Turning, she faced the boy again and resumed her "laying an egg" expression of concentration. "I want you *out* of there!" she growled.

The boy shifted in his seat again. It was subtle, but it appeared that there was some kind of interior struggle going on with him. "Is it working?"

"Keep going," Stone said, his voice even. He was watching the boy as closely as she was. "Try touching his forehead. Might help you focus."

Verity looked like that wasn't her first choice for something to do: the boy's face was dotted with a nasty case of acne. But after a moment she reached out and tentatively put one finger in the middle of his forehead. "Out!" she ordered again.

The boy's squirming grew a bit more pronounced. He appeared to be fighting his way to consciousness — or something inside him was trying to fight its way out. So far, Stone's spell was holding. "It's not working," Verity said under her breath, her voice thick with concentration.

"It is," Stone murmured. "I can feel — something — trying to fight you. Keep going."

Verity leaned forward, putting her hands on each side of the boy's head. "Leave...him...*alone!*" she yelled in frustration.

Suddenly without any warning, the boy lunged forward. Jason hadn't tied his hands tightly, since all he was trying to do was keep him upright in the chair. Nobody had noticed that while they were all focused on his face, he had apparently been busy working his hands loose from the bindings. Flinging his arms forward, he locked his hands around Verity's neck and the two of them over-balanced and went over backward with a crash.

Jason moved almost instantly, leaping forward and grabbing the kid's arms to loosen his grip on his sister. The kid, though skinny, fought with the strength of a madman, his eyes blazing with hatred. "You—can't—stop us!" he spat out through gritted teeth.

Stone was only a little slower than Jason, moving in to grab the boy's other arm. Together they managed to pull him off Verity, who skittered away, puffing and scared. They struggled with him as he flung his body back and forth, apparently heedless to any damage he was doing to it. His only obvious motivations were to escape and to injure as many of his captors as he could before he did it. "Do something!" Jason yelled to Stone. "Unless you want me to clock him one!"

Verity, however, had gotten back to her feet. She was regarding the kid with a mixture of anger and disgust. "Get out of there, damn you!" she yelled. "I'm sick of screwing around with you!" She closed her eyes and *pushed.*

Just as suddenly as he had lunged from the chair, the boy went limp in Stone's and Jason's arms, his head slumping forward. At the same time, a dimly glowing ball of energy shot up out of him, hovering above his body for a few seconds. Like the one before, this one made a few quick and desperate darts around, hovering in front of each of its captors in turn, and then exploded in what looked like a very feeble and silent white firework.

Verity let her breath out. "I...I did it," she said, like she hardly believed it herself.

"That you did," Stone said, puffing. Together with Jason he hustled the unconscious boy back into the chair. He checked to make sure he still had a pulse and was breathing, then turned back to Verity. "Nicely done. I was even able to get a couple of readings — though I didn't expect him to go after us like that."

Jason was looking at Verity with concern. "Are you okay? Did he hurt you?" He shot a nasty glance at the boy, obviously thinking about giving him a good swift kick or two for his trouble.

She felt at her neck, then shook her head. "No, just scared me. He didn't get a very good grip. That was pretty freaky."

Stone nodded. "But the important question is — do you know what you did now? Do you think you can duplicate it at will?"

"I'm — not sure," she said slowly. "But I think maybe I can. I did what you said — just pushed with my mind. But it seems like it takes some kind of scary thing to make it work right. Like I need to be afraid it's going to hurt me or somebody else."

"Hmm. Well, that's better than nothing, I guess. It will have to do for now." He motioned toward the boy. "Come on — let's get him back to the van. We need to take him back where we got him."

"Why can't we just leave him here?" Jason asked. He obviously wasn't feeling too much like making life easy for this kid.

"Safer to take him back. I don't think he'll remember any of this — he'll probably think he just passed out from drinking too much beer, or fell asleep. But we can't give him too many reasons to question that — like waking up in a location he has no knowledge of. That can bring up awkward complications."

"Okay, whatever." He got the kid under his arms and hoisted him up, then hung back as Verity left the room first and headed toward the van. "Hey, Al?"

"Yes?"

"Did you really have any idea that her being a mage would make this any easier?"

"Of course not." He raised an eyebrow. "She might be bright, but she's seventeen. I've got a few years of deviousness on her yet."

Jason grinned and resumed dragging the boy out of the room.

28.

After collecting Lissy (who was asleep, still clutching her glow stick) and Susanna (who guiltily scrabbled around trying to put out her cigarette before she got caught with it), they were able to drop the sleeping boy off in a shadowy corner near the side of the haunted house without incident. Of course, a little concealing magic never hurt. "So now what?" Jason asked as they were once more on the road, heading back to the Forgotten's current location to drop off their two guests. "Do you go back and try to work out how to build your cage?"

"Exactly," Stone said. "Hopefully by the time I finish, Lamar's feelers will have come back with some solid information about where we need to look for our big baddie."

"Well, I hope it doesn't take too long," Jason grumbled. "I'm getting sick of being cooped up in the house, even though I know it's not really safe to make too many appearances out in public right now."

Stone nodded. "I know, and I sympathize. But you're right—it wouldn't make sense to go through all this effort to deal with the Evil, only to have you two get picked off by a couple of DMW because you simply had to go to the cinema."

Once again they were met by a small party of Forgotten before they even parked the van. Marilee and Benny looked relieved that Lissy and Susanna had made it back safely. "No problems?" Marilee asked as they all went back inside to say their goodnights, and Stone broke off to go have a quick chat with Lamar.

"Nothing," Jason said. "But Al says we can't really do anything else until we get more information about where the Head Evil Thing is hanging out."

Marilee nodded. "I know. We've put the word out to every Forgotten group we know, but nothing's come back yet. As Lamar said, I think a lot of them are afraid. They don't think it's a good idea to poke at the Evil. We've spent so long hiding from them that going after them seems—suicidal." She sighed. "Still, though, I'm confident that something will turn up."

"I hope so," Jason said.

Stone spent the next three days once again splitting his time between his magic setup in the family room and his bedroom office with the door closed. The only time he came up for air was to disappear for about half an hour after Verity complained of being bored and running out of new and exciting recipes to try. "Here," he said when he returned, handing her a small stack of leatherbound tomes. "Start reading these. They'll give you some of the basic theory and concepts behind magic. It'll give you a leg up when you're ready to begin your studies."

She riffled through one of the books, wrinkling her nose in distaste. "These look like math books," she complained.

"Magic has a lot of math in it," Stone told her. "Might as well get used to it if you want to be any good."

She grumbled something noncommittal, but she did take the books with her to her bedroom.

On the third night, Stone was a little late for dinner. Jason was about to go hunt him up when he came down the hall and dropped into his chair, plunking a small object down next to his plate.

Jason looked at it curiously. It looked like a small open cube a little smaller than a child's building block, comprising eight crystals of varying hues held together by gold, silver and copper wire. He was about to ask what it was when he remembered what Stone had been doing all this time. "Wait—that's the cage?"

"That's it."

Verity regarded it with a tilted head. "It doesn't look very powerful," she said dubiously. "I thought it would be—bigger. How's it work?"

"Well, it needs to be small so we can take it wherever we need to go without someone noticing it. Since I don't expect we'll be able to lure our big Evil out of his hidey hole, we'll likely have to go in after him. And if he's some sort of powerful entity like a police chief or a politician, walking in with a large strange-looking object hardly seems prudent, does it?"

"So how's it work?" Verity asked again. She reached out tentatively and, at Stone's nod, carefully picked it up and examined it.

"It's attuned to the wavelength of the Evil, at least as much as I could determine it through my brief experiments with our young friend. When activated, it will create a magical field that, if we're fortunate, will contain any specimens of the Evil that happen to be nearby."

"Is it powerful enough?" Jason asked. He, like Verity, was dubious—the thing looked like something a moderately talented beginning jewelry maker might cobble together from spare parts.

"Well, the power doesn't come from the object, but from me," Stone said. "The object merely focuses it and attunes it to the proper energies." He took it back from Verity, holding it up in his palm. "It also, I believe, has another serendipitous side effect."

"What's that?"

"I'm not positive since it's impossible to test it here, but I'm fairly sure that it will resonate when it's near the Evil."

Jason's gaze on the little thing sharpened. "You mean it'll buzz or glow or something when it's near somebody who's possessed?"

"That's the theory. If it works, it solves another problem that I was concerned about—that wherever our quarry ends up hiding, we'd have to take one or more of the Forgotten with us to help triangulate on its precise location."

Jason let his breath out slowly. Yeah, the thought of having to drag Lissy and Susanna into a police precinct or an office building or some other restricted place didn't sound like anything any of them was in a hurry to do. Something else was bothering him too, though: "Well, yeah, that's a good thing. But this whole thing seems pretty sketchy. You keep saying things like 'if I'm right' and 'if we're lucky' and 'I can't be sure, but—'" He shook his head. "It sounds like one big magical house of cards that will crash and burn on us if one of these 'maybes' or 'I hopes' of yours is wrong."

If he was hoping for some reassurance from Stone, he didn't get any. "You're absolutely right," the mage conceded. "And I'm afraid that's the best we're going to get. We can't spend too much more time planning—every day we take is another day that something could go wrong. Especially with Lamar putting out feelers among other Forgotten groups. No offense intended to our friends, but having a whole army of mentally unhinged individuals in on the fact that we're planning to hunt down and execute our enemy's leader does not fill me with warm feelings of confidence."

Either by coincidence or by design, they didn't have long to wait. The next morning when Verity went out to get the paper, she found a small triangle-and-rays symbol chalked on the front porch next to it. She quickly called

Stone and Jason out to look at it, and Stone looked satisfied. "Aha," he said. "It appears that we have our sign."

"You think they've found something?" Jason asked.

"Let's go find out."

The Forgotten were still in the same place; apparently they either felt safe at the mall storeroom or else were risking remaining there a bit longer than was technically prudent so that Stone and the others could easily find them. As usual, the reception committee came out to meet them; this time Lamar himself was among the group. "Good morning," he said, smiling. "I see you got the message."

Jason handed over the large box of donuts and pastries they'd bought on the way over, and they all trooped back to the storeroom. "You found him?" Stone asked when they were all settled in their usual corner with Lamar and Marilee.

"Or her?" Verity added.

"Well—yes and no," Lamar said. "We're closer, but we still have more work to do."

Stone raised an eyebrow. "What do you mean? You haven't found him yet?"

"We've narrowed it down," Marilee said. "It took awhile because he's not nearby. We're pretty sure that he's in San Francisco. Or she," she added, with a smile toward Verity. Then she looked serious again. "It took a while to get the information back because the Forgotten over there are very frightened. Apparently it's much more dangerous to be homeless in San Francisco than it is on this end of the bay. Many of them—not just Forgotten, but homeless in general—disappear without a trace. And naturally the police can't be bothered to try to figure out why, so the Forgotten learn to keep their heads down."

Jason looked disappointed. He was sure that they were finally going to get the answer that would lead them to their quarry, but now it seemed like they still had a long way to go. "San Francisco's a big town," he said. "We can't exactly drive around with Lissy in the backseat looking for readings. I'm betting there are tons of Evil in San Fran."

"Well, it's a start," Stone said, trying to make the best of it. "Do you have contact with the Forgotten up there? Can you ask them to help us narrow things down a bit?"

"We're already doing that," Lamar said. He sighed. "I'm sorry. I wish we could move faster, but there isn't really much else we can do."

"It's okay," Jason assured him with a sigh, trying to hide his frustration. The thought of having to go back to the rental house and spend an indefinite amount of time puttering aimlessly around trying to kill time was a tiny version of hell for him. He wanted to *do* something. "We know you're doing your best."

"We're going to have to move again," Lamar said. "We've stayed here too long." He gave Stone a small piece of paper. "Here's where we're going next. It's in Mountain View."

Marilee started to speak, but then she happened to notice something and quickly struggled to her feet. "Hey now," she called, heading off at a quick waddling pace.

The others turned to see what she was so agitated about, and all of them had to grin. The black kitten had somehow gotten herself stuck headfirst in one of the shopping bags hanging off the side of Marilee's cart, and her tiny legs were pistoning around trying to get purchase, while her stubby little tail waved in agitation. Marilee quickly dug her out and set her on her feet, where she proceeded to look around with proper feline indignation and then began licking her back leg as if to say, "I meant to do that."

Stone chuckled. "Another intrepid explorer foiled in her plans," he began. "She—" But then he stopped. "What is it?"

Marilee had turned to come back to where they were sitting, but she only made it a couple of steps before stopping again. For several seconds she just stood there, looking deep in thought. Her expression glazed over as if she were seeing something far away, and then without a word of explanation she turned her back on them and moved back over next to the cart.

"What's she—?" Jason started, but Lamar put a finger to his lips, watching her intently.

Her back still to them Marilee stood regarding the cart for several more seconds. Then she reached out and plunged her hand into one of the several shopping bags she had attached to various points around its perimeter. She rooted around a bit, after a moment coming up with a piece of glossy paper in black and white with garish red highlights. Then she turned as if nothing out of the ordinary had happened, returned to the group, and plopped back down next to Lamar.

"What have you got there?" Stone asked her, curious.

She handed it over without a word. The glazed look was still in her eyes, but it was fading.

Stone took it and smoothed it out. His eyes darted back and forth as he took it all in, and then he raised an eyebrow and put the paper down so everyone could see it.

Even at first glance it was obvious that it was a flyer for some sort of nightclub. They were all quiet for several moments as they read over the copy:

R. L. KING

EXCLUSIVE BAY AREA ENGAGEMENT

-NIHIL-
-VERZWEIFLUNG-
-RAZORBABIES-
ONE NIGHT ONLY
Fetish Wear Strongly Encouraged

WILL TO POWER
Free Your Urges!

The flyer was accompanied by several dark illustrations in pseudo-fascist style. The date for the show was the following night.

"Look at the address," Stone said softly. There was an odd note in his voice.

Jason's eyes widened. "It's in San Francisco."

Verity was staring at Marilee. "You—find things in your cart," she said, like she couldn't quite believe it. "I've seen you do it before. Could this be—?"

Marilee's expression had returned to normal by now. She looked at the flyer almost as if she'd never seen it before. "It—could be," she admitted. "Sometimes I just—find things. Things I need. Even though I don't ever remember putting them in there."

Jason was looking at Stone. "Why would she have a flyer for a show at a club in San Francisco?" he asked. "Do they advertise down here?"

"They might, if it's a big enough show," Stone said. "But this does seem quite a coincidence." He looked at the flyer again. "I've heard of this place. Some of my students talk about it occasionally."

"What kind of club is it?" Jason asked. "*Fetish Wear Strongly Encouraged?* Is it some kind of S&M dungeon?"

Stone nodded. "Yes, among other things. The upper part—the main part, actually—is apparently a large nightclub that features bands that play dark music. Gothic, industrial, that sort of thing. Lots of bands imported from Germany and Scandinavia. Occult Studies tends to attract people who enjoy that lifestyle. Some of them are Wiccans, some are goths—some of them just like anything that's spooky or mystical or 'evil'." He put finger quotes around the last word. "And some of them just like dressing up in studded leather, black trench coats and too much makeup."

"But what about the rest?" Jason asked, trying not to notice the fact that Verity was looking far more interested than she should in this whole topic.

"The rest is a bit foggier," Stone said. "From what I understand, the lower level of the club is invitation only, and caters to what a couple of my students call 'the scene.'"

"The scene?" Jason was perplexed. The kind of clubs he frequented were more properly called 'bars,' and the music played there was generally of the garage-band heavy-metal variety.

"It's a BDSM sex club," Stone said, "For people who are into leather and whips and tying each other up and playing slave and master. That sort of thing."

Jason was silent for several seconds. "And he's in *there*?"

"It sort of makes sense, doesn't it?" Verity said, speaking up for the first time. "They like pain and misery and strong emotion. What would be a better place to get a steady source of that than a place where people go to hurt each other and get hurt on purpose?"

"She's got a damned good point," Stone agreed, nodding. He looked at Marilee. "You've done this before, then?"

"Yes," she said. "Lots of times. I usually find things that our group needs—coupons, sometimes old tools or a hat or socks or that kind of thing. Occasionally a little bit of money. It's never anything very valuable, or new—just stuff I might pick on the street. Except that I never remember picking it up after I find it in there."

"Interesting..." the mage said softly. "So—if this ability of yours helps you find the things you need, then—we're in need of locating this person, and you find a flyer for a club in the very city where he's supposed to be." He looked at Jason. "I'm inclined to take a chance on this," he said. "I wouldn't believe it if I hadn't seen some of their abilities firsthand. But this just seems like too much of a coincidence not to follow up."

"So—we're going to an S&M club," Jason said. He didn't sound at all enthusiastic. "Are you sure about this, Al?" He glanced at Verity, unable to hide his big-brotherly concern. "It's probably 21 and over. Verity probably can't even get in."

Verity rolled her eyes. "Come on, Jason. I spent the last five years in the nuthouse and even *I* know about fake IDs. We'll just have to get me one."

"Yeah, I guess," Jason grumbled. "And where are we gonna find 'fetish wear'? I don't even know what that is. I'm not going *anywhere* in skintight spandex pants and a leather harness, and there's no argument about that. The Evil can take over the world before I'll do that."

Stone chuckled. "I don't think it will come to that," he said. "I'm not exactly enthusiastic about the idea myself— I'm a bit old for this sort of thing—but we'll do what we have to. As I said, I have some students who are familiar with the place—or at least the club. I'll give one of them a call for advice. They can probably also give us the basic layout of the place so we don't have to go in blind."

Lamar and Marilee had been watching them, saying nothing. Now, though, Lamar spoke up. "You—don't intend for any of us to go with you to this place, do you?"

Stone shook his head. "No," he said gently. "You all have done enough already, and we can't begin to thank you for it. There wouldn't be any point in putting you in further danger. In fact, I would say that it would be best if we didn't contact each other anymore until after we've checked this place out. Of course, if you need help you have only to call."

Both Lamar and Marilee looked relieved. "I do hope this is what you're looking for," Marilee said, nodding toward the flyer. "I hope you can do it. And I'll pray for your safe return."

Spontaneously, Verity threw her arms around the old lady and gave her a hug. "You keep yourselves safe," she told her, her voice shaking a little bit. Then she pulled back and smiled. "Hey, you don't happen to have a fake ID with my name on it in that cart, do you?"

29.

"You're sure about this?" Jason asked. It wasn't the first time he'd done so.

It was eight o'clock the night after they'd last seen the Forgotten. He, Verity, and Stone were in San Francisco, in the front room of the small suite they'd rented at a motel that wasn't too far from the club. "Jason, stop being a wuss," Verity told him, rolling her eyes. "And quit worrying about me. I'll be fine."

Stone's students had come through not only with information about the club and advice on what to wear so they would blend in as much as possible (and where to buy it), but one of them had also put him in touch with an art major who was known in student circles as a wizard with fake IDs. The young woman was a little hesitant at first when approached by a professor, but changed her mind when Stone offered to pay double her normal fee. She had produced an extremely realistic-looking driver's license by early that morning, proclaiming Verity to be 21 years old.

Verity had enjoyed the subsequent shopping trip immensely; her two male companions, not so much. Stone and Jason spent much of their time trying to be as inconspicuous as possible and not to look like they were as uncomfortable as they were. Verity, meanwhile, moved around the stores like she'd spent her life there, picking out items not only for herself but for them. When she'd finished, both of them had to admit that she'd done a good job finding them outfits that wouldn't make them feel completely ridiculous: for Jason, she'd chosen black jeans, a studded black belt, combat boots, a tight black T-shirt with the logo of an industrial band Jason had never heard of, and a black leather biker jacket (she'd declared that his own leather jacket, which was brown, was simply "all wrong.") She had even more fun with Stone, deciding that he needed to look "more formal." When she got done with him, he looked quite reminiscent of a German SS officer minus any of the Nazi iconography. She'd put him in a black military-style tunic, black pants tucked into tall shiny black boots, and an impressive-looking black overcoat. When he got a look at himself in the mirror, he raised an eyebrow. "Where's my bloody riding crop?" he asked, half sourly, half amused.

Verity herself looked like she was finally able to dress the way she wanted to. Her outfit consisted of her own black biker jacket that was very much like Jason's, a tight leather top that laced up the front, a black leather spiked dog-collar choker, black miniskirt, fishnet stockings with artful holes in them, and her black Doc Martens. Jason took one look at her and started to say something, but her glare silenced him. He had to concede, albeit grudgingly, that she carried the look off. She didn't look vulnerable — she looked completely in control of herself and more than a little intimidating. It scared him a bit. What was his tomboy kid sister turning into?

She had also picked up some hair dye and cosmetics, and when they got back to the hotel after deciding to permit themselves dinner at a good restaurant for a change, she locked herself in the bathroom for an hour while Jason and Stone sat out front and went over the crude map of the club that the student had given them. Unfortunately they hadn't been able to track down either of the two other students who were familiar with the lower level, but at least they wouldn't have to go in completely blind.

Stone was arranging his various magical items in the pockets of his overcoat when Verity emerged from the bathroom. He and Jason both stared at her with wide eyes. She'd dyed her hair jet-black and used some sort of gel to spike it up into points, and done her face in dramatic makeup that made her look paler than she was and emphasized her large dark eyes. Her lips were blood red. "Whatcha think?" she asked grinning.

"I think you're having entirely too much fun with this," Stone told her.

"Well, you *did* say we had to blend in, right?"

Jason didn't say anything. He wasn't sure what *to* say, and a little afraid that if he spoke up, he might say something he'd later regret. In many ways, this new transformation in his sister was causing him more mental difficulty than the entirety of the insane and magical proceedings that he'd been dealing with for the past couple of weeks. *She's growing up,* he told himself sternly. *You can't keep treating her like she's twelve, even though that's the last time you really knew her. You have to let her grow up, even if you don't like the way she's doing it.* He knew that in less than a month she'd be eighteen and technically he wouldn't have any control over her anymore—not that he did now. "We ready to do this?" he finally asked.

Stone, who'd been smiling at Verity's enthusiasm, sobered. "Ready as we can be," he said.

Will to Power was on the waterfront, a mile or so off the main part of the Embarcadero. Here, glitzy souvenir shops and seafood restaurants gave way to derelict warehouses and ugly looming industrial buildings. "Definitely not the posh end of town," Stone commented. "But that's not too surprising, given its focus."

They were in a cab; the driver was a dark-skinned Middle Eastern man who barely spoke English, but who had given them a very strange look when they'd told him their destination. He didn't comment, though. *Probably gets all kinds of tourist weirdos,* Jason thought.

He leaned back in his seat and looked idly out the window as the cab picked its way through the thick Friday night traffic; he hadn't been to San Francisco since he was a kid up here with his dad for a vacation, and he didn't remember much about it except the Golden Gate Bridge and the tourist part of Fisherman's Wharf. They had come past the Wharf, but they soon left the lit-up tourist area and moved into a part of the docks where most tourists weren't brave enough to venture these days. He wondered if he could spot any of the Forgotten symbols, then almost immediately noticed one spray-painted on the side of a rotting warehouse: the circle, X, and squiggly line. Bad place. Danger. He touched Stone's arm and pointed it out; the mage nodded. "I've been noticing them for awhile," he murmured over Verity, who was seated between them.

"All the bad ones, I take it?"

He nodded soberly. "Haven't seen any others. Wherever this place is, the Forgotten seem to avoid it like the plague."

Indeed, they had not seen one homeless person or group for the last fifteen minutes, despite the fact that the buildings they were passing were rundown and many were abandoned. It looked like a prime area to be colonized by a few enterprising Forgotten groups, but yet there were none in evidence. "Weird," Jason said. "I wonder if even the normal homeless groups avoid it."

"Quite probably. Remember what Marilee said about homeless people up here disappearing without a trace?"

"You think that has something to do with this club?"

Stone shrugged. "No idea, but I wouldn't be surprised."

Jason sighed. "You know, I'd give just about anything right now to be able to call in some heavy hitters on this. It feels wrong to me to be playing Batman, trying to solve

R. L. KING

this on our own. We ought to be able to call the cops, or the government, or somebody who's better equipped to deal with it. It just feels wrong that they're the ones we *can't* call, because they're probably mixed up in the whole thing and there's no way to know who's clean and who isn't." He shook his head and dropped his voice even further, glancing at the cabbie to make sure he wasn't listening. "You know, taking care of this guy, whoever he is, isn't going to solve the problem. There's still gonna be all the second-tier Evil in the cops and the politicians and the business leaders. What's to say that one of them won't just step up and take over the operation?"

"That's a damned good question," Stone said. "And I don't have an answer for you, except to say that, honestly, this probably *won't* end it. The best we can hope is that it tosses whatever organization they have into disarray for awhile, and perhaps gives us — and others — time to deal with what's left before it can reorganize."

"That doesn't sound very encouraging." Jason shook his head, still looking out the window.

The cab was slowing down now, working its way over to the right lane. Stone, Jason, and Verity all switched their attention to the front window. "Here it is," the cabbie said, double-parking next to a group of motorcycles.

Jason didn't know what he expected to see, but it wasn't anything like the reality. The club was in a large old industrial building of indeterminate type, its entire front-facing wall painted black. "WILL TO POWER" shone in glowing purple neon above a set of windowless black padded double doors, and a poster-sized version of the flyer Marilee had pulled from her cart was tacked up behind glass to the right of the doors. Even from inside the cab the three of them could hear the pounding beat of the music, muted but still quite loud. A large crowd was milling around outside, smoking and chatting. Most of them were dressed similarly to Stone, Jason and Verity: lots of leather, military styles, skintight vinyl, and goth-wear. Most were young — early to mid twenties — but there were a surprising number of people Stone's age or even older.

The exited the cab and Stone paused to pay the driver while Jason and Verity got a look around. Jason noticed two beefy guys in tight black club-logo T-shirts and jeans standing on either side of the doors. He watched for a moment as a group went up to them, noticing that they were collecting the cover charge but didn't appear to be paying that much attention to checking IDs.

Verity tapped his arm. "Look," she whispered, pointing.

Jason looked. They were very hard to spot this time, chalked nearly at sidewalk level on the side of the building near the corner and very small, only three inches or so high. But there were five of them in a row: "Bad Place" Forgotten symbols. "This must be a *really* bad place," he muttered under his breath. "I hope that means we picked the right one."

Stone rejoined them. "Shall we, then?"

The bouncers didn't give them a second look — including Verity and her fake ID — but just collected their money and waved them in with a muttered "Enjoy the show." Beyond the padded doors was a steep black-painted stairway lined with posters and flyers from bands who had played at the club previously, along with a lot of graffiti. Most of the latter seemed to be names and phone numbers, band names, and general obscenities regarding one band or another. Jason didn't spot anything that looked like gang tags, and surprisingly he could find no evidence of Forgotten symbols. When he mentioned this to Stone as the three of them were borne along up the stairs by the rest of the crowd, he shook his head. "If you were Forgotten, would you have any desire at all to come in here?"

"Good point," Jason had to admit. Both of them practically had to shout over the music.

The stairway ascended what appeared to be one or two floors and then opened out onto a large clear space. The music, no longer muffled even by one wall, was nearly deafening now. The three of them stepped out of the flow of traffic and moved off to the side so they could take in the scene.

It was impossible to see everything from where they were—it was evident that the place was designed in such a way that it wouldn't allow unrestricted sightlines to much of anything. There were no windows. The only things they could see clearly were the enormous purple-neon-rimmed bar on the other side of the room, and the stage far off to their right. Small tables dotted the landscape, spread out and hidden back in alcoves so no more than two or three of them were near each other, and all around them people stood in little knots holding drinks or writhed on what was apparently a large dance floor in front of the stage. The band currently performing consisted of a slim young woman behind an impressive looking synth, a dark-haired man in sunglasses playing guitar, another man they couldn't quite see on drums, and an animated lead singer with short-cropped bright blond hair and a vaguely military-looking outfit. There was no way to make out any of the song's lyrics between the distortion, the volume, and the fact that the lead singer was growling into the mic. The audience was eating it up, though, from the look of things.

"Where do we start?" Jason shouted over the music.

Verity tapped his arm and pointed over to an empty table near one of the walls. They quickly moved over there and commandeered it. Once they were seated, Jason leaned in toward Stone and yelled, "Is your magic thing buzzing yet?"

Stone raised an eyebrow, but pulled the little cube out of his pocket and held it in one hand, shielded by his other. The crystals were glowing faintly. "It is," he said. "Doesn't surprise me—I wouldn't be at all surprised to find a decent contingent of Evil in here."

"That doesn't help much," Jason said. "What do we do—just wander around until we find something? I don't want to split up." At Verity's glare, he glared right back at her. "I'm sorry, V, but I'm still responsible for you for another month, and there's no way I'm gonna let you wander around a place like this by yourself."

"He's right," Stone said. "I don't think it would be the safest thing for *any* of us to wander around here alone. It's unlikely we'll be spotted or recognized, but if that were to happen I think our chances would improve significantly if we remained in a group."

Verity nodded reluctantly. "Yeah, I guess you're right. Most of these people look like fun, but I've seen a few sleazeballs too."

"I don't think what we're looking for is out here, though," Stone said. "We need to investigate the dungeon area."

"Where is it?" Jason asked. The crude map that Stone's student had provided did not include the entrance to the dungeons. "We can't exactly walk up to somebody and ask, 'Hey, can you tell us where the bondage dungeon is?'"

Verity grinned. "Sure we can. You just have to do it the right way." She started to stand, then waved Jason off as he reached for her to pull her back down. "Just keep an eye on me. I'm not going far." She pointed at a balding middle-aged man dressed in a leather jacket with a mesh shirt underneath, too-tight pants, and a dog collar similar to hers. He was standing about ten feet away from their table on the periphery of the dance floor. "Gonna go talk to him for a minute." Before Jason could protest further, she was gone.

Jason and Stone did not take their eyes off her while she sidled up to the man, close enough that their leather-clad shoulders touched, and appeared to be saying something to him. Everything about her body language suggested that she found him the most attractive man in the club, and it was everything Jason could do not to leap up and punch the guy's lights out. "Steady," Stone cautioned. "Let's see if she can pull this off."

The man's pasty face broke into something resembling a leer as it became clear that this attractive young woman seemed interested in him. He said something to her, to which she replied with a predatory smile. He said something else, pointed across the room toward the bar, then reached out as if to touch her. She danced deftly out of his grasp, shaking her head and waving her finger at him in a 'naughty boy' gesture. He looked briefly crushed, then brightened, said one more thing to her, and moved off into the crowd.

Verity came back over to the table about three seconds before Jason was about to jump up and drag her back. She dropped down into her seat with a long sigh. "What a perv," she said, wrinkling her nose. "I took a chance—with an outfit like that he might have just been a leather daddy with bad taste in clothes, but no, he was a straight perv. I told him I was looking for a little more interesting action and he practically drooled on me."

"Did you find out where the dungeon is?" Stone asked.

She nodded. "The entrance is over there past the bar. It's on the first floor, which is why we had to come up here to get to the club. There's no other way in for the public besides through here. Supposedly you don't get in without an invitation, but he said you can bribe your way in, and women and cute guys pretty much just have to smile at the door guy." She looked the two of them up and down. "I think you two qualify. We should be okay."

"How did you get rid of him?" Jason asked, hooking a thumb toward where Perv Guy had disappeared and ignoring what she'd said about him and Stone.

She chuckled. "Oh, that's easy. I told him to get out of my sight. I think he thought I was a dominatrix. Which means he'll probably be looking for me once we get in there, but I'll just tell him to lick my boots or something and we'll be good to go."

Jason looked at her sideways. "You know way too much about this stuff. I'm not gonna ask you where you learned it."

She shrugged. "Hey, it was pretty boring when I was in the nuthatch. I did a lot of reading."

Stone stood. "Well, then. I don't know about the rest of you, but I can think of many places I'd rather be spending my time. So shall we get on with this?"

Jason was all for that. The sooner they got done and out of here, the happier he'd be. This wasn't his kind of club even if it *wasn't* a haven for Grand Poobah Evil of this part of the state, and much as he was loath to admit it to himself, Verity's comfort level in here was not sitting well with him at all. He wondered sometimes—often, actually—how she was managing to deal so well with the aftermath of the five years she'd gone through. Nobody just shrugged off that kind of situation. He kept catching himself watching her as if expecting her to lose it any minute. The fact that she hadn't yet he attributed less to Stone's blocking magic and more to a growing fear that it was building up and getting ready to blow at the smallest provocation. *Can't worry about that now, though,* he told himself sternly, hurrying to catch up to Stone and Verity. *Gotta deal with this now. Time for the rest of it later.* He might not be able to cast lasers from his hands, but his fists were in pretty good shape and he wasn't about to let anything happen to Verity and Stone while he still had the power to stop it.

On the far side of the bar, obscured to them from where they'd been sitting by the seething crowd, was a door with an unobtrusive "No Admittance" sign. Like the rest of the place it was painted black, and it looked like it led to the kind of hallway you'd go down to get to the restrooms. The only thing that indicated that it might have other purposes were the two beefy guys dressed in tight leather pants and harnesses that showed off their impressive physiques. They lounged on either side of the door, drinks in their hands, doing their best to look like a couple of club patrons who'd simply decided to hang out here for awhile and watch the show. Stone motioned for Verity and Jason to stop as they drew up to the bar. "Order us something," he muttered under his breath to Jason. "I want to get a read on them."

Jason moved over to the bar, Verity following closely; it was crowded, but they were able to worm their way in before too long. He ordered a beer for himself and a Guinness for Stone; Verity looked like she was going to try ordering something alcoholic but at Jason's glance decided it wasn't worth the effort and instead got herself a sparkling cider. By the time they made their way out of the crowd and back to Stone, he appeared to have finished whatever he was trying to do. "Anything?" Jason asked, handing him the Guinness.

Stone nodded. "The one on the right appears to be Evil, though I can't quite be sure. At least one of them is, for certain. They're too close together for precise evaluation. We need to be careful."

"Could you tell if they like girls or boys?" Verity asked.

Stone looked surprised. "Erm—why?" When she didn't answer right away, he shrugged. "I think they're straight. At least judging by the leers they were directing at two scantily clad young ladies I saw trying to get in, while completely ignoring their male companions."

She grinned. "Let me handle this, then." she said. "Just follow me and play along." She looped her arm through Stone's and began moving toward the guards.

As the three of them approached, the guards casually moved toward each other to block the door. "Hey, you two," Verity said with her best wolfish grin.

The two men looked her up and down. "Haven't seen you around here before," the left one said.

"I'm new in town, and looking for a little action," she said. Her expression suggested quite effectively what sort of action she was looking for.

The other guard indicated Stone and Jason. "Who are these two?"

She smiled, squeezing Stone's arm. "He's my...date. And he," she added, pointing at Jason, "is my bodyguard. He makes sure everybody plays nice, you know?"

Jason pulled himself up to his full height, moved a little closer to Verity, and glared at the guards. This was a role he could play with ease.

"So what do you say?" she asked them, reaching out to tweak the closest one's nose, then let her finger continue halfway down his chest. "You going to let us in so we can liven the place up a bit?"

The two guards looked at each other for a moment, then the one she'd tweaked shrugged. "Sure, why not? You're gonna have to pay for your friends, though. Twenty bucks cover, each." He leered. "Or you can leave them here and go on in yourself..."

"Oh, that's quite all right," Verity said. "I like having them around. Pay the man, will you?" she said to Stone.

"Of course," he murmured, handing over the money. The guards stepped aside.

"Oh, look," Jason said when they were safely past and the door swung shut behind them. "A *pretend* basement this time. This is really getting to be a theme."

Stone grinned. "Well, it *is* San Francisco," he pointed out. "Not too many real basements 'round here, what with the earthquakes and all. They have to make do."

Ahead of them was a short hallway lined in more band posters and ending with a staircase down. The music was a lot quieter here, but there was an odd odor: a mixture of vinyl, body oil, and what smelled like incense. Jason was getting a very bad feeling about this, but there was nothing to be done about it except to follow Verity and Stone down the stairs. The main source of his concern was the fact that if this really was the only public entrance to the dungeons, then the door above them was the only exit from this place that they knew about. He never liked going anywhere dangerous that only had one exit. Once again he wished he'd been able to obtain a pistol, though he had to admit that getting it inside this place would have been close to impossible unless Stone had more magic tricks up his sleeve than he was admitting to.

At the foot of the stairs was a wide doorway that opened out onto a large clear space that had been divided by barriers that reminded Jason of the ones at the hospital where Willow had been, except that they were taller, more substantial, and painted black. The music was louder in here, but different: still dark, but more ambient and instrumental, with a hypnotic driving beat. The walls were black too, with flashes of neon scattered around for effect. The ceiling was dotted with strobes and black lights. The whole effect was disorienting, eerie, and very strange. "Where the hell do we start?" Jason asked.

"Let's look around a bit," Stone said, stepping aside to allow a couple to move past them. The man was naked except for a tiny thong, sandals, a ball gag, and a dog collar; the woman was dressed similarly to Verity. She held the end of a leash attached to the man's collar and was pulling him along. Neither of them acknowledged Stone and the others, but the man looked utterly blissful. Off to their right was a large table covered in safe-sex literature, boxes of condoms, small individually wrapped disinfectant towelettes, and rubber and latex gloves. A poster above the table depicted a couple of indeterminate genders engaged in enthusiastic sex and read in large purple letters: "Play Hard! Play Safe!"

Jason took a deep breath. This wasn't going to be easy. He'd been to strip clubs many times before and always enjoyed them; he'd even once spent the night with what he jokingly called "commercial affection" when he'd been at a particularly low point in his love life. But this—he shuddered a little. "You can't get any kind of good read down here, can you?" he asked Stone hopefully.

The mage shook his head. "No, not where we are. There are definitely Evil here, but no way to tell where or who. Come on. The sooner we get this over with, the sooner we can get out of here."

Oddly, it made Jason feel a little better that Stone didn't seem to be enjoying himself here either. Even Verity was looking a little freaked out—he imagined that whatever idea she had about how these places were supposed to work didn't match up with the reality. "The floor is *sticky*," she said, wrinkling her nose and picking up one of her Doc-Marten-clad feet as if she'd stepped in a pile of dog leavings.

"Come on," Stone said grimly, and started off to the left. The other two hastened to follow him.

For the next twenty minutes, all three of them got a crash course in a subject they all would have preferred to avoid. As it turned out, the dividers were there to delineate spaces both small and large. The small ones, equipped with beds that were little more than stained mattresses on cheap frames, had black curtains in front of their entrances and were obviously meant to be used by groups of two or three people. The larger ones, which ranged in size from a medium sized room to a large garage, were set up for various "scenes": one contained a wooden rack with leather straps and an assortment of whips and floggers neatly arranged on a table along one side; one was set up like a medical office with a surgical bed, a collection of wicked looking instruments on a tray, and a glaring overhead light; another was, with the help of artful painting on the barrier walls, designed to look like a prison cell and contained a large metal cage in the back that was occupied by a naked man who appeared to have been left there alone.

Stone moved staunchly along, occasionally stopping for a discreet consultation of his magical detector. For the most part, none of the dungeon's denizens seemed to mind the presence of others; only one couple glared at them and sent them off with an angry "Fuck off!" when they glanced into their open cubicle. The others either ignored them or, in some cases, seemed to be glad for the audience. One woman who was obviously an exhibitionist perked right up and put on a show for them as they went by, draping herself around her leather-clad "mistress" with great enthusiasm. An attractive middle-aged man dressed in a quasi-military uniform similar to Stone's offered the mage a proposition that he politely declined, whereupon the man smiled ruefully, bowed, and faded off into the darkness.

At one point, much to their consternation, they developed a fan club: three small, thin men in briefs and flip-flop sandals spotted them and began to follow them around, making all sorts of inappropriate comments and invitations with wide, cheerful smiles. They didn't seem to discriminate on their choice of partners, directing their invitations at all three of them equally. Jason was a few seconds from informing them that if they got near Verity again he was going to punch their teeth in one at a time when they suddenly spotted a blond shirtless man in short shorts and immediately hurried off to follow him, waving jaunty goodbyes at Stone, Jason, and Verity.

"You getting anything?" Jason asked again as he watched them go. The urge to take a shower, preferably in disinfectant, was growing by the minute.

"No..." Stone was looking a little confused. "This is...odd."

"What? *Everything's* odd in here."

"No, no. That's not what I mean." He held up his detector. "I'm getting readings, but they're faint. As — strange as this is here for us, these people are clearly enjoying themselves. Even the chap who was getting his bare bum whipped so enthusiastically by that large woman — didn't you notice? He looked like he was having the time of his life, and so did she. I can't say for sure, but I would be very surprised if any of the participants here were Evil, nor many of the spectators."

"Yeah," Verity added, nodding. "I see what you mean. We haven't seen anybody like that kid at the haunted house, just standing around watching and getting his jollies — and even if people were watching, nobody's really getting hurt. Not permanently, anyway. Do the Evil get off on pain if the person *enjoys* being hurt?"

"Could we be in the wrong place?" Jason looked concerned now. "What about Marilee and her cart? I mean, I guess everybody misses sometimes, but—"

Stone wasn't really listening. He appeared to be deep in thought, staring at but obviously not seeing a lurid poster for a band called "Dark Desires" on the wall in front of him. Finally he shook his head as if trying to rid it of cobwebs. "I don't understand this," he said. "There are definitely Evil here—I'm getting readings and I've no reason to doubt them. But the concentration—it's not as high as we were led to expect."

Verity started to say something, then held up as two women, their arms draped around each other's shoulders and passing a marijuana joint back and forth, moved past them. When they were gone, she said slowly, "Well...the Evil do get off on any kind of emotions, right? Not just the bad ones. They just like the bad ones better. But it's kind of hard to make a place where there are bad emotions all the time. We tried to think of one before, and the best we could come up with was a haunted house."

"Or some sort of asylum or prison," Stone agreed. "But what are you getting at?"

She shrugged. "I don't know exactly. I was just thinking—maybe this place is kind of like—broccoli or something."

Stone and Jason both stared at her like she'd sprouted antennae. "What?" they asked in near-unison.

She grinned sheepishly. "Sorry, sorry. Sometimes my shorthand gets me in trouble. What I mean is that if they need strong emotions to live and it's sometimes hard to get the bad ones they really like—then maybe the kind they get here are something they *need,* even though they don't like it as much. You know, like eating your broccoli when you don't have any candy bars."

"Verity, you're weird," Jason told her.

"Indeed she is," Stone agreed. "But she has a point. Perhaps what they've got set up here is a place where they can get a fairly constant influx of emotional sustenance — not what they prefer, certainly, but enough to keep them going until they can *get* what they prefer."

"So does that leave us back at square one?" Jason asked, hoping very much that it didn't. He wasn't sure how much more of this kind of detective work he could stand.

"Not necessarily," Stone said, pulling out the detector. "We just need to figure out where the Evil activity is coming from, if not here."

"Some sort of secret part of this building?" Verity asked.

"Possibly," Stone said. "Let's spend a bit more time investigating this area down here. Look for any unmarked doors, areas that don't seem to get a lot of traffic — anything that looks out of the ordinary." At Jason's roll-eyed look, he grinned. "All right, *more* out of the ordinary than just about everything else 'round here. Better?"

Jason didn't answer that.

"I'm going to try something," Stone told them. "I didn't want to do it before because it has its own problems associated with it and I didn't think we needed it before, but I think we do now."

"What's that?" Verity looked interested.

"Come on," he said, gesturing toward an empty cubicle. They moved behind the black curtain and he closed it behind them. "I have a spell — it's a concealment spell, but not invisibility per se."

"You can make people invisible?" Jason asked.

"I can, but it requires a lot of energy and it's almost never practical for anything more than a few seconds. No, this is more like a misdirection than true invisibility. Somewhat akin to what the Forgotten can do to make people not notice buildings. It's essentially a stronger version of the concealment spell I've been doing on the car for awhile now. Surprisingly, it's a lot harder to do it on people than it is on cars. People rarely notice cars anyway, unless they're looking for a specific one."

Verity cocked her head. "You mean you can make it so people don't see us even though we're not invisible?"

"Essentially. It's risky, especially in crowds, because it doesn't make us incorporeal. If someone runs into us, or we speak right next to them, they're going to notice us. But it will help us fade into the background a bit and perhaps make it so we can see things that we might not have seen if people were aware of us."

Jason gave him a look. "Al...I can think of at least a dozen times in the past few days where that would have come in really handy. Why didn't you tell me you could do this before?"

"Because a few days ago I didn't have the items I've been building, and it's damned tiring to keep even a simple spell like that going if I have to power it myself — especially if it's covering more than one person." He raised an eyebrow. "Jason, before I met you and got caught up in your little web of insanity, I was a humble university professor. My magic was more of the experimental variety. I'm not an action hero, and I'm not a voyeur. I don't exactly get much call for using that kind of spell."

"So let's try it now," Verity said eagerly. "What do we have to do?"

"Stay close to me, and whatever you do, stay out of people's way. Stay close to the walls, and if a large group is coming, duck into one of the cubicles until they pass by." Gesturing, he chivvied the two of them into standing next to each other, then moved in front of them. He held up his hand and moved it slowly over all three of them.

Jason noticed that the blocky purple ring he wore glowed slightly. In a few seconds, he lowered his hand. "There, that's done."

"I don't feel any different," Verity said. Experimentally she held up her own hand as if expecting not to be able to see it.

"Well, you wouldn't, would you?" Stone said. "Trust me, though, it's working. Remember, stay close. You don't have to be touching, but don't move more than a couple of feet away. Let's go."

They moved back out of the cubicle into the hallway (which fortunately was still unoccupied) and set off. "Let's investigate as much of the area we haven't already seen as we can," Stone muttered. "I'm convinced there's something down here we're not seeing."

"Wait a sec..." Jason said, stopping. Stone, in front, had to stop fast to avoid moving the spell effect away from him.

"Don't do that," he said irritably. "Didn't you hear what I just said?"

"No, this is important," Jason insisted. "You said 'something down here we're not seeing'."

"Yes, and — ?"

"What if you're not the only mage here? We know they've got at least one good one, or they did anyway, before Verity evicted him. Who's to say he hasn't been reoccupied?"

Stone stared at him. "You know, I didn't even — "

" — think of that," Jason finished. "Yeah. I didn't either, till you said that. But remember that door in that restaurant? The one with the gateway? Or you and your crypt? What if there's a hidden door around her somewhere?"

"Unlikely," Stone said slowly. "But possible."

"Why unlikely?"

"Because that sort of thing is white magic, not black. Remember I told you permanent magic isn't something black mages can do? It's one of their biggest weaknesses. That kind of concealment magic is permanent, or at least long-term."

"So you're saying they can't do it, or just that it would be hard?"

Stone thought about that for several long seconds. "I don't think it would be completely impossible," he said at last. "But it would require an immense amount of effort. They way their magic works, they probably would have had to kill at least one person to get the power to even begin it, plus put their mage — or mages — at some personal risk. So they would likely save it for something they wanted to conceal very much."

"Can you find it?" Jason asked. "If it's here, can you find where it is?"

"Not directly. Not without a lot more equipment and time than we have."

Jason sighed, looking disappointed. Then he perked up. "But if they've got some kind of hidden entrance to something, maybe if we poke around enough we'll spot someone using it."

"That's much more likely. Come on. Let's go. It doesn't take a lot of energy to keep this spell up, but I can't do it indefinitely."

They moved off again, carefully staying close to walls. and keeping their eyes open for anything that looked out of the ordinary. They were lucky in that most of the patrons of the dungeon seemed now to have moved off into their various cubicles or larger areas, so there weren't many people wandering the halls. They did have one close call when the middle-aged man from whom Verity had first gotten the directions to the dungeon's entrance came weaving around a corner and nearly blundered into them, but they quickly ducked into a nearby cubicle and managed to avoid him. Jason got one look at the couple inside and averted his eyes. He was an open-minded kind of guy and firmly believed that anything consenting adults wanted to do together was absolutely a-OK, but that didn't mean he wanted to watch it. In any case, he doubted that they would have noticed the arrival of a platoon of Marines, given how caught up in each other they were.

It took them another twenty minutes or so to carefully explore the rest of the dungeon area. It wasn't as large as they'd initially thought—the maze of black dividers distorted its dimensions and made it seem much bigger than it really was. They glanced inside the large scene areas, peeked discreetly into the cubicles, and investigated both the men's and women's bathrooms. For this latter activity they had to drop the spell and hope for the best—Jason was highly reluctant to let Verity out of his sight long enough for her to check out the ladies' room, but in the end he had to relent. He and Stone hovered nervously outside the door, earning themselves a couple of sour looks from female patrons who had to walk past them to get inside, and were just about to go in after her when she emerged. "Nothing to report," she said. "Three or four women putting on makeup, a couple using the stalls, no extra doors or windows or anything. Just looks like a bathroom that really needs cleaning."

Jason nodded. They'd encountered similar in the men's room, except that two of the stalls were obviously in use for romantic encounters ("Why would they want to use the bathroom stalls when they've got a whole *club* to use?" Verity asked in distaste). Again, no extra doors or suspicious looking blank walls.

Stone sighed. "I'm running out of ideas," he said. "We've checked out the whole area. Either we're missing something, there's nothing here to find, or it's upstairs in the nightclub. We—" He stopped, because Verity had just poked him hard in the arm. "What?"

"Shh," she whispered urgently, pointing. She'd turned to look behind them while Stone and Jason were looking ahead. The two of them turned, and Jason had to stifle an exclamation of surprise.

Coming down the hall and moving like they owned the place were two young men. Their body language didn't suggest that they were a couple, but rather a clear contempt for their surroundings. As they moved closer, it was obvious to all three of the concealed watchers that they were both dressed in identical black leather jackets with the red-and-black circle logo of Dead Men Walking. The three watchers flattened themselves against the wall, holding their breath as the gangers moved past. If the gangers noticed them, they made no sign of it.

When they drew past, Stone pointed at them and nodded. Taking the cue, the three of them detached themselves from the wall and quietly followed, leaving about ten feet between themselves and the gangers. The music was so loud that they weren't concerned about being heard, but they still made every effort to move as quietly as they could.

Perhaps surprisingly given their usual propensity for causing trouble, the gangers didn't do anything overtly threatening. They didn't poke into the cubicles or otherwise disturb any of the dungeon's patrons. They simply moved down the hallway, then took a left at an intersection. Stone and the others picked up their pace a bit to follow; their previous investigations had shown them that this particular hallway was flanked by the long wall of one large closed scene area on the left side (a quick peek inside had shown it to be an elaborately staged church/funeral setup complete with open casket at the front, with its entrance on the hallway from which they had just turned) and three smaller cubicles on the right. The wall at the end of the hallway was blank, and if Jason's sense of direction was any good—which it usually was—it was the outer wall of the club.

Stone and the others hung back to watch what the gangers did. The pair moved past the first two cubicle entrances without a glance toward them; their destination seemed to be the third cubicle. One pulled a folded cardboard sign from his pocket and affixed it to the curtain with two safety pins; it read "Closed for Cleaning." Then both of them moved inside. As soon as they disappeared through the curtain, Stone motioned Jason and Verity forward. They quickly closed the distance and moved in close so they could see through the gap in the cubicle curtain. They glanced at each other, wide-eyed, when they saw what was happening.

30.

The far wall of the cubicle wasn't a divider, but rather a continuation of the solid wall that represented the outer boundary of the building. Stone and the others had checked this cubicle before and the wall had been resolutely blank, but now one of the two gangers was on his knees fiddling with something under the bed, while the other waited with clear expectation near a spot in the middle of the wall. After a moment, just like in A Passage to India, a section of the wall shimmered and a door came into existence where none had been before. It was a boring metal door with the word "Maintenance" on the outside. As soon as it appeared, the standing ganger fumbled in his pocket, pulled out a key, and opened it. He held it open to wait for his companion to get up, then the two of them went through it. From the other side of the cubicle curtain, Stone made a quick gesture at the door, and it stopped an inch before clicking closed again. The three of them waited anxiously to see whether the gangers noticed that it hadn't closed.

"Holy shit," Jason whispered after several seconds. "It's just like the door at the restaurant. They're even using the same Maintenance trick."

Stone shrugged, moving inside. "Who looks in a maintenance closet?" He glanced around. "Get me something to block this door open."

Jason pulled the threadbare pillow from the bed and tossed it to Stone, who used it to prop the door and let his spell holding it open drop.

"Where could they be going?" Verity asked. "Secret room?"

"Let's find out, shall we?" Stone said. "Let me go first—if it is a secret room and they're in there, I can likely take them out faster than either of you two can. Be ready, though."

Silently, he moved forward and pushed the door open. Jason kept a close eye on him, while Verity watched the cubicle curtain to make sure nobody else was coming in. After a couple of tense moments, the mage's whisper came back through the open door: "Come on in, and close that door behind you."

Quickly Jason and Verity followed him through the door. Jason picked up the pillow and tossed it back on the bed, then let the door click shut.

They were standing at the top of a long metal stairway. Their steps echoed eerily as they made their way slowly down about a floor's distance, until they were standing in a short concrete tunnel. The tunnel was completely featureless except for some pipes running along one wall and a bare incandescent bulb hanging overhead. Ahead about fifteen feet they could see a tee intersection; the bulb's light didn't reach far enough to illuminate well what was beyond, but it looked rougher and didn't appear to be made of the same concrete as their current tunnel. The air down here was chilly, and there was a faint hint of a breeze.

"What...*is* this place?" Verity whispered, wrinkling her nose. "Smells like — garbage. And seaweed."

Stone moved forward, keeping close to the wall of the concrete tunnel until he reached the intersection. Cautiously he peered around in both directions, then pulled his head back. "It's brick," he said, his expression troubled. "If I didn't know better — and I'm not so sure I do — I'd say it was a storm sewer tunnel, and a very old one. I'll bet if we follow it toward the ocean, we'll find that it lets out there."

"Why would they have a storm sewer attached to a nightclub?" Jason asked, confused.

"I don't think it's in use anymore—and it appears that this concrete section isn't part of the original design. I can't see the other end of the brick tunnel—I think it might be blocked. Come on. Let's check it out. This is very strange." But instead of moving forward again, he suddenly put his hand to his chest. Before Jason could ask if something was wrong, he pulled out the small cage/detector. The crystals were glowing more brightly now. "Whatever it is," the mage said softly, "I think we're heading in the right direction. Look sharp and stay close. Remember, they have mages too."

Staying close together, they first made a right turn. The tunnel, which was round and lined with brick and not tall enough for Stone or Jason to stand fully, extended for about twenty or thirty feet, then stopped abruptly. It was very obvious that it had been blocked off on purpose; the opening was filled with concrete that looked much newer than the bricks. "This place looks *really* old," Verity said, nervous. "Are you sure it's safe? If we had an earthquake right now—"

Stone glanced up. "They've reinforced it. Look."

The other two looked up as well, and sure enough someone had added metal bracing to the top of the tunnel. Like the concrete, it looked much newer than the brickwork. "Curiouser and curiouser," Stone muttered. "Come on." He changed direction, moving down the tunnel in the direction of the ocean. "I think we'll find a—" he started, but then stopped moving.

Jason and Verity nearly ran into him. "What?" Jason hissed, but he didn't have to ask. Looking over Stone's shoulder, he saw another hole in the side of the tunnel, this time on the other side and about twenty feet down in the ocean direction from the tunnel from which they'd just emerged. This one wasn't lit, which is why they'd almost missed it. "Another one?"

"It appears that the club and something else are connected via these tunnels," Stone said. He was looking very grim now. "And look—I was right. The sewer exit out to the ocean is blocked." He pointed, and his companions looked. The end of the tunnel was covered by a very formidable looking metal grate, the spaces between the bars so narrow that nothing bigger than a large rat or a small cat would be able to make it through. Most of the lower part of the grate was choked with garbage, seaweed, and other debris. They could hear the sea lapping beyond the opening, but it didn't reach this high.

Verity glanced from the opening to the new tunnel. "Did anybody even notice what was next door to the club?" she asked.

Both Stone and Jason shook their heads. "Probably another warehouse," Jason said. "But I didn't see. I was too busy looking at the club."

"Same," Stone said. "We could go outside and look, but I don't think it's wise. I'm not sure I could get us past that door again if we let it lock, and it's too risky to leave it open."

Jason nodded reluctantly. "Yeah...I think we'd better just move forward." He looked troubled. A very large part of him wondered what the hell he was doing, leading his sister into something like this that was almost certainly highly dangerous. He knew there was no point in going without her—she was the only one among the three of them who had a shot at ending the Evil's hold over this area—but that didn't make him like it any more. He pulled a small flashlight from his pocket, switched it on, and moved forward with the others into the second concrete tunnel.

As they expected there was another door at the end of it the second hallway, very similar to the one in the other tunnel. "What if it's locked too?" Jason whispered to Stone. "Can you pick locks with magic?"

The mage shook his head. He put his finger to his lips and moved forward, putting his ear to the door. He listened for almost a full minute, then turned back to the others. "I don't hear anything," he told them. "Of course, that doesn't mean much. We're going to have to take a chance again. That's assuming the door is unlocked. If it's not, we'll have to wait for someone else." He reached out to the door handle. All three of them held their breath as he turned it.

It turned easily, and he swung the door minimally open.

Jason let his breath out. This was it. Only half conscious of what he was doing, he slipped his hand into the pocket of his jeans and pulled out his knife. Then he nodded to Stone.

The mage slowly opened the door a bit more. It was quite heavy, but moved silently on well oiled hinges. When he saw no movement inside, he pushed it open the rest of the way and motioned for the others to move in fast. When they were all inside, he swung the door closed with a soft click.

They were standing at the foot of another metal stairway like the one inside the club. Moving slowly, they ascended it and found themselves in a long narrow hallway only about four feet wide that stretched off to their left. The wall on the near side was solid; the other one was wooden and looked more temporary. Both were painted with years' worth of faded graffiti. Another naked incandescent bulb illuminated the area.

"Do you smell something weird?" Verity whispered.

Stone nodded, looking grim. "Something's died in here, I think," he murmured back.

"Oh, man...I hope it's just a rat or something," Jason said, glancing around nervously.

"Shh," Stone whispered. "We have to get out of this hallway. It's too narrow—even with the spell up, we're sitting ducks if anyone comes in."

They moved quickly to the other end of the hallway. Jason was looking everywhere at once, afraid that someone would ambush them even though Stone's magic was concealing them. His gaze settled for a moment on the graffiti—it was a mishmash of gang symbols (all of them DMW), crudely painted horror imagery like severed heads and fanged demons, and obscene words. What he didn't notice were any Forgotten code symbols. Not even one. "I'm starting to wonder if we've found the DMW's gang clubhouse," he muttered. The idea did not appeal to him in the slightest.

At the end of the hallway was another door, but this one was much less substantial than the heavy metal one at the entrance. It was made of wood and had a cheap-looking knob without a lock. The smell was getting worse; whatever had died here had probably been here awhile. The putrid stench mingled unpleasantly with the odors of must, mildew, and far-off seawater. Stone stopped and listened at it again. "Put your light out," he whispered, then turned the knob.

Again, the door opened easily. This seemed odd to Jason—if they were hiding something (or someone) in here, why leave all the doors unlocked? *Maybe the magic door in the dungeon is the only way in,* he decided. *No point in locking the place up if they're the only ones who can even find it.*

They paused for a moment to orient themselves. Directly to their left, along the same wall, was a large heavy pair of double doors. These were firmly closed and locked with a thick chain and a padlock the size of a man's hand. "Nobody's getting in that way," Jason whispered.

"Or out," Stone agreed.

Verity was looking in the other direction. "What *is* this place?" she asked, pointing. Off to the right was a large open area; it was dimly lit by another of the ubiquitous incandescents, this one hanging high above them. Scattered around were what looked like broken racks and fixtures, along with a significant amount of trash and debris. Directly in front of them were several wooden workbenches built into the wall. They too were covered with broken items and more debris. Occasionally they could hear the faint skitter of rats or mice moving around.

"It doesn't look like a factory or a warehouse," Jason said under his breath.

"Doesn't smell like it, either," Verity said. The stench was getting stronger, beginning to overpower the mildew and must.

"I think," Stone said slowly, as if talking to himself, "that it's some sort of theater."

Jason stared at him. "Theater?" He looked around, confused. "Here? This is the warehouse district."

Stone shrugged. "We just came from a nightclub. It's not uncommon to repurpose old warehouse or factory buildings. I think we're in some kind of backstage or workshop area."

"I think he's right," Verity said. She pointed up. "Look at all the catwalks and rigging and stuff up there. It all looks pretty messed up, but—"

"Come on," Stone said. "Let's keep moving."

"Wait!" Verity whispered urgently. "I think I heard something!"

Instantly all three of them went quiet, fading back until they were standing with their backs to the padlocked double doors, as far from the door in which they had entered as they could manage. For several seconds they heard nothing but the rustling of the mice, but then off to their right came the sound of voices. The three watchers huddled together and strained to hear what they were saying.

There were two of them, both young and male, and they were coming from a shadowy area directly in front of the watchers. "Gotta get back," one was saying. "Got another pickup in an hour."

"Good," the other one replied. "These ones are gettin' boring. Ain't got much left in 'em."

The first one laughed. "Need to figure out how to make 'em last longer." They were approaching now: ahead of Stone and the others was a short stairway, and the two men were descending it. As they reached the ground it was clear that they were the same two DMW gangers who had gone in ahead of them. They made a left at the foot of the stairway without noticing the watchers, headed straight for the door where they had come in. They went quickly through and closed it behind them.

Stone and the others stayed where they were for several more seconds to make sure they were gone, and then Stone pointed toward the short stairway. "I think that's where the action is," he whispered. Jason nodded.

Moving slowly, they crept along the wall. Jason's head was moving on a swivel again, trying to see everywhere at once. The light in here was very dim, and it would be easy for someone (or multiple someones) to be hiding in the shadows waiting to ambush them. He brought up the rear of their little procession while Stone took point; if Verity noticed that she was being protected from both sides, she didn't comment on it.

The stairway was skeletal and made of metal. Stone pointed upward. "Backstage area, most likely," he whispered, and began ascending. It was impossible to be completely quiet on these stairs, but they did the best they could. When they emerged at the top they were standing in a sparsely lit, wide open area. Stone had been right: this was the backstage area. Like the workshop it was strewn with debris, broken objects, ripped clothing, and similar objects that had survived whatever ransacking the place had undoubtedly experienced at some point in its history.

They couldn't see out very far, since there were no lights out in the auditorium. Once again they stopped and listened. For several seconds they thought they wouldn't hear anything, but then something came from far on the other side of the building: a faint sound that could have been a heavily muffled yell or scream.

Jason stiffened. "Did you hear that?" he hissed.

"Shh," Stone murmured. "Yes."

Verity poked Stone in the arm. "Take off my block," she whispered. "Just in case."

The mage nodded. Quickly turning back to her, he put his hands on either side of her head and stared into her eyes for a few seconds. "There," he said. "Remind me to put it back up when this is over."

Jason was impatient. "Come on," he whispered. "Somebody's hurt over there. Let's go see what's going on." As scared as he was, the thought of action was energizing him. All this sneaking around in the dark was making him much more nervous than if he just had something to punch.

"Easy." Stone held up a hand. "Don't lose your head now." Jason could see that he too was looking grim.

Verity, meanwhile had spotted something off to the side, in the shadowy backstage area off to their right. "Is that—a body?" She pointed into the dimness, grabbing Jason's arm.

"What? Oh—probably just a pile of debris," Stone said, though he did move off a bit to investigate the bundle. He stopped before he reached it, though. "Or…" he added in an emotionless tone, "It's a body."

"Holy crap." Jason came up next to him. He tried to shield Verity from the sight, but she was having none of it. She moved in alongside of him and stared down.

The body was that of a man of indeterminate age, with the wild beard and ragged clothes that clearly marked him as someone who'd seen hard times. From the look of things he hadn't been dead that long. "Forgotten?" Verity whispered.

"No way to know," Stone said. He looked up, his gaze quickly sweeping the area around him. "I don't like this at all. Come on—let's keep going. We can't do anything to help him now."

"Why would they just...dump a body in the hallway like that?" Jason asked whispered.

"Perhaps they didn't. There's always the possibility that he died of natural causes, or a drug overdose." Jason gave him a 'you can't *possibly* believe that' look, and he shrugged. "I didn't say it was likely—I said it was possible. Now hush. I think we're getting closer."

They continued picking their way through the back-stage area, mindful of the debris on the floor and looking even more carefully than before to make sure they didn't stumble on any more dead bodies. All three of them kept casting glances out into the stage area and the auditorium beyond, even though they couldn't see anything and no one could see them if Stone's magic was holding. Jason couldn't shake the feeling that somebody up there was going to pin them in a spotlight any minute now, revealing that the whole place was crawling with DMW and other Evil just waiting for the chance to pick them off .

This didn't happen, though. They made it across without incident and found another metal stairway, a mirror of the one they'd just come up, leading back down on the other side. "Part of this place has to be underground," Jason whispered, pointing at the stairs. "This thing goes down too far to just be ground level."

"Partial basement," Stone agreed, also whispering. "Too dangerous to build real basements 'round here, with the earthquake potential."

As silently as they could, the three of them picked their way down the staircase. The light was brighter here but still high up. Ahead of them was a closed metal door; off to their right, down a short hallway, was a second less substantial one. "Which way?" Jason asked.

Stone was about to answer when another sound cut through the silence: another low moan like the one they'd heard before. Directly in front of them this time, it was a little louder than the previous one, but clearly still muffled.

Jason pointed wordlessly toward the door. "I wish we had a way to know if there's anybody in there," he whispered.

Stone put up a finger and glided forward, motioning for them to come along. Once more he put his head against the door and listened. There were more moans now; even those who weren't directly listening could hear them. And then, suddenly, a scream of agony. Still muffled. Whatever was going on in that room, it was heavily soundproofed. "Clearly they don't want whatever they're up to in there getting out," Stone said grimly.

"What do we do?" Jason asked. "We can't just bust in. We have no idea how many of them are there. It might be a trap."

"Wait," Stone said, again flattening back against the wall. "Let's see if anyone comes out."

Jason was sick of waiting, but he didn't see any other option. Reluctantly he followed the mage to the wall, and Verity came along with him.

After about five minutes, though, nobody had come out. The sounds continued, however: moans, screams, the sound of someone sobbing, all damped by whatever soundproofing they had in the space behind the door. Jason fidgeted, becoming more and more driven to do something with each passing minute. Finally he let his breath out in a rush. "I can't do this, Al," he said in a harsh whisper. "Something's going on in there — sounds like they're killing people. I can't just sit here and *wait.*"

Stone took a deep breath and nodded. "All right. Let me try something." He pointed over toward the underside of the backstage area — the space beneath where they had come down the metal staircase. "You two hide yourselves there, so they won't see when the door opens. I'm going to try to open it magically if it's unlocked, and see if we can flush them out. Be ready, though. Depending on how many of them there are, I might not be able to deal with all of them on my own."

Jason and Verity quickly crossed the hallway and hid themselves behind some debris under the stage, both focusing hard on the closed door. Stone, his concealment spell still active on himself, moved behind the stairway itself where he had a good view of the door. "Ready?" he whispered.

Jason nodded, clenching his fists, his entire body feeling like a spring ready to uncoil. He could feel Verity standing tensely next to him. "Go," he hissed back.

Stone raised his hand. For a few seconds nothing moved, and then the heavy door flew open and slammed into the wall behind it.

31.

Several things happened simultaneously at that point, the first being that the corridor was flooded with light from the room beyond. The screams and moans, which had been attenuated by the closed door, grew immediately louder and more urgent. And they were joined by more sounds—cursing and harsh yells of surprise. "What the fuck—?" Then came the sound of running feet and the hallway was suddenly full of leather-jacketed figures.

Jason, glad to finally have something to *do,* launched himself out from cover and smashed into one of the figures, slamming it into the wall and reveling in the satisfying melonlike *thunk* as the ganger's head hit the wall and he dropped.

They made surprisingly short work of the remaining gangers—there were actually only four in total, though the narrow hallway initially made them look like more. Stone dispatched two with magic, and Verity took out the last one when he tried to ambush Jason, concentrating for all she was worth and *pushing* with her mind until the glowing ball of Evil was ejected violently upward from his body. The ganger dropped bonelessly and the shimmering ball erupted into nothingness.

The three of them stood puffing in the hallway. "What are we gonna do with the rest of them?" Jason demanded. "We can't just leave them here. They might wake up. Verity, can you—" he put his hands to his head and mimed an explosion effect.

She shook her head. "I don't think so. Not when they're unconscious."

"Help us!" came a desperate scream from inside the room. "Oh, God, please, help us!"

"Drag them inside," Stone ordered. "At least we can keep an eye on them in there." He grabbed hold of one of the smaller gangers and began following his own order.

And then he stopped, halfway in and halfway out the door, as the sounds of increasingly panicked screams continued to echo around them. "Bloody...hell," he breathed.

"What?" Jason dropped his ganger and poked his head around the doorway, past where Stone was blocking it. He too stiffened and stopped moving. "Holy shit..."

"What's going on?" Verity didn't have space to shove past the two of them, so she couldn't see.

"*Please!*" The screams from inside were near-hysterical now.

Jason shoved Stone bodily inside and the two of them for a moment could not do anything but stare. Verity moved in next to them and gasped.

They were looking at what could only be described as a torture chamber, or a charnel house. It was a large room, probably used previously as a communal dressing area for the theater. Now, though, the far wall was lined with large cages, each one containing a captive. Metal hooks hung from the ceiling, on which various severed and rotting human body parts had been skewered. Wooden and metal apparatus, some of it looking like it had been brought in from the dungeon next door, occupied most of the room's open space, including one that looked like a rack and contained messily eviscerated male body with its entrails pulled out and draped over the edges. Inexplicably, several padded armchairs lined the near wall. At the far end of the room was a closed door, next to which were stacked three naked bodies, also obviously dead. The stench of decay in here was nearly overpowering.

Stone, Jason, and Verity took all this in in the space of a few seconds, and then they were moving again. "Verity, watch the door," Stone ordered.

"Get us out of here!" screamed a man. "Please, oh God, let us out!" Like the other captives—three men, two women, and a boy of about twelve—he looked ragged, dirty, and terrified.

"Where's the key?" Jason called. All the cages were locked with chains and padlocks. He was struggling hard to keep his gorge in place—there wasn't any time to waste losing his dinner. Inexplicably, his mind flashed back to the haunted house—how *clean* it had looked compared to this, how different the smell of popcorn·and sawdust had been from this nightmarish stench of blood and fear and excrement.

"On the wall by the door." The man was sobbing with fear, but obviously trying to keep it together. "Quick, before any more of them come!"

"Anyone in that back room?" Stone demanded.

"N-no," said one of the women. "That's—where they store—bodies."

Jason was already moving, snatching the key off the wall hook where it hung. He hurried over and began unlocking cages, starting with the young boy. "How did you get here?" he asked.

"Snatched," the man sobbed. "All of us. They—they grab homeless people. Runaways. People—people nobody will miss."

"And torture them?" Jason demanded.

The woman nodded. She was white as a ghost. She pointed vaguely at the body parts on meathooks. "They...like it. Doing that to people. They—"

"Any of you Forgotten?" Stone cut her off. He kept shooting glances back toward the door as if expecting more DMW to come in.

Most of them looked perplexed, but one thin young man who looked ill nodded. "I am."

"Can you—do anything?"

Jason was still unlocking cages; as he did each one, the occupant came tumbling out, staggering with fear. "Nothing—useful," the young man said. "I'm sorry..."

"It's all right," Stone said grimly. "Come on—we need to get out of here."

Verity, meanwhile, was rifling through the unconscious DMW gangers' clothes. "Hey!" she called. "I found a gun!"

Jason spun. "Give me that," he ordered. She handed it over readily and he inspected it, checking to see if it was loaded. "I thought the DMW didn't use them," he said. "But I'm not gonna look a gift horse in the mouth."

Stone was checking out the rest of the room. "Are you sure there's nothing useful in that room?" he asked the captives. "We've not much time."

"Just bodies, I think," the man they'd first been talking to said.

Stone sighed. "Cover the door, Jason," he said, and moved over to check. Jason got a quick glimpse of something red as he opened the door and a horrible smell, worse even than before, fetid and coppery and almost tangible, rolled out. When Stone closed the door and turned back to the group, even his normally unflappable demeanor was slipping. "Let's go," he said in an odd tone. "Nothing to save in there."

"Wait!" It was the young boy who spoke this time.

Stone turned to him. "What?"

"There's more of them here," he said. "Mister—you're not gonna believe me, but—I saw Gordon Lucas!"

"Who?" Stone asked.

But Jason and Verity were both staring at the boy like he'd sprouted a second head. "Gordon Lucas? The talk show guy?"

The kid nodded. "Yeah. That's how they got me. I went to one of his homeless benefit things, tryin' to get some food. His people asked me a bunch of questions, and then when I left, I got grabbed by those guys on my way back to where I was stayin'." He pointed at the gangers. "I didn't think it was connected 'til I got here. I been here awhile before the rest of these guys got here, and I seen him. He comes in here sometimes! In this room! They torture people and he sits there and—and—and *watches!*" Tears started to run down the boy's cheeks.

Stone's eyes widened. "The philanthropist?" Suddenly he clapped his hands to his forehead. "Of course! It all makes sense. Who else could possibly be less obvious, but more logical?"

"Wait a sec," Jason said. "*Gordon Lucas* is the Big Evil? The guy who used to have the talk show? The guy who gave it up a few years back to devote his life to helping the poor?"

"Quit—a few years ago!" Stone almost yelled it. "I remember it now! It was all over the news. Everyone was so surprised he'd quit at the top of his popularity. *Why would he do that?* everyone was asking."

"Because he's possessed!" Verity filled in. Her eyes got big too. "And he's *here?* In this building?" She stared at the boy.

"I don't know who Gordon Lucas is," said the first man, "But there's a guy who comes in sometimes—a couple of them. One looks like a movie star—older guy, tan, gray hair, big teeth—"

"That sounds like Lucas," Jason said.

"The other one's—this mousy-lookin' guy in a suit."

"I think he's a mage," said the Forgotten man. "The mousy guy."

Stone's expression hardened. "Come on," he said quickly. "Jason, any more guns on those gangers?"

Verity answered: "I checked them all—just that one. And no extra ammo that I can find."

"All right," Stone said. "Jason—and you," he ordered, pointing at the first homeless man. "Drag them into those cages and lock them up. We have to get you out of here, and fast."

Jason and the man did as directed, and Jason pocketed the key when they were done. The other homeless people huddled together, still looking terrified. Everyone was trying hard not to look at the grisly body parts swinging on the overhead hooks. "How are we gonna get them out?" Verity asked. "We have to—do what we came here to do. And we haven't seen any other exits except through the club. We can't send them through there. They'd get grabbed again as soon as somebody spotted them."

"We—" Stone started, but he didn't get a chance to finish. Suddenly from the hallway outside came the far-off sound of running feet and yells. "Damn!" His gaze darted back and forth between the people in the room. It locked for a moment on the boy. "Did Lucas say anything about where he is when he's not in here? When was he here last?"

The boy looked panicky. "Uh—uh—" He was almost hyperventilating—Stone's intense focus was spooking him almost as much as the torture chamber. "He was here—like an hour ago. He—said something about the office. That's all! I'm sorry!"

"It's all right, it's all right." Instantly Stone turned away. "You lot might need to hide for a bit. The only exit we know isn't feasible to use right now."

Jason was peeking around the doorframe, gun ready. "I don't see them yet," he reported. "But they're getting closer."

"All right, everybody out," Stone ordered, making shooing motions. "Directly across from this room is a stairway, and underneath that is an under-stage storage area." He motioned to the prisoners. "You go there, be quiet, and wait. Try not to get noticed." He pointed at the Forgotten man. "I'm going to guess you don't have a concealment power."

The man shook his head, looking miserable. "I—I'm good with animals."

"Great," Stone snapped. "If they have a dog, we're set."

"Go!" Jason called urgently, trying to keep his voice down. "Go now. They're getting closer. I think they're on the stage!"

Stone, Jason, and Verity herded the homeless group out and directed them under the stage. "Al—can you conceal them if you're not with them?"

"No, I—wait. Yes I can." The mage fumbled in his pocket and pulled out a small crystal wrapped in metal wire. He passed his hand over it, muttered something, and handed it to the Forgotten man. "Hold on to this, and stay together," he said so the others couldn't hear. "It will help conceal you, but it's not foolproof, nor is it invisibility. Just hide in the shadows and stay quiet. We'll be back for you when we can."

"You're a—" said the Forgotten man, taking the crystal.

Stone nodded. "Now go."

"Al, they're getting closer." Jason sounded nervous, though less so than before now that he had the gun out.

The Forgotten man nodded and quickly took charge of the group, urging them under the stage. After a few seconds they faded into the shadows.

"Don't you need that crystal?" Verity asked Stone. "Isn't it one of your power objects?"

"I have a few more," he said. "Don't you worry about that."

"Can you conceal us again?" Jason asked.

"I can try, but it's not going to work very well if they're looking for us. Come on. We need to find this office. I don't know if Lucas is here now, but if he is, we have to find him."

The door at the end of the hallway to the right of the torture chamber burst open, and three DMW gangers poured through. "There they are!" one of them yelled, pointing. "Come on!"

Jason grabbed Verity's arm and pulled her quickly up the stairs to the backstage area. Stone remained for a moment, crouching down and launching a spell at the three. One of them grabbed his head and dropped to the ground. The other two staggered, but kept coming. "Come *on*, Al!" Jason yelled. Stone quickly backed his way up the stairs, and Jason grabbed him and pulled him the rest of the way.

"I wonder how many of them there are in here," Jason said, ducking back to the side. "I don't want to shoot anybody unless I have to, but—"

The remaining two gangers, realizing that plunging madly up into the midst of a group containing at least one mage wasn't the wisest course of action, had slowed down now. Jason and the others could hear them cautiously working their way up the stairs. "We have to find the office," Stone whispered. "Before Lucas gets wind that something's up and makes his escape."

"Come on." Jason pointed behind them, toward where the actual stage was. The curtain had long since rotted away; it hung in musty shredded ribbons high above them. "I'm guessing it's up front."

One of the gangers chose that moment to poke his head around the corner. Stone, who'd been waiting for just that, plugged him with a spell. They were rewarded with a grunt of pain and the sound of the other ganger retreating back down the stairs. "Come on!" Jason hissed again.

The three of them hurried across to the front of the stage, staying in the shadows off to the left backstage area and taking as much care as they could manage not to trip over the various debris strewn on the wooden floor. The floor itself made ominous creaking noises under their feet and sent up puffs of dust at their every step; Jason hoped it hadn't rotted out to the point where they risked falling through if they hit a bad spot.

Stone was scanning the auditorium. There wasn't much light so all he could make out were vague shapes. "Most of the seats are gone, it looks like," he muttered. "Probably stolen over the years. We need to stay to the sides — if anyone's watching, they'll pick us off with ease in the middle."

"That's a long drop down," Jason said, pointing at the front part of the stage.

"We can do it," Verity said. "Come on, let's do it before that other guy gets brave again."

They moved forward, cautiously, continuing to stay to the left. Soon they reached the point where they'd have to break cover if they wanted to get down off the stage. "All together, then," Stone said. "I'll try to conceal us, but don't count on it. Get to cover fast."

"One — two — three," Jason whispered, and they jumped.

They hit the ground and moved off to the left, and not a moment too soon. The sound of gunfire erupted from somewhere ahead of them, and muzzle flashes appeared at the back part of the theater, high above the auditorium.

"They're in the control booth!" Stone yelled. "Move! We have to get to the front!"

They moved, crouched low and running as fast as they could go in the darkness, while bullets pinged off the wall behind them. They didn't stop until they'd reached the back wall. "We're under them," Stone said, puffing a little. "They won't stay up there long. Be ready."

"Where's the stairs up?" Jason demanded, looking around.

"Other side—has to be," Verity said. "I don't see 'em here."

"Might be inaccessible from here," Stone said, trying to look everywhere at once. "I don't see the offices, either. Must be upstairs as well."

"If there's only one exit from up there we might have 'em cornered," Jason said, already moving.

"Don't count on it," Stone said.

"Got 'em!" yelled a voice—from behind them. All three of them spun to see a group of three DMW gangers rounding the corner—just as they heard more footsteps from the direction in which they'd been heading.

"Fuck, they've got us surrounded!" Jason yelled, bringing the gun barrel around to aim at the group in front of them.

Stone was looking grim. "Deal with the group in front," he ordered. "I'll take care of the ones behind." And before either of the other two could protest he was off, back the way they'd come.

Jason didn't like this at all, but he didn't have time to say anything about it. The front group of gangers was now rounding their own corner—there were four this time, and one of them had a gun. "Down, V!" he yelled, reaching around to shove her toward the floor. Dropping to a crouch he aimed his own gun, allowing his well-honed instincts and muscle memory from his time in the Academy to take over. Focusing on the ganger with the gun, he squeezed off a round.

There was a deafening *bang!* and the ganger spun, dropping his gun and screaming in agony. Verity watched from the floor wide-eyed, her hands clamped over her ears, then leaped back up again.

The other three gangers hadn't stopped, though. They surged forward, yelling obscenities and pulling knives from their jackets. Verity was able to evict one of them before he reached them, and he too dropped as the Evil left his body. The other two launched themselves at Jason, who pulled the trigger again.

Click.

Wildly, he glared down at the gun. He'd checked it! It had a full clip! But his quick glance told him what he needed to know—the thing was in terrible repair and probably hadn't been cleaned or maintained in ages. He didn't have time to worry about it now, though—one of the gangers had his hands around his neck, and the other one was going for Verity.

Enraged at the thought of these lowlife scum touching his sister, he lashed out with his fist and caught the ganger in the stomach, then brought both hands together and forced them up between the ganger's arms. The ganger's hold broke, giving Jason an opportunity to aim a heavy-booted kick right at his gut. The ganger staggered back, stunned, and Jason spun to face the other one.

Verity was in trouble. She was obviously trying to do her mind push to cast out the Evil, but the ganger in her face was playing hell with her concentration. She was backstepping, but the ganger was almost on her when suddenly he pitched forward and hit the ground with a crash at her feet, revealing Jason standing behind him, puffing, holding the barrel of his gun in a hand protected by the sleeve of his leather jacket. "You okay?" he asked.

She nodded quickly. "Yeah. I—couldn't—"

"It's okay. You're new at this. Come on. Let's find where Al got to."

But he'd forgotten momentarily about the stunned ganger. "Jason, look out!" Verity yelled, but too late. The ganger plowed into Jason from behind, taking both of them down.

Jason hit the ground hard, but again his instincts took over and he rolled forward, pitching the ganger over his head and quickly leaping back to his feet. "I hear more of them!" Verity called.

"Fuck!" Jason spun sideways to keep both directions in sight at once. The formerly stunned ganger was getting back to his feet, and three others were coming around the same corner. "Do you see any guns?"

Verity didn't answer. She was concentrating again, and this time it worked. One of the three stopped, screamed, and fell to the floor. The other two looked momentarily panicked, and then both of them went for Verity. "Get the bitch!" one yelled.

Jason lunged forward and planted a fist right in the middle of the ganger's face. His nose exploded in a spray of blood, but he tried to keep coming. All of them were like madmen now. "No!" Verity yelled, and focused on the uninjured one. Like his friend, he clutched his head and fell down to his knees, not quite unconscious but looking bewildered.

"Come on!" Jason yelled, grabbing Verity's arm. He'd spotted a stairway up just around the corner—it must be the one that led up to the tech booth and the offices above them.

"Wait! What about Dr. Stone?" Verity protested.

Jason looked around wildly, but he didn't see the mage. He could hear the sounds of combat, though, back the way they'd come. He was about to turn around and sprint back in that direction when two more gangers came up the hall. He snatched up the ganger's dropped gun, hoping it worked better than the one he'd been using, and dragged Verity up the stairs. "We should be able to see better from up there!" he told her as she tried to protest again. "The booth is open to the seats!" He had to hope that with all the magical focus objects and doodads Stone had been making the past few days he had enough punch to deal with the gangers, at least for a little while.

The stairs this time were a proper stairway, not the metal skeleton version that was backstage. Jason took them two at a time, still grasping Verity's hand tightly. At the top he glanced around the corner to make sure no one was lying in wait for them, then shoved Verity behind him. One of the gangers—the one with the exploded nose—was still coming, flying up the stairs half-blinded from the blood. Jason kicked him in the chin and sent him rolling head over heels back down, where he landed against his bewildered de-Eviled friend and didn't move. "What the fuck is going on?" the bewildered ganger yelled to nobody in particular. "I just want to get the hell *away* from these fuckin' loonies!"

"You know another way out?" Jason yelled down to him, pointing the gun at him. "Tell us, and I won't kill you!"

"Uh—" The ganger's mouth was hanging open, his breath coming so hard his whole body was bucking. "Uh—just the club. The rest of it's sealed tight. They're fuckin' *crazy!*" Without waiting to see if his answer was sufficient to keep Jason from shooting him, he ducked back around the stairs and took off.

Jason didn't follow him. Instead, he turned and hurried down the narrow space that was the tech booth. It was nearly empty now—the boards were still there, but they'd been long ago gutted of any electronics or anything else of value. The only other feature was a closed door halfway down the back wall—probably where the offices were located. Verity was crouched in a threadbare folding chair, peering over the top of the half-height wall that separated the booth from the auditorium. "See anything?" he demanded. He took in the scene quickly: there were narrow catwalks that extended out from the booth on either side, crisscrossing high above the auditorium. He could see the remnants of broken light fixtures still hanging from them, but it was hard to tell if they were safe enough to trust any weight to. He hoped he wouldn't have to find out.

"They're underneath us, I think," she said, pointing. "I can hear them, but—"

Jason was about to reconsider his reluctance to try out the catwalks in hopes of getting out where he could see better when suddenly a figure flew through the air down below and crashed in a heap in a pile of debris where there used to be seats. "What—?"

The figure scrabbled to its feet, revealing itself to be a stunned ganger. Another dark figure vaulted over a small pile of broken wooden bits and faced back toward the area under the tech booth. It raised its hands and what looked like blue lightning crackled around them, arcing back and forth between them. Jason and Verity, watching from far above, could see by the lightning's flickering illumination that it was Stone. His face looked positively manic, his hair disheveled, his eyes burning with intensity. He roared something they couldn't understand and lashed out—the lighting flew from his hands and slammed into whatever was out of sight. There were two screams, and then silence.

"Holy shit," Jason breathed. "Remind me not to get on *his* bad side."

"Come on," Verity urged, pulling on his arm. "Let's get back down there and help him. We still gotta find the big bad."

434 | R. L. KING

Jason paused long enough to check that there wasn't another stairway on the other side — as far as he knew, the only way out of the upper floors was down the one they'd just come up — and then he hurried to follow his sister.

He overtook her halfway down the stairs. "Let me go first," he told her. "In case anybody's —" As he reached the foot, he sensed something in his peripheral vision, off to his left. "Down!" he yelled, flinging himself sideways.

His quick response most likely saved his life. He felt white-hot pain erupt across the upper part of his arm and spun around just in time to hear Verity scream "No!" and see a ganger holding a knife drop, clutching his head. A quick glance at his arm told him the knife had found a target; blood was already running down his sleeve. He couldn't worry about that now, though. There was a second ganger, lunging toward him and trying to pin him to the wall. Jason lashed out with a kick, sending the kid careening back into the opposite wall with a grunt, but he quickly recovered and plowed back into Jason.

Jason kept waiting for this one to slump down too, but he didn't. Maybe Verity's power had to have a brief time to recharge. In any case, he couldn't worry about that right now. The ganger had both of his arms pinned to the wall now — he was skinny and unhealthy looking, but he had the strength of a madman. Jason's arm where the knife had slashed it was alight with pain. He had to do something fast or —

The ganger suddenly lurched sideways, roaring and spinning to face Verity, who's just hit him over the head with a piece of broken wood she'd picked up in the hallway. It wasn't enough to take him out, but it was enough to get his attention. Yelling obscenities, he raised his hands and moved toward her, Jason momentarily forgotten.

"Bad decision, asshole!" Jason yelled, clocking the enraged ganger with the butt end of his gun.

The ganger staggered toward Verity who, finally getting it together, grabbed both sides of his head and yelled "Out!" The shimmering Evil flew free and exploded, leaving the ganger in a heap.

For a moment both of them stood there panting. Verity quickly looked back and forth, then moved toward Jason. "Let me have a look at that," she said. "He got you."

Jason, who was pale and still puffing, shook his head. "We—gotta find Al," he got out. "Can't—stop."

"Screw that," she said. "He was doing fine, and you're not gonna be any good to him or anybody if you bleed to death. We have a minute. Now off with that sleeve." She steered him over toward a shadowy alcove.

He sighed, allowing himself reluctantly to be steered, already shrugging out of his bloody jacket sleeve. His arm was on fire, streaked with blood running down toward his hand.

Verity quickly examined the wound. "It doesn't look too bad," she said. "I wish we had some antiseptic or something, but we don't so we'll have to make do. Tear off part of your T-shirt."

He did as he was told, quickly ripping several inches off the lower part of his black shirt and handing it over. She took it and quickly wrapped it around the wound, tying up a crude but reasonably effective bandage. "That won't hold long," she said, "but hopefully it won't have to. Come on."

They could still hear sounds of combat as they hurried around the hallway under the tech booth. They burst through the crazily-hanging double doors leading to the auditorium, both of them looking wildly around trying to spot gangers, Stone, or anybody else.

It didn't take long to find Stone: he was off on the far right side of the auditorium, crouched behind another pile of debris. While Jason and Verity watched, he flung another bolt of energy at something unseen and was rewarded by a grunt of pain and a yelled obscenity. The two of them were poised to run out and join him when suddenly a bright *something* flew down from above and hit the mage square in the chest. Jason and Verity could see a look of utter astonishment cross his face right before he slumped.

32.

"Take him to the office!" yelled a voice from the same direction as where the bolt had come from. "Leave him alive!"

"That guy's in the tech booth!" Jason whispered, pointing up. "There must be access to the office from up there behind that door. Come on!" He hurried along the wall over to the right side, trying to get to Stone before the gangers did. As soon as he stepped out from cover, though, shots rang out. One tore into the wall not a foot away from him. "Shit!" he called to Verity. "Stay down! They're on the stage!"

Sure enough, he could see at least three gangers leaning out from cover in the backstage wings. Another muzzle flash bloomed and another bullet hit the wall near him. He quickly ducked and skittered back along the back wall to join Verity on the other side of the door. "We have to get to Al," he said.

"They'll have to go up the stairs," she said. "Unless they have a back way in."

Jason nodded. "Come on. And be careful. Look sharp."

They pushed back through the double doors into the hallway and started off to the right toward the stairs when two more gangers rounded the corner behind them. Verity's head whipped back and forth. "Run for it or fight?"

Jason swore. How many of these gangers did they have? It seemed like they had an unlimited supply--or more likely, the word was getting out and more were coming in through the club entrance. They needed to deal with this fast. He spun and fired an erratic shot toward the two gangers, who ducked back around the corner. There was no way he and Verity could make it to the other corner before the gangers could get a shot at them if they had guns. And already the gangers who had Stone had had enough time to hustle him upstairs. "Go!" he told Verity. "Just to the corner. I'll cover you. Go now!"

She did as she was told. He could feel her hand squeezing his good shoulder, and then she was off. A ganger poked his head around the corner; Jason fired another shot and he quickly ducked back. Jason began backstepping toward Verity, keeping the gun trained on the space around the far corner. At least this one seemed to be working, but he only had a couple more rounds and no extra clips. "Anything?" he called softly back to Verity.

"Clear," she called back.

"Okay, go around. I'm coming now." He could sense that he was only about ten feet from the corner, and took the chance that if they'd had guns, they would have used them by now. He turned and sprinted the rest of the way, executing a quick turn around the corner. The stairway, empty now, lay ahead of them. "Come on," he said. "Let's go while it's clear."

She started up the staircase, but almost immediately stopped short, causing Jason nearly to run into her. "Keep going!" he snapped, still afraid that the two gangers would make their appearance — possibly with reinforcements by now — any second.

"Wait!" she called. She was ducking down, scrabbling at something on the floor. "Be careful. Don't move! You'll step on it!"

Jason froze, wondering what she'd found. Another gun? A dead body, or part of one? One of those incendiary grenades the DMW seemed so fond of? (He was very grateful they didn't seem to be using them in here, given the fact that the whole building was made of old dry wood.) "What is it?" he demanded in a harsh whisper.

She scooped something up and held it so he could see it. It was the small crystal-and-wireframe cube Stone had been carrying. "The cage?" he hissed.

"It must have fallen out of his pocket when they were carrying him," she said.

"Or he dropped it on purpose," Jason said eagerly, feeling heartened by the thought. If he'd dropped it on purpose, it meant two things — he didn't want Lucas and his cronies finding it on him...and he was still alive.

"Jason!" Verity yelled, pointing over his shoulder.

He spun. In his surprise at finding the cage he had momentarily forgotten about the gangers, and they had taken that opportunity to make up lost ground. The two of them came pounding up the stairs, screaming and waving knives. Verity evicted one of them just as he reached her, shoving his unconscious body back where it smashed into his friend and took him tumbling down. Jason plugged him without a second thought. He was beyond caring about who he hurt at this point — his only objective now was to get to the office, rescue Stone, and deal with Lucas. Oh, and get the hell out of here and as far away as possible. That, too.

"Go, go, go!" Verity urged, already pounding the rest of the way up the stairs.

"Wait!" Jason yelled. "What if there's — "

"It's clear!" She was already at the top. "Come *on*. We have to hurry. They won't be expecting us this soon!"

The tech booth was clear except for a pile of ashes and clothing that used to be a ganger — one that hadn't been there last time they were there — draped across the ruined board. The door halfway down the back wall was closed. Verity grabbed the knob. "Shit, it's locked!"

"Back up," Jason ordered. It didn't look like a metal door — just a standard interior model. Verity stepped back and he wound up and kicked, just like they'd taught him.

The door splintered away from the frame and flew open. Both he and Verity ducked off to the side in case anybody was waiting for them.

Nobody was. The hallway beyond was deserted. There were two more doors, one on either side. "Which one?" Verity whispered.

Jason was about to say he didn't know when he spotted something—a faint flickering glow coming from beneath the one on the left. He pointed silently toward it, and she nodded.

"Do we just break in?" she whispered. "Can we even do that?"

Jason looked down at the gun in his hand. He double-checked it--still only one more bullet. "Whatever we do, we gotta do it fast." No sound was coming from the other side of the door—either it was soundproofed or they just couldn't hear. Oddly, they couldn't hear any gangers coming up the stairs either. Had they given up? That hardly seemed likely. He didn't have time to think about it now, though—Lucas and his people could be killing Stone as the two of them dithered over what to do. "Get ready," he told her.

And he rushed forward and kicked the office door open.

It's amazing the amount of detail you can process in the space of two seconds. That was about the amount of time Jason had to notice the detail in the office: Stone bound and unconscious on the floor, his longcoat with his magical items tossed in a far corner; a large desk, behind which stood a tanned, gray-haired man with movie-star features twisted into a rictus of hatred; another man, unassuming and mousy-looking, standing over Stone; the slumped dead form of another DMW ganger, his eyes fixed open in surprise nearby; a shimmering, glowing *thing* on the far side of the room, surrounded by flickering candles.

A shimmering—

Oh, fuck—

"Holy shit, it's a portal!" Jason yelled.

Verity pushed in past him. "What? What are you—" Her eyes fell on the mousy-looking man and widened in shock. "Oh, my God, Jason! That's the guy from the basement! At the halfway house!"

"Kill her!" screamed the man with the movie-star looks that Jason and almost every other person in America had seen for years smiling out at them from TV talk shows, telethons, magazines, and billboards. "Kill the girl!" he yelled in tones completely alien to the soothing, pleasant baritone with which he had interviewed the country's entertainment royalty and addressed the country's social problems.

"Verity! Go!" Jason yelled. He was already swinging the gun around to cover the mousy man, who must be the mage and was thus the stronger threat at the moment. "You try it, asshole, and I'll plug you before you can get the spell off!"

"Wait!" A weak voice called from the floor off to Jason's left.

Jason didn't take his eyes off the Evil mage. "Al?"

"Can't—kill him," Stone got out with difficulty.

"What the hell? *Why not?*" The Evil mage was hovering there, obviously reluctant to make a move with Jason's gun trained on him.

"Can't—Cage—"

"I have it!" Verity yelled from the other side of the door. "I picked it up!"

"See?" Jason said, still without turning. "We can—"

"No...we *can't,*" Jason could hear Stone shifting in his bonds, and the mage's voice took on a strained urgency. "Only—one. Must—save—"

"Only one? What the hell are you—" And then suddenly he realized what Stone meant. The cage. It was only built to hold one Evil. If they killed the mage and evicted the Evil from him, they'd either have to let it go free to take up residence elsewhere, or capture it and have nothing in which to capture the Evil possessing Lucas. "Shit!" he yelled. "Al, what—"

And it was then he made his mistake. The shock of what Stone had said caused Jason to turn toward him as he spoke. It was only for a split second, but that was all it took for the man driven by a panicked and nearly immortal force to take his chance. The Evil-possessed mage leaped forward, faster than one would have thought it possible for such a small and unassuming man to do, and clamped his hands on Jason's shoulders. "Now, you die!" he hissed. His burning gaze locked on Jason's, he leaned forward as if in expectation—

—and nothing happened.

Jason had no idea what the man had been trying to do, but he didn't let him get in another chance. The man was off balance, obviously shocked that whatever he'd been attempting hadn't worked as planned. All at once Jason had a crazy idea. An insane idea. An idea that couldn't possibly work. And yet—

Roaring with rage, ignoring the throbbing pain in his arm and the fact that it was bleeding again, Jason flung his arms around the man and bull-rushed him forward—straight toward the portal.

At the last moment, the Evil mage realized what Jason was doing. He screamed, struggling madly in Jason's grip, but Jason was stronger. "No, you fool!" he yelled. "You don't know what you're—"

Jason let go, shoving him forward. For a moment he teetered, arms flailing almost comically as he made a desperate attempt to regain his balance. His thin hand locked around Jason's wrist as he went over backwards. Jason planted his feet, suddenly fearful. If he went over too, if he touched that thing—

—And then Verity was there behind him, grabbing him around the middle. The Evil mage overbalanced and his tenuous grip loosened. His screams echoed around the room, and then his head broke the shimmering surface of the portal and the screams silenced as if someone had hit a switch. The rest of him followed. The portal flickered crazily like a TV set that couldn't tune in a station. It crackled, and the swirling surface roiled and surged. Verity staggered back, shaking, trying to get as far away from the portal as she could.

"You—fool," Stone said faintly from the floor. He was trying to struggle up, but his bonds were preventing him from doing so.

"What the hell is going on?" Jason demanded, his gaze darting back and forth between Stone and Gordon Lucas.

"They've—tried to construct a temporary portal," Stone said. He looked pale and he was bleeding from a cut on his head, but he appeared to be gaining strength. "It's—failing."

33.

"Holy crap," Jason breathed. "What happens if it fails?"

He didn't get a chance to answer before Gordon Lucas spoke. "You won't leave here alive," he said. His voice sounded calmer now, and Jason could definitely hear the beloved talk-show host and philanthropist behind the mad words the thing inside him was saying. "The others will be here soon. Even if you kill me, you know I won't be truly dead. It will be unfortunate to lose this vessel—it's served me well and it will be difficult to find another that will be as suitable. But no matter. A temporary setback at best. And now I've got all three of you here."

"Al?" Jason sounded urgent. "The portal?"

"If it goes, it will—take out most of this building," Stone said. He glared at Lucas. "Including you. Not—just the vessel. All of you."

Lucas grinned, showing large white capped teeth and somehow making the handsome face look macabre. "How little you know, mage. Just keep talking. They'll be here soon."

Jason glanced nervously toward the door. Where *were* the DMW? Why hadn't they come? Why couldn't he hear anything outside?

"You might as well put that gun down, boy. You aren't going to use it on me and we both know it."

"Like hell," Jason snapped, not lowering the pistol from where he had it aimed at Lucas's heart. "You make a move, I'll blow you away."

"No you won't, or you'd already have done it," Lucas said. "A failing of your kind—you always want to preserve the vessel. Don't you see that this is all you are good for—to be vessels?"

"Yeah, talk it up, scumbag," Jason said. He'd noticed that even Lucas now seemed to be casting furtive glances toward the door, as if he too were wondering where his backup was. "We got time." Without turning, he said to Verity, "V, can't you—?"

"Trying," she muttered, her voice thick with frustration. Stone was silent; Jason could see him past Lucas, and he looked like he'd passed out again. That wasn't good.

"Ah, yes," Lucas said. "I should attend to the girl. I don't know where you got that annoying power of yours, but I really can't allow you to keep it. You've caused me and the others quite a lot of inconvenience." He rose from behind the desk and smiled at Jason. "Go ahead and shoot me if you want to. Even if you wound me and I don't die right away, your mage friend is right—that portal *is* going to lose its structural integrity soon, now that you've killed the only one who can control it. Are you going to take the chance that I'll survive it, even if this vessel doesn't?" He moved around the desk and looked at Verity. "You, however, are different. I need to ensure that you are dealt with. No more inconvenient escapes for you." He stood over her and smiled. "And your fear as you die will make me stronger. That's the best part." He stepped forward—

Stone, directly behind him and far from unconscious, lashed out with his bound feet, catching Lucas hard in the backs of his knees. The Evil roared something in a language that none of them understood, pitching forward toward Verity, reaching out with his arms toward her—

"NO!" Verity yelled. She closed her eyes and *pushed* with everything she had. The effort was clear—this was no simple ganger. Lucas's handsome face contorted into ugliness, something inside him struggling against her. Jason watched in horror as his features twisted and became inhuman. He heard something crack; when blood appeared at the man's mouth, he realized that Lucas must have been clenching his teeth so hard that he'd broken them — or maybe his jaw. Verity's face was screwed up in concentration, sweat beads bursting out on her forehead. "You — get — the fuck — OUT!" she screamed, emphasizing her words by pushing out physically with her hands on his chest.

Lucas screamed too — it was a sound unlike any of the three of them had ever heard. An inhuman, alien sound of rage and agony and shock. His hands flew up and clutched at his head, his nails ripping the tanned skin which sprouted blooming bloody wounds in their wake. He looked like he was trying to pull off his own face. Then his whole body went rigid and he fell backward, crashing into the desk. The old wood broke and splintered into a heap of cracked debris, Lucas's twitching body in the midst of it.

And *something* broke free of it and flew upward.

It wasn't an indistinct ball of white mist like the evicted gangers had ejected. This one glowed a sickening reddish-purple hue, bright as a light bulb but somehow not illuminating the rest of the room. It looked like a small unhealthy sun hovering there in the air, appearing for the moment to be disoriented.

Jason was not idle. He leaped across the room, pulling out his knife and getting behind Stone. The mage had been bound with plastic zip-ties; Jason sliced through the one holding Stone's hands behind his back, and he quickly pushed himself up to a sitting position while Jason worked on his feet. "Quickly!" Stone yelled to Verity. "Before it escapes! Cage!"

Verity, momentarily shocked by what she'd seen, quickly recovered her senses. Fumbling inside her jacket, she pulled the little apparatus out and tossed it to Stone, who caught it deftly. Shaking free of the bonds that Jason had cut from his feet, he struggled up and held the cage aloft near the hovering form. Breathing hard, he began reciting an incantation in the same odd language Jason had heard him use before. His eyes were fixed on the Evil, unblinking and intense.

The glowing ball obviously had some knowledge of what was in store for it; it tried to make a break for it, first heading toward the door and then changing direction abruptly and darting toward the portal, which was now rolling and surging with alarming frequency. It moved toward Jason, then toward Verity, who glared at it and waved it away. Then, finally, it began to move, slowly and protestingly, toward Stone and the cage he held.

It looked like the world's strangest tug-of-war match, or like an odd fisherman trying to land an even odder fish. The glowing ball would draw closer, then move away a bit. Each time, though, the distance at which it pulled away was a little smaller than the distance in which it was pulled toward Stone. Closer and closer it got to the cage, its light flaring first purple, then red, then a clashing mix of the two. If it were possible for a glowing ball of energy to panic, then it was very clear that was what this one was doing. Stone's arms were shaking with the strain of focusing his will on the ball. He was fixed on it and nothing else.

So was Jason—until he smelled something burning. He allowed himself a quick second to glance to the side, and what he saw made his blood freeze. The force of Lucas's body crashing into the desk and destroying it had propelled chunks of dry rotting wood off to the side, knocking over two of the candles near the portal. A small blaze was forming, fueled by the dry wood of the floor and the desk. "Al!" he yelled. "Hurry it up!" He snatched up the first thing he could get his hands on—Stone's coat—and threw it over the flames, trying to muffle them.

It was too late for that, though: the coat caught fire and the flames began to spread.

"No, Jason!" Verity wailed. "The crystals—"

Too late, Jason realized that all of the crystals and other objects Stone had created to help him channel magic had been in his coat. He tried to grab it back but the fire was already flaring up around it. "Al!" he yelled again.

It wasn't clear whether Stone had heard his words or noticed the loss of his items, but something in Jason's urgency must have gotten through. He tightened his grip on the cage, gritted his teeth, and leaned forward, passing the little cage through the roiling mass of purple and red. Something screamed—it was more in their minds than an actual physical sound—and then the glowing ball blinked out of existence, reappearing in miniature form inside the cage. Stone dropped to his knees, puffing and pale, his head bowed. He stuffed the cage inside his pocket.

Verity grabbed his arm and tugged. "Come on," she urged. "We gotta go. I don't know what that thing in the corner is, but it doesn't look healthy. And the place is on fire!"

Those last words finally seemed to reach him. With effort, he dragged himself to his feet. "Let's go," he agreed. "Where's my—" His gaze fell on his jacket, which was blazing merrily now. His expression hardened, but there was nothing to be done about it now. "No matter. We have to get out of here before that portal blows."

"Or we burn to death," Jason muttered. "Let me take point, in case there are any more of those gangers out there. With any luck it'll take awhile for the fire to spread and we can find another way out. How long before the portal goes, Al? Do you have any idea?"

Stone sighed. "No way to know. From the look of it, maybe fifteen minutes. If we're lucky." He hurried out behind Jason.

"Wait!" Verity stopped said suddenly when they were out in the hall and about to pull the door shut.

"*What?*" Jason was trying not to panic, but it was getting harder.

"What about Lucas? He's still in there! And he's not Evil anymore!"

"Oh, crap!" This is one of those times when Jason really hated having an overdeveloped conscience. "Crap. We can't just leave him." He was already spinning around to head back in. Stone followed, with Verity bringing up the rear.

Lucas was conscious again, and standing near the fallen DMW ganger. He was unsteady on his feet, his face was bleeding from where the Evil had torn at it, and his expression was one of abject horror. He held a gun loosely in one hand. "Don't shoot!" Jason yelled. "We gotta get you out of here."

"Out?" Lucas seemed to be barely aware that he was talking to anyone. Tears began to run down his face, joining with the blood and staining his expensive suit. His eyes traveled around the room, taking in the portal, the dead ganger, the growing fire. "My God. What—what have I done?" His voice was a dead monotone, his eyes haunted.

"Mr. Lucas—" Jason took a step forward, not taking his eyes off the gun in the man's hand. "Just—"

Stone came up alongside him. "He's not coming, Jason," he said gently. He looked at Lucas, and some understanding seemed to pass between the two of them. He touched Jason's arm. "Come on—let's go."

"But—"

Lucas raised the gun—but not to point it at Jason or Stone. Instead, he raised it to his own head. "I'm so sorry..." he said softly.

"No!" yelled Jason, diving forward, but it was too late. The gun went off, taking the side of Lucas's head with it. Blood and brains and perfectly coiffed silver hair flew out, staining the walls and, even more sickeningly, speckling the miasmic surface of the failing portal and slowly absorbing through and disappearing. Jason stared in shock, moving closer to Stone in an effort to shield Verity from the sight. For once, she didn't protest. Lucas's body crashed twitching to the floor for a final time, the flames licking at his legs and alighting the fabric of his suit.

"Guys—come *on!*" Verity urged, near hysteria, grabbing each of them by an arm and tugging. "We have to *go!*"

As one, the two men turned and hurried after her. "How are we gonna get out?" Jason said, scanning the area ahead of them for gangers. "We can't go through the club. And we still gotta go back for the prisoners."

"If they're still alive," Stone said grimly. He was staggering a bit, as was Jason, but they both moved as fast as they could down the stairs. Jason half-expected to see gangers any second, but so far all they encountered were the bodies—unconscious or dead—of those they'd already dispatched. Jason and his overactive conscience felt a twinge of regret that there was no way they'd be able to get them out—after all, it hadn't exactly been their fault that they'd been possessed by extradimensional horrors—but there was no helping it. If they found a way out and the place hadn't gone up yet by the time he got Verity out safely, he'd consider coming back in for them. Otherwise, all bets were off.

By the time they made their way to the ground floor and down the hallway toward the shop and where they'd left the former captives, they could already smell smoke. "I don't think we have too long," Jason said in an urgent tone. "I know smoke rises, but this place is in bad shape.

That whole second floor section—the whole fucking *roof*—could come down once that fire takes hold." He raised his voice as they reached the under-stage area. "Come on out, you guys!" he yelled. "We gotta get out of here fast!"

A few seconds passed, and then the bedraggled group of former captives came picking their way out through the debris, led by the Forgotten man. All of them looked considerably less shellshocked and terrified than they had when Jason, Stone, and Verity had left them there. "What happened?" the bearded man asked. "Can we go now? Is it safe? I smell something."

"The place is on fire," Jason said. "We have to get out fast. Did you see any gangers?"

"We took out a couple of them," the bearded man said, looking proud. "They didn't see us, and we took a chance."

"How are we getting out?" asked one of the women, frightened. "Did you say the place was on fire?"

"I can smell the smoke too," said the young boy.

"Al," Jason spoke up. "The crystal you gave him—can you—?"

Stone shook his head. "It's tuned for concealment, not combat. It—"

He didn't get to finish. Suddenly the air was filled with yelling voices and pounding feet. "There they are!" a voice cried. "Get 'em!"

Everyone spun in the direction of the voices in time to see three gangers skidding to a stop at the top of the metal staircase above them. Two of them reached in their jackets. "Die, fuckers!" yelled one.

Jason reacted instinctively, firing at the one who'd yelled with his last round while shoving Verity violently to the side behind a large broken light fixture and diving on top of her. "*Down!*" he screamed, unable to stop the second ganger before he flung something into the midst of the group.

Stone reacted fast, grabbing the arm of the nearest prisoner — the Forgotten man — and launching the two of them forward to roll under one of the wooden workbenches. The rest of the homeless group wasn't so lucky. The incendiary grenade hit the ground between them and exploded, and suddenly the air was full of agonized shrieks and the smell of burning flesh and hair as the remaining former captives caught the brunt of the grenade's effect. The hallway lit up with flames, fanned further as the terrified, dying people ran around in a desperate and futile attempt to outrun the inferno. Verity screamed, trying to shove her way out from under Jason, to get to them, to do something — anything — to help. She glared at one of the gangers and evicted his Evil with barely a thought. The remaining ganger, seeing now that by tossing the grenade where he did, he had cut off his only escape route, stood for a moment in indecision at the top of the stairs. Stone rolled out from under the workbench and plugged him with a spell, staggering back into the wall and sagging against it. The ganger dropped off the edge and crashed to the ground, his own clothes catching fire too.

"Al!" Jason screamed, scrambling back to his feet and yanking Verity up with him. "What do we do?" His head jerked madly around, looking for an escape route, wanting to help the dying people but knowing he couldn't. He had never felt so impotent — and now their one last desperate escape route, the tunnel back to the club, was engulfed in flames. Above them, they could hear faint popping sounds followed by a muffled crash. The smoke and the stench of burning bodies was filling the air. "What do we do?"

Stone was breathing hard, coughing, obviously trying to keep it together despite the fact that he was almost as panicked as Jason was. "The doors!" he said, pointing at the firmly chained metal double doors.

"They're locked, Al! No way I can break that down!"

"Can *you* break it?" Verity demanded to Stone. She too was coughing from the smoke, her eyes streaming. "With magic?"

"I—" Stone started to say something, then realized he had no other choice but to try. He took a few steps in the direction of the doors, braced himself against the back wall, and focused his gaze on the door. His eyes were streaming too, and his head wound was bleeding down his face—angrily he brought his arm up and swiped the smoke-induced tears away, then put both hands together and pointed them at the door.

The lock rattled, then fell back with a thud. The doors didn't move. Stone slumped back against the wall, white and shaking. "I can't do it—" he breathed, coughing. "Not without some sort of focus—"

"They're all gone, Al! You have to—" Jason stopped. "Wait! Al! You said you can use people, right? To power spells?"

Stone stared at him. "What?" Then he shook his head. "No! I won't—I won't do it. I don't have the control—"

"You *have* to do it!" Jason yelled. "You don't have any other choice! If you don't do it, we're all dead!" He leaped across the hall and grabbed Stone's shoulders, getting right up in his face and shaking him. The flames were getting closer, the smoke thicker. Around them, the wooden building cracked and popped. Jason thought he heard another explosion upstairs. "Damn it, Al, *do it!* Use me as a power source, and *get that door down!*"

Stone glared at him for another couple of seconds, and then something hardened in his eyes. "God *damn* you, Jason!" he hissed, half sobbing. His hands came up and with surprising strength he spun Jason around, gripping his shoulder in a viselike grasp with one hand while focusing both his gaze and his other hand on the door. Verity and the Forgotten man watched, horrified, nearly heedless of the fire now. They knew that this was their last chance and, one way or another, it would all be over soon.

For a moment nothing happened. Jason could feel Stone's hand shaking as it grasped his shoulder. He forced his eyes shut and concentrated as hard as he could on giving whatever power he had to Stone to use. He didn't care if he died now, drained of all his vitality, if it meant getting that door open and getting his sister and the others out safely. The sacrifice would be worthwhile. An absurd thought flitted through his mind: *You can't say I never gave you anything now, V.*

Stone barked out a command, thundering it at the top of his lungs and nearly deafening Jason. Instantly a loud *BOOM* split the air, drowning out the sounds of the fire, the moans of the dying, the muffled explosions. Jason's eyes flew open in time to see a massive bolt of glowing magical energy arc out from Stone's hand and hit the door. The lock hissed and deformed and cracked open like it wasn't even there, the heavy chains dropping away like two dead snakes. "*Go! Go! Go!*" Verity cried in near panic, throwing herself against the right-side door's exit bar. It flung open and she nearly fell over in her rush to get outside.

The fire flared brighter with the new influx of oxygen from outside, licking at their clothes and singeing their skin. Stone's hand dropped away from Jason's shoulder. Jason, stunned, looked down at himself in amazement. He wasn't hurt—well, not aside from his bleeding arm and all the other bumps and cuts and bruises he'd taken inside the building. Whatever Stone had done to him—the thing that under the best of circumstances was supposed to drain him of his vitality to the point where he'd take days to recover—hadn't even made him dizzy. *What the hell —?*

Stone had recovered his senses sufficiently to shove him hard in the back. "Outside, you fool!" he ordered. The Forgotten man was already in motion too, casting a quick regretful glance back toward the burning forms of his former companions before ducking outside the door. Jason allowed himself to be shoved, and in a moment the four of them stood, pale and shocked, in the cold night air. Far away, they could hear the sounds of sirens. Someone must have seen the fire and reported it.

Jason was breathing hard, coughing, bent over with his hands on his knees. "Holy crap, that was close," he got out between breaths. "We—"

Stone ignored him. "You," he snapped at the Forgotten man. He was white as death, barely able to get words out. "Focus. Concealment." He held out his hand impatiently.

Fortunately the man seemed to make sense of his ravings. Reaching in the pocket of his ragged jacket, he pulled out the crystal Stone had given him before and dropped it in the mage's hand. Stone muttered something over it and then started moving. "Come on," he said, without waiting to see if they followed. "We don't want to be nearby when that place blows."

The four of them made it halfway down the block on the other side of the building away from the club when the top front part of the theater building imploded with a crash that shook the area like a minor earthquake. The entire front end of the building fell down into itself, collapsing and sending up choking plumes of thick dust into the night sky. Flames shot up from the front end to mingle with those that were steadily consuming the back part of the building, joined briefly by shafts of weird flickering multicolored light that winked out in mere seconds. The sirens were getting closer.

Jason sagged back against the side of a building and just watched the theater burn. He kept shaking his head, unable to form a coherent thought. Verity too watched the building, tears streaming down her cheeks for which the smoke and fire couldn't take full credit. The Forgotten man, shaking and confused, merely stood there and stared at nothing in a state of near catatonia. And Stone, staggered from exhaustion, watched Jason, an odd expression in his eyes that nobody else noticed. They all stayed that way for a long time, hiding there in plain sight as the fire trucks and police cars and the media vans and gawkers moved in to take over what had been nearly deserted streets.

34.

If the proprietors of the upscale steakhouse in Palo Alto had any issues with the strange collection of individuals who trooped up into their private second-floor meeting room the following night, they didn't mention them. Given the large sum of money the organizer of the event had paid them to provide a lavish dinner and otherwise stay out of the way as much as possible, they contented themselves with hoping that the group would at least remain back there and stay away from the rest of the clientele.

Stone had been unusually quiet for the remainder of the previous night as they had hailed a taxi and ridden back to their hotel suite in San Francisco, and equally quiet on the drive back to the house in Mountain View. They'd given the Forgotten man a ride to the area where he last remembered seeing his friends—they were able to follow the chalked signs and reunite him with a small group of ragged men and women who were shocked and surprised to see him. Stone, Jason, and Verity didn't remain to swap stories; Stone silently handed him a couple of bills with a nod of thanks, then just as silently went back to the car and waited for Jason and Verity to join him.

Jason and Verity didn't bother him. They too weren't feeling much like talking; reeling from all the shocks of the evening, they simply sat and stared out the window as the lights of the freeway flashed past. Jason found himself a little astonished that anything as normal as traffic could be happening around them after what they'd been through. He wondered if anything would ever be normal again. He knew the screams of the dying, burning people in the building would haunt him for many years to come, and his mind wouldn't stop going over ways in which he

R. L. KING

could possibly have saved them. Saved the boy, at least. Verity seemed to know what was on his mind, for at one point during the drive her hand had crept across the seat and settled on his own. He'd smiled faintly at her but said nothing.

The next day passed in a bit of a blur. They tended their wounds, slept a lot—though fitfully—and waited with trepidation for the phone call that would indicate that someone had seen them near the theater building, that the police wanted to talk to them, that somebody had spotted Stone doing magic. But the call didn't come, and as the day went on they began to relax, just a bit.

Stone had disappeared for an hour at midday; Jason didn't ask him where he went, but when he returned he announced that they had a dinner engagement that evening. Jason suspected he knew what it was about, but again didn't ask. It was a strange feeling, and he thought both Stone and Verity shared it—that it wasn't time to talk about it yet. He wasn't sure what they were waiting for, but perhaps this evening would reveal it. When they arrived at the steakhouse and spotted Lamar, Marilee, and the rest of the Forgotten group huddling nervously outside near the back of the parking lot dressed in shabby but clean clothes, he knew he was right.

Now they all sat in the wood-paneled room, the kind of room where business deals and decisions affecting thousands of people were made over cocktails, staring down at the plates of appetizers the tuxedo-clad waiters were placing in the middle of the long table, and they waited. Of Lamar's group, only Lamar himself looked like he'd ever been inside a place like this; the others were shifting in their seats nervously and clearly feeling out of their element. Jason, nursing a beer and feeling out of place himself, wanted to force Stone to speak—but he knew the mage would do it in his own time.

Stone didn't say anything until the waiters had finished bringing in the appetizers and the drink orders. When the door closed behind them, he looked around the table. "Please," he said, his voice oddly soft. "Eat. Enjoy. The food here is very good."

Tentatively, the others began passing around the dishes. "Dr. Stone," Lamar said at last. "Is it over? Is that why you've asked us here?"

Stone stared down at his plate. He hadn't joined in partaking of the food yet, though he had already polished off half a large drink. He sighed. "No. It's not over. Not completely. But it's a good start, at least for awhile." He looked over across the table. "Jason, if you would be so kind—"

Jason wasn't quite sure what he meant for a moment, but the Forgotten were all starting to ask questions now and he realized what Stone wanted. The mage still didn't want to talk, to explain, to answer questions. "Yeah," he said.

With the help of Verity, he explained to the Forgotten what had happened. Their voices shook as they got to the part about the fire—by mutual agreement following a quick glance at Stone, they didn't mention anything about the failed portal. All around the table, tears sprang to the Forgotten group's eyes as Jason told them about the ones who didn't make it out. "How horrible, how horrible..." Marilee sobbed, fumbling in her single tote bag for a tissue.

"I can't believe it..." Lamar said softly, shaking his head. "Gordon Lucas...I don't think any of us ever suspected—He must have used non-Evil to run his events, or someone would have noticed..."

"No doubt," Stone said, speaking for the first time. "I doubt they'll be able to identify his body in that wreckage, but I suspect that the Evil involvement in that organization confined itself to the upper echelons. It's brilliant, really—giving them access to the very people they wanted to destroy without causing any suspicion. I'm quite surprised he didn't get hold of more of your people."

"He'd have to be careful," Marilee said. "Forgotten look out for each other. If too many of us started to disappear, especially after attending one of his events, the groups would get suspicious." She sniffed, wiping her eyes with her tissue. "But with him gone now—"

Jason sighed. "I don't think it'll stop it completely. The DMW are still out there, though I'm guessing there are a lot fewer of them now, and without their leaders they might go back to being disorganized again." He shrugged and looked at Stone questioningly.

"You're still not safe," Stone said, his normally animated tones still sounding oddly dulled. "But I think for awhile you're safer. Until another of those things shows up to fill the vacuum. But who knows how long that will take? Who knows if there even *is* another one? There are so many things about these entities that we don't know." He had already explained to Jason and Verity earlier that he had put the cube in a safe location where he could keep an eye on it to see how long it took the spirit inside to die, but there was no need to go into that kind of detail here.

The waiters arrived again shortly to begin bringing the main course, and for awhile everyone was silent again as they ate. The Forgotten, faced with the best meal many of them had ever seen in many years, polished off the food with gusto. Jason, Verity, and Stone, still haunted by the images from the previous night, merely picked, though both Stone and Jason ordered second drinks. When things began to wind down and the waiters returned to pick up the plates, Jason leaned over toward Stone. "Can I talk to you for a couple of minutes?"

Stone nodded, getting up. The banquet room had a small balcony for guests who smoked; he led Jason out there and stood staring out over the back parking lot, waiting.

Jason took a deep breath. "Are you okay, Al?"

"Why do you ask?"

"You've been acting—weird since last night."

Stone raised an eyebrow at him. "Haven't we all?"

"Al—"

Stone sighed, staring down at his hands. "I've been thinking about what happened."

"What—"

"About how I got that door open."

Jason rolled his eyes. "I'm *fine*. I know you didn't want to do it, but if you hadn't, we'd all be dead. It was worth it."

Now Stone turned to face him. He had that burning, intense thing going on with his eyes again. "Don't you see, Jason? That's the thing. You're *fine*."

"You're being cryptic again. Spit it out. What's going on?"

"I could have killed you. But I didn't. And it wasn't because I had the control. I didn't have it. Something— protected you. Jason," he said, reaching out to grip his shoulders. "If what I think is true, it's—amazing. Unprecedented."

"*What?*" Jason tried and failed to keep the frustration from his voice.

"Don't you see? If this wasn't a fluke, some sort of anomaly—it means that it's possible for you to power magic without suffering psychic drain. And that—" He shook his head. "That is—astonishing. There's no other word for it."

Jason stared at him. "No way," he said. "Can't be." Something came back to him from last night. "Wait a

R. L. KING

sec—I *know* it can't be. I think that's what that Evil mage guy tried to do to me. Remember he went for me right before I shoved him through that portal? He tried something but it didn't work. He looked freaked out, like he was amazed it didn't work. That's how I caught him off guard."

Stone's intense gaze was fixed on him. "That's what happened? I was a bit out of things at the time. You—he tried to—"

Jason nodded. "Yeah, I think so. I can't think what else he was trying to do. He—" He stopped, because Stone's expression had just gotten very strange. "Al?"

"Jason—could I try just a small experiment? It might hurt a bit, but if I'm right about this, it won't."

"Uh—sure?"

Stone took a deep breath. He reached out and gripped Jason's arm, focusing his gaze on one of the potted plants that stood guard on either side of the balcony. "Work with me here," he murmured. "If you sense anything, don't fight it." He stared at the plant for a moment, and after a few seconds it exploded with a soft little *whoosh* and disappeared. He spun to face Jason. "How do you feel?" he demanded, urgency in his tone.

"Um...I feel fine. Why?"

Stone nearly sagged, having to grab the balcony rail for balance. Jason reached out to take his arm. "Are you okay? Did casting the spell—"

"No!" Stone was breathing hard, his eyes alight with some sort of mad energy. "Jason!" Again, he gripped Jason's shoulders, shaking him with intensity. "It worked!"

"What worked?" But then it clicked. His own gaze locked on Stone's. "You mean—I can be a mana battery and it won't hurt me?"

Stone took a moment to get himself together before answering. "I think so, Jason. And—I think you have to *want* it! Which means that nobody can do it to you against your will!" Excitement rose in his voice. "It must be your mother. You're not a mage—you can't be—but she must have given you this."

"And it didn't—hurt your soul to do it?" Jason demanded, fighting his way past how absurd that sentence sounded when exposed to the air.

Stone shook his head. "I—I don't think so. That was powerful magic last night. More powerful than anything I've ever done without a ritual. And—I feel *fine*. I feel *right*." He took more deep breaths. "Jason—I don't know if you want to continue with this. I wouldn't blame you if you wanted to just leave this whole area behind you and forget you ever saw any of this. You can do it, if you want to. But if you don't want to—if you want to stay here and help me—we could be quite a team. The Evil are still here. We've not gotten rid of them yet. To do that, we need to find out where they came from. And that's what I'm planning to do."

Jason stared at him, stunned. Truth be told, he hadn't given any thought at all to what he was going to do now that this was over. He had begun to think it would *never* be over, so he'd never have to worry about the future. But now, did he even *want* to go back home to Ventura and resume his safe, boring life of freelance mechanic jobs and Friday night bar fights? "I—"

"Before you answer that," came a new voice from the doorway, "You might want to hear something."

Both men turned; Verity was standing there, watching them. Jason had no idea how long she'd been there, how much she'd heard. "V?"

She didn't address Jason, though; she addressed Stone. She took a deep breath. "You said before I could pick somebody to train me for magic. Will—will you do it, Dr. Stone? I don't want to go back home. There's nothing for me there. I don't think there ever was, after—what happened to me. I want to stay here and learn magic, and help track down the Evil and get rid of it. You know I can help. And if you can teach me how to control this ability of mine better, then I'll never have to worry about them."

Jason's eyes widened. "V, you—"

"It's not your decision, Jason," she said softly, but firmly. "I'm eighteen in a month. This is what I want to do. You can either stay here too, or you can go back home. I hope you'll stay, but even if you don't—I am. I've made up my mind." She looked at Stone. "So...will you?"

Stone didn't answer for a long moment. He looked at Jason, then at the pot that had formerly held the disintegrated plant, and then finally at Verity. "It won't be easy," he said at last. "You'll work harder than you ever did in your life. I've not had an apprentice in many years, but I've been told I'm quite the taskmaster. And I've been on my own for so long that you'll probably find me very difficult to get on with after you've gotten over the novelty of it all."

Verity grinned. "You won't make me do your laundry, will you? Or call you 'Master'?"

Stone's eyebrow quirked up. "And if I did?"

She thought about that a minute. "I guess maybe, all things considered, it'd be worth it. But you'd better watch out once I'm fully trained. I'm gonna give you a run for your money."

For the first time in a long time, Stone smiled too. "I don't doubt it, my friend. I don't doubt it at all."

Jason looked back and forth between the two of them, took a deep breath, and shrugged. As usual, he knew the choice he'd have to make even though he wasn't completely sure he liked it. Even when compared to everything they'd been through in the past few weeks, he suspected life was about to get very interesting.

Acknowledgements

Just wanted to say "thank you" to a few folks and entities who've either helped out with this book or who've influenced it in some way.

First of all, Dan Nitschke, my spousal unit and best friend. He puts up with a lot from me, doesn't bug me too much about all the writing I do when I get working on something, and provides an editorial ear to help me find the little errors and hiccups in my plot.

Mary Decker and Marty Costello, who were kind enough to answer a couple of my cop-related questions (and Mary is always happy to talk about writing, since she does it herself and understands!)

The Shadowrun universe (currently licensed to and published by Catalyst Game Labs), which I've loved since it came out in 1989 and always will. My first five online novels were all written in this universe, and my longtime readers will recognize a couple of major characters from those novels who've been "transplanted" and in some cases renamed in order to let me use them in an original setting that I could sell.

Michaela Eaves, a fantastic artist and fellow Shadowrun fan—when I realized I needed a cover for this thing so it didn't look like every other generic self-published book around, she was the first person I thought of. Check out her website at *michaelaeaves.com*.

My beta readers, who helped me find all those annoying little errors—and some larger ones—that you never see yourself: Dan Nitschke, Michaela Eaves, and Lisa Gray (and Jeff Gray, who didn't actually read it yet but who provided general encouragement).

Pandora Radio (specifically my Alan Parsons Project channel) for providing background music.

All my Facebook friends who've encouraged me in my quest to finish this thing, which started out as a NaNoWriMo project and ended up as something more.

And finally — you! I thank you for taking a chance on an unknown book, and I do hope you enjoyed it! I'm planning at least two more in the series, so check back if you liked this one!

If you have questions, comments, want to tell me I screwed up on something, or otherwise want to share your opinions with me, you can reach me at *rat@areyouforgotten.net*.

--Rat, May 2012

About the Author

So, yeah. I hate referring to myself in the third person. (I go by "Rat," by the way, which is a long story.) I've been writing strange and twisted little tales ever since I got my hands on a pen and a piece of paper sometime back in the Jurassic Age.

My first "novels" were abysmally bad Star Trek fanfic, followed by some original stuff that will never see the light of day, followed by the discovery of the *Shadowrun* RPG universe where I got brave enough to write and web-publish a full-length novel. Failure of my readers to point, laugh, and throw things at my head encouraged me to write four more (check them out on *magespace.net*, where they're all available as free ebooks — if you liked Dr. Stone, he got his start there, under a different but recognizable guise).

Professionally, I've done some freelance writing for the *Shadowrun* game — you can find my work in many of the sourcebooks from the 2001-2006 timeframe. I'm getting (slowly) back into it again after a few years' hiatus.

Otherwise, when I'm not writing weird stories my "real job" is technical writing for a large database company in the Silicon Valley. When I'm not doing either, I can usually be found playing various MMOs including World of Warcraft, Star Wars: The Old Republic, and The Secret World, playing with my cats, or hanging out with my extremely understanding spouse.

Made in the USA
San Bernardino, CA
28 December 2013